This is a work of fiction. Names, characters, places, and incidences are either the product of the author's imagination or are used fictitiously, and any resemblance to actual persons living or dead, business establishments, events, or locales, is entirely coincidental.

Cover Art—Beautiful Book Covers by Ivy

Character Art—Leraynne S.

Developmental Edits and Proofreading—Rachel Throp

Copywrite/line Edits—Jessica McKeldon

ISBN 979-8-9925456-3-0 (ebook)

ISBN 979-8-9925456-4-7 (paperback)

To my mom.
Wish you were here.

RISE OF THE SIRIN

Trigger Warning: This is a Dark Fantasy Romance. While the relationship between the MCs isn't dark, there's a recurring theme of non-consent and on-page rape of the MMC.

Golden rays breached the ocean's surface, transforming the murky depths into a hazy green. Underwater, Eislyn closed her eyes, focusing on the tingling sensation traveling over the nerve endings below her skin. In a soft flare of light, her sealskin pelt magically peeled away from her body. With it, she shed her animal form and swam the rest of the distance with her human limbs.

Rising out of the ocean, she stepped onto the shore of the remote island. Her mate, Ronan, walked along the rocky beach with his pelt draped over his arm. The morning sun blanketed his nakedness in its heavenly glow, and ocean water dripped from his long, dark hair down his back, over his muscular buttocks and thighs. Eislyn pressed her fingers to her bare breast, attempting to contain the love brimming in her heart.

As if he could feel her stare, he turned his head to flash her one of his charming grins. Like all Selkies, his canines were sharp and pointed, but the rest of his teeth were bright and white and very human-like.

They were neither seal nor human. They were both—shapeshifters, for lack of a better term. So long as they had their skins, they could change between forms. Without their skins, they'd be stuck in their human bodies, always longing for the sea. Stories of Selkies stranded on shore without their pelts were a favorite cautionary tale from parent to child.

Eislyn lowered her lashes as she blushed, having been caught shamelessly ogling her partner. She wouldn't have minded being stuck as a human so long as Ronan was by her side.

He cleared his throat. "Ya know I love it when you stare. And I love it even more that it still flusters ya." His heated gaze traveled the length of her willowy figure and back up again until he found her eyes. "It's chilly. Let's gather some wood, and then I'll show you what I've been dreaming about all day."

A thrill rushed along Eislyn's spine while the rest of her body flushed in anticipation.

The couple was one year into their exploration of the world—a journey very unusual for their kind. Most Selkies preferred the comfort and safety of their homes off the shores of Scotland and Ireland. But she and Ronan—they were different. Their longing for adventure was what had initially attracted them to one another. It had nothing to do with the fact he was the most beautiful creature she'd ever seen, or that a mere glance from him made her weak with desire.

Barefooted, she tiptoed around the slippery seaweed and black rocks speckled with razor-sharp mussels. Along the way, she quickly filled her arms with driftwood as Ronan made a fire ring with some of the smoother rocks.

Temperature, in the ocean or on shore, didn't affect them while wearing their sealskin pelts, but when they removed their fur and transformed into their human bodies, it did. Not as much as it would've a regular human, but a fire would be pleasing, nonetheless.

Most of their kind preferred their animal forms, feeling safer in the water than on land. Over the centuries, they'd suffered much at the hands of humans—not only for the price of their pelts, but man's desire to wed or bed the mythological shapeshifter known for their seductive beauty.

Stopping next to Ronan, she bent over and let the driftwood tumble from her arms. Ronan was crouched in the sand with a small log pinned under his feet, a stick perpendicular between his palms, and a bunch of dry grass where the two met. Furiously, he rubbed his hands together and soon struck a spark.

Once the fire was going strong, he stood. Firelight reflected orange in his large, ebony eyes while a smile sharpened his cheekbones and masculine jawline. "Now, come here my love," he growled. "I have needs." He arched a suggestive eyebrow.

Her toes curled into the sand, and she bit down on her bottom lip. She stepped toward him. "As do I," she answered.

"And I plan on fulfilling every single one. Perhaps more than once."

After a year together, she knew Ronan was not one to make false promises.

Hours later, as the sun traversed over the rugged mountain peaks, they lay naked and satiated on the shore.

"If you only knew how much I love you," he whispered, tipping the end of her nose with his finger, "you'd run."

Laughter bubbled from her chest. He often teased her that she was the object of his obsession, and running was the last thing she planned on doing.

She flung herself over his bare chest and met his gaze. She fiddled with the wavy hair in front of his ear and tucked it out of his face. She wondered if all of it would be wavy if it was shorter. "Not without you, I wouldn't."

Love, desire, hope, and home flashed in his eyes, and she knew his feelings mirrored her own. She loved him to the ends of the earth, and he returned that love in droves.

Interrupting their moment, a menagerie of birds began to circle overhead, throwing ominous shadows over the ground. A small unkindness of ravens settled into the upper branches of a gray, skeletal tree. They cocked their heads and stared with black, glossy eyes but stayed unusually quiet.

A heaviness coiled in the hollow of Eislyn's throat and goose bumps peppered her skin. "We should go." She pushed herself up from Ronan's chest.

"Why?" He chuckled. "Because of the birds?"

She could see he was trying not to smile at her discomfort, though he was failing miserably. She smacked his arm playfully.

"They're birds, lass. They can't harm ya."

And just as he said it, all at once, they flew away and disappeared from sight.

The tension in her shoulders eased but the sense of dread didn't vanish even though their audience was gone. To distract herself, she ran a fingernail over his skin and traced his rippled abs. He groaned and relaxed into her touch, only to tense up a moment later.

"What?" she asked.

Abruptly, he sat up and pushed her off him. He stood, frozen on the rocky sand with his ear angled toward the dark forest beyond.

Concerned about his strange reaction, but more concerned there may be danger near, she scrambled up and scanned the area. But she could find nothing unusual. Though, when she stopped breathing, she could hear a faint melody traveling over the ocean breeze. The tune was gut-wrenchingly mournful, full of love and loss.

Panic flared and the hairs on her nape rose.

Of all the islands, in all the world, they had chosen to rest on a prison.

Eons ago, the Gods had decided to incarcerate their most dangerous creation.

Sirins.

In Eislyn's opinion, the Gods should've destroyed the wretched creatures. They were half woman, half bird, and used their seductive voices to enthrall men. Once within their grasp, they used them for sex and then killed them. Eislyn believed it was the Sirin's revenge because the Gods had denied them men of their own.

"Sirins!" she screamed, attempting to gain Ronan's attention.

But it didn't work.

Without giving her a second thought, he ran off into the trees, barefoot and naked. She fled after him. When she caught up, she grabbed his arm, trying to stop him, but she was no match for his strength, and he threw her off and kept running toward the music. She dove for his legs. In a quick back-kick, he planted the heel of his foot directly between her eyes. Pain exploded while bright stars and tiny birds flashed. Then the world went dark as she passed out.

myka

With her head cradled on a luxury down pillow, sleeping soundly on Egyptian cotton sheets, the sharp *ring, ring, ring* of the phone startled Myka from her slumber. Her hand batted around the side table, searching for the phone. "What!" she snapped when it was by her ear. As she sat up, the curly cord caught on the edge of the nightstand and almost toppled it to the floor.

"Ms. Vukovic?" said a man with a sexy foreign accent.

"Yes." She repositioned the phone and ran her fingers through her short, blonde hair, messing her longer bangs into place.

"This is Mr. *Whateverhisnamewas*." All she remembered was it sounded like the name of a French spy. "You need to meet me in the penthouse."

To prevent the four members of the rock band, Burning Brenda, from getting into trouble after their Anchorage concert, Myka, their manager, had booked their overnight lodging forty miles away in the tiny town of Girdwood, Alaska. Population: 1,360. How much trouble could the 1992

Grammy winner of the Best Rock Album of the Year find in this remote ski town?

Dread sloshed in her stomach as she set the receiver on its cradle. She was about to find out. With a deep breath, she held her hand against her chest, allowing a moment to maintain composure. Once her emotions stabilized, she threw on her clothes from the night before. She slipped her arms into the sleeves of her black leather jacket and found the nearest elevator. It wasn't her first rodeo—between the band's growing popularity and their overflow of cash, these calls were becoming more frequent.

The elevator stopped with a ding and opened. She muttered under her breath while hurrying to the end of the hallway. Stopping in front of the penthouse suite, her stilettos squished into the brown carpet, wetting the tips of her exposed toes with cold water.

Not bothering to wait for *Mr. Whateverhisnamewas,* she pulled the new fancy key card from her pocket and opened the door. Beyond the huge windows, a magnificent backdrop of snowcapped mountains and cornflower-blue skies mimicked a fairy tale.

Only the beer cans, soggy chips, and peanut shells littering the soaking-wet carpet were able to tear her away from the view. Milk sat open on the dining table next to half-empty bottles of booze and a spilled box of cereal. She picked out a handful of pastel-colored marshmallows and popped the sugary sweetness into her mouth. Cheesy puffs and bright-colored chips stained the kitchenette countertops a toxic orange.

Gus Gus, the bass player, lay spread-eagled and naked on the couch. His latest conquest was passed out on top of him with her head lolling between his legs. One of her false eyelashes had shuffled to the side of her cheek, looking eerily like a spider, and something mysterious stuck her frizzy bleached hair to the side of her face.

"You stupid Mother Francis..." Myka let the words fade as the hotel manager breezed into the room, followed by an obscenely strong dose of cologne.

He cleared his throat. "You know you are not welcome here again." Too bad his sexy accent didn't match the person. He was short and bald with hairy ape hands.

"I understand." She pressed against her eyelids with the pads of her thumbs. They'd been kicked out of hotels before. She was starting to lose count. "You have our credit card on file. I'll get them up and gone as soon as I can."

He scowled. "You do that. We need to get this room repaired immediately. The hotel is full for the summer." He smoothed out his ridiculous handlebar mustache before he scurried away.

She picked up the phone on a nearby table and dialed for help. Her foot tapped into the wet carpet—*splat, splat, splat.*

Gus Gus stretched out on the couch and farted against the leather. The woman lying on top of him smacked her dried-out lips together.

"Nick, Nicky..." Myka sputtered into the phone, trying to control her gag reflex.

"What's up?" Nick, the lead guitarist and the only responsible member of the band, answered.

"They've destroyed another room. I need help getting them out."

A heavy sigh traveled over the connection. "Really? I thought for sure this time they'd behave. I'll be there in fifteen."

After he hung up, she paused in front of the arched

windows, breathing calmly and counting to ten. Vacant ski lifts hung, forgotten, above the peaks of the Chugach Mountains. A few random hikers, dressed in neon colors, trudged up the slope instead of riding the massive tram slowly ascending to the top. She pinched the bridge of her nose and grudgingly tore herself away from the scenery.

Tiptoeing to the bathroom, she opened the door to find Tony, the drummer, sprawled out in the tub. Running water flowed over the side of the bath onto the marble floor. *Yes, it is slippery when wet.*

A groupie clung to the toilet, passed out with her head hanging over the side, praying to the porcelain goddess. Chunks of vomit clung to her long, dark hair. Tony and another woman lay unconscious in the tub snoring. A heavy coat of mascara ran down her ultra-pale face giving her the look of an aged rock star only with perky, expensive breasts. Myka turned off the running water spilling over the side of the tub and causing all of their problems and left them to prune longer.

She stopped in front of the bedroom door and hesitated. She knew what she'd find inside—the same scene she'd found one too many times before. Even after three years, her throat seized to the point where she couldn't swallow from the pain of her broken heart. It didn't matter that she'd initiated the breakup, it hurt nonetheless.

Self-respect dictated that she mustn't wait for Nicky. If she did, it would be admitting she still had feelings for Andrew Arie. Lately, she spent half of her days listing all the reasons why she should avoid him and his unwanted effect.

Her eyes blurred over in a moment of weakness, and a punch-drunk smile curled her lips as she remembered the first time she'd seen him. It was the summer between her junior and senior year of college...

Walking home from her waitressing job, she heard the telltale scream of an electric guitar entering the seventh level of hell, followed by the low thrum of a bass. A drumbeat pounded in her chest, urging her to rock her head to the familiar beat. Somebody's stereo was a thumpin'. At least that's what she thought until she came around the corner and spotted a rock band playing outside their open garage doors.

The hazy afternoon light reflected like molten chocolate on the lead singer's long hair. He stood, legs shoulder-width apart, wearing nothing but beat-up jeans tucked loosely into open-laced combat boots. He wore no adornment, only black and gray tattoos that covered both arms and crawled onto his chest. Wisps of sun and shadows danced over his body, accentuating gleaming muscles. He threw his head back as he wailed into the microphone, then flung his long hair forward, tossing it to the beat.

Despite the heat, goose bumps scattered along Myka's skin, and a thrill boiled in her stomach. When they finished playing, she held up a finger and said, "Give me ten minutes. I have people."

Running to her dad's law practice two blocks away, she burst in, dashed past his receptionist into his office, and grabbed his keys from the hook next to the door. She told him it was of the utmost importance for him to follow. He shook his head and complied. Being the youngest, and the only daughter, her father tended to indulge her wishes.

When they got back to the scene of her discovery, she pointed at the lead singer and said, "One song. Your choice. You already impressed me, but now for the hard part—impress him."

He threw her a charming smirk as he picked up a T-shirt hanging over the half-stack amplifier and threw it on, covering up his golden washboard stomach, smooth chest, and many of his tattoos. He stalked up to the mic, lithe like a cat, and looked at his bandmates before he turned back and counted. "One, two, three."

The guitarist hit hard right out of the gate, his fingers plucking the strings as he evaporated into the music. The fuzzy redhead standing to the side needed to shave his scant beard, but his lack of personal style didn't hinder his ability to slap the bass. The drummer, with his hair greased back mafia-style and a ridiculous number of gold chains around his neck, did not need to tell her which side of the tracks he hailed from.

Her knees buckled slightly when the first few notes registered in her brain. The fates have aligned, she mused. How had he guessed her favorite singer?

His eyes never left hers, and everything faded to black except for him and his voice. Chills crawled down her spine and goose bumps again peaked on her flesh. Parts tingled that shouldn't have, just from the sound of his voice.

Myka's dad listened intently, then after they finished, he asked if they had any originals. And that was where it all started...

And *this* was where it was going to end. Right here, right now, in this Alaskan hotel room.

Determination strengthened her resolve. She reached for the bedroom door handle, but it slipped away, and she stumbled into Drew's hard body. He caught her, his hands burning her shoulders as he steadied her. She pushed away, giving him a dirty look as if it was his fault.

"Hey," Drew said, coming out the door and purposely shutting it behind him. He wore nothing but black boxer briefs and a smile he reserved for Myka—the one that broke her heart over and over again. He ran his hand through his hair, pushing the thick strands from his face. "Whatcha doin' up so early?"

As always, the deep raspy tone of his voice raked across her skin, making her insides quiver. She clenched her teeth, warding against the sensation. "Are you kidding me? The hotel manager just kicked us out."

"Why? We kept it down like you asked." He reached out to touch her cheek, but she shied away. Hurt flashed across his handsome face but vanished quickly behind his dark-blue eyes.

She exhaled violently and pointed to the floor.

"Oh, yeah, I guess that might do it. Sorry." A sheepish half-smile rose on his sleepy face as he splashed the water with his foot. He walked over the squishy carpet and opened the door to the bathroom. When he spotted Tony and his ladies, Drew looked back at her and asked, "Uhhh...do you think I could use your shower?"

"Fine." She scrubbed her hands up and down over her cheeks. She was such an enabler.

"Ya gonna come with me?" he asked almost innocently.

She turned her back. "No. I have work to do. Somebody has to get you idiots out of here."

"Oh, all right." He sounded disappointed, maybe a bit frustrated. He went back into his room, grabbed some clothes, and quickly snuck a kiss on her forehead—some form of apology—before he left.

Myka woke up the three groupies and sent them on their way before entering Drew's room. She flipped on the light and blinked to make sure she wasn't hallucinating. The room was empty. Only one side of the bed had been disturbed. That usually wasn't the case. Drew always had hordes of women flocking to him.

According to her superstitious grandmother, Baba, it wasn't just because he was gorgeous, talented, or rich, it was because the blood of a Sirin ran through his veins. Baba studied mythology of all kinds, though she was most interested in stories from the *old country*. Folklore from Kievan Rus'—a medieval stronghold that once encompassed parts of Finland, Russia, Ukraine, and many other Slavic countries—was her specialty. And Sirins—women with bird bodies but human heads and chests—were her favorite. Legends said that because Sirins had no men of their own, they lured human males away with their hypnotizing voices. Then, like a black widow spider, they procreated with them and killed them afterward.

Baba insisted that was the real reason people were irrationally drawn to certain humans or celebrities. They had the magical *it factor* that came from mythical blood. With rock stars, it was their voices. They opened their mouths, and people would follow them to hell and back.

Baba said their family was part Sirin as well, and therefore, Myka would never be vulnerable to their charms. It came in handy as the manager of a rock band. It made her resistant to every celebrity she'd ever known, except for Drew. Moth meet flame.

She tore open the blackout curtains and the morning sun poured in, the golden rays heating her chilly skin. Even though it was summer, it wasn't warm. She tossed the pillows back on the bed and pulled up the crisp sheets. Before leaving the room, she lifted Drew's down pillow, the one he always traveled with, to her face and inhaled deeply. It smelled like him, his cedarwood and spice cologne with a hint of the strawberry-scented shampoo he'd stolen from her.

She closed the door softly behind her and leaned up against it. Something like relief flooded her system. He'd slept alone, as he had for the last few months. Not that she was counting. She bit the inside of her cheek and balled her fists. *How am I going to control these feelings again?* Oh, hell, she was lying to herself. She'd repressed the feelings at best, but she'd never truly be over him. He was the one.

In an attempt to distract herself from the building grief, she hurried to the kitchen and pulled a pitcher from the cupboard. She filled it with cold water.

Wearing a smile that might've been slightly manic, she stood over the top of Gus Gus and poured the water over him. It wouldn't hurt the floor, and after what had happened on that couch, they probably owed the hotel a new one.

"What! What the fuck!" Gus Gus sputtered as he scrambled up.

A sick sense of pleasure warmed the cockles of her heart. "Go to your room and put some pants on." She threw him a towel so he wouldn't shock the other guests on his way there.

Still coughing, he hissed, "You can be such a bitch." He wrapped the towel around his waist, covering his pasty buttocks. He picked up his wet leather pants off the floor and hung them over his arm before he left.

He didn't mean it. They loved her, and they knew everything that she did for them, but after this, she was done. She didn't get paid enough to babysit three—not including Nicky—grown men who perpetually acted like spoiled teenagers. *Okay*, so she *did* get paid enough, but that wasn't the point.

Nicky showed up dressed immaculately in designer

jeans, a pinstripe shirt, and Italian leather shoes. He didn't always look the part of a rock star—and he certainly didn't act the part. He was more like a sexy Latin supermodel with the disposition of a saint. For that, she was thankful.

He helped her lift Tony out of the water and dress him in a hotel bathrobe. Tony's mafia motif hadn't changed much in the last few years, though his hair was long and tightly permed now, affording him a few more inches in height.

"You know, Nicky, sometimes I think I've seen more twigs and berries than a porn star."

Nicky half choked, half laughed while Tony snarled his lip. He wanted to throw her a witty comeback but was smart enough, for once, to keep his mouth shut. He was learning.

After the penthouse suite was empty, she stormed back to her hotel room, her irritation growing with each step. It was her own fault. She was the one who kept going back for more. She took a few centering breaths before quietly opening the door.

Drew was sitting on the plush white bed watching a documentary about Alaskan wildlife. Droplets of water ran from his dark hair, down his chest, over his rippled stomach, into the towel around his waist. She tore her eyes away from what lay beyond, back to the artwork on his arms. On Drew's impressive right bicep was his most recent tattoo—a wolf with pitch-black eyes.

He caught her staring at it, and he reached up and tapped his arm. "You know this one's for you, right?"

The sincerity on his face made her heart flip but it only fueled her anger. They used to joke he would get a tattoo of a wolf for her, and she would get a lion for him—the correlating meaning behind their surnames. Once upon a time, she had been his wolf, and he was her lion. How fitting. She was an animal that found its one true partner and mated for life; he was an animal surrounded by a harem, happiest when balancing multiple women.

"Whatever," she said, doing her best to ignore him.

"Hey," he said, standing up. "Sorry about that." His eyes darted to the ceiling.

She pursed her lips and raised her eyebrows.

He held open his arms, beckoning with a come hither of his hands.

"Seriously? I'm mad." She tossed her ruined designer shoes across the room. They slammed into the wall with a thump and slid to the floor.

He smiled despite her attitude. "I know you are but come here anyway."

She had a hard time resisting him. And since she was leaving—even though he didn't know it yet—she desperately wanted one more hug. Against her better judgment, she melted into his embrace.

He smelled clean, like hotel soap and *her* shampoo and conditioner. He rested his chin on the top of her head, which was not easy for many men to do. Myka was 5'10" without shoes. His long arms engulfed her, making her feel small. He held on tightly as he nuzzled his face into the crook of her neck. His breath tickled her skin as he inhaled deeply, then exhaled slowly. A tsunami of longing washed over her. He cautiously kissed her neck all the way to her face, leaving sparks in their wake as if testing the waters. The rapid rhythm of her heart pounding between her ears was deafening—so loud she was afraid he could hear it. When he licked her bottom lip, her breath hitched. With no resistance, his soft lips parted hers and his tongue gently wove its way inside. He tasted like cinnamon toothpaste and everything she'd ever desired. Her brain and scorching flesh screamed to give in.

Just.

This.

Once.

Heat flared through her and the deep throbbing between her thighs became impossible to ignore. He stepped in closer, pressing his hard body against her, causing his cotton towel to slide to the floor, leaving him naked.

Panic rose. Okay, perhaps it wasn't panic, but this had gone too far. All she'd wanted was a hug. Correction—all she'd *needed* was a hug. She wanted much, much more.

But a moment of pleasure wasn't worth a lifetime of pain.

Shoving him back firmly, she shook her head and retreated to the bathroom, locking it.

She rested against the door, panting. *Please don't knock. Please don't knock.* Because if he did, she wasn't sure she was strong enough to resist the temptation much longer. She gripped her fists into her hair and glanced up. *God, why can't I just hate him?*

The realization that the wall she'd built between the two of them was crumbling around her in a useless pile of rubble was enough to warrant her resignation. She decided, then and there, that her five-inch patent leather stilettos, which were no longer made for walking since they were ruined, were finished. And so was she.

drew

Drew grabbed the towel off the hotel room floor, got dressed, and tried not to think about Myka on the other side of the door. She infuriated him sometimes. Just when he thought he was about to break through her defenses, she'd pull away and shut him out again. His life would be so much easier if he could get over her. But he couldn't. It wasn't like he hadn't tried.

He ran his fingers through his damp hair and gripped the back of his neck. There was nothing more he could accomplish by hanging around, so he tossed his bag over his shoulder and headed to Nicky's room. He knew better than to stay and wait. He had already pressed his luck. If he wanted Myka back, he was going to have to advance slowly, carefully.

It'd been three years since she had broken up with him. She'd ended their relationship with no warning. She'd simply walked away and locked her heart up in a ball of ice. He knew he deserved her cold demeanor now, but back then, he hadn't deserved it. He'd loved her, desperately, still did, but to this day, he couldn't figure out why she'd stopped loving him. He'd worked hard to get her—harder than any other girl had ever made him work.

As he walked down the hallway toward Nicky's room, he smirked, nostalgically recalling the first time he'd seen her.

She leaned up against the maple tree in front of Nicky's house. A hot summer breeze shimmied through the leaves, doing its best to cool him off on the sweltering day. Her arrival didn't help his heat level. She was slightly intimidating, though he didn't like to admit it. He wasn't sure if it was her looks, or her height, or the effortless confidence she oozed as she watched them through mirrored sunglasses. She wore cutoffs, a tank top that hugged her luscious curves, and flip-flops. Her long, blonde hair was pulled into a high ponytail.

When they finished playing their song, she strolled over, pushed her aviators on top of her head, and said, "I have people. Give me ten minutes, and I'll be back."

"So does this mean no more playing in dive bars?" he asked, not ready for her to leave.

She stopped and slowly turned around, peeking above her sunglasses that were already back on. "Only if you're good enough."

He threw his head back and laughed. "Baby, I'm better than good."

Ten minutes later, the band had an impromptu audition in front of her dad.

She was right. She did have people. Her uncle had been a hugely successful country musician before he'd died.

After a whirlwind ride, much of which Drew didn't even remember, she and her father had them in front of a record label with a signed deal. He, Nicky, Gus, and Tony asked her to be their manager. He was the only one who regretted it. He knew better than to mix business with pleasure, but the more he got to know her, the harder it became.

The day they signed their first record contract, she suggested they throw a bash to celebrate.

"Let's have a big party and invite all your friends," she offered after the paperwork was finalized and had been approved by her father, who was still, to this day, their legal counsel.

"You know, to be honest, I would rather have it just us," he said. "The ride's been so crazy, I want a moment with all of you to let our success sink in."

That night, they celebrated together around a crackling bonfire next to a remote lake. After everyone else had passed out, Drew picked up his old guitar and sang one of Myka's favorite ballads. Nighthawks warbled on backup while they swooped in the dark sky. As he played, he watched Myka stare at him through the dancing flames. He loved the way she could hang with the boys—no makeup and ponytail, a crude sense of humor, and thick skin. But when she dressed up, she took his breath away, even if she didn't know it.

For months, they'd bantered and flirted harmlessly. But as she sat on the sand, leaning up against the log with a cold beer in her hand, he knew he couldn't pretend she was one of the guys any longer. Or just another girl.

After the song ended, he helped her off the ground, catching a whiff of her sweet citrus perfume mixed with campfire smoke. If she were anyone else, he probably would've made his move then, but he was nervous. What if she didn't like him like that? She flirted with all of them. But he swore there was a connection only they shared.

They rolled out their sleeping bags next to the fire and laid down on top of them, staring at the stars. "You know, I've been thinking about asking you out."

Silence—except for the crackling of the campfire, loons cooing on the lake, and the occasional splash of a fish.

"You know, out? Like on a date," he said with his hands tucked behind his head. A ball of nerves settled in the hollow of his throat. The nice breeze floating through the whispering trees helped cool the perspiration on his forehead.

"Hmmm," she said.

"I've been thinking you should say yes." He chuckled. His heart pounded, even over the calming effects of the alcohol. Normally girls asked him out. He watched the stars flicker in the sky and thought to himself, Twinkle twinkle, little star...*as she made him wait anxiously for an answer.*

She laughed. "I'll think about it."

She kept Drew at arm's length for the longest time, but he eventually broke down her walls, only to have her shatter his heart later. And though their breakup wasn't his idea, he'd been paying the price for three years...

Drew dispelled his memories from the past and looked to the future. Now that last night's concert was over, he couldn't wait for this vacation to really begin. Myka had planned an epic Alaskan adventure for all of them. Only hours from now, they would be miles away from civilization, practically alone on an island, for a little fishing and a much-needed escape from the chaos. This weekend, he would make his move. Only moments ago, as he held her in his arms, he had been able to tell her determination was waning. He knew some part of her still loved him. Now, he just had to convince her she could trust him.

He had a plan. By the end of this week, she would be back in his arms, firmly under his spell. *How could it not work?* he thought arrogantly. *I am Andrew Arie, lead singer of Burning Brenda, the 1992 Grammy winner of the Best Rock Album of the Year.*

Myka huffed, her bangs ruffling over her forehead, as she waited on the band. Even though most of them were hungover, her motley crew sauntered out of the hotel looking like an album cover—just regular dudes in battered jeans, T-shirts, each wearing a flannel in various states of dress. The unusual part was the crowd of fans staring and whispering excitedly. The guys, all good-natured attention whores, posed for pictures, rock star-style with their tongues out and finger signs cast. Cameras flashed as admirers caught it all.

"Okay, guys, enough," she said to the boys while every woman and a few men in the growing crowd glared at her. "We have a plane to catch."

Drew's ponytail, hanging through the opening in his baseball cap, swung gently behind him as he strutted toward the limo. How he pulled that off without looking like an idiot was beyond her. But he did. At least he hadn't permed his hair like some other rock stars. He waved again at his fans before he nudged Nicky out of the way so he could scoot next to her, sitting far closer than necessary. He smiled, waggling his eyebrows like a nutjob.

He was on a mission—Myka wasn't blind. But no matter what her heart desired, she couldn't allow it to happen again. Falling for him in the first place had been a mistake. Not resigning after she'd broken up with him was a choice. One she regretted.

He settled into the seat, resting his thigh against hers. Where their legs touched, heat flowed like a slow-acting poison, leaching methodically into her veins and weakening her resolve. Her pinky finger, only a millimeter away from his, beckoned for her to take it. To end the torture. Attempting to distract herself, she stared out the window as the limo hummed down the winding highway.

Glacier-lined peaks rose like titans out of the ocean, guarding the narrow inlet. Bald eagles dotted the shoreline, encouraging tourists to stop on the side of the road and snap pictures. The limo driver pointed out a pod of beluga whales surfacing like white blocks of ice in the water. They all shimmied to one side of the car and pressed their faces to the glass.

When the show was over and they settled back in their seats, Drew laid his hand on her upper thigh. She pursed her lips and tried focusing on the tide rolling over the dangerous mud flats they'd been warned about. According to the chauffeur, many people had been sucked into the silt, thinking it was safe. It was akin to love.

Drew's thumb, heavily calloused from years with the guitar, skimmed her leg. She kept her breathing steady, despite her racing heart. His touch, like water caressing the sand, was systematically stripping her of her strength. In the end, water always won, either by wearing you down, weaving around, or penetrating the smallest cracks. That was why she had to leave. Her heart wouldn't survive the battlefield again.

A sting of melancholy tugged at her soul while listening to the guys' endless chatter. They bantered back and forth like prepubescent boys competing by writing their names in the snow. Funny how she'd always felt like one of them—minus the equipment, of course.

After one of the longest hours she could recall, they finally arrived at the Anchorage airport, where they boarded a private jet for the remote coastal town of Sitka, Alaska.

Once seated, Drew stretched out beside her, his long legs comfortable thanks to the copious amounts of room only a large bank account could afford.

She gazed out the oval window, admiring the scenery, and ignored him as they took off. There was something on his mind. She wished he would spill his guts and get the drama over with. But he had an infuriating amount of patience. A hunter by nature, he could wait out his prey, stalk you like a panther—because that's what he reminded her of—slowly, silently until you were so paranoid and twitchy you would bolt at your own shadow. Patience— that's how he'd gotten her to go out with him in the first place. And even then, when she was young and dumb, she had known he was dangerous. She had the emotional scars to prove it.

"What's your problem?" she spat at him as a leggy flight attendant placed a glass of soda in front of her on the table.

He glanced down at Myka, his dark-blue eyes looking deceptively brown, and cracked a lopsided grin. He said nothing. But even that burrowed past her defenses.

She held his gaze for a beat to prove he wasn't getting under her skin before she took a sip of soda and drifted deep into a memory. The first time she'd noticed the true color of his eyes was the morning after he'd asked her out.

The sun peeked over the dark treetops and crawled onto her face, waking her up. She gripped her sleeping bag and rolled over onto her side. With no one watching, she admired Drew under the dawn's light. He was curled up on his side, facing her with his trusty pillow, the one he carried even now, tucked up under his head. Some of his dark hair spilled over his face, gently rising and falling with his breath. His thick, black eyelashes cast shadows on his cheekbones. A couple of days of no shaving left a sexy scruff on his chin, framing his lips. If he wasn't so good-looking, his mouth might have been a smidge too big for his face.

He took a deep breath and opened his eyes. He raised one eyebrow when he caught her staring. "You see something you like?"

"Your eyes are blue," she said, almost offended by not noticing earlier. She spent a lot of time trying not to stare at him. But it was hard not to. Plus, add in that voice and the fact that he was genuinely a nice guy—a hazardous combo, at least to her heart. And she didn't want to be one of those groveling girls willing to do anything to gain his attention.

He cleared his throat. "Yeah, same as always."

She squinted to make sure she was right. "I thought they were brown."

"Surprised you noticed since you avoid looking at me. Your eyes are black." He reached out and touched the tip of her cold nose with his finger.

"Yep, just like a demon." She tilted her head back, doing her best impression of an evil laugh. He'd noticed she didn't look at him...

Abruptly, Myka rose from her seat and scooted past him to use the lavatory. He growled low in his throat as she walked away.

She couldn't help herself, so she turned to yell at him. "You know those shenanigans," she swirled her finger in the air, "don't work on me!" But unfortunately, everything he did worked on her. All she had to combat his charm was her stubbornness—the cut-off-your-nose-to-spite-your-face kind.

"I know," Drew grumbled, looking properly reprimanded. "But nothing I do seems to work on you anymore."

Little did he know. But hey, at least she was faking it well.

"Man, what the hell did you do to her this morning—or not do?" Gus Gus ribbed as she stomped away. "Why don't you two just bump uglies? Get this over with already so we can *all* stop suffering!" Gus Gus was the blurter—what went through his mind came out of his mouth. At least she always knew what he was thinking, for better or worse.

She slammed the bathroom door shut and splashed some cold water on her face. The sexual tension between the two of them had always been explosive even though they'd only dated for a few months. When she'd broken it off, they hadn't even had sex yet. It was Drew who'd insisted they take things slow when she'd admitted she was a virgin.

She patted her face dry with a paper towel, wondering if they had just scratched the itch, if the tension between the two of them would've naturally faded. For some reason, she doubted it—at least on her end, because she loved him even now. She was smart enough to realize, given the chance, she could've lost herself to him, body, mind, and soul. But a girl like her could never keep a man like him. Since their breakup three years ago, he'd dated only supermodels and actresses. And if *they* couldn't hold his attention, what made her think she could? She took a deep breath and let it out slowly, knowing she'd done the right thing, even if it still felt wrong.

After the laughter died down, she ventured out.

The flight attendant hovered over Drew, batting her fake eyelashes and giggling like an idiot while she mixed him the hair of the dog.

Myka snatched her soda off the table and switched seats to the back of the plane. Somewhat alone, she shut her eyes, refusing to pay them the slightest bit of attention. The purr of the jet engines had almost lured her to sleep when she felt a gentle tap on her shoulder. She squeezed her eyes tighter before she opened them.

"Here," Drew said. He handed her her cassette player with earphones. Inside the deck was a homemade tape on which he'd recorded all the songs he knew she loved, even if he hated them, and some of his favorites too. A few months ago, he'd given it to her like they were in junior high. He was thoughtful like that. And painfully cute.

Begrudgingly, she thanked him.

"Can I sit?" He rested his hand on her shoulder, sending tingles all the way to her toes.

"Whatever." She hoped she sounded indifferent, not pouty.

"Oh, you smell good." His deep voice plucked that particular string—the one that made panties around the world drop. He leaned his head toward her neck, his breath spilling hot on her flesh. "Is that the perfume I got you?"

It wasn't like she couldn't see what was going on—the gifts, the compliments, his subtle touch. It wasn't going to work this time. Last week, he told her she had the most beautiful hair he'd ever seen. She'd whacked it off the next day into a pixie cut with longer bangs, bleached it from its natural dark blonde to platinum.

"What do you want?" she sighed.

He laughed under his breath and sat next to her. "Nothing." Even with the amount of room on the private jet, he invaded her space as their arms touched.

"You've got to be kidding me, right? Go back to your seat." She shut her eyes so she didn't have to see his handsome face.

"For the next hour, all of the seats are mine. Burning Brenda chartered the plane. We have enough money now, thanks to you. Remember?" His cockiness only added to his charming demeanor. It was frustrating, especially when she was doing her best to dislike him.

"You know what I mean. Go. Now." She pointed to their previously abandoned seats.

"No."

Myka's eyes snapped open. He stared—not in a fierce, challenging way, but more like he was trying to figure out what was going on inside her brain.

She wasn't going to back down from his puppy dog stare. "Fine." She put on her headphones, slipped the volume all the way up, and pressed play. A song that she loved—and he hated—blared through the little speakers. She reclined her seat.

He started singing even though he strongly disliked her classic country music. Without shame, she turned down the volume and let his amazing voice bathe her skin. It permeated her pores and settled into her bones. Soon, the rest of the boys joined in.

Times like these brought her to her knees. Just like the

night when Drew sang to her under the stars. She'd known he was talented—they all were—but until that moment on their celebratory camping trip, she hadn't realized how talented he truly was. The depth in which he sang haunted her long after his voice faded. Like he felt every word—the pain, the joy, the demons.

That was the night he surprised her by asking her out. Sure, they'd flirted, but she'd flirted with all of them. She'd thought he saw her as another dude, or at least a little sister. After months of *thinking* about it, she finally gave up and said yes. She'd wanted to say a resounding *yes* right away, but that little rule about not dating coworkers had stopped her. Too bad she hadn't stuck to her guns and heeded her sound advice.

Soon, the plane skidded to a landing and the doors opened, letting them out onto the small tarmac. Descending the stairs, she welcomed the cool mist on her parched face. The air was heavy and smelled of rain, earth, and saltwater with a slight tinge of jet fuel. The mountains, snow clinging to the tallest peaks, repeated like sharks' teeth, row behind row. If she were only a tad taller, she could've reached up and touched the low-slung clouds that circled the endless summits like a smoker's rings.

Inside the tiny airport, a large, weathered man with a bushy red beard followed by a husky strolled up to her and held out his hand. "Myka, I presume. It's nice to finally meet you."

"You too, Paul. And this must be Denali." She offered her hand and let the dog smell her before she petted its head. Myka quickly introduced the rest of her crew. They all gave Paul a hearty handshake and told him how much they'd been looking forward to this trip. She shooed them away by insisting they load their bags into the back of the old, beat-up van waiting for them.

"Is everything a go as we discussed?" Myka whispered when the others looked away, then handed Paul an envelope.

He tucked it inside his coat pocket and patted it. "Yes, boss, you leave the rest to me. Hop in." He winked before he climbed behind the wheel.

It only took a few minutes to drive over to the harbor. Soon, they pulled up next to dozens of float planes. Paul directed them toward a red and white aircraft and told Tony to sit in the back seat with Denali because he weighed the least. Gus Gus and Nicky were to hop in the middle, and Drew was to sit up front because at 6'5" with muscles to spare, he was the heaviest.

"Wait, where's Myka going to sit?" Drew said.

"I'm coming back for her, along with the rest of our gear," Paul answered smoothly. "She wanted you gentlemen to be together. Don't worry, I told her where to get the best coffee." He tossed her the keys to the van.

"I don't know..." Drew stammered, stepping toward her, seeming uncomfortable with the situation. Creases lined between his brows as he searched her face. "I don't want to leave you."

She bit back the desperate words on the tip of her tongue—*I don't want to leave you either*. "I don't remember asking your permission," she said instead. She pulled up the hood on her rain jacket, shielding him from her peripheral vision, afraid that if he looked into her eyes much longer, he would know something was amiss. With the flip of her hand, she dismissed him.

"Okay," he said, climbing inside the cockpit.

She waved as the float plane traversed the water and then slowly took flight like a goose.

Now that he was gone, tears pooled in her eyes, and her chest shuddered as she held back a sob. She had to remind herself this was the best for both of them. And though she'd played him like a fiddle, she hoped he and the boys would have the trip of a lifetime.

drew

Drew blew Myka a kiss through the aircraft window as they pulled away from the dock. She waved but wasn't smiling. Though she looked calm, her energy had hummed with anxiety all day. He could feel it—he always could—like a nest of angry hornets behind his ribs. Something about this situation troubled him. But as they took off, the knot clenching in his stomach slingshot to his throat and pushed Myka's anxiety away, replacing it with his own fear. He attributed it to being a celebrity on a small plane. The number one cause of death for a rock star was drugs—followed closely by small plane crashes.

They sliced through the low, gray clouds like a hot knife cutting butter. Below, he caught glimpses of small islands dotting the blackened sea and boats plowing through the whitecaps. He was almost happy to be flying instead of down there, probably getting seasick.

About the time he grew slightly confident they might get

there alive, the plane caught a pocket of turbulence and dropped. Everyone but Paul panicked and cussed.

"Never been on a small plane before, boys?" Paul chuckled calmly over the headset.

Drew shook his head and cracked his knuckles, then wiped his sweaty palms on his jeans. "We try to avoid them. They have a bad track record in our circle."

"Well, it's a bit cloudy so hang on, it's going to be bumpy. But after tomorrow, the weather forecast is quite spectacular. Unusual, really. That Myka has good timing."

That she does, Drew thought, letting his mind drift back to her. Two weeks in a remote Alaskan lodge full of fishing, whale watching, kayaking, bear viewing, and whatever else everyone wanted to do. No TVs. No phones. No media. No outsiders to distract Myka.

Who would've guessed that a woman would end up being his drug of choice. And Myka was the fix he craved. Simply being near her made his body almost hum, like all the electrons inside of him sped up, creating a frenzy of sorts, an effervescence. It was an invigorating feeling, but at the same time, almost uncomfortable. Sometimes, the desire to touch her became so intense it was all he could think about. But the minute she was within reach, the uncomfortable sensation abated, immediately replaced with a clear-headed euphoria. Touching her was indescribable. He'd figured with time, the feeling would dissipate, but to this day, just catching sight of her made his heart rev.

Drew breathed a sigh of relief as the plane, slowly this time, dropped in elevation. They curved around a circular island nestled among other atolls. His muscles unclenched significantly when they touched down inside a calm, protected cove and motored up to a wooden dock alongside a gleaming white fishing boat. The briny ocean air slapped him in the face as he jumped down and helped the others out.

After Tony's feet hit the dock, he puked over the side into a tangle of seaweed. His olive skin, a shade greener than normal, almost matched the ocean's tone.

"Feel better?" Drew chuckled.

"Bite me," Tony said with a grin and wiped his mouth with the back of his hand.

Out of the small cargo hold, Paul handed each of them their bags. Drew tossed his over his shoulder, prepared to rough it. Myka had warned them about the lack of *necessities* and the outhouses. But honestly, he was looking forward to going back to the basics. He'd grown up, not poor, but not quite middle class either. His parents owned a small farm, though both had had side jobs to make ends meet for their family. A smile twitched at the corner of his lips. That wasn't the case any longer. Once Burning Brenda signed their record deal, he'd insisted his parents quit and focus on the farm. It brought him a huge measure of happiness to see his parents in their true element.

"Holy shit! This place is bitchin'!" Gus stopped abruptly in his black and white sneakers. "Dude! Myka was fuckin' with us! I believed her when she said we'd be going old school."

"She never ceases to surprise." Nicky chuckled.

"Ain't that the truth," Tony said. "Thank God! This city boy was worried there for a second."

Bleached skeletal remains of washed-up driftwood were scattered over the rocky beach. Exposed tree roots, where the rocky shoreline changed into the land, resembled clawed hands digging into the rough sand. Beyond that, nestled into the forest amongst the towering spruce trees, sat a massive lodge with huge, round logs, a green metal roof, and a stone chimney spilling out a curl of smoke.

With their bags over their shoulders, they trudged up a couple flights of stairs to the expansive front porch. Floor-to-ceiling windows reflected the cloudy sky and the deep-green ocean. A rock firepit, built between curved benches, and a hot tub on the cedar deck, took advantage of the glorious views. Bright-colored flowers overflowed from the whiskey barrels and hanging baskets. Flora, fish, spruce trees, and day-old campfire perfumed the great outdoors.

Drew stopped and took a deep breath, enjoying the scent.

Paul's wife, Barb, met them at the door. Her curly hair was pulled back into a tight ponytail. She patted down some wayward frizz with no success before she held out a calloused hand to each of them and welcomed them into her home.

The heat from the massive stone fireplace warmed Drew's chilled skin.

A colossal moose head hung above the hearth and a few bear skin rugs, with attached heads and long, yellow canines, decorated the surrounding logs. The smell of cookies wafted from the kitchen, making his mouth water.

Drew grabbed a treat when Barb held out the plate. He asked Paul, "Are you going back to pick up Myka now?"

Paul reached for the cookies, only to have his hand slapped away by Barb. "These are for our guests," she scolded. Paul grunted and took one anyway.

He wiped the crumbs from his beard before digging into his battered jacket and removing two envelopes. "Here." He handed one each to Drew and Nicky.

Drew turned it over to find his full name typed on the front. Just as he started to rip it open, Paul said, "Let me show you to your accommodations."

He stuffed it in his pocket, sure that it was just a cautionary policy letter—*please don't do this; please don't do that*—and followed Paul up the stairs to Gus's, Tony's, and Nicky's rooms on the second floor. Then Paul showed Drew to the guest suite on the third floor. Even though Myka had rented the entire lodge, Drew had high hopes he could convince her to stay with him.

He tossed his bags onto the log-framed bed before he turned to thank Paul and ask him again if he was going back for Myka, but Paul had disappeared.

Drew sat down on the chair in front of the toasty fire with his eyes closed, rubbing his sternum. Even though they were no longer in the air, he couldn't get rid of the weird anxiety humming behind his ribs. It was as if his bones were prison bars and his emotions were rioting convicts. Leaving Myka behind in Sitka set his teeth on edge. For the last month, he'd had a hunch she was going to quit the band, but Nicky had assured him that wasn't the case. They had a tight relationship, so he was going to have to trust that Nicky had the inside scoop. He'd also hinted that if Drew wanted Myka back, now was the time to act.

Three years ago, when she'd broken up with him, he'd been surprised that she continued to manage the band. But she had always been close to Nicky, Tony, and Gus as well. Not that he wasn't grateful—though seeing her that often caused him pain.

Directly after the breakup, she'd avoided being alone with him. She'd refused to take his calls, immediately lashed out if he cornered her, and finally, she'd threatened if he didn't abide by her wishes, she'd quit.

In a desperate attempt to keep her near, he'd only talked with her when other people were around. And to ignore his broken heart, he'd distracted himself with famous women and partying. Lots of partying. The Band-Aid wasn't working any longer. It never really had. It had only numbed the pain for a while before it returned with a vengeance.

What he needed to do was to win Myka back.

Though it would be much easier if he knew what he'd done wrong in the first place. He hadn't cheated on her or raised a hand to her, and he never would. They'd never even had an argument—or at least one he was aware of. Things between them had been going perfectly. And then she'd dropped the bomb out of nowhere. She'd used the excuse that she couldn't date him and manage the band successfully. Her career was more important. Even then, he didn't believe her, but he couldn't force the lie out of her without fear that she'd quit.

During their vacation, he planned on discovering the truth so he could fix whatever he'd broken. If the last three years had proven anything, it was that he was a better man with her by his side. He loved her. He'd spent the last three years pouring his heart and his soul into every verse he sang, hoping she could hear—*feel*—his desperation. Hoping she'd recognize his cry for help. That he couldn't live without her.

How was he going to get her back?

Not yet having the answer to that question, he pulled the letter from his pocket and finished ripping it open. He unfolded the paper and instantly, he recognized the handwriting. All capitals and to the point. His stomach churned and the blood drained from his face, leaving him lightheaded. The last time Myka had penned him a letter, it hadn't gone well. She'd said their relationship had to end because her job meant more to her than he did. Well, it had gone something like that. He clenched his teeth and prepared for the inevitable.

Drew,

This is my official resignation letter. By the time you return home, I will have the position filled with someone more qualified than myself. I wish you all the best of luck. I'm truly sorry that I'm no longer able to manage Burning Brenda.

(Nicky is reading his letter right now. You know him well enough to know he knew nothing of my plan. He may be my friend, but first and foremost, he is your best friend.)

Now for the important part—the only person you have to blame is yourself!!! If you'd just left our past where it belonged!! I can see what you're trying to do—the gifts, the flattery, the looks, the touches. If you ever loved me—STOP. PLEASE. I'm begging you.

Myka

DREW FELT A STAB TO HIS HEART, A LITERAL PHYSICAL BLOW, LIKE A razor slicing with a quick sting that grew more painful with time until it throbbed with every beat of his heart. Maybe she didn't love him back? But he couldn't set aside the feeling that she was running because she did.

He stumbled to the bathroom and fell to his knees before vomiting. A hangover, plus a plane ride and a broken heart, didn't sit well with his digestive system. He rinsed out his mouth, then paced in front of the huge windows. The weather, which hadn't bothered him moments ago, now reflected his mood—dark, gray, and brooding.

They had something special together and she knew it whether she was willing to admit it or not. She was the only woman he would ever love. The high he got simply being near her fed his soul. No other woman could take her place. He'd already tried that avenue. *Repeatedly*. It had failed miserably.

As far as he was concerned, they were *not* over. Even if he had to kidnap her and whisk her off to a deserted island. That's what he would do.

She'd fallen in love with him once. He could get her to do it again.

myka

Myka lounged on the bed in the downtown Anchorage hotel with a cold washcloth over her puffy red eyes. There was something soothing about the smell of white towels washed with bleach.

Her letter to Drew wasn't going to be a hit. If she'd stayed on the island with him, her note would've been a challenge. A game she couldn't win. Though she was the one who'd broken up with him over a bogus excuse, her heart would not survive a rematch. She loved him to the bottomless depths of her soul. She always would. But she couldn't change him—wasn't sure she even wanted to.

He was a rock god. Women flocked to him; men bowed before him. He had an unusual combination of exquisite talent, arrogance, charm, and humility. Even the most venomous critic was putty in his hands. He always said, "*A sincere conversation without judgment could solve a lot of differences.*"

She'd taken his words to heart when it came to business

but ignored them otherwise. When Myka was presented with an emotional disturbance, her defense mechanism was to shut down. Disengage. If she ignored the problem for long enough, it would disappear. Her mom once said she'd gotten that negative trait from her dad.

For the last three years, she and Drew had managed to keep a tolerable, professional distance. His initial anger, she could deal with. The recent sadness in his eyes, the renewed interest—she couldn't. They both needed to move on. Perhaps with some distance, it could be done.

Originally, she'd planned on flying home to upstate New York immediately, but amongst the chaos, she'd forgotten to book a return flight. It was peak tourism season in Alaska and the soonest one she could get was three days away.

She'd decided to spend a few days in the land of the midnight sun, exploring. Then she'd head back home to find them a new manager. Preferably a man. Getting another job wouldn't be a problem with her experience and connections. Over the last few years, she'd had more than a handful of musicians try to lure her away from Burning Brenda, but leaving them had felt like abandoning her family.

Though, sometimes you had to do what was best for your family—even if it caused pain.

To distract herself from wallowing, she played tourist. She'd driven north to Talkeetna. The day had been clear, and Denali, the tallest mountain in North America, stood magnificent in the distance. Next, she'd headed south and taken a glacier tour out of Whittier and kayaked a small part of Resurrection Bay. On her final full day in town, she'd biked the Tony Knowles Coastal Trail and hiked Flattop as advised. The view of the surrounding town, mountains, and the ocean had been to die for, though the climb was precarious.

A thunderous pounding on the hotel door startled her from her stupor. Her muscles protested violently as she climbed out of her snuggly bed to answer it. She did a little dance as she shuffled forward. Breakfast.

Instead, she was greeted by a handsome Alaska State Trooper—blond, tall, crew cut.

"Miss Vukovic?" His voice was as sexy as he was.

"Yes." She patted her hair down, wishing it wasn't sticking up like a rooster's tail.

"I'm Officer Miller. I'm sorry to tell you, but your colleague, Mr. Arie, has been reported missing. I'm here to escort you to the plane we have waiting."

She gripped the doorframe. "What? What do you mean missing?" A ball of panic twisted in her throat and tightened, cutting off her ability to speak.

"Miss, I'm afraid I don't have much information at this time. How long until you can be ready?"

"Fifteen minutes," she squeaked.

His eyes, stopping on the absurd amount of luggage scattered behind her, rose in disbelief. "I'll meet you in the lobby. Pack light. I'll make arrangements with the hotel to send the rest of your belongings to the lodge."

She ran to the bathroom to brush her teeth and wet her hair before frantically throwing random things into a smaller case. She shimmied into jeans, a sweater, and some flat-heeled boots and then dashed from the room.

The trooper waited in the lobby as promised, seeming surprised she had five minutes to spare. He held out a hand for her bag and led her to his squad car. Her breath hitched when she saw the Pontiac Trans Am with a star logo and

Highway Patrol Interceptor splashed across the door, waiting for them in the parking lot. It was Drew's favorite car.

Officer Miller threw her bag in the trunk. No wonder he'd arranged to have the hotel send her luggage later. There wasn't enough trunk space to fit all her things.

After buckling her seatbelt, she bombarded him, her voice rising with every question. "Where is he? How long has he been gone? How did he go missing?"

"He was kayaking with friends. My understanding is one minute he was there, the next he was gone." By his stony expression, she suspected there was more to the story. "The Coast Guard is there searching already," he said as if trying to reassure her.

"Oh my God. Oh my God." She gripped her knees and started hyperventilating. "I shouldn't have left. This is all my fault!" Her heart slammed against her chest and guilt cloaked her shoulders.

"No, miss, it isn't. Things like this happen here in Alaska all the time. We'll find him."

She noticed he didn't say "alive."

The trip back to Sitka passed in a blur. She managed to keep her growing terror contained except for the perspiration stinking up her sweater.

Paul, the owner of the lodge, met her at the airport and pulled her into a bear hug. She did her best to hold back the tears. Denali, his husky, rubbed against her thigh as she petted the dog's thick fur in search of comfort. She and Paul had spent hours on the phone, planning this vacation for the boys. It had taken a lot of secrecy and trust to pull this kind of thing off without the media finding out. From the beginning of the process, she had known Paul and his wife,

Barb, were the people for the job. Sincere and steady—that's the kind of folks they were.

After Paul drove her and Officer Miller to the harbor, they hopped in the float plane and flew out to the lodge. A large number of small boats patrolled the waters below. She quizzed Paul on the circumstances, but he didn't have much more information than the trooper did. "We're gonna find him," Paul growled over the headset.

Again, she didn't give way to her fear. She nodded as unshed tears burned the back of her nose. She might've enjoyed the scenery if it hadn't been for the hysteria strangling her ability to breathe.

As they landed near the picture-perfect lodge, her fog began to dissipate. Barb greeted her on the dock with a strong, reassuring hug, but it didn't make Myka feel any better. With her spine straightened, she put on her big girl panties and walked toward Nicky, who was running down the planks followed closely by the other two.

Stumbling to a stop, they all started babbling at once. Nicky yanked her into his arms, while the other two hugged her on each side. One big family—that's what they were. And she was going to break up that family. A sob caught in her chest, but she clamped it down before the emotions spilled.

"Whoa, one at a time. What happened?" she said, muffled in Nicky's shoulder. He was a few inches taller.

"We went kayaking. He was in front of us one minute, then he disappeared the next." Nicky pushed her back, his green eyes clouded with fear.

"What do you mean disappeared?" Officer Miller said.

"He was there one minute and gone the next!" Gus Gus yelled, running his hand through his frizzy red hair.

Dark circles marred Tony's under eyes, and Nicky's normally immaculate appearance was off.

Officer Miller asked, "Were you drinking?"

"No," Tony snapped.

"Anthony." Myka glared, mimicking his scary Italian mother.

He sheepishly hung his head. "We might have been a little stoned."

She glanced at Nicky.

"What? We're on vacation and it's mostly legal here. At least, according to the locals." He shrugged. Not that being illegal would've stopped them.

"Where were you when you lost him?" Miller said.

"We didn't lose him! He vanished. Kayak and all." Nicky cracked his knuckles like he did when agitated.

"Okay. Where?" Miller said calmly.

"We headed out in the morning with enough supplies to camp on one of the islands nearby. I already showed the Coast Guard where we were. We never made it. I sent Gus and Tony back for help, and I stayed put so we wouldn't lose the exact spot where Drew disappeared."

Oh, thank goodness for Nicky's logic, she thought.

"He was gone, but so was his kayak." Nicky rubbed his hands over his scruffy face. She wasn't used to seeing him anything but composed and flawlessly groomed. This look actually suited him nicely—stocking cap, ugly rubber boots, and a soft flannel shirt. A rugged outdoor model. He paced over the dock, his feet slapping the wood every time he took a step.

"Were there any islands nearby that he could have made it to?" she asked.

"Yes," Nicky answered as his shoulders drooped.

"What can we do to help?" Myka asked Officer Miller.

"Stay here and wait to see if he comes back."

She wrinkled her nose. "Really? We're going with you to search."

"No, I'm sorry, but you're not." He towered above her, which furthered her irritation.

"Uhhh, yes, we are." She folded her arms.

"No. Do you really think *you*," he said, looking at her dressed in what she perceived as casual clothes, "are going to be any help? With our luck, you'd get lost too. Now please stay here and help Barb feed the search party."

"Screw you," she muttered under her breath as she beckoned for Nicky, Tony, and Gus Gus to follow. Taking *no* for an answer wasn't her strong suit.

They huddled together on the deck around the firepit as a buzz of action took place on the dock and in the house.

"Okay, where's the island? Can you find it yourselves?" She started sketching out a mental plan.

"Yes, I can find it," Nicky said. "It's not far from here. We kayaked out to it once already." He peeled the seed pods off a pine cone. He didn't do well without something in his hands, though usually, it was a guitar. Half the reason he was so talented was because he practiced obsessively. They didn't get their record deal on Drew's vocals alone.

"Good. Pack what you need, and we'll take kayaks out again. I'll figure out how to get Barb's help."

"No," Nicky said. "Let me handle that. We've become friends."

Nicky always made friends with older women. Myka figured it was because he'd grown up without a mom, and that's why he tended to gravitate toward them. Truthfully, there wasn't a woman he couldn't charm—or a man for that matter.

"Go put your things in your room, and we'll all meet back here in half an hour. I'll have supplies. And hey," Nicky stopped her, "put your things in the room on the third floor."

There was only one room on the third floor, and Drew's things were already strewn across the bed. She shook her head and dropped her bag on the floor with a thunk. Nicky would never stop pushing them together. He always said she and Drew were destined. Fated. An example of true love. Nicky was a silly romantic, and though he usually had good instincts when it came to matters of the heart, in their case, he was mistaken.

Crumpled on the nightstand, next to an empty beer bottle, was her resignation letter. She picked it up and smoothed it out before folding it and sticking it in her pocket.

She repacked her bag, adding some of Drew's things. She borrowed one of his baseball caps and an old, ratty flannel shirt that had seen more than its fair share of concert stages. She'd bought it for him years ago because lavender looked nice on him. Everyone gave him crap when he wore it, but it didn't seem to bother him because, obviously from the tattered hemline and holey cuffs, he wore it a lot.

She buried her face in the material as unwanted tears leaked between her closed lids. His cologne still permeated the fabric. *She had to find him. She had to.* She couldn't live in a world without him. It would be comparable to living in a world without light. Breathing air without the ambrosial scent of nature. Or listening to music without sound. *She wouldn't do it.*

She met the boys under the lodge's front deck, where they were loading up red and yellow kayaks with fresh water and food. Barb loaned her a pair of ugly rubber boots, some black rain pants, and a raincoat in case the weather got bad. Barb said things could change quickly in the last frontier.

Myka already had everything else stuffed into her back-pack and thrown into a waterproof bag—more clothes, cheap sunglasses, a tape deck with the cassette Drew had recorded for her, matches, her watch, and a tiny pocketknife she'd purchased in Anchorage.

In the midst of the chaos, nobody noticed as they dragged the kayaks down the beach. Slimy rocks covered in seaweed slipped under her boots, making the short jaunt perilous. She pushed her boat into the water and fastened the neoprene skirt.

Nicky pointed toward a tiny dot of an island that was easily a mile away, and they pushed off. Her paddles dipped effortlessly into the ocean as she settled into a rhythm. The sun's rays penetrated the first few inches of water, revealing a brilliant jade, only to be sucked into the dark, murky depths like a black hole. In the distance, the sunlight glinted off the almost glass-like surface. Under normal circum-stances, she would've enjoyed herself, but the fear clogging her throat prevented any measure of joy.

Seagulls called from above and a couple of bald eagles rested amongst the crown of a tall spruce tree. Their white heads appeared to be floating while their dark feathers blended seamlessly with the branches. When an otter popped up unannounced about twenty feet in front of them, she stifled a scream. It floated on its back with its dinner gripped in its paws while its teeth crunched loudly on the shells.

Once they made it to the first island, they skimmed the shoreline, following it around to the other side. A large orange jellyfish pulsed silently under her kayak, its long tentacles lazily trailing behind.

"We were headed to those over there." Gus Gus pointed to an outcrop of islands in the distance. "But we only made it halfway."

Her breathing lagged and her heart sped up all at the same time. She didn't want to think this could be Drew's watery tomb. A surge of dread flashed along her nerve endings.

A couple of small planes and a helicopter buzzed overhead, but surprisingly, there were very few boats in the area.

"Why are they not searching here?" she demanded.

"They did yesterday," Nicky said. "They think we're mistaken about where we lost him and it must have been somewhere else because they found nothing. No signs of Drew *or* the kayak."

She gazed into the blackened depths of the icy Alaskan ocean and whispered a small prayer. "Please, God." Then she dipped her paddles back into the water and took the lead. Her arms held up fine, but her legs began to form pins and needles from sitting in one position too long. She didn't want to fidget for fear of tipping into the water. Sweat beaded on her brow and upper lip as she embraced the physical exertion and pain. Anything to keep her mind off Drew.

Cold water snaked down her arms into her pushed-up sleeves. She paddled faster and sloppier. Behind her, the boys cussed as salmon jumped out of the water, occasionally hitting their kayaks headfirst on the hard plastic.

The ocean breeze whispered over her skin, trying to lull her into a false sense of security. Its caress held promises of healing, if she would only let it. But if Drew were lost here, these pristine waters would only fuel her nightmares. Alaska had a harsh beauty. Unparalleled splendor blinded many from its darker side. One wrong move and she would kill you, so she'd been told.

Soon, Myka was startled out of her reverie when she heard the whooshing and crackling of static on a radio. She tipped her ear toward the belly of the kayak, thinking Barb might've packed a walkie-talkie in her waterproof sack.

When she looked up, she twitched with surprise and squinted in confusion. Directly in front of her sat an island that she'd swear wasn't there a second ago. She turned to question the boys, but a foggy film, alive and glowing like the skin of a bubble, swayed and shimmered. It separated her and her friends. The hairs on her flesh rose from the electricity snapping in the air.

"Nicky!" she screamed, paddling furiously toward them.

The closer her boat got to the bubble, the louder and brighter the shield burned. Try as she might to break free, it nudged her around its circular web, not allowing her to escape. She watched through the glowing film as Nicky raised one hand to shush the others.

"Nicky, can you hear me?" she yelled. She stopped paddling and drifted.

"Yes, but we can't see you. Where are you?" he shouted back. Even though he was only about twenty feet away, he sounded like he was on the other side of a child's tin can and yarn phone.

She waved her arm in the air like the sweeping motion of a windshield wiper. "Right in front of you. Twenty feet at twelve o'clock."

"No, you're not!" he screamed, staring through her like a blind man.

"Listen, calm down. I am. This is what must've happened to Drew too. I don't know if they have some freaky phenomenon here, but I can see you, even if you can't see me. Please don't panic. Can you still hear me?"

"Yes, but barely." She could tell by the exaggerated movements of his lips that he was hollering.

As the bubble squeezed tighter, pulling her further from Nicky, her calmness fled and altered into a stabbing terror, unleashing panic. Not considering the consequences, she unlatched the neoprene skirt and wiggled out of her life vest. If she couldn't go through, she was determined to go under. She tossed herself into the ocean before rationality got the better of her.

Once she hit the water, common sense returned, punching her in the chest, taking her breath away. As she sank into the icy waters, the cold dug its claws into her skin, robbing her instantly of dexterity. *What had she just done?*

Her legs and arms flailed wildly, pushing her toward the surface to catch a sufficient amount of air. The waves, which had looked mild while in the kayak, were much bigger now that she was struggling to stay afloat in raingear and rubber boots. Nasty saltwater slopped into her mouth and burned her eyes and nose. She gulped the biggest breath she could manage before she dove under again. Her hands rammed into the flexible but impenetrable shield and bent her fingers backward sharply. Unfortunately, the bubble didn't stop at the water's surface. She tried kicking, but her legs were a set of lead weights and all other body parts were numb from the cold.

Slowly, she began to sink. Using one foot, then the other, she clumsily slipped off her boots to lighten her load. She kicked hard toward the murky green light above. Her lungs screamed for oxygen. Her head popped above the water's edge just as her body involuntarily inhaled. Gasping, she gulped mostly salt water. She splashed, coughed, and gagged.

Once capable of catching a real breath, she scanned for her kayak, but it was gone. Though the small island wasn't far away. She prayed she had enough strength to swim to shore. From the cold, her fingernails had turned blue, and she couldn't feel anything except for her teeth violently chattering.

On a high point of the wave, she forced her arms to swim, but something grabbed her ankle and pulled her down into the vast abyss below.

drew

Drew woke up on a soft, down bed wrapped in a fur blanket and wearing only his boxer briefs. The pelt caressed his skin, silkier than anything had a right to be. The only light in the windowless room came from a shelf twelve feet above the floor, lined with candles.

Confused, he sat up, studying the small area. The white gossamer curtain that separated the washroom from the rest of the space swayed in the candlelight, moving gently to a mysterious breeze. On a wooden cabinet, below a warped mirror, was a marble basin with a cloth folded over the side.

The last thing he recalled was spending the morning kayaking, hunting for a secluded place to escape. The media. The fans. The critics. An oceanfront campfire, a few beers, and the advice of his brothers was the solution. There, he would do some soul-searching.

They'd picked a distant island, and he'd led the charge. Around two hours into their trip, an unusual number of birds had started circling overhead. He'd looked up to see what all the racket was about, only to look back down as he'd sliced through a strange glowing bubble. On the other side, an island had mysteriously appeared out of nowhere.

He'd screamed at the boys, but they had been too far away to hear him. He'd waved, but they didn't see him. As he was trying to figure out what the hell was happening, a prickle on his skin alerted him to something unseen. The hair on his arms rose like the anticipation before the pleasure. A lover's caress.

Then he heard singing. The sound of heavenly voices pumped like a drug directly into his veins. The melody flowed from his ears, down through his core, into his groin, around his heart, and finally, to his brain. A high that he'd never beheld before. His desire to follow became an obsession.

A fixation.

He'd paddled ruthlessly until he hit the shore of the small island and jumped out of his kayak, not bothering to pull it up onto the beach. He'd dashed down the worn path, pausing momentarily to throw off his rubber boots, which had been thwarting his progress.

As the singing grew louder, his obsession turned to madness. Tree branches slapped across his face as he ran until his feet bled and his lungs screamed for air.

Stopping in front of three totem poles, he dropped to his knees, panting, sinking into the mud. The wooden owls on top of each pole, wings expanded, stared at him with large, yellow eyes and circular black pupils. Under each owl was a different species of bird—an eagle, a raven, and a hawk. Carved at the bottom of all three poles were men crouched in pain or perhaps fear, a silent scream ripping from their lips.

That was it. That was the last thing he remembered.

The sound of shuffling outside of his room brought him back to the present, and he quickly scooted out of the bed onto the bearskin rug. He was woozy as if he'd taken prescription painkillers. His feet were bandaged, but he felt no discomfort. He clenched his teeth, determined to take out whoever came in.

Three years of training with some of the world's best MMA fighters would come in handy today, he thought. The exercise and focus had helped him combat his stage fright. He leaned forward, balancing on the balls of his feet, poised to use his skills.

Until a tiny figure floated into the room. "Stay back," she said. Her voice, low and guttural, cloaked his body like liquid night—dark, sexy, and dangerous. "I come in peace. I'm here to bring you some food." Her eyes roamed his face, down his chest, past his abs, and paused slightly lower. She licked her blood-red lips and slightly shivered as she set the plate on the floor.

He cocked his head, blinking, trying to clear the drug haze. The woman had wings—angel wings. They peaked slightly above her head and draped down, almost touching the floor. Black and shiny, they glimmered like an oil spill in the candlelight.

"What the fuck?" was all Drew managed to say as he backed up a step.

She smiled, and her dark eyes, lined with thick black lashes, smoldered. "I love rock stars. They're my favorite. We haven't had a new one in thirty years," she purred, twirling her black hair around her finger and then brushing it over her plush mouth. Her pale skin almost matched the sheer, gauzy toga pulling tightly over the curves of her figure.

"Where am I?" Drew asked. He pressed the tips of his fingers together in the prayer position, though he wasn't praying, he was preparing.

"Don't come any nearer," she warned, smiling like it was a dare, not a command. Her tongue darted out, wetting her bottom lip.

"Where am I?" he repeated, locking eyes with her, giving her his signature come-hither look. He needed answers, and if he had to use his looks and charm to get them, so be it. He lowered his head, raised his eyebrow slightly, and smirked with interest. Even though she was a stunningly beautiful creature, vile goose bumps peppered his arms. She gave him the full-on stalker vibe. And as a musician, he'd learned how to spot the crazy train a mile away.

Her lids drooped as she reached for her ample breasts, circling her nipples through the fabric. She arched her back and moaned.

"Rave!" squawked a blonde angel woman hovering outside the doorway.

Rave's eyes snapped open, landing right on him. "Sorry, soldier, maybe later. But I'll be thinking about you tonight when I touch myself." She backed toward the door.

The blonde shooed her out, then said in a soft voice that was higher pitched than he expected from someone with such defined shoulder and arm muscles, "Eat. I'll be back for you later."

He wasn't sure if it was a threat or a promise.

She closed the door.

His stomach growled as the smell of grilled fish reached his nose. To prevent further injury to his feet, he walked over carefully and grabbed the plate off the floor.

He stopped to double-check the lock. Just because. But he already knew it was bolted.

myka

Shivering on the rocky shore next to a small campfire, Myka awoke dressed in only her underwear and wrapped in a blanket. On closer inspection of the short, soft fibers, she realized it was a fur pelt.

Cautiously, she sat up and glanced around. Relief flooded her veins when she spotted her kayak safely on the shore out of the way of the incoming tide. But every other instinct she had screamed—Run now! Get in that boat and paddle for your life!

But her desire to find Drew trumped her fear. Someone had to be nearby and maybe they could tell her what was going on. "Hello?" Her voice seized like she'd swallowed razor blades instead of seawater. "Hello? Anyone there?"

She waited for a minute, hoping someone would answer. When they didn't, she rose from the rocky beach, her joints creaking and her muscles complaining. She tiptoed to the other side of the fire where her clothes were laid out on a log. The orange and yellow flames crackled and popped, shooting sparks into the air. Ashes floated aimlessly on the breeze, landing on her grody hair and parched skin. Her fingers were stiff as she struggled to pull on her damp jeans and sweater.

Since her rubber boots were in the ocean, she dug through her backpack, which had somehow made it to shore safely, and slipped on the pair of sneakers she'd packed. Then she wrapped herself back in the warm fur and stayed near the fire as she contemplated her situation.

Something unpleasant nagged at her gut and an ominous shiver tumbled down her spine, but not because she was cold. The sensation radiating from this island was comparable to stepping inside a house and intuitively knowing it was haunted. But she had questions, and it might have answers.

She folded the borrowed fur and placed it on the log for whoever had pulled her out of the ocean, away from death's door. She glanced again at her kayak and swallowed hard. She wanted to get back into it, but she'd already tried that route and failed. The only reason she was alive was because someone, or something, had saved her.

She dragged her boat over the rocks, through a narrow forest of gray skeletal trees and long swaying grass, until she found a good spot to hide it. She couldn't afford to lose her only mode of transportation.

Her breath froze when she caught sight of another kayak buried under some brush. She checked over her shoulder before she dug inside the other boat and came up with Drew's pack. She hugged it to her chest and crumpled to the ground, silent sobs of relief racking her body. He was here, somewhere. Alive. When her tears subsided, she opened his sack to see if there was anything useful in it besides clothes.

Buried at the bottom was the photograph of them together attending the Grammys.

The night she'd dumped Drew.

He stood with his arm wrapped around her waist, posing on the red carpet. Bulbs flashed and paparazzi shouted his name, trying to get him to look their way. Drew was sexy, yet still boyish and innocent in his designer tux with his hair pulled back from his face. She stood next to him wearing a full-length violet dress and four-inch heels. He was staring at her, smiling, and ignoring the camera.

Afterward, she snuck off to the restroom. For some reason, nerves affected her bladder. As she stood inside one of the private stalls, struggling to get her zipper up, she heard a couple of gigglers arrive.

"Can you believe Andrew Arie brought his manager as his date?"

"You know why she got the job, right?"

A beat of silence passed as if someone might've shrugged.

"Her uncle was James Austin. The famous country singer who died like ten years ago."

"Oh, yeah. I remember that."

"Nepotism works every time."

They giggled. "Ain't that the truth."

"I just don't understand why he brought her. That boy could have anyone, and he chose a cow."

"I know, right? Can you say moo? Maybe he likes big girls."

They giggled again.

"It won't last long. Every woman out there wants a piece of that pie. She doesn't stand a chance. When he breaks her heart, she'll quit and crawl back to the herd."

"Good riddance."

Mortification rose up Myka's neck and chest before settling hot on her cheeks. Did everyone think she got the job because of her family connections? So what if her uncle was famous? She was the one who'd spotted Burning Brenda's talent. And yeah, sure, she was a bit overweight compared to most everyone else in attendance, but in the real world, who wasn't? Her Baba said they came from sturdy stock, and she was never going to be skinny, but she was by no means as heavy as they were insinuating. She was tall and thought of herself as curvy, voluptuous, not fat. Even if she were, who were they to judge with their sunken collarbones and every rib showing? She thought they could all use a snack, but she would never say that out loud. Because it was rude and none of her business.

But she had been twenty-one at the time, and to her shame, she'd let their words fester and rot the entire night. Maybe Drew was dating her because she'd given Burning Brenda their big break? Maybe he'd felt as if he owed her? Earlier, when he'd visited her hotel room while she'd been getting ready, he had said that he owed everything to her. That he was standing on *that* stage because of her.

As each Grammy was awarded, she questioned her worth. Her self-esteem withered, pulling her into a dark hole of reality.

He was desired by the world's most beautiful, powerful women, and Myka couldn't compete. Those catty girls had opened her eyes, even if she didn't like what they'd had to say. He would've eventually dumped her for someone better. So she'd decided to give up before she lost.

At the end of the night, when Drew was surrounded by admirers, she'd excused herself and left a letter in her hotel room telling him she couldn't date him and do her job properly.

She'd lied.

But she'd lived the lie for so long that it had become her truth, warped and ugly as it was. She couldn't face the pain that her lie, and low self-esteem, had caused.

And ultimately, Drew's track record proved that Myka was right. After they'd broken up, he jumped from one supermodel to the next and then traded that one in for an actress. The guys used to joke about Drew's flavor of the week.

As she stared at the photo with a trembling hand, guilt snaked its ugly tendrils around Myka's sorrow, not exactly strangling it, but warping her emotions into something worse—regret. Had she made the biggest mistake of her life breaking up with him three years ago?

Having thought she'd lost him forever put things profoundly into perspective.

But two things could simultaneously be true.

She loved him.

And yet she suspected her love would never be enough.

When she'd ended their relationship, she had almost destroyed herself in the process. If they got together again, and he dumped her, she feared complete annihilation.

It was enough to make her run again—this time far away and for good. But not until he was safe at home, back on the stage where he belonged.

She stuck the picture in her pocket, wanting to keep it close, but it felt wrong, like she didn't deserve the memory. She swallowed the gaggle of emotions and tucked it back into his bag.

After grabbing food, water, and the basic survival kit from the kayak, she followed the shoreline until it forced her into the woods. She trekked through bogs, over stumps and rocks, then battled vicious barbed plants that made her question the sanity of the rescue.

A large flock of birds darkened the sky and soared overhead, calling and screeching, freaking her out even more. But they were just birds, not bears. She had to keep reminding herself of that as images of the dagger-like canines on the bearskin rugs back at the lodge danced through her mind.

There are no bears on these tiny islands, right?

Small cuts in her skin screamed, not only from sweat, but from the saltwater left behind. When the sun started to go down sometime around ten o'clock, she needed to rest, at least for a few hours. Her muscles were starting to shake, and her stomach growled. She set up a small campfire, ate a few granola bars, drank some water, and curled up on the cold ground near the fire. Mosquitoes bombarded her now that she'd stopped moving and was no longer near the ocean breeze. Unfortunately, the smoke from the campfire only deterred them so much. Roughing it sucked.

She pulled the hood up on her rain jacket, tightened it under her nose, and sucked her hands up in the sleeves to hinder the biting bugs. She tucked Drew's flannel shirt under her head and promptly fell asleep. If something decided to eat her, be it a bird or a bear, she was too tired to care.

myka

Curled in a fetal position on the damp, moss-covered ground, Myka melted into a reoccurring dream of her first date with Drew.

"What's this for?" Myka asked as her mom handed her a packed overnight bag just as the doorbell rang.

Instead of answering the question, her mom opened the door.

Drew waited on the bottom step, wearing a big smile, standing in front of an RV.

"Have fun," her mom said, ushering Myka outside.

She glared at her mom on the way out, mad, but not really. What kind of parent did something like that—shove their twenty-one-year-old daughter out the door with possibly the hottest guy on the planet and tell them to have fun?

"What's going on?" she asked Drew.

He shrugged and threw her a charming smirk. "You told me in order to go on a date with you, I had to come up with something original. Remember? You gave me a list of things you didn't want. No dinner, movie, flowers, or jewelry. So buckle up, we're going on an adventure." He waved his hand toward the RV like a game show host.

Myka shook her head in complete disbelief, but she was intrigued. "How did you rent that thing at twenty-three?"

"Seriously?" He clutched his chest as if she'd insulted him somehow. "Actually, I bought it, so I didn't have to worry about it." He opened the passenger side door and closed it after she hopped in. He picked up her bag and placed it in the back before he climbed into the driver's seat and took off down the highway.

"Really? Your first house is an RV? You're a closeted redneck! I knew it!" She slapped her leg. "Please tell me you're not going to park it at your parents' farm and live there," she razzed.

They both laughed so hard their eyes watered, and she worried he was going to run off the road.

"You know I'm not going to sleep with you because you have a sweet ride, right?" she said, half joking with him, because her thoughts often traveled that forbidden path.

"Yeah, I know, but hey, you can't fault a guy for trying." He sent her an overexaggerated wink like a fool. He was ridiculous but so flipping cute she could barely stand it.

The RV was really nice. Small, but top-of-the-line finishes. Easy to maneuver and park, but had everything someone would need for a long weekend. She could see him living in it. That's the kind of guy he was.

"Where are we going, if you don't mind me asking?"

"Well, you said you didn't want jewelry, but you said nothing about gems," he said.

"What? Gems are jewelry. And why would you need an RV for that? You're not making any sense, Drew."

He held up a hand. "Semantics. Hear me out. You don't need an RV if you're going to buy gems, but we're going to dig for our own." A grin spread across his face.

She closed her eyes momentarily. "How in the whole wide world of dates did you come up with this?"

"I watched a documentary," he said, so proud of himself. "And with this beast," he patted the dashboard, "it'll be easier to avoid people."

He had a point. After their first single hit the Billboard charts and raced to the top, it was getting harder and harder to go anywhere without fans recognizing him. He was hard to forget even before he was famous.

Thankfully, as of yet, he did pretty well disguising himself in a baseball hat and sunglasses. Though it was hard to hide the 6'5" and tattoos.

They spent hours on the road discussing their future. Not "their" future, but the future of the band. The only stops they made were to fill up with gas and switch drivers.

Around eight o'clock, they pulled into a nice North Carolina campground that Drew had reserved. Once everything was hooked up, they lit a fire in the pit, grabbed some beers, and roasted hot dogs.

When they started yawning, they went inside to figure out the sleeping arrangements. Drew told her to go shower, and he would make the pull-out bed to sleep there. When she came out, he was standing in front of the bed, rubbing the back of his neck.

"What's wrong?"

He didn't have to answer. His accommodations were at least six inches too short.

"You did this on purpose!" She stomped her feet, pretending to throw a fit.

He turned to look at her, his eyes big, round, and horrified.

She laughed hard in his face. "Dude, I'm just messing with you. The bed is a queen. You stay on your side, deal?"

"You're lame." He chuckled.

They crawled into bed and she separated them with a line of pillows, afraid of what would happen if she didn't have the barrier.

The next morning, she awoke to him staring at her through sleepy eyes.

"What are you doing?" she asked.

"Just looking." He reached over to push the hair out of her face. "I love how you have dark eyebrows, but your hair is light." He traced her brow with his finger. Butterfly wings beat against her stomach walls. "It's so unique with your black, demon eyes and poufy lips." He jumped out of bed and grinned, showing off his straight white teeth.

Years of geeky braces, Nicky had told her.

At the emerald mine, they rented a bucket and a shovel. One of the employees escorted them through the woods to a private site in the middle of an open field—basically, an area of red clay that mimicked the surface of Mars.

Drew handed her the shovel. "Great practice for if I ever piss you off." He winked.

They switched places often, giving the other a break. They picked up interesting rocks and tossed them in the bucket. Neither of them knew what to look for. Even though sweat poured down her back, soaking into her shorts, she was having a fantastic time. Being with Drew was effortless. It was like hanging with a best friend, except one she couldn't stop staring at, especially after he removed his shirt. Sweat glistened on his golden skin and all she could think about was running her fingers over his abs. Bump, bump, bump. His basketball shorts hung low on his hips, making her wonder how easy it would be to slide them off.

He turned his ball cap backward and wiped the sweat from his brow with a T-shirt before he held out his strong arms. "Okay, your turn."

She took a swig of water and then poured the rest of the bottle over her head, trying to cool off—in more ways than one. The heat was no joke.

"Holy hell," he muttered as he helped her down into the small hole. Instead of climbing out, he placed his dirty hands on her arms and asked, "Will you be my date to the Grammys? If you don't go with me, I'm going to have to ask my mom." His face morphed into false sadness.

"I'm sure there are plenty of girls willing to go with you." He had his choice of women.

"Yeah, there are, but I want to go with you. Mom's my second choice. Don't worry," he said, holding up his hands, "she already knows this."

Myka nodded.

"Soooo...is that a yes?" His voice held a smile.

"Yes."

She watched his eyes dilate, even in the scorching sun, as he leaned in and kissed her. And all that time, she'd thought the North Carolina sun was hot. But that one kiss set her insides on fire. His lips were gentle, tickling, almost like a feather running across her sensitive skin. Shivers ran down her spine, directly between her legs, despite the blistering heat and nearly one hundred percent humidity. One hand slid up her arm to her face, then behind her head, grabbing a fistful of ponytail as his other hand gripped tighter on her arm, almost becoming painful.

Soon, though, the dream warped into a nightmare.

Drew's fans gathered around them. They yanked on her hair, tore at her clothes, and slapped her. She struggled to get away until she realized she was no longer dreaming...

Her dream had literally become a waking nightmare.

Her eyes popped open just in time to see a fist slam into

her face. Pain cracked the bridge of her nose and blood gushed as darkness imploded.

Myka came to, naked and shivering on a cold dirt floor. Sharp pebbles bit into her flesh as her eyes darted around the space. Her pulse thumped loudly between her ears. Past a set of iron bars, torches hung on the stone walls. They flickered, casting long, eerie shadows. Bruises, in the shape of small handprints, painted her skin, and scratches, those strongly resembling fingernails, etched her arms. She swallowed, trying not to gag as metallic-tasting blood trickled down the back of her throat. She got up off the damp floor and limped to the iron gate, wondering where the hell she was.

"Son of a beehive!" she cussed as she shook the cage wildly. Clanking metal on metal echoed along the corridor.

She stuck her face close to the bars and peered down the torch-lined hallway. The walls curved sharply, obscuring her view. Her prison cell was wedged like a slice of pie with no windows and sat at the far end beyond two others that were empty. She ran her hands over the rough walls, pushing on stones, searching for weakness. The smell of mold and earth saturated the humid air. Moisture seeped between the cracks, but not enough to pool on the floor. Her toes were frozen to the point of numbness while her teeth chattered so loudly in her skull, she thought they might break. She rubbed her hands over her arms to create some heat, but she wasn't sure which was worse: the cold or the pain.

More light flickered in the passage, and she snuck to the far rounded corner of the cell, pressing her back against the frigid wall.

Beyond the bars, a tiny figure holding a torch came around the bend, gliding over the dirt floor. Myka gasped when the creature turned away and stuck the torch into the wall slot.

Soft, gray wings folded compactly protruded from her back and almost touched the ground. Silvery-brown hair, reflecting in the warm light, tangled amongst the feathers as she bent over and laid a leather pack on the ground.

Myka's breath escaped violently and her legs buckled. She held on to the wall so she didn't fall.

Sirins.

Baba's stories were true. They resonated through her mind as her heart slammed against her ribs.

Mythical winged women, who were half bird, half human, who hypnotized men through song. Once under a Sirin's thrall, there was no escape. They would seduce the men and kill them afterward. Occasionally, when a union was fruitful, and a child was born, the Sirins would leave it in the woods as an offering to their gods. Somehow, some-way, once in a while, a child would survive, and that's why people like Baba, Drew, and Myka existed—descendants of the Sirin. Myka had always pretended to believe Baba because she'd gotten angry when she didn't.

"Oh, goodness, I don't know why they do this." The Sirin's voice sounded full of pity when she saw the state Myka was in. "Are you okay?"

It took Myka a second to realize the creature was

speaking English with a slight Eastern European accent. She hugged her arms tight around her boobs and didn't answer.

"Are you okay?" the Sirin asked again, slower this time. She looked up at Myka with round eyes that were a hint too big for her heart-shaped face. She couldn't have been an inch over five feet tall.

Do I look okay? Myka thought sarcastically. Then she decided to be nice, having heard you catch more flies with honey. She assumed it was the same for birds. "No."

The Sirin dug through her pack and pulled out a blanket and a gauzy gown. Dried mud flaked off the bars as she passed them through. "Here. Put this on and wrap the blanket around you."

"Where am I?" Myka lost her modesty and lifted the gown over her head. It fit tight through the chest and hips, but it was better than nothing.

"The island of Pan. It means paradise."

Somehow, Myka had never pictured paradise looking through prison bars. "Am I dead?"

"No."

"Can you let me out of here?" Myka asked.

"Not yet, but hopefully soon. I can stay here with you for a while." The Sirin reached into her bag, pulled out a few tiny crab apples, and handed them through the bars.

Myka's stomach growled. She choked back a laugh, thinking of Adam and Eve in the Garden of Eden—aka Paradise. But the Sirin didn't look like a snake, and Myka was starving, so she ate it. Tart juice ran down her chin, and she wiped it off with the back of her hand before she licked it clean.

She looked up to find the Sirin staring at her with her doll-shaped lips agape.

"Sorry, I was hungry," Myka said.

The Sirin shook her head, short and quickly, like she was resetting her thoughts. "No, that's quite all right. I understand." She handed Myka a piece of shortbread through the bars. "What's your name?" She sat down on the dirt outside of the cell and pushed her wings over like someone with long hair might do to get it out of the way.

"Myka," she answered, wondering if she should have lied. "Yours?" Myka sat down too.

"Anserlee." Torchlight flickered over her face, giving her an unearthly glow. She looked like an angel sitting there in the dirt with her luminescent skin and soft, downy wings.

"Do you have any other humans here?" Myka asked, fishing for clues. She needed to escape, and Anserlee was the only source of information thus far.

She cocked her head sideways as creases formed between her eyes. "Yes, we have a few."

"Are they all locked up like me?"

"No, most are free," Anserlee said, drawing it out like it was a wonderful thing.

"When can I leave?"

"Oh. Nobody ever leaves." She tilted her head to the other side and smiled, staring at Myka like she might be crazy. "Soon, you won't want to leave either."

anserlee

Anserlee handed the young woman a gown and a blanket, wondering how long the Matriarchs planned on keeping her in the dungeon. She hated the way the raptors had treated their newest captive, depositing her in the prison cell as if she were garbage. Her heart had ached when she'd found her cowering, naked in the corner, with her battered arms hiding her breasts. She was as tall as most men, and her hair was short, but her body was soft and curvy in all the right spots.

Anserlee cringed with sympathy when the woman painfully pulled the gown over her head, exposing, for a moment, her full, unmarred breasts. She admired the human's soft, golden skin that was practically hairless until the small dark patch between her legs. A twinge of jealousy flared as she looked longingly at the smooth calves that led to orange-painted toenails.

They talked for a bit until Anserlee got up and dusted off. She fluffed her feathers to remove any lingering dirt.

"Don't worry, I'll be back soon. Is there anything I can bring you?"

"Water?" Myka cleared her throat.

Anserlee nodded, not trusting her voice. The purple ring around Myka's neck upset her. She questioned why they had to treat the woman so poorly and keep her in the dungeon while they held the handsome young man on the second floor, which was a luxury by comparison.

She huffed as she walked up a semi-circular flight of stairs, flanking the outside walls of the tower. Levels two and three were configured in an S-shaped pattern with a hallway down the middle and rooms on either side. They maintained these rooms for captive men until they could be trusted not to flee. Floor four was used for auditions, and five, six, and seven belonged to the Matriarchs. On top of the tower was an open-air veranda they used for festivities and celebrations.

As she trudged upward to report her findings to the Matriarchs, the passageway became lighter and brighter. Unlike the first three stories, the others had huge arched windows that ran equally spaced around the tower.

She stopped in front of the double doors on the fifth floor, knocked, waited ten seconds, then let herself in. She spread her wings, flying through the large hole in the center of the ceiling. The Matriarchs' accommodations had no stairs—a safety precaution to keep out humans. If the men weren't under a Sirin's direct control, they could be dangerous left to their own devices. Not surprising, considering what most of them went through.

Curving around the fireplace were three circular pits carved into the stone, lined with furs, feathers, and silk pillows. Each Matriarch rested comfortably inside a nest with their feet tucked underneath them and their spotted wings circled up over their laps.

Gleaming weapons and priceless works of art, from tapestries to paintings—most stolen from the modern world—lined the stone in between the distorted glass windows. Coronas of soot from the torches stained the ancient walls.

Unlike the rest of the Sirins, who looked like women except for their wings, the Matriarchs seemed more bird-like than human. Instinctually, the flock knew the Matriarchs were their leaders, the same way a predator knew their alpha. According to the teachings, the Matriarchs were created by the Gods as the wise old owls, while the rest of the Sirins, at some point in time, had been born. Anserlee was around two centuries old. Eventually, the monotonous years began to blend and she often lost count.

Myka was the first bright spot she'd had in decades.

In unison, the Matriarchs peered up from their books and studied Anserlee with their unblinking eyes. Their movements were as one, and they made all flock decisions collectively. Their voices worked, not only on men, but on all of the Sirins as well, giving them total control. If one of them stepped out of line, the Matriarchs were the judges, the jury, and the executioners. Anserlee had witnessed their powers only once. Thirty years later, she still couldn't get the images out of her head.

There were other islands out there like Pan, spread throughout the world from the Caribbean to the Mediterranean to Antarctica. They each had their own trio of Matriarchs, all wise old owls, no matter the location.

Without prompting, Anserlee began her report. She'd held the position of Lead Healer long enough to know the drill. The Matriarchs did far more listening than speaking. She cleared her throat and began. "The young lady, Myka, is doing well. She's not combative or as confused as she should be. I have a feeling she might know more about us than most humans do. I would like to take her to the springs to clean up and help her heal from the rough treatment she received earlier. Then perhaps set her up on the third floor, where she will be more comfortable?" She maintained her neutral tone. The Matriarchs didn't approve of emotion. Especially when it came to their captives.

They all tilted their heads slightly and definitively blinked their golden eyes with round pupils.

The middle one answered, her voice soft and very human but her accent very heavy. "Yes, but take a couple of raptors with you. We hear the woman is quite large."

Without any formal dismissal, they promptly went back to reading their books.

Though in a hurry to return to Myka so she could provide her with pain relief, Anserlee took her time leaving. Anything out of the ordinary was sure to capture the Matriarchs' attention. And that was the last thing she wanted to do.

TEN

myka

M yka had fallen asleep against the stone wall, cuddled in the warm, fur wrap. Anserlee was practically in front of her before she noticed her this time.

Anserlee crouched next to her cell, her wings smudging over the dirt floor. "Okay, I have to lay out some ground rules," she said. "I conferred with the Matriarchs, and they said after I get you cleaned up, I can house you on the third floor, which is lavish compared to this. But you will have to obey the rules." Anserlee handed Myka's sneakers through the bars.

Myka was anxious to make her escape but the only way to succeed was with some rest and a plan. And the only way to come up with a plan was to cooperate. *For now.* She had to know what she was up against.

"And what are the rules?" Myka slipped on her shoes and tied the laces.

Anserlee wrapped her dainty fingers around the iron bars. Her nails were neatly trimmed and clean. "Don't try to run. Because if you do, they *will* kill you. It's not like we have a shortage of women here." Her thick, feathery lashes fluttered. They were a hair short of brushing her brow bone.

"I guess that sounds easy enough." Anserlee wasn't bluffing. Myka was surprised that whoever had captured her earlier hadn't killed her. They certainly weren't gentle. Her nose ached with the beat of her heart, and she wondered if it was broken. "And?"

"That was the most important one. But there are a few niceties to follow that will help you in the future. Don't speak unless spoken to; do not make eye contact unless spoken to; and please, whatever you do, if you are spoken to, answer with respect. Some will try to goad you and some will outright insult you. Do *not* rise to the occasion. It will only end with you back down here...or worse."

"For goodness' sake." Myka inhaled deeply, catching the scent of lavender amongst the damp, musty dungeon.

Anserlee clasped a tiny hand over her chest. "Please, not all of us are that way. Matter of fact, most of us aren't. But the few who are make up for those who aren't."

"Okay. I can follow your rules." Myka had spent what seemed like a lifetime catering to divas and biting her tongue. Ha, ha, who was she fooling? She rarely kept her opinions secret. But she could handle a few days.

"Outside, I have two guards waiting to accompany us. They shouldn't give us any problems, but if you try to escape, their orders are to kill."

Myka gave her a mock salute before she stood. She cracked her knuckles and stretched prudently, looking down upon Anserlee's diminutive frame.

"No!" Anserlee's voice echoed harshly off the stone walls.

Myka's eyes widened.

"I saw the way you looked at me. You think you'll be able to overpower one of us because of your size. *That* is what I'm talking about. *That* is what will get you thrown back in here or worse. Because of your immunity to our voices, they will use strength to subdue you."

"Sorry," Myka said. But she really wasn't. Drew had taught her some of his MMA moves for self-defense, and if she got the chance, she wouldn't hesitate to use them.

Anserlee pulled an ancient set of skeleton keys, ornate and rusted, out of her pack. They jingled as she opened the door. With a wave, she motioned for Myka to exit. Once free of the bars, Anserlee held her palms out. Myka placed both of her hands into Anserlee's tiny, warm ones. Within a millisecond, Anserlee's hands darted to the top of Myka's wrists and held on while she twisted. Myka crashed to her knees. A sharp, stabbing pain ran all the way to her shoulders and down her spine, causing her to holler. Then, as quickly, Anserlee let her go.

"Come with me," Anserlee said in her singsong voice as if nothing had happened.

Myka stood up and brushed the pebbles from her knees. She needed to master her facial expressions better if she wanted to avoid that again.

They climbed a set of semicircular stairs to the next floor, where Anserlee opened an unlocked door. Myka stepped into the sunlight and cringed, shielding her eyes with her hand. *My retinas*, she wanted to scream. Slowly, she parted her fingers, letting her vision adjust to the light, and took a breath perfumed with evergreens, damp earth, and the sea.

A series of tree houses, all connected by suspended

wooden boardwalks, sagging slightly toward the middle, loomed over her head. It was like a spiderweb starting at the massive stone tower, then branching out in all directions, deep into the forest. The birdhouses—she laughed internally at her joke—were identical: moss-covered roofs, wooden shake siding, oval windows with flower boxes, and arched front doors. It was spectacularly whimsical.

Waiting outside were two minuscule women. Each had curly, brunette hair and brown eyes. Myka caught a quick glimpse of the broadswords strapped between their silky wings before she turned around to follow Anserlee down the path.

Occasional footsteps and laughter echoed from above. There was no visible way to access the tree houses on foot, but if you had wings, you probably didn't need a ladder. As they got farther from the tower, the underbrush became thicker, funneling them onto winding trails.

Draping moss occasionally tickled her exposed neck, forcing her to duck lower. Fungus grew like steps up the older tree trunks, while bright-orange mushrooms with yellow dots flourished randomly along the forest floor. Bits and pieces of sunlight penetrated the canopy, scattering across the lengths of Anserlee's hair and wings. Whiffs of sulfur permeated the air long before they found the steaming hot springs.

"Wow, this is quite a way to go for a bath," Myka said.

"There are ones closer, but I thought the seclusion would be preferable." Anserlee slid out of her pack. She set it down on a large rock next to the steaming, turquoise water. She nodded to the two sentries behind them, but when Myka turned around, they'd disappeared. She wrinkled her forehead, wondering where they had gone.

"All right, get in," Anserlee said.

Myka didn't appreciate the audience, even if she didn't know where they were, but complaining wouldn't change anything. She took off her shoes and tugged the gown over her head, tossing it aside. She dipped her foot into the hot water, testing the temperature. Stepping into its almost too-hot embrace, she welcomed warmth for the first time in days. It penetrated deep, defrosting her brittle bones. Mist enveloped her as she swam to the far side of the hot springs.

Anserlee stood on the bank wearing a pleased smile. She sat down on a lichen-covered rock next to her pack and unlaced her leather boots.

"I thought birds didn't like water," Myka said, hoping Anserlee had a sense of humor.

Anserlee pulled her boots off and held her foot out. Myka didn't even have to put on her game face. Baba had already told her about *the feet.*

Anserlee laughed—though it kind of sounded as if she were honking. "Some of us like it more than others." Her feet were narrow at the heel and wider at the ball, with three webbed toes and narrow, curved nails. The skin on her legs, from mid-calf to her toes, shifted from cream to a buttery yellow, ending in a subdued orange. She held one foot up and wiggled her toes. She slipped out of her clothes, grabbed a leather bag, and swam across the springs toward Myka.

"Wet your hair." Anserlee poured something into her hand.

She cozied up behind Myka and started scrubbing her scalp. Her strong hands left Myka in shivers, even in the hot water.

"Why is your hair so short?" Anserlee massaged a

flower-smelling concoction into Myka's tresses after she helped her rinse the shampoo.

"Because he likes it long," Myka said before she caught herself.

"Is he the one you're running from?"

Myka nodded. *Or running to.*

"Well, you won't have to worry about that anymore." Anserlee kneaded her fingers down Myka's neck to her shoulders.

Myka took a deep breath and allowed herself to relax.

Little did Anserlee know, that was why Myka was here —to rescue Drew. She knew if she was being treated this well, then he was being treated better. So, for the time being, he was safe. Unless all the stories Baba had told her were wrong.

"These are healing nicely." Anserlee inspected the scratch marks on Myka's arms.

Myka looked down, surprised that they were almost gone. "How did they heal so fast?" she asked.

A clueless look rose on Anserlee's perfectly arched brows, and then she pointed innocently to the soap. Her wet hair draped over her small, pert breasts, and Myka found herself missing her long hair. Anserlee's skin, even more amazing in the light, was poreless, like she had been carved from a flawless slab of marble.

Anserlee added soap to her hands and swiped some over the bridge of Myka's nose before working on the marks around her neck. She closed her eyes as Anserlee massaged along her collarbone then back down her arms. With each pass, the pain and tension in Myka's body retreated.

"Okay, lean back and rinse your hair, then we better go," Anserlee said.

They got out of the springs and dried off with soft towels. Before Anserlee dressed, she opened her wings and flapped them furiously, sending droplets of water all over Myka's dry skin. A hazy rainbow sparkled in the mist, shrouding Anserlee in a heavenly glow. All she was missing was the halo.

"Sorry." She bit the side of her lip. "I didn't mean to get you wet again. I didn't even think."

"It's fine," Myka said. The sight of her outstretched wings was almost worth drying off again.

On the way back, Myka remained silent, trying not to be obvious that she was scoping out her surroundings, wishing she'd picked a different career path. How was managing a rock band going to get her out of this situation? One way or another, she'd figure it out.

anserlee

The two guards left as Anserlee entered the tower with Myka in tow. On the second floor, they passed a door with a latched iron padlock.

"Is anyone in there?" Myka pointed.

"Yes, a human man stumbled upon us the other day. Rumor has it, this one is a famous rock star." Anserlee attempted to keep the judgment out of her tone. She didn't approve of their practices, but it was safer to mind her own business. The Matriarchs had taught them long ago not to question their judgment. Not that Anserlee had learned the hard way herself. She'd witnessed the punishment that went with a dissenting opinion. The Sirins who'd protested the harsh treatment of men had been banished from Pan, forced to live outside the barrier as a bird. She shuddered at the thought. Though Anserlee disagreed with their opinions, she was smart enough to keep her mouth shut.

"Who is it?" Myka's ebony eyes sparkled with curiosity. She paused by the wooden door and rested her elegant fingers against the surface.

It wasn't often people with Sirin blood crossed the magical shield protecting their remote island, let alone two in a matter of days. The coincidence was bizarre, but Anserlee knew they couldn't possibly be acquainted. Two Sirin-blooded people in the greater world would repel one another—polar opposites, like magnets on the wrong side, forced together. It just couldn't happen. Even if Drew and Myka had met at some point in their lives, they could never be friends, no more than a lion could love a lamb.

"His name is Andrew Arie. He's the lead singer for Burning Brenda." Anserlee ushered Myka up another set of stairs.

"Oh, wow," Myka said, sounding impressed. "Everyone knows who he is. How do *you* know who he is?"

"Because in our bird bodies, we can fly through the shield. That's how the Matriarchs keep informed. Every month, scouts from here, usually ravens or raptors, are stationed in random locations in the Northern Hemisphere. Later, they return with their findings, and others are dispatched."

"Oh." The disbelief on Myka's face suggested she was skeptical. "So, are you like bird...birds on the outside? Or do you keep your human," she twirled her finger near her head, "ahh, brain?"

"We keep most of our facilities, but our instincts become stronger, and we see the world through a very different lens."

"Will you keep Andrew Arie here forever then? People are searching for him." Myka's tone took on a sharp edge.

"I assumed that's how you got here—as a part of the search team?"

Myka paused for a moment, then answered brightly,

"Yeah. Of course that's how I got here. How else would one get here?"

Anserlee brushed past her strange reaction, chalking it up to the *situation* and sleep deprivation. She unlocked the door to the room on the third floor. "And yes, to answer your question, Andrew will stay here forever. No one ever leaves." Though it wasn't quite the truth. In a different colony near the Caribbean, they had a famous musician who'd figured out how to pass through the barrier in his human form. Nobody knew for sure how he managed, and so far, he was the only one who'd succeeded.

She moved aside and allowed Myka to enter first.

"In that cabinet over there, you'll find some more gowns. Here, sit." Anserlee patted the fur blanket on the bed before grabbing a mug out of the other cabinet. She filled it with water from a faucet and sprinkled some scented herbs over the top of the surface. They sank to the bottom before she handed it to Myka. "Drink this."

"What is it?" Myka held on to the cup and stared into it suspiciously.

"It's going to help you sleep. You're going to need it. Tomorrow's a big day."

Anserlee was pleased that the marring around Myka's neck had faded significantly. With a good night's sleep, it would be gone by morning.

"What's tomorrow?" Myka asked.

"Tomorrow, they decide who will be his partner for the audition."

"Whose partner?"

"Andrew Arie."

"A singing audition?"

Anserlee avoided the question with a nonchalant, "Mmmm. Drink it," she encouraged.

Myka put the cup to her lush lips but hesitated.

Anserlee brushed Myka's bangs out of her face and held her cheek in the palm of her hand. Her skin was warm and soft. She stared into Myka's deep, dark eyes, endless midnight pools, and smiled sadly. "If I wanted to hurt you, I would've done it already."

Myka's eyes snapped wider at her bluntness before she shrugged and tossed the drink back.

Anserlee took the cup and set it on the nightstand next to the bed. "Sleep well. I'll see you in the morning."

She gently shut the heavy door and stood there for a moment before she locked it from the outside. She hated the thought of keeping Myka prisoner, but it was safer for her. She dropped the key into her pocket, thankful there was only one copy. She clenched her fists, then opened her hands and shook out the tension before heading to the fourth floor.

She stopped for cleaning supplies and fresh linens along the way before continuing up the stairs. Usually, the task of preparing *the room* was someone else's job. Her station as Lead Healer was well above janitorial work, but for the rest of today, Anserlee wanted to be alone and get her hands dirty. There was something rewarding about good old-fashioned manual labor. Plus, she wanted to make sure the job was done to her standards. If Myka was the chosen one, then Anserlee wanted to make sure the accommodations in the room were perfect.

As perfect as the dreadful room could be.

She set the supplies on the floor and stood in front of the two-way mirrored glass separating the spaces. She pressed her hands against its cold surface. It would have been a beautiful room, tranquil even, if it wasn't for the horrors that took place inside. She ran her fingers downward over the glass, making a high-pitched squeak and leaving smudges behind. She needed to clean it anyway. She loaded up her arms before entering.

The dirty deeds done in this room lingered in the air long after the show had ended. The horrors. The screams. The begging. And finally, the submission. They were branded into the cold, stone walls. A stain that, no matter how hard Anserlee scrubbed, could never be erased.

She propped the door open so air would flow through. She leaned over the fireplace to scoop out the ashes into a wooden bucket. Next, she dusted, then swept and mopped the floor. Sadness crept over her as she threw fresh linens onto the bed and fluffed the down pillows. She flew around the room, making sure all the candles on the upper shelf were new so they wouldn't burn out before the event finished. No session had ever gone that long before.

Though it was pointless, she hoped Myka wouldn't be picked for the audition with Andrew. If Myka were chosen, her life would go from uncomfortable to downright dangerous. Some of the other Sirins didn't like competition, especially from a human.

When Anserlee completed her tasks, she went outside and flew up to the boardwalk. Wood creaked under her steps, and true birds sang amongst the branches as she headed home to her nest. She nodded politely at the sisters she passed by but refused to engage in conversation. The day weighed heavily on her wings, and she didn't have anything left to give. She craved privacy more than most, probably because she cared for her sisters all day long. She was the nest's Lead Healer in the art of medicine, responsible for their overall health.

Upon waking this morning, the Matriarchs had alerted her that another human had been captured. Because of the odd coincidence of two washing up on their shores, the Matriarchs immediately assigned to her the complete well-being of the woman. All Anserlee's other tasks had been distributed to her underlings.

What made her suspicious was Myka's acceptance of it all. She knew more than she was saying. Most human women—not that there'd ever been many—panicked. And none had ever lived long. But Myka seemed remarkably fine. It could be shock—but in Anserlee's opinion as a healer, she didn't think so. She would bet Myka had believed in Sirins before she arrived. Did Myka know that she, herself, had a small amount of Sirin blood running through her veins? It was the only way anyone could cross the protective barrier onto the island.

A coy smile played on her lips as she opened the door to her quaint tree house. Over the last two hundred years, she'd been assigned other humans before, men and women, but none had burrowed under her skin instantly the way Myka had.

Her Amazonian goddess size was only a fraction of Anserlee's fascination. Myka's icy composure might've been the rest. Most of the time, Anserlee spent weeks, if not months, calming the women down. The men were easier because all she had to do was sing and they fell under her spell. But it was a lie. There was no challenge in making somebody want you or love you when their heads could be turned by a song.

Humans who had Sirin blood running through their

veins could never be attracted to one another. For some reason, one repelled the other. Sirins themselves were also polar opposites. They could work together, they could play together, they could even have a sexual relationship, but there would never be a connection or a bond like the one they could have with a human.

In the beginning, it wasn't just sex that made men precious to Sirins, it was the connection. Eons ago, before the Gods imprisoned them, there were stories about the love affairs between Sirins and their men. How they escaped the colony so they could be together and not have to worry about another Sirin singing to their man. After their race was locked behind the barrier, the male pickings got slim, and somewhere along the way, that connection had been twisted and warped into what it was now.

Unfortunately, love and escape were no longer possibilities. Except for the one anomaly in the Caribbean, the only way to leave the island was to turn into a bird and fly far, far away.

But because of her Sirin blood, Myka could live an exceptionally long life in Pan. What if Anserlee could give Myka a reason to want to stay?

drew

Drew lay sprawled out in his bed, dressed in a pair of linen pants and a shirt, bored as shit. Every morning, before he awoke, his dirty clothes had been removed and clean ones were left in their place. He'd already explored the room, searching for any weaknesses in the stone, but found none. Unfortunately, the breeze shifting the curtains came from the small crack under the bolted door.

He tucked his hands behind his head, humming a tune he couldn't get off his mind. He itched for a piece of paper and a pencil so he could jot it down. This was the first time in a couple of days he felt clear without the foggy company of drugs. He still didn't know where he was, who these women were, or what they wanted with him. His gut, rife with anxiety, told him he wouldn't like the answer.

He hadn't seen anyone since Rave and the blonde woman had brought him dinner the first time. Now, his meals just miraculously showed up on the nightstand, as if he'd fallen asleep and awakened to food. He realized he was in prison, even if it was a five-star facility.

Adrenaline flared as jiggling at the door startled him. He sat up, and for a split second, considered bum-rushing the person on the other side but decided to stay put. *For now.*

Through the entry walked the angel with the quiet, yet high-pitched voice. Her leather boots, with ties coiled around her calves, were silent on the stone floor. The hem of her belted tunic hit mid-thigh and flicked with every step.

"Drew, I'm Gilda, and for this evening, you will be in my care. I'm going to need you to accompany me." Her shiny, blonde hair blended almost seamlessly with her metallic wings. Her eyes, glistening like a fine whiskey, looked almost burdened by her thick, flaxen eyelashes, and her skin glowed in the candlelight as if she'd bathed in liquid gold.

"Where?" Drew pushed himself up against the carved headboard and crossed his arms.

"It is time to prepare you for the audition selection." She sat down at the foot of his bed and folded her hands as if ready to answer his many questions. Her fingernails were black, curved, and sharpened to a point like talons.

He swallowed. "The what?"

A soft smile arched her lips. "Do you know where you are?"

"Uhhh, no…" Drew said.

"Well, that doesn't really matter anyway. But what you *are* matters. We are Sirins, and you have our blood running through your veins."

Drew sat up straighter as a distant memory trickled forth. He vaguely remembered when Myka had told him he must be part Sirin with a voice like that, but he'd laughed her off. Even after she'd tried convincing him with her Baba's wild story about the mythological creatures that were half bird, half woman, who used their beautiful voices to enthrall men. Apparently, they didn't have any guys of their own so they sang like the pied piper. And dudes followed. She'd even gone so far as to tell him that sometimes, if the Sirin got pregnant, they would leave the child outside as an offering to their gods. She'd been pulling his leg...or had she?

"You are rare, though. You got close enough to hear us sing. Centuries ago, we could sing to whomever we chose, but the Gods decided to lock us up. Now, the only people who can hear our call have Sirin blood running through their veins. And even if a normal human could hear our call, they wouldn't be able to pass through the barrier that has imprisoned us on this island. We're only able to escape when we shift into our alternate form, that of the bird."

Drew began to say something, but was quickly cut off by a wave of her hand.

"Yes, yes, all of us have two forms—one human while we're on the island, and one bird which allows us to cross over to the outside world. Our goal when we leave Pan is to find those with a drop of Sirin blood and monitor them. Thankfully, most of you are musicians and we only focus on the men. As you will soon see, there are more than enough women on this island. When one of you on the outside dies, one of us in our bird form is always watching. Waiting. As you die, we collect your soul before it has a chance to move on."

His eyes slivered and his jaw dropped open in horror. "Uhhh, how in God's name do you collect someone's soul?"

He wondered if they were the spawn of Satan, who was, after all, a fallen angel.

"We swallow the soul and fly back home, where we transform into our human form. Then three months later, a baby boy is born. One who will grow into the man whose soul we took. They age quickly until they hit approximately thirty. They have memories of their previous life without the complication of people thinking they're missing. Because their dead bodies are left behind."

Drew's mouth watered as his stomach roiled. He shook his head. *No way. Not possible. She has to be lying.*

"You, on the other hand, have people searching. Some of them fine young men." Her lips curved into a hungry smile, and she ran her tongue over her white teeth.

"I thought you sang to the men then killed them?" Drew asked, having recalled Myka's tale with clarity. He now began to worry for Gus, Nicky, and Tony's safety. They were out there searching for him. He was sure of it. A cold sweat beaded on his forehead. His only solace was knowing that they didn't have Sirin blood, otherwise they would've passed through the barrier with him. And thank God Myka was long gone, because according to her Baba, she carried Sirin blood too.

"We never kill them on purpose. Eventually, our love wears them out and they...well, they give up and die." Her lower lip pouted. "Long ago, we would sing, and men with or without Sirin blood could follow our call. Back then, swallowing a soul was the last resort. A desperate measure. But now, it's all we have—unless someone *like you* gets within earshot."

Drew's nostrils flared. "How do people not know about this?"

A chirp-like laugh bubbled from her chest. The sound made his groin tighten in a perverse, unwanted way. It felt dirty, and invasive, and was followed by self-deprecating guilt.

"Actually, you musicians make it simple. How many of you die of drug overdoses? Even if you're surrounded by other people, they're all high." She raised a sharp eyebrow. "Rarely do they even notice there's a bird nearby. Others die in car accidents, plane crashes, suicides...really, it is easy. And perhaps people over time have noticed us. Why do you think ravens and owls are known as the harbingers of death?"

"If you can control men with your voices, why don't you just lure those with Sirin blood here so you don't have to steal souls?" The idea of losing one's soul seemed worse than the situation he was currently in. Because when he escaped, he could go back to his former life.

"First of all, in our bird forms, we're just birds. Our speaking voices only work in this form. And in this body, I can't leave." She gestured to herself. "Our islands are so remote that very few humans ever find them. If they do, the chances of them having Sirin blood is exceedingly rare."

"It just feels like a disgusting, incestuous ring," he snapped.

"That's not how it works. We just swallow the soul— our genetics don't mix. And besides, whoever carries the child opts out of ever sleeping with them, despite not truly being their mother. We do have standards."

"If you say so," he muttered. "But I could still be related to any one of you."

"There are a lot of islands, so your lineage being from this one is minuscule. And even if your ancestor came from here, it was probably hundreds of years ago, so at the worst, we'd be distant cousins. Any more questions?"

He shook his head, more from disbelief than as an answer. "No." Truthfully, there were a million questions swirling around his brain, but between his queasy stomach and the pain building in his temples, he couldn't fasten any of them down. He was still having problems coming to terms with her explanations. Because nothing that she said was remotely believable. Yet he believed every word.

"Good. Let's get you ready for the festivities."

He tensed, wondering if *festivity* was a code name for orgy or massacre. Sex or death? "Festivities for what?"

"I told you—the audition. First, we eat, then you sing, then the Matriarchs decide who will be your partner."

He ran his fingers through his long hair in frustration. He threw off the down blanket, stood up, and started pacing. The cold stone floor, along with the crisp air, cooled him down quickly. "Look, I don't mean to be rude, but am I putting on a show?" He certainly hoped that was the case and not the other horrors running through his head.

"Yes, but perhaps not the kind of show you're accustomed to. It seems that Rave didn't tell you."

"Tell me what?" He stopped in front of Gilda and stared down at her. She was tiny, but the self-assured way in which she presented herself hinted she was not to be messed with. Two types of people often carried themselves as such— those well trained in any form of fighting or martial arts, and predators.

"You will be auditioning for buyers. The highest bidder wins. We will bid on you to gain your services, but first, we need to see if you're worth the gold." Her eyelids lowered, slivering almost shut, and a disturbing sigh escaped between her lips.

Drew swallowed, his Adam's apple bobbing slowly. "Do you mean as a singer...or a slave?"

She laughed again. This time, he gritted his teeth to ward off her effect. "Hmmm, we are not communicating well. Let me be blunt." She rose from the bed and stood toe to toe with him, her gaze traveling slowly up his body until meeting his eyes. "Your audition will be you and a partner copulating so we can see how much you're worth. Plain and simple. We want to know how good you are in bed. Usually, your audition would be with one of us, but unfortunately, a couple days after you arrived, a human woman conveniently washed up on our shore. Most of the time, the Matriarchs will opt for one of them to be your partner if they're still alive," she flicked her hand in the air, "so the rest of us don't squabble for the honor."

Blood drained from Drew's face, leaving him lightheaded, and his pulse jumped, kicking viciously under his jaw. He knew of only one woman who would scour the ends of the earth to find him even though she swore she didn't love him. His stomach cramped and his heart seized. *Please,* he begged whoever might be listening, *don't let it be her. Anyone but her.*

"How did she get here?" Drew asked, his voice coming out breathless.

"Apparently, she's of Sirin blood, too, and crossed through our barrier. You couldn't possibly know her though; she must've been an extra in the search for you. Luck be a lady, for the three young men traveling with her, they couldn't get through. Oh, what I would do to them." The golden feathers of her wings vibrated as she shivered.

Drew turned and bowed his head so Gilda couldn't read his face. Tony, Gus, and Nicky were safe from these creatures. It was Myka he was worried about. And he was curious as to why they didn't think he could know her. His instincts hollered for him to keep his mouth shut.

"Snap, snap. We need to clean you up. The event begins tonight." Gilda unlatched the door and beckoned for him to follow. "If you behave, I'll let you enjoy this not under the influence of the song."

"Enjoy what?" The hair on his arms raised in alarm.

"Not what you think, though you might like it." She eyed him eagerly. "I am under oath not to touch you like that. My job today is to simply groom you and prepare you." Her heated gaze rested on his crotch. "Although I'm not going to lie, I will be bidding on you."

"Who are you?" he asked rhetorically. He'd had millions of women look at him like that before, but none had made him feel degraded. Sure, they were looking at him for sex, but he had had a choice in the matter. Here, he was afraid he didn't.

He took his emotions and wrapped them up in a tight ball to bury them deep in the recesses of his heart. He needed to keep his wits about him if he wanted to survive long enough to escape. And that's exactly what he planned to do—find Myka and run. First, he needed to test Gilda's ability to control him. There was no way he could fight the monster under the bed without bringing it into the light.

"What if I don't want to come with you?" He schooled his face into boredom, then crossed his arms and planted his bare feet.

"I am Gilda, Head of the Raptors. And you don't have a

choice. If you refuse, I will sing. But if you come willingly, you'll be able to remember everything."

"So if you sing, I'll forget?"

"If that's what I want. We all have several tones that do different things. The voice I'm using now has no effect on men whatsoever. But I have another tone that will control you, and one that can make you forget, and another one that will do both at the same time. Which shall it be?" She glanced over her shoulder as she held the door open.

"I think I'll come willingly, for now." Drew slipped his feet into some weird leather shoes by the door.

Gilda led him down the stairs to the ground floor where they exited the stone tower. As they walked, he marveled at their tree houses and all the beautiful women staring down at him from the boardwalks. The sun crested over their heads, shoulders, and wings, basking them in a heavenly glow. Revulsion tasted sour in the back of his throat—they were the opposite of angels.

Gilda clapped her hands sharply at all the gawkers from above. "All of you will disperse and continue about your business or none of you will attend the festivities later," she snapped.

"If you're the boss, why are you in charge of dressing me up for tonight?" He didn't bother hiding his disdain.

"Because, Andrew, I'm one of the few who will be able to control myself around a specimen like you."

He stumbled. Were they all just going to jump him and force him to perform? The horror. That ball of emotion he'd so neatly put away threatened to explode. He clenched his fists and his jaw, neither action helping the pounding headache at the base of his skull.

She escorted him to a small hot spring hidden inside a

dark cavern. Wavering lights from the lanterns hanging on the stone walls glistened off the wet rock. Droplets of condensation plopped into the steaming aqua waters and the smell of rotten eggs flooded the thick air.

Gilda stripped off her gown, folded it, then laid it neatly on one of the wooden benches that surrounded the hot spring. Next, she sat down and began unlacing her knee-high leather boots. "Turn around," she ordered.

When he didn't comply immediately, she said it again—only this time he didn't have a choice. His brain argued but his body did as he was told—something akin to being a puppet on a string, only he was conscious. He tried to fight it but failed miserably. It was as pointless as trying to control the beat of his heart. Fear flooded his system as the precariousness of this entire situation truly dawned on him. She'd taken his free will and tossed it out the window as if it weren't even a struggle for her.

"Now turn back around," she said.

He rotated slowly, able to act on his own again.

She stood in the pool, the water just above her knees, her golden hair floating alongside her. She was fit like an athlete, with small breasts and a hard stomach that led to a slight curve of her narrow hips. "Are you coming?" she asked, her voice breathless and husky.

For a moment, he wasn't sure what she meant. He scooted backward, away from her, fight or flight mode activating.

She started to hum low in her throat.

Embarrassment blushed his cheeks as he felt himself growing hard, though he didn't think it was of his own accord. His head and heart screamed, "*No*," but his other head wasn't listening. She was as beautiful as she was repulsive. He wasn't even remotely attracted to her, not emotionally nor physically—when he was in control.

To hide his body's betrayal, he dashed into the hot pool.

A mixture of terror and rage pulsed through his veins as he tried ignoring Gilda's predatory hands while she washed his hair and then moved on to his body. How was he going to get himself out of this situation? More importantly, how was he going to save Myka?

THIRTEEN

myka

Anserlee arrived at Myka's door early the next morning and escorted her to a small room in the tower that smelled of dried flowers and herbs. Muted sunlight flooded the space and reflected off a large, warped mirror hanging from the wall. Dust particles and tiny down feathers floated in the sun's golden haze. Boar hairbrushes, ribbons, and a pot of beeswax with a candle heating it from below sat on a table under the mirror. Open shelves held corked glass bottles filled with oils and perfumes. A chair, tucked under the desk, and a long wooden table layered with furs were the only furniture pieces.

First, Anserlee ordered her to climb onto the table, then proceeded to wax her legs and other sensitive bits before performing a facial and rubbing a spicy-smelling oil into her skin. After she styled Myka's hair and added a small amount of makeup to her face, she brought her back to her room and began to dress her.

"I don't understand why you're doing all of this."

Anserlee had been quiet and withdrawn all morning, but Myka needed some answers.

"You must be beautiful for the audition selection tonight." Anserlee flipped through dresses in the armoire, making faces while shaking her head at each one.

"Really? Can't see what difference it's going to make." She'd seen some of the beauties on the island of Pan. Nothing Anserlee could do would make her stand out, or more like blend in. The fact that Myka stood a hair under six feet tall and had no wings made her conspicuous enough.

Anserlee ignored her and pulled a filmy, purple gown out of the cabinet. "This will look lovely on your skin." Myka couldn't argue since it was her favorite color.

Myka held her hand out and pulled the dress over her head.

Anserlee's expression switched from pleased to what seemed like an unusual combination of sadness and resolve. She reached out with a finger and ran it gently over the side of Myka's cheek before trailing the back of her nail across her bottom lip. A shiver rushed through Myka as she dropped her gaze.

"Sit." Anserlee pointed to the bed. She placed a pair of black ballet slippers in front of Myka and laced them up her legs, tying them behind her knees. She clasped a single black pearl on an almost invisible chain around Myka's neck, the jewel resting slightly above her breasts. The finishing touch was a delicate gold belt wrapped around her waist with the ends draping down to the bottom of the dress.

Anserlee stepped back, observing her handiwork. "Come. You're ready." The tiny furrows between her brows and pursed lips suggested otherwise.

The dress swished around mid-thigh as Myka followed

behind. Trepidation spasmed inside her stomach from the unknown.

Anserlee led her outside the tower, where two Sirins waited for them. They stared at Myka with blank faces, but she could tell behind their warm, brown eyes, they were sharp and intelligent. They all had the same poreless skin, only in varying shades of perfection. Whereas Anserlee looked to be carved from marble, these two reminded her of polished bronze. Sunlight reflected copper off their feathers.

Myka gasped as each one grasped her under an armpit, spread their wings, and lifted her off the ground as if she weighed nothing. Her feet dangled uncomfortably like a pendulum and her guts took a nosedive as they rose. She did her best not to look down. It took less than thirty seconds to arrive at the top of the tower.

The roof was probably close to the diameter of two football fields, but round. The view from the top overlooked the valley, out into the sparkling ocean. A circular stage cloaked in black curtains sat in the center, surrounded by a green blanket of unkempt grass and clover.

"What is going on? Some kind of celebration?" Myka gestured toward the venue.

"Something like that," Anserlee said cryptically. "Everyone's here for the concert."

Myka's heart palpitated and her breathing shallowed at the thought that Drew might be there. Of course, the Sirins would want to show off their latest addition. She scanned the area quickly, but other than the vendors peddling their colorful merchandise and food from small booths, they were the only "people" she could see.

Myka's mouth watered when the aroma of barbecue hit her nose, followed by her stomach growling in agreement.

"Would you like something to eat?" Anserlee placed her tiny hand on the small of Myka's back.

"No, thank you." While her body might want food, she didn't think it would stay down long with the nerves bouncing inside. She prayed Drew would be there too. She desperately needed to see him to make sure he was okay. She hadn't asked about him again because the possibility of them knowing each other was an *impossibility* to the Sirins. It was the only advantage they had.

Anserlee led her by the hand along a stone path around the perimeter. They stopped in front of a booth selling fresh honey attended by a tiny, beautiful woman without wings. She smiled at Myka, a real smile, not a threat hidden within a smile. She couldn't possibly be human. She was too perfect—like a tiny porcelain doll with flawless skin and eyes that were more orange than brown. Myka wondered if somehow, she'd lost her wings. Despite the warm day, a shiver burrowed under her skin.

"Is she a…?" She ticked her chin toward the woman when they were out of hearing range.

"Yes. She just got more of her father's attributes than her mother's."

Bile heaved, burning the length of her esophagus, when she realized that the girl's father was human and more than likely dead. At least according to Baba's stories, sirins were the black widows of the supernatural realm.

"Does her voice work like yours?"

"No. Only those of us born with wings seem to have it. I suppose it's possible, but I've yet to see it."

Quiet singing floated through the air, notes so beautiful, Myka wanted to capture them and hold on to them forever. Multiple feminine voices added layers upon layers of depth to the unknown tune. Anserlee joined in as they continued their walk through the marketplace. Myka ran her hands up and down her arms, trying to abate the goose bumps.

Muted pottery, the colors of earth, water, and sun, were for sale next to handmade jewelry pounded from gold and silver. Gauzy clothing, hanging from wooden racks, blew gently in the breeze. Delicatessen retailers sprinkled randomly throughout varied the smells in the air from sweet to spicy.

"How do you buy things here?" Myka picked up a robe. The fine silk, an intense shade of cobalt, felt almost nonexistent between her fingers, like water flowing through her hands.

"With gold, jewels, or services." Anserlee snatched the fabric away. She folded it and placed it back on the blue pile between the ruby-red robes and the vibrant green ones. The colors were so brilliant they seemed fake.

"My apologies," Myka mumbled to the girl selling it. She didn't know what to call the ones without wings. She tossed Anserlee a dirty look for her rudeness. "What if somebody buys something with services then doesn't repay them?"

"The punishment is so severe, it has never happened. That's not how things are done around here," Anserlee snapped.

"Wow," Myka whispered under her breath. She wasn't sure what she'd done to upset Anserlee, but whatever it was, she was mad.

Most of the Sirins wandering through the festival had wings of muted tones—browns, grays, blacks, and whites. A few, however, had wings the most beautiful shade of blue and eyes that matched. It was arresting against their dark skin.

When the place started getting crowded and Myka began drawing too much attention, Anserlee dragged her toward the stage. They followed the stone walkways with moss growing between the cracks until Anserlee pushed her down on one of the front benches in what felt like a child's time-out. A set of stairs connected every aisle to the stage, and the configuration reminded her of a five-pointed star. Anserlee sat stiffly beside her, staring forward. The rise and fall of her chest was the only thing that separated her from a statue.

As more Sirins arrived, instead of getting louder, everything hushed in a quiet anticipation. Though Myka refused to look, their stares burned a veritable hole in her back.

The ever-present breeze vanished, and all of the noise was suctioned from the world. The wind rustling through the trees, birds chirping, insects buzzing, and singing—all gone. The absence of sound screamed unnaturally in her head. She yawned to make her ears pop.

From behind the black, velvety curtains, notes from what sounded like a twelve-string guitar pierced through the silence almost violently. She recognized the song instantly—most Americans would have, as it had been played on the radio for going on forty years—but she didn't feel sick until she heard his voice. Whoever was singing sounded identical to her late uncle, James Austin. Sweat slicked her forehead and the nape of her neck as rage gathered in the pit of her stomach. Her Uncle James had written that song for his wife, Myka's auntie, not for these blasphemous women. They were not worthy of his music.

Myka clenched her hands into tight fists, digging her nails into her palms. It took every ounce of strength she had not to stand up and scream. She knew it couldn't really be him—he'd died in a small plane crash more than thirteen years ago. That knowledge was the only thing that kept her seated.

Tears streamed down her face as the song ended. She'd loved her uncle, and getting over his death wasn't something she'd yet accomplished.

Anserlee elbowed her gently and whispered in her ear, "Isn't he amazing? Besides Andrew, he's the most recent addition."

Myka's head snapped toward Anserlee, and if looks could kill, she would've burst into flames. Uncle James's music had helped shape her childhood. She remembered twirling over their freshly cut lawn, belting out his songs at the top of her lungs, or sitting around a campfire, strumming a guitar as everyone else sang along.

Myka was eleven the day her uncle died. All of the next week, she'd refused to come out of her room, nor did she attend his funeral. Instead, she'd held her own, alone in her room, listening to his music on her boom box.

Anserlee's eyes widened at Myka's anger.

What she couldn't understand was how they'd found someone who sounded exactly like him. Her uncle was dead. For the first time in her life, she was happy about it.

The next performer behind the black curtain, she didn't recognize so readily. She couldn't put her finger on the voice, but she knew she'd heard it before.

But the third singer—she knew he was there before he even opened his mouth. *Hallelujah.* Her heart stumbled and her energy, her soul, her essence, whatever it was, reached toward the stage as if it wanted to spring from her chest and wrap around him. Even though they'd only dated for three months, she could *feel* him. It was the same as always. From the very beginning, and even after she'd broken up with him, it was like a rope of electricity tethered them whenever he was near. It used to freak her out until she'd gotten used to it. She'd never said anything to Drew about it. She didn't want him to think she was strange. She'd attributed it to the Sirin blood inside of both of them. Not that Drew would've believed her then—bet he did now.

Drew used no instruments save his voice. His dark, raspy tone washed over her and flowed down her spine like molten gold.

After his last notes died away, the curtains opened. The velvet fell to the ground in slow motion and pooled like a shimmering black lake around his feet. In an odd combination of joy and terror, Myka's throat twisted, leaving behind a knot she couldn't swallow away. Tears burned the back of her nose, welling in her eyes as her chin trembled.

Drew stood, centered on the platform, glaring at the crowd of ogling Sirins. She wasn't sure what was worse, that they'd cut his beautiful hair or that he was completely naked.

Her muscles tightened, ready to spring from her seat and shield him from their prying eyes. But if she did, then someone was bound to figure out they had a history. Anserlee had said their Sirin blood should repel one another, not attract. Myka's gut instinct screamed at her to stay put despite her desire to protect him. When their eyes met, she held his gaze for a split second before she looked down. Not that she didn't want to see him. But not like this, she didn't.

Suddenly, the stage parted like an earthquake separating the ground, except for the small circular island where Drew stood. Three identical, winged women flew through the hole in the floor. After the stage came back together, they floated down and touched the ground in front of him.

Silver braids woven with flowers and jewels crowned their heads. Each one of them had a different color of gem dangling in the middle of their forehead. Otherwise, Myka couldn't tell the three apart. Round, amber eyes with large black pupils, sharp almost hooked noses, tiny lips, and the grayish undertone of their skin made them appear less human than the others.

"Who are they?" Myka whispered in Anserlee's ear.

"The Matriarchs," she answered with a slight tremble.

Before Anserlee could say more, the center one started speaking. "Ladies, this is the specimen you will have the opportunity to bid on come the new moon." Her voice was thick with an Eastern European accent.

The crowd broke into frantic shouts and catcalls, and the smell of lust tainted the air.

Slowly, the small stage behind the three women descended and Drew disappeared, but the Matriarchs remained.

Myka let out a big sigh and dabbed at her eyes. At least he was alive, and as far as she could tell, unharmed.

"Now let's bring forth our first prospect," one said, throwing her arm up toward the blue sky. Diamond rings on each finger caught the light, tossing a rainbow over the crowd.

Whoops and hollers broke out as the first beauty took the stage. Her black hair contrasted with her white skin, and the ridiculous amount of jewelry she wore flashed in the sunlight. It was as if she hadn't been able to decide which trinket or bobbles to wear so she'd opted for all of them. Once on the platform, she spread her black wings and flapped them slowly, shades of blues and greens reflecting on her feathers. A slight breeze passed over Myka's skin. The three Matriarchs walked around the first contestant—for what, Myka still didn't know—bobbing their heads up and down and blinking wide.

Next, they summoned a Sirin with flaming-red hair and even paler skin under a ton of freckles. The audience hooted for her but not as loudly as they did for the first woman. She spread her wings, but unlike the previous Sirin, they didn't match her hair at all. They were spotted with black and white and not as big.

"And for our final contestant—Anserlee, will you bring forward the human?"

The dryness in Myka's throat prevented her from swallowing. She didn't budge. *This is not happening.*

Anserlee politely, with a firm grip on her arm, lifted her from the bench. "Either you do this willingly or the Matriarchs will ask for help." Anserlee smiled, though her eyes were serious. She rose and yanked Myka by the arm.

Myka flashed Anserlee a nasty look. She could've given her some verbal forewarning. Like *you're one of the contestants*, instead of just hinting at the possibility.

As they stepped onto the stage, dead silence greeted them. Moisture slicked under Myka's breasts and in the small of her back. She shrank under the gaze of the three women circling her, studying her intently. They picked their legs up quickly and then paused before they put them down, like a chicken. She almost expected them to stop and scratch the ground for bugs.

She choked back laughter, but not because any of this was funny.

One of the Matriarchs stopped in front of her and

grabbed her arms in her cold hands. Myka twitched. Wide yellow eyes stared up at her, unblinking until she started nodding. "We thought it would be you, but now we are positive it has to be you." She tossed her hands into the air, playing to the crowd. "The human is a virgin," she yelled, offering Myka up like a sacrificial lamb.

FOURTEEN

drew

Drew ran his fingers through his short, shaggy hair as Gilda led him back to his room. They'd cut his long hair—just one more violation to add to the list.

"That got them worked up," Gilda whispered under her breath, and the feathers on her wings fluffed.

"What happens next?" Drew tightened his robe around him. He felt dirty and vulnerable—two feelings which had never occupied the same space in his mind—until he'd arrived here.

"The three ladies will be brought to your room, and you'll declare your choice. The Matriarchs make the final decision, but they consider your wishes. We do want your best performance, after all."

Above, the monsters were choosing who he would sleep with. He prayed it wouldn't be Myka. Not that he didn't want her, he did, but he didn't want her to have to go through that kind of humiliation. It was bad enough being on display, naked, in front of those cheering, leering women, let alone having to *perform* in front of them.

Gilda left him alone in the room, the soft click of the lock reminding him he was a prisoner. He tossed his robe on the floor and threw on a pair of linen pants and a loose-fitting shirt. He sat down on the edge of the cushy bed, elbows on his knees, and rested his forehead in his hands.

The lead weight clogging his throat dropped and settled in his gut when he realized Myka was coming to the room. Usually, the thought of her made his heart race, but under the circumstances, all he could find was a debilitating fear.

He swallowed the bile burning the length of his esophagus.

He was right about the human woman who'd washed up on the island shortly after he'd arrived. It was Myka. What he couldn't understand was, when he was on that stage, why had she refused to look at him?

He didn't have much time to process the information before the door unlocked and Gilda escorted Rave, five other Sirins, and Myka into his room.

"Drew, these three are our Matriarchs, and this is Anserlee." Gilda tipped her chin toward the three strange-looking women and the beauty with her hand resting protectively on the small of Myka's back. "You have already met Rave, and this is Forest, and the *human*," she said, like it was a dirty word. "These are your choices. Take a moment, introduce yourself, then inform the Matriarchs of your wishes."

He swallowed and rose from the bed. He wiped his sweating hands on his pants. The quicker he picked, the sooner everyone would leave him alone. Or at least he hoped.

He strolled over to Rave. "So we meet again." He took a lock of her silky hair in his fingers and brushed it over her shoulder. Disgust shivered over his arms, but he managed to hide it from his face.

"That we do." Rave smiled, gazing at him intensely with her hooded eyes.

He shook his head and moved on to the next woman. He held out his hand, and she placed her fingers in his. She was chilly to the touch as if she'd been outside in the cold for too long. "I'm Drew." He kissed her smooth, soft skin.

"Forest," she said as she squeezed his hand before she let go.

The creepy crawlies didn't trickle down his spine as they had with Rave.

Next, he moved to Myka. The ever-present humming over his skin buzzed frantically, reminding him that she was near. He'd often wondered if she had the same physical reaction to him as he did to her. He'd never asked, because if she didn't, he didn't want to seem odd.

She looked directly at him, communicating nothing through her stare, and she shook his hand firmly, politely, like he was a stranger. He could only assume she was pretending that they didn't know each other for a good reason.

"Myka," she said. "It's nice to meet you, though I'd rather it was under different circumstances." She rolled her eyes. "I love your music. It speaks to my heart." She clutched her chest.

His soul begged him to reach out and hold her. It took every ounce of control he had not to force her into his arms. All he wanted to do was to shout, *Myka! I choose Myka! Every time.* But he loved her enough not to put her through the torture.

Before he chickened out, Drew turned to the Matriarchs. "Forest. I choose Forest."

Forest's face lit with delight, then flashed in fear as she glanced at Rave. Rave's eyes gleamed and her ruby-red lips flattened.

"And why Forest over Rave?" the middle Matriarch asked, as if gathering facts, not sating her curiosity.

"I believe we'll be well matched. I'm afraid Rave," he said, glancing at the seductress, "would eat me alive. And this is my audition."

Rave's temporary anger seemed mollified by the statement but not entirely pleased.

"But the human is a virgin. We would like to observe how you handle that. It allows us to see how much control you possess," said another Matriarch.

For a moment, Drew paused, his brows furrowing. They'd only dated for three months, and he knew, at the time, Myka was a virgin. It was part of the reason he'd wanted to take things slow. He hadn't wanted her to feel as if she'd missed out on something by not having more experiences—from dating to foreplay to more than just sex. His plan had been to build a relationship to last a lifetime. And in show business, a stable foundation was the only way couples survived. From the beginning, he'd envisioned a future with them together. Forever. But Myka had made it clear that she didn't agree with taking things slow. She'd made it very difficult to stick to his guns and he'd often wondered if he'd sabotaged himself by refusing her.

So how could she still be a virgin? She was twenty-four

and had dated countless men. But now that he thought about it, the longest she'd dated anyone was about three months. Which was about three months too long, as far as he was concerned. Still, he knew the Matriarchs must have been wrong about her virginity.

myka

For a moment, the only sound in the room was the whoosh and thump of Myka's pulse as it filled the silence. Thankfully, she was positive she was the only one who could hear it. She had been prepared for Drew to choose one of the others to audition with.

She could tell they had an unspoken agreement of *it's safer* that they didn't know each other. If they had to perform together in any artistic medium—dancing, singing, whatever—there would be no hiding the kind of chemistry they had—the long-term kind forged in respect, combustible attraction, and if she was being honest, love. So much love. At least on her end. But she wasn't prepared for the *she is a virgin* crap again.

Drew had no right knowing that about her now. He'd known about it then, when they'd dated. But she'd spent three years seeing other men to prove she'd gotten over him. It wasn't like she'd kept *it* on purpose. She just couldn't find anyone she wanted to be with. Most had been wonderful guys—good-looking, great jobs, funny, and generous. Despite that fact, they had each been missing the one thing she was searching for—they weren't him.

When he touched her, her body, and something deeper, perhaps her soul, instinctively responded. As if he was the yin to her yang. Every nerve ending tingled, driving an ache deep inside her soul. It wasn't simply physical—it was emotional, spiritual. And only one person could fill that need.

Andrew Arie.

Myka willed her face to stone, pretending not to be upset at them spilling her secret. She really didn't understand what all the fuss was about anyway.

"We shall inform you of our decision tomorrow morning," the Matriarchs said before they strutted out of the room with their entourage following.

Myka turned and looked at Drew one last time before Anserlee shut the door behind her. His eyebrows were creased together, but when he caught her eye, his full lips softened into a sweet but worried smile.

Myka kept her silence until she and Anserlee arrived at her bedroom.

"Why do they keep telling everyone I'm a virgin? I don't see what difference it makes. Besides, the only thing virgins are good for is being sacrificed at the altar. Right?"

Wait.

Myka's heart skipped like a flat stone thrown over a lake, only to sink seconds later. Were they going to make Drew kill her in some sort of sick ritual? She shook her head. No. Not possible. Because he'd actually chosen Forest, and they wouldn't sacrifice one of their own, would they?

Anserlee choked and then recovered with a cough. "My dear Myka, no one is going to die." She stopped suddenly, then laid a sleeping gown on Myka's bed before turning her way.

"Well, what are we doing? Singing, dancing, reciting a sonnet, perhaps?" she said, going back to her original thoughts. The tension in her shoulders eased.

"Here." Anserlee patted the bed where she had pulled back the covers. "I think you need to sit down."

"Nothing good ever comes from sitting down," Myka snipped, her qualms returning.

"Yes, well, sit down anyway so I don't have to look up."

Myka tore off her dress and scurried into her nightgown. Then she sat on the bed and Anserlee began gently unlacing her black ballet slippers. Her cool hands soothed Myka's feverish skin, and she closed her eyes, hoping to ward off the headache stabbing behind her eyes. She propped a pillow on her lap and draped her arms over it.

After Anserlee had removed both shoes, she stayed cross-legged on the floor, looking up at her with soft gray eyes. She massaged her feet with her strong, tiny hands. "If the Matriarchs choose Forest, she will not be singing, dancing, *or* reciting poetry with Andrew."

"What will they be doing then?" Myka whined, rubbing her temples. Anserlee needed to get on with it.

Anserlee pursed her lips and an audible breath rushed out of her nose. "First, the chances of them choosing Forest for his partner are nonexistent. They will choose you."

"Will you please just tell me what we'll be doing!" She pounded the pillow with open palms, a hint of lemongrass and lavender escaping under the beating. Horrible visions of having to battle Drew like an MMA fighter raced through her throbbing head. She didn't have to worry about him hurting her on his own, but these women could control him with their voices. He might not have a choice.

Anserlee avoided Myka's eyes, instead staring past her head at the stone wall while her hands paused with the foot massage. "You will have to sleep with him while we watch."

Myka's exhausted brain pictured them snuggled up together under a thick, down blanket next to a cozy, warm fire. Exactly like the lodge they'd left only days ago. Which seemed like years ago.

"Sex, Myka," Anserlee snapped. "You will have to have sex with him while we watch. Then we will bid on him to see who is next in line for the pleasure of his company. This will happen on the full moon, which I believe is a couple of weeks from now. The Matriarchs like the anticipation to heighten. The higher the bidding, the more that goes into the community coffers."

Myka's brain shuddered, trying to process the information properly. The pillow, quickly becoming her safety blanket, squished under her embrace. A knot formed at the base of her throat. For a second, she questioned why Drew hadn't chosen her. He'd made it very clear he wanted her. Now, when presented with the perfect opportunity, he'd bailed. But she knew him better than that—he'd chosen Forest to save Myka the humiliation. She cherished her privacy, and the notion of having sex, first time or not, with an audience, was unbearable. She liked the idea of MMA fighting better.

"Will you be bidding on him?" Myka squeaked out, jealousy ripping through her heart.

Anserlee rose from the floor and grabbed a mug from the cupboard. She filled it with water and sprinkled herbs over the surface. She swirled the cup around and handed it to

Myka without saying a word, then walked to the door and stood in front of it. Her silver wings drooped. "I don't like men like that," she said quietly before she left the room.

The door lock clicked while Myka struggled to wrap her mind around what Anserlee had said. Fortunately, whatever herbs she'd given her worked quickly, and Myka fell straight to sleep.

MYKA AWOKE THE NEXT MORNING, GROGGY AND CONFUSED ABOUT where she was. For a second, everything in her life was as it should be. Then it all hit her like a slap in the face.

She gripped the blankets in her hands, her knuckles whitening under the pressure. They were going to force her to sleep with Drew while they watched. Sex with him wasn't the problem. Sometimes all she could think about was having sex with him. But doing it in front of strangers, freaks—that was an issue.

She crawled out of the cozy bed and began pacing barefoot on the cold stone floor. Maybe she was worrying for nothing. There was a small chance that Forest would be chosen. Her hackles rose and her eyes slivered at the mere thought of Forest in bed with Drew.

She ran her fingers through her hair and squeezed at her scalp. The need to get out of there hit harder with every beat of her pulse.

Anserlee had said they had two weeks until the big event. And Myka still didn't have the slightest clue how she was going to pull off the great escape.

The door opened and Anserlee glided through. She carried breakfast in one hand, Myka's backpack over her shoulder, and a pair of rubber boots slung over her forearm. Myka wondered where she'd found them. The last time she'd worn them, or a similar pair, she had been trying not to drown.

Anserlee dropped the boots on the floor with a slap, then placed the food on the table and motioned for Myka to sit.

"Where did you get those?" Myka pointed at the boots.

Anserlee tossed Myka's backpack on the bed. "I found them on the shoreline next to the firepit you built when you ended up here."

Myka didn't build the firepit, but kept her mouth shut, wondering who had. Excitement trembled her hands. She hadn't seen her things since she'd gotten here. Inside were modern clothes, rain gear, and a real toothbrush.

Anserlee sat down at the small round table, each of her wings touching the floor on either side of the wooden chair. "Eat," she said.

Myka took a bowl of steaming oatmeal and poured in some fresh cream, a pat of butter, and a swirl of golden honey. "Where does all this food come from?" She was curious, and it seemed a harmless place to start gathering information.

"We have farmers, hunters, seamstresses, healers, builders, and anything else you might need. Our lifestyle is basic and simple. Pretty much what your life might've looked like if you'd been born a couple hundred years ago. The upper echelon, the winged Sirins, all live in the nests—the tree houses," she clarified. "The others live farther out."

"You mean the women without the wings?" Myka stirred her food but didn't take a bite.

"Yes, but only those of us with wings are allowed to bed a human male. That way our blood never becomes too diluted."

But somehow it does, Myka thought. "Anserlee, I don't understand how this," she said, holding her empty spoon and waving it about, "all works. This world. How do you keep hidden? How do the men get here? How do some of you not have wings?"

"Whoa, one question at a time. I'll answer what I can." Anserlee raised a dainty hand to slow her down, then sprinkled cinnamon on her oatmeal. "Do you remember coming through a static skin of sorts when you got here?"

Myka nodded.

"That's what protects us and keeps us hidden from humans. I don't know where it came from, why it's there, or how exactly it works. Though I have a few guesses." She took a bite and swallowed before continuing. "Over the years, staying hidden has gotten more difficult with the population increase. When one of you goes missing, you have more resources for rescue. Of course, Andrew was far too tempting to ignore. A rock star with Sirin blood this close to our shores?" she said as her eyes widened in amazement. "Unheard of. He is a complete soul, not a half-soul like we're used to."

Anserlee proceeded to shock Myka with the tale of how they got men to the island of Pan. First, scouts, in their bird forms, were assigned to individual males around the world with Sirin blood—mostly musicians, but sometimes actors or politicians. Second, they stalked their prey and waited for them to die. Then, in their final moments of life, the Sirin swallowed the soul of the dying man. Finally, for the strangest part yet—three months later, the Sirin who had swallowed the soul gave birth to a baby boy. That was how half-souls were created. But complete souls, like Drew, were far more valuable. And practically unheard of because all the islands were in such remote locations.

It explained why in so many cultures birds were a direct line to the afterlife.

Myka's eyes narrowed in horror. "How do you know who to watch?"

"Well, I would think it's quite obvious, don't you?"

Myka raised her brows and nodded. Now that she knew to look, she could probably tell which stars had Sirin blood running through their systems. For some reason, there were a few musicians and celebrities that she felt an aversion to. It wasn't like they didn't like each other, but there was always a force pushing her away from them. It made for an excellent business relationship because there was no sexual attraction to get in the way.

One older but quite famous rock star had always joked with Myka, calling himself crazy because she was the only beautiful woman he didn't want to sleep with. But then why did Myka feel so opposite about Drew? She now knew for a fact he had Sirin blood. To the contrary, she'd always been *pulled* to him. Every cell in her body pointed to him like a magnet toward true north.

"What about Drew? Have you been watching him?" Myka tapped her index finger on the wooden table.

"Sort of. We assign scouts based on recklessness. There aren't enough of us to cover every man with Sirin blood at all times. We started out following Drew closely, but then we stopped because he's tame for a musician. He doesn't use regularly—so many of them die from drug overdoses. It's only a matter of time with heavy users. Plane crashes are another easy target for us. No people around to witness what we do, and birds are not suspicious outside."

Hot acid shot up Myka's throat. Her Uncle James had died in a plane crash, and he most certainly had Sirin blood. So it *could* be him that she'd heard at the audition. Him—but not really him. Myka's mouth watered and she swallowed repeatedly, trying not to puke. The back of her nose prickled with tears, but she pushed them away. She didn't have time to cry if she wanted a means of escape.

"What about the women without wings? How does that happen?"

"Well, sometimes a union between a Sirin and a man will be fruitful. It's not often, but if the baby's a girl, she stays whether she's born with or without wings."

"And if the baby is a boy?"

"They're all born without wings. They are taken away. Don't ask me more." Red flushed up Anserlee's neck, and she gripped her spoon until her knuckles whitened.

Myka's nostrils flared and she grimaced. She didn't need to pursue that line of questioning. If what Baba said was true, they left the boys alone in the woods as a sacrifice to their gods. But someone had to save them—it was the only logical explanation as to how people like Myka and Drew existed. If her theory was correct, it proved people could get beyond the barrier in human form. That tiny bit of information settled in her gut like a diamond buried in a mountain of coal.

"What is your job here?"

"I'm the Lead Healer," Anserlee said.

"Oh, I should've known," Myka muttered, still trying to figure out how to broach the pink elephant in the room. She gave up and came out with it. "Who did they pick?" She raised her eyes from her untouched breakfast.

Anserlee's wings drooped. "You. They picked you." Sadness clouded her voice.

"Mother Francis! That's stupid. Do I have any say in this?" Myka stood up and leaned against the table with her palms flat on the rough surface.

"No," Anserlee said with a heavy sigh. She motioned to Myka's food. "Sit. Eat." Her silvery-brown hair was braided into a thick rope and wrapped around her head like a halo. "You need to be very careful now. Chances are, Forest won't bother you, but Rave will. She has two weeks to see to your demise."

"What do you mean? She wants to kill me?" Myka's appetite, meager a moment ago, completely vanished. She slumped back in the chair.

"Yes, that's precisely what I mean. With you out of the way, her only competition is Forest. And Forest would step down just to avoid the confrontation. Rave has a reputation for getting what she wants by any means necessary." Anserlee reached across the table and took both of Myka's hands in hers, stroking her skin with her thumbs. "Don't go anywhere without me or a guarded escort."

"How do I go anywhere? I'm locked up."

"From now on, your door will be open. You will assist me during part of the day, then you will spend time with Andrew so the two of you will have a chance to get to know each other before...well, you know." She averted her gaze.

"What if I run?" Myka flicked a raspberry off the table. It splattered against the stone wall and dropped to the floor, leaving a pink stain in its place.

Anserlee shook her head. "Run if you want. You can't

escape. The barrier around the island is designed to only let people with Sirin blood in. Unless you can change form, you will never leave."

Myka caught her breath and almost broke out in tears. She couldn't tell whether Anserlee was lying, being naïve by burying her head in the sand, or if she really didn't know that people had escaped from the island. She bit down hard on the side of her cheek, soft skin crunching between her teeth. She tasted blood on her tongue. Not willing to accept that fate, Myka silently vowed to find a way off this hellhole or die trying.

"Are there more of you elsewhere?" Myka asked.

"Of course. There are small communities of Sirins all over the world. The Matriarchs are always owls, but all the birds on Pan are native to this area. It's the same everywhere because native birds are inconspicuous. That's how we know what's going on in your world. That's how we are able to harvest souls so easily."

"Has anyone ever escaped?" Myka pushed again.

"No," Anserlee snapped a little too quickly. "I already told you—no one ever leaves."

Myka held Anserlee's gaze for a few uncomfortable seconds to see if she would crack. When she didn't, Myka asked, "What kind of bird are you?"

Anserlee's dainty eyebrows arched. "Seriously?"

Myka shrugged. How was she supposed to know?

"I'm a Greater White-fronted Goose."

"Oh. Oh?" Myka scrunched her face. "Yeah, I can see that." She liked the idea of Anserlee being a goose—such beautiful birds. But then she remembered Drew's mom had a pet goose named Cecilia and that bird was downright frightening.

Which still, kind of, reminded her of Anserlee. "What about Rave? No, wait, that's pretty obvious, right? And to think I used to love ravens," Myka mumbled. "What about Forest?"

"A red-breasted sapsucker."

Myka snorted and Anserlee glared.

"And that scary blonde with Drew all the time?" Myka shivered at the thought of that woman. She reminded her of a golden gladiator with wings. Something about the way she walked and the tilt of her head and shoulders screamed predator.

"She's the most dangerous of us all—a golden eagle."

"Huh. I would think a bald eagle would be more dangerous."

"Well, you would be wrong. Have you ever seen golden eagles hanging out at the dump scavenging food?"

Myka shook her head and shrugged a shoulder. She'd never thought about it before. Birds were birds. The only time she'd been around any was at Drew's house. Carly, his mother, loved birds. They owned a small farm outside of town where she had ducks, geese, fancy chickens, and a Catalina macaw named Boss. He was some kind of special bird that was in her will because he would probably outlive her. He was like a dog, only louder and bossier, hence the name. He'd never warmed up to Myka, but he loved Carly and Drew.

"Bald eagles enjoy each other's company, while goldens don't. Bald eagles fish and scavenge for the most part, and goldens don't. They hunt their prey with single-minded precision. They are brutal and dangerous. Stay far away from her."

"What about Drew? Will he be okay?"

A breath of air shot from Anserlee's nose with a *hmph*. "He has something she wants. You don't."

"What about—" Myka started to ask.

"Enough questions." Anserlee held up her hand, ending Myka's inquisition. "Come on, we're going to go to my house to see if anyone needs my services."

Myka yanked Drew's lavender flannel over her linen dress and threw on the brown rain boots. She followed Anserlee through the tower to a door that led directly to the hanging platforms. The rain had stopped, but a cool dampness hung in the air. The walkway, slippery from the moisture, swayed and bounced enough that she had to grip the handrail to keep from falling. It hadn't seemed so high when she stood on the ground.

It took around ten minutes to get to Anserlee's tree house, which led her to believe Pan might be larger than she'd previously imagined. They entered through a double-hinged barn door. She ducked to get inside. The ceiling height was high enough for her to stand up, but if she stretched her arms, she could touch the exposed beams above her head.

Myka walked across the floor, avoiding a wooden table scarred from years of use, to the stone fireplace. Open cupboards, full of mismatched vials in an array of colored glass, ceramic, and carved wood, hung on the walls above the base cabinets.

Wood smoke and strange herbs overpowered the little room. Myka sneezed into her sleeve and stopped in front of the built-in bookcases on either side of the fireplace. Medicinal books, leather journals, well-worn poetry, and classic tales were packed tightly on the shelves.

"This is my treatment room. Upstairs are my living

quarters." Anserlee grabbed two aprons hanging from a coat rack. "Throw this on, then we'll be ready."

Soon, Sirins came pouring in with all kinds of strange ailments—missing feathers, burns, animal-related accidents, and even one looking for birth control.

Her cheeks heated, but then a measure of logic trumped the anger. At least that Sirin was being careful. Better than getting pregnant by one of the human men on the island and sacrificing your child to the gods.

Myka ignored them as best she could while still trying to help Anserlee. Some of the women pretended she didn't exist, but others made rude, ugly comments. Surprisingly, Myka kept her head down and mouth shut.

After they were all gone, Anserlee said, "I'm pleased you were able to keep to yourself today. I know that must've been difficult." She unwound her braid and ran her dainty fingers through the wavy length.

You're telling me, Myka thought.

"Now it's time for me to take you to the rock star," she spit out, like the words were dirt in her mouth.

"His name is Drew," Myka said. "And I don't know why you're so angry about it. I'm the one who has to fuck him with those bitches watching." Her filter, which she prided herself on, had finally broken, and she let loose with the cuss words.

"Oh, good, there you are. I thought all those hours of silence might have softened your temperament." Anserlee tossed her hair over her shoulder and gestured for Myka to exit.

She led Myka back to the tower and stopped in front of Drew's room. Myka's heart fluttered in her chest frantically and she could barely swallow. She laid one hand on the door, ready to go inside.

"You will have two hours every afternoon for the next two weeks to get to know one another. You can wander around by yourselves, but remember what I said earlier—you need a raptor for your safety."

"Do we have to have an escort?" Myka pressed her forehead to the cold wood of the door, wishing Anserlee would get on with it so she could finally see Drew.

Anserlee hesitated. "No. It's not required. Like I said before, there's no way for you to leave this island. If you run, they will find you. Being the Matriarchs' choice will only protect you so far. If he tries to run, all we must do is sing to him. But if you do it, some of the Sirins may use it as an excuse to kill you."

Myka rolled her eyes.

Before she could enter, Anserlee grabbed her hand. "Please promise me you will always have an escort!"

"Fine," Myka snapped, knowing she wouldn't keep her promise.

"Oh, I almost forgot to tell you—"

"Are you kidding me right now? Let me get on with this." Her desperation shone through, and Anserlee's eyes narrowed to a sliver.

"You can't have sex with him until the audition night. Owls' orders." Anserlee clasped her other hand on top of Myka's as if she might've felt sorry for her. "Listen to me—if you do, they'll burn you at the stake."

"Yeah, yeah, whatever," Myka said, pulling out of Anserlee's grasp. She opened the door and quickly shut it behind her to keep Anserlee from following.

Drew stood up from his bed, his hair perfectly messy,

bedhead sexy. His eyes lit up and a smile of relief flooded his gorgeous face. "Fuck it," he said, holding out his arms, taking large steps toward her.

Excitement tickled Myka's stomach like it did every time she saw him. Even if the sensation wasn't wanted. Tears filled her eyes and her bottom lip began to quiver uncontrollably.

The consequences be damned, she thought as she threw herself into his strong arms.

drew

"Shhhh, baby, it's going to be okay," Drew said as he held Myka, her tears soaking into his shirt. He squeezed her hard, resting his chin on her head. She fit perfectly in his embrace.

"What if they're watching?" she asked between sobs. Her shoulders shook and paused as she drew deep breaths between waves.

"Don't you worry. I'll tell them you just needed a human shoulder to cry on." He petted her hair, trying to calm her down, never having seen her this upset before. She always had it together, even when she shouldn't. He had to keep calm for both of their sakes, and it was about time she let him be the emotional rock.

He held her until the sobs became quiet hiccups, then ceased. "Come on, let's sit." He gently took her hand and guided her to the bed. He helped her sit, but stayed standing, facing her.

"We need to get out of here. We need to get out of here," Myka whispered, crossing her legs underneath her, rocking back and forth. "And that was my Uncle James singing up there, wasn't it?" Her voice trembled.

"I believe so."

"We must get out of here. And we have to take him with us!"

"I know, baby, I know," Drew soothed. But he didn't agree with all of Myka's statements. He'd seen some of the men who'd been there for a long time. They were physically and mentally past the point of no return. A madness of sorts swirled behind their eyes, and they were prone to violent fits of outrage. He'd watched as one Sirin had utilized her voice to keep a man from yanking his hair out by the roots and digging his eyes from their sockets. But now wasn't the time to disagree with Myka.

He pressed his hands against her cheeks, wiping her tears with his thumbs. "We're going to figure out something." He didn't even know where to begin. The only hope was that yesterday, they'd moved him into a new room, one with a window. Today was the first day his door had been unlocked.

"Anserlee told me there's no way out unless we can shift into birds, like they can. But I know she's lying, because somehow, some way, somebody got out. Otherwise, we wouldn't be alive. Maybe we could run in the night." She looked up at him, hopeful. Sunlight, peering through a crack in the clouds, shimmered over her face, lightening her eyes to a deep, coffee brown.

"We can't. Gilda said we have our freedom in the day, but the doors will be locked at night. For both of our protection." The window in the room was large enough to crawl through, but secured with iron bars, so unless he could figure out a way to remove them, that wasn't going to work either.

Gilda had laid the law down with him earlier that morning—sleep with Myka before the special night, she dies. Refuse to sleep with Myka at all, she dies. Not that she cared whether Myka died or not. She'd actually told him she thought it would be better if she did. She said Sirins should have the pleasure of his company, not a lowly human. How ironic, since he was human too.

Anger boiled like lava in his gut at the idea of the Sirins touching Myka. If they hurt one hair on her head, he was prepared to burn the place down. Though he'd yet to figure out how. Their ability to completely control him was terrifying. It amazed him how easily he submitted even when they didn't use their powers on him. It was as if doing what they wanted without their influence somehow gave him the feeling of having a choice. It was an illusion. But fighting them was worse. It was like being locked inside a car driving off the edge of a cliff whether he wanted to or not. His brain screamed at him to stop, but his foot pressed harder on the gas pedal.

She reached out and traced her fingers over his newly healed tattoo. He'd gotten the wolf with dark eyes to represent her—another desperate attempt to announce his feelings without having to speak to her. If she were to look closely, she'd see her name inked in the outline of its fur. A permanent reminder that he loved her regardless of their romantic commitment.

"What are we going to do?" Myka asked again.

"Today, we're going to do nothing." Drew put a finger on her soft lips to stop her from protesting. "Today, I'm going to hold you. And you're going to let me." It had been so long since she had allowed him to hold her for any length of time. He laid her down and snuggled in behind her. He spooned his body around hers and nuzzled his head into the back of her short hair. It had grown quite a bit since she'd cut it off. Her darker blonde roots created a long shadow under the platinum. A faint smile pulled at his lips as he inhaled deeply. Lavender had replaced the familiar scent of strawberry in her hair.

Finally, after a few minutes, her body relaxed, and her breathing returned to a normal rhythm. He traced his finger around her slightly pointed ear and along her jawline. Her skin was hot to the touch, almost feverish from her crying. He kissed the back of her head and took it as a good sign when she didn't tense up.

"Why did you really break up with me?" he whispered, cursing himself as her shoulders stiffened. He needed the truth if he was going to have any chance at fixing what went wrong.

"I don't want to talk about it," she snapped, attempting to sit up.

"Please. I don't know what the outcome of all this is going to be, and I need to know what I did," he begged. "One minute, everything was fine. I thought for sure that was the night. I had plans for us." Plans that only he knew about. He placed a gentle kiss behind her ear. Maybe he did like the short hair—it gave him easy access to her long neck.

She muffled her face into the down pillow. "I told you— my career was more important, therefore, what we had needed to end."

"Then why bother coming after me?" He dug deeper.

"Because you're my friend."

"No, Myka, I'm not. I've never been your friend. I've

never *wanted* to be your friend. From the beginning, I wanted more. I *still* want more. So stop lying to me. Why did it need to end? What we had, or still can have, is rare." His voice faltered as all his pent-up emotions lay bare on his tongue. "What did I do to make you give up on me? You told me you could never be with a guy like me. What did you mean?" he whispered.

"Please," Myka said, curling up into a ball. "I don't want to talk about it."

"Fuck! Myka, I deserve the truth." He climbed on top of her and straddled her hips so she had to look at him. He placed his hand under her chin and brought her head up. His concentration veered off course. How long had he waited to get her in this position? The heat from her skin burned through his flimsy linen pants. Her thick black lashes had dried in spiky clumps from her tears and her dark eyes shone glossy, glaring up at him. The tip of her nose glowed pink and he still thought she was the most beautiful woman in the world.

But beauty was only the tip of the iceberg with her. Underneath that shell was so much more. She was one of those women who always had it together. In times of panic, she was calm. In heated arguments, she maintained the level head. They'd always joked she was the ice to Burning Brenda's fire. The only person who could keep the band from self-immolation.

She sucked her bottom lip and clenched her eyes shut as if she couldn't look at him and speak the truth. "I saw you that night with them. They were right."

"What do you mean? Saw me with who? Who was right?" Drew asked, his brows puckering.

"I saw you surrounded by beautiful women, famous

women. They were all staring at you with hero worship, laughing at everything you said, and I knew at that moment I couldn't compete with them. I didn't want to." Her voice dropped to a stubborn murmur.

"Where did those kinds of thoughts come from? Certainly not from me."

She shook her head.

"Come on, what are you really trying to say? So I was talking with a whole bunch of women. It wasn't like I was screwing any of them." He leaned down closer to her face. "Look at me," he demanded.

"I couldn't be with you—" Her voice hitched, then a calm settled over her features as she secured her emotions behind the mask he'd become so familiar with. "I couldn't be with the man every woman in the world wanted. I couldn't compete with that. I saw you that night surrounded by them, and I didn't want to take that away from you. How could I? You worked so hard for it."

Shock coursed through him. He was also slightly offended, which wasn't easy to do. "Are you kidding me? I think your bullshit reason was better than this one," Drew said, getting off her.

He planted his feet on the stone floor and stood with his arms crossed, immobile with his emotions. Originally, she'd told him in a letter that she chose her work over him. For her to stay on as their manager, they'd needed to end their relationship. It was a professional call. She couldn't maintain both. And they all knew Burning Brenda couldn't survive without her. She was the glue that kept them sane. She was the buffer to the outside world—a world where hate and jealousy could poison the best of friends. She had never let that happen. If any one of them started having issues, Myka had sat them down to hash out their differences. No matter how painful. *"Communication,"* she always hounded, *"is the key to making this work in a world that thrives on misery and drama."*

He turned and glared at her as she sat up. "So let me make sure we're clear. What you're saying is—you punished me as the criminal before I *ever* committed the crime?"

"I suppose you're right," Myka said quietly, looking away. "But I also didn't want to be in your way. I wanted you to enjoy every aspect of your success."

"That wasn't your decision to make," Drew growled, pacing with his hands on his hips.

He didn't even look up as she got off the bed and tiptoed to the door. She'd wasted three years because she thought he should *hook up* with other women. All because of his success. All he'd wanted was her. Then and now. But it didn't ease the fury lodged in his chest, growing stronger with every step. The time she'd wasted. The pain she'd caused them, or at least him. She preached communication —but she didn't fucking practice it when it came to them.

"You know, Myka," Drew said quietly, reining in his temper—though it still bled through in his tone.

She stopped with her hand on the door handle as she slipped on her boots.

"We've been through a lot together. And I know many things about you, but I never took you for a coward."

She bowed her head and her shoulders sagged.

The door shut behind her softly.

He assumed she would go back to her room. Once he'd calmed down and gathered his thoughts, he'd go find her. They were going to talk about this whether she wanted to or not.

Even when they'd dated, she'd tended to shut down if a conversation between them went too deep. It was as if she wore invisible armor to protect herself and she could only let someone get so close. He wasn't going to give her a choice this time. He had nothing to lose—she'd already quit.

In the beginning, the challenge of her shield had called to him—he was man enough to admit it—but soon, it had become more than that. When he was around her, he felt good, not just physically because of the strange buzz he had while next to her, but emotionally, she made him feel safe, as if he could truly be himself without fear of judgment. Fuck was he wrong. If she'd thought all he wanted to do was screw famous women, then she didn't know him at all.

Drew sat down on the bed, resting his face in the palms of his hands. He ran his fingers through his messy hair, then grabbed some and pulled. "Fuck!" He stood up and punched the stone wall, leaving a smear of blood behind.

He had a feeling more was troubling her. She'd mentioned something about *they*, though she hadn't explained who *they* were. What had they said to make her flee? At that point in time, he'd had no skeletons in his closet. Though now that he thought about it, Nicky had mentioned a time or two that Myka's self-esteem wasn't nearly as strong as Drew thought it was.

At one point, after a particularly brutal writing session with the guys, Nicky had pulled him aside.

"Dude, what the hell was that?" Nicky asked.

"What?" Drew said, though he knew what Nicky's problem was—too much of his personal life was sliding into their songs. His depression and anger were slowly suffocating him. Like he was lying on his back in quicksand with no plans to escape—and he was taking the band with him.

"Those were some dark lyrics. I mean, that last song—ouch. I'm worried about you. The path you're traveling is dangerous."

"I'm fine," Drew said, shrugging off Nicky's concerns.

"You're not. And neither is she. I don't understand either of you right now." Nicky crossed his arms.

"Shall I clarify it for you? I'm in love with her, and she hates me. I don't know what I did wrong. She won't talk to me, she won't even stay in a room alone with me. It makes me feel... alone."

"Honestly, I'm not sure you did anything wrong. I think there's something deeper going on with her. I've tried to talk to her too, but she freezes up and pushes me away. I think someone or something got to her. You know, her self-esteem isn't as good as you think it is."

"She's got the best self-esteem of anyone I know."

"Dude, she doesn't. She's just better at hiding her weakness behind that wall of ice."

But she was the most confident woman he'd ever known, so much more than any movie star he'd ever met. Or dated. Or screwed.

Or was she?

"Shit!" He punched the stone wall again. After she had broken up with him, he'd done exactly what she'd expected him to do. What a fool he'd been. He rested his head against the bloody wall and swallowed back tears. He'd taken her insecurities and rubbed her nose in them. No, he'd held her head under and drowned her in them.

Afer shutting the door calmly, Myka ran down the hallway to the stairs that led to the second floor. Her promise to Anserlee to find a guard evaporated because, at that moment, she didn't care about her safety. She ran toward the blinding sun until she stumbled upon a trail. The path steadily darkened, making it hard to see through her tears, but that didn't stop her. She bounded over the ground, slipping and falling on exposed roots and rocks. The rain boots were not running shoes. She brushed the mud off her hands and knees and continued to jog until she was well past the tree houses. Her goal was to get as far away from there as she could.

Twenty minutes later, beams of golden light stabbed through the canopy as the tree line abruptly ended in a small, open meadow. The sun warmed the air while evaporating the earlier moisture into a hazy glow.

Trees stood guard around the field, lush with gently waving grass and purple wildflowers. She weaved her way to the other side, letting the top of the plants tickle her hands. Water from the tall grass brushed against her dirty legs and dampened the hem of her shirtdress. She picked the biggest tree, its width an easy five feet across, and leaned against it to catch her breath. Tears ran down her skin, burning over the well-worn path. She used the sleeve of Drew's flannel to dry her face.

Her secret was out, and Drew knew that she was a coward. But she hadn't told him all that had happened. She'd never told anyone. When she'd overheard those women gossiping about her in the bathroom the night of the Grammys, it had damaged her self-esteem. She had only been twenty-one at the time, and negative remarks, even from strangers, were easy to believe. They'd said she'd gotten her job because of who her uncle was. They'd said she wasn't good enough for Drew. They'd said she was fat. They'd wondered why he would choose her when he could have anyone. She'd immediately begun to question if he was dating her because she was the one who gave Burning Brenda their big break. Was it out of a sense of obligation?

Instead of tossing their opinions where they belonged—in the trash—she'd taken their words to heart. Her insecurities had killed whatever they could've had. Now that she was older, she regretted her actions and could see their comments for what they were—pure, unadulterated jealousy. Though she was too proud to admit it, and it felt easier to outrun her past instead of facing it. She had always been good at taking charge and dealing with other people's problems. But her own, she often buried deep where she could ignore them.

And if she was being honest, the thought of having a relationship with Drew now terrified her. Walking away from him the first time had destroyed her, and to put herself in that position again—even deeper—she wouldn't survive. But what if her fear was keeping her from the kind of love she'd always dreamed of? She really was a coward.

She scanned the meadow through a pool of tears and jumped when she saw Drew run out into the field. Her heart hiccupped. Maybe now would be her chance to fix what she'd broken, to stand up and take responsibility for her poor choices, even if they were made with the best of intentions.

When he spotted her, his shoulders slumped with relief. Afternoon sunlight flared around him as he strode toward her, long legs pushing through the quaking grass and flowers. His hair, normally dark, reflected bronze in the misty light. He might've looked ridiculous in the flowing tunic and linen pants if he'd been anyone else. But he looked like a Roman god who had descended from the heavens.

"Myka—" was all he said before she tried interrupting him.

"Drew, I am so—"

"Don't you ever do that again to me! You may be my manager, but you don't get to make those kinds of choices for me. I—" Instead of continuing his train of thought, he grabbed her by the shoulders and fiercely kissed the rest of her apology away.

Tingles flowed like a waterfall over her shoulders and blood rushed between her ears.

Needles fell from the branches as he constrained her tight against the tree. He captured her hands and lifted them above her head as he pushed his knee between her legs. His kiss was hot, angry, demanding—holding her hostage. He didn't ask for permission. To be honest, she didn't think he wanted it. He bit her bottom lip and then sucked on it as his free hand wound through her hair. Pulling her head back and tilting it sideways, his lips moved over her jaw to the sensitive skin of her neckline. Myka's mouth burned from his three-day scruff, and she licked her lips, longing to taste him again. His breathing slowed as he rested his head in the crook of her neck.

She started to talk again, but he raised his finger and pressed it against her mouth. "Give me a second," he said, his voice gruff.

Finally, after their hearts stopped racing, he lifted his head and looked down. He pressed his hands on her shoulders, keeping her in place. "I'm the one who needs to apologize," he said.

She started to shake her head.

"No, hear me out. I'm an idiot. After you broke up with me, I did exactly what you expected me to do."

He lifted her chin and kissed her tenderly on the nose. His cheeks were flushed under his golden skin and the ends of his hair curled in the humidity. She'd always wondered if it would be wavy if he cut it off. When it had been long, it always curled slightly at the nape of his neck and beside his ears.

"But I didn't act that way for the reasons you think. You believed I would do it anyway, so you were trying to escape the pain before it happened. I get it, but I don't agree with you. I would've never cheated on you." He pressed his forehead against hers. "I slept with those other women so you would want me." He held up his hand to stop her from protesting. "I know, I know. It sounds stupid. I thought if you saw how they desired me you would get jealous and come back. I see now how wrong I was." He pulled away from her forehead and stared at her with his sad blue eyes as she picked a small twig from his hair before she brushed his damp locks off his face. "I should've fought harder. I should've never given up. I should've whisked you away and forced you to talk to me then."

She began to speak again, to tell him how wrong he was. Their breakup was all her fault. But she was older now, and those words that had flayed her insecurities bare no longer held the power they once had. She needed to grow up and let her mistakes come to light. She needed to trust he was the man she'd always believed him to be.

"No, no, no," he said quickly, pressing his finger against her lips, shushing her. "Because there's only one woman I've ever loved, and now I'm afraid I might've screwed up so heinously that she may never forgive me."

Myka realized she hadn't just lost the battle—she'd lost the war. She'd tried for years to get him out of her head. But it was never her head that had been the problem—it was her heart. He owned it, and even after all this time, it had no plans to evict him.

She'd paused for so long that he lightly shook her by the shoulders. "Did you hear me? *I love you.* I think I have since the moment I saw you. Are you listening? Can we start again...you and me?"

She couldn't let fear rule her life any longer. And at the possibility that this might be the only chance they ever got, she nodded, hoping that she'd be enough. Not only for him, but herself too.

He leaned in and kissed her again, gently this time, his lips feathering against hers. "Don't. Ever. Do. That. Again," he said firmly.

The growl in his tone had her toes curling and her nether regions begging.

She clasped her hands behind his head and drew him closer, forcing him to shut up. She pressed her hips against him, feeling his erection through her flimsy dress. She realized she would probably regret her rash behavior, but she had loved him for so long. If at some point he got bored with her, she would have to deal with the broken heart then, because she couldn't deny him any longer.

He groaned as his hands found their way under her gown. His calloused fingers scraped against her bare skin, squeezing hard around her waist. Slowly, he inched up until the weight of her breasts rested on his hands. His lips never left hers as he explored the depths of her mouth. Myka's body ached for him, throbbing with every beat of her heart.

Both thumbs skimmed over her nipples, warranting an uncontrolled whimper from her throat. With no protest, he slipped his hand under her bra and did it again, pausing, rolling his fingers until she leaned her head back, gasping for breath.

He grabbed his flannel shirt that she was wearing and slid it off her shoulders. He tossed it carelessly to the ground, then did the same with her dress. He reached behind her and unsnapped her bra, letting it fall. Goose bumps rose as the cool air hit her skin.

"Amazing," he said, standing a foot away. His eyes crawled over her almost-naked body. Her breath trembled under his scrutiny, but nothing in his gaze suggested that he saw anything other than perfection. "You are beautiful. I knew you would be. It seems as if I've waited a lifetime to see you like this."

He crashed into her and kissed her neck as his hands held up her breasts. He slowly lifted one to his mouth and licked the tip with his searing-hot tongue. Her knees buckled. Then he drew back and blew cold air, causing her nipple to pucker even harder before he came back for more. He sucked gently as his other hand lightly trailed down her stomach, pausing to slide under her panties.

The emotional shield she wore to protect herself dissipated, and she melted into bliss. She couldn't concentrate on anything but the pounding in her head, the pounding in her heart, and the pounding between her legs.

With no more hesitation, he swept his fingers over her, sliding through the wetness as she wound her hands into his hair. Moans tore from her throat. He switched to her other breast as she gasped and spread her legs slightly. "Please, please. Oh, Drew, don't stop."

Gently, he rubbed her clit, swirling and lightly pinching, adding pressure, releasing pressure, until the world ceased to exist. He grabbed her nipple between his teeth and tugged to the point of almost pain. Just enough, but not too much. As her body was about to give in, he inserted a finger. Her breath caught and she arched forward as he inserted another, filling her, stretching her walls. The palm of his hand rubbed against her clit while he pumped his fingers deeper. Harder. Bark from the tree bit into her naked skin, adding to her pleasure. She could barely keep her legs beneath her as stars flashed behind her closed eyes. Time suspended as her body tightened and shock waves of ecstasy pulsed through her. She realized this was only the start of what could be. She should've known how easily he would be able to do that with his fingers. If he could make a guitar scream and cry so effortlessly, why should she be any different?

She bit her lip, savoring the tingle that coursed through her being. When she opened her eyes, Drew stood before her, only inches away, sucking on his fingers with a look of satisfaction on his face. He leaned in and whispered, "I have been dying to taste you."

"I want you," she whispered back. "Now." She wouldn't be fully sated until he was inside of her, claiming her.

He groaned and raked his hand through his hair. "We can't."

"Why not? Of course we can," she insisted, ignoring Anserlee's warning. "Nobody is out here but us. And anyway, we might as well practice before we have to do this in front of a live audience," she said with a knot forming in her stomach.

"You would think, right? But no, we can't. They already laid out the ground rules for us and they want you a—" He paused, cocking his head and raising a sharp brow. "By the way, how did that happen? Not that I'm complaining. Believe me, there were several of your *boyfriends* I contemplated killing." He chuckled.

She shook her head. She thought the answer was pretty obvious. "You know there were a few you weren't very nice to."

"Are you going to answer me, or are you going to deflect?"

"Deflect."

He cocked an eyebrow. She knew him well enough to know he wasn't about to let it go.

She swallowed her pride. "They weren't you."

The emotions that traveled behind his eyes were easy to discern—pain, relief, joy, hope. But then again, he'd never tried to hide them from her. She'd been the one hiding the entire time.

And though they couldn't sleep together—because she

really didn't want to burn at the stake—there was nothing stopping her from returning the love.

She grabbed Drew by the shoulders, rotated both of them around, until he was pushed up against the big tree. She placed her hands on either side of his cheeks and brought his lips to hers. Tasting herself on his lips drove her wild. She lifted his shirt over his head and tossed it onto the growing pile of clothes. She kissed her way across his neck, over his smooth chest, and down his rippled stomach to the small line of hair above his linen pants until she was kneeling. He rested his hands on the top of her head, caressing his fingers over her scalp. She started to untie the bow, but he snaked his fingers through her hair and squeezed, pulling it tight.

"Ouch!" she said, before he yanked her up by her hair. "That hurt! What are you doing?" she yelled.

All emotion had vanished from his face and his eyes stared, vacant of any recognition. He blinked sluggishly like an old-fashioned doll with plastic eyelids and a row of heavy lashes.

"Drew? Are you okay?" Myka asked hesitantly. She waved her hand in front of his face. It was like he'd been shut off.

He didn't acknowledge that she'd said anything, but he released her hair, ran his hands down the sides of her head, and rested them on her shoulders.

For a quick second, behind his eyes, she caught a flash of fear, before his hands clasped around her neck and began to squeeze, cutting off her ability to scream. To breathe.

EIGHTEEN

anserlee

Anserlee flew quietly behind Myka after she ran out of the tower. She'd been standing guard, sure that the promise Myka had made to her earlier was false. But Myka didn't realize how much danger she was in. Rave wasn't the type of Sirin to lose.

Wind flowed under her wings, and she followed as far behind as she dared. She hung close to the treetops, sometimes hitting the crowns, causing tiny pine cones to drop to the forest floor. When Myka stopped across the open field, Anserlee settled herself amidst the boughs of the tallest tree and waited. A gentle breeze swayed the treetop while the birds and bugs resumed their serenade, having paused for only a moment. Yellow pollen coated the needles in their fine dust, making the fragrant air cloudy. Through her blurred vision, Anserlee watched Myka slump against a tree.

Justifiably, the girl needed some time alone. She'd been through a lot lately. Pulled into a world where she wasn't wanted. Forced to do things no woman should have to. While Anserlee mostly enjoyed her life in Pan, she could see

154

how it would be a prison sentence for a human, male or female.

Andrew Arie was a complete soul and could return to his life without question. But escaping was nearly impossible and had only happened once before to an adult male. And not to a complete soul, but to a half-soul. Thankfully, it hadn't been from her community that he'd escaped. Somehow, he and his blue suede shoes had done it time and time again, but he'd always returned to his colony eventually. His sightings had been a source of contention amongst the Sirins and were famous throughout the world.

Anserlee shook her head, sick with the consequences of his first escape. One of her Matriarchs had been dispatched to oversee the situation since it involved so many Sirins. She'd chosen Anserlee to accompany her to the tiny Caribbean island, because, as a goose, she had superior navigational skills.

After they'd arrived and the evidence had been gathered, the Sirins found responsible for the incident were punished. Images of that day flashed in Anserlee's mind.

Four of the Sirins chained to the silencing pole were already crying, though they'd stopped begging for their lives. Unlike the tower in Pan, this colony gathered on a series of decks, platforms, and gazebos built over the turquoise waters. One Sirin, her head held high and her dark eyes defiant, stood straight despite what was about to happen.

The Matriarchs, who were the only ones who could control other Sirins with their song, began to sing, their voices otherworldly and violent. The melody urged Anserlee to destroy her wings even though she wasn't included in the directives. She bit down on her tongue, the pain making it easier to disregard the orders. The four, already crying, immediately began to pluck out their feathers. The defiant one snarled, her lips pulling back from her teeth. Ignoring the Matriarchs' orders was painful in itself. But after a long few seconds, she succumbed to their orders. Despite the agony, not a tear fell down her tan, freckled cheeks. One by one, they plucked out each feather until their wings were left bony and naked, the pink flesh raw and bleeding.

Anserlee, not nearly as strong, had to blink back tears of her own.

When the shaming was finished, a Matriarch from the offending colony brandished a curved sword. Its blade flashed in the Caribbean sun. Without a second thought, she grabbed one of the Sirins' wings and pulled it tight before the metal sliced through the joint with the crack of breaking bone. A bloodcurdling scream tore through the tropical air. Blood sluiced down her back and legs, draining through the decking. She passed out in a heap when the Matriarch grabbed her other wing to finish the job. The remaining Sirins began to sob and again started begging for their lives. But not the defiant one.

Her eyes met Anserlee's and held, as if she could tell Anserlee wanted to plead for their lives again, as she'd done at their trial. What was happening to them wasn't fair. Anserlee had been there for the entire thing, and though the King of Rock 'n' Roll had escaped on their watch, he'd returned home. But the Caribbean Matriarchs saw no shades of gray, only black and white.

Many of the Sirins watching vomited, but Anserlee managed to keep the contents of her stomach in place. Once they finished cutting the wings off the crying Sirins, they turned toward the defiant one.

The Matriarch adjusted her grip on the sword handle and said, "Pippin. Pippin. Pippin," she repeated. "This one's going to hurt." For some reason, Anserlee didn't think the mother was talking about the physical pain, but instead referring to the loss of one of their most trusted Sirins. She was their head of security—the same as Gilda. Though it seemed, from all that Anserlee had learned, that they managed their jobs very differently.

As the blade separated flesh from bone, the defiant one opened her mouth and screamed, but it wasn't the sound of pain. She'd used her voice, that of a peregrine falcon, as her final farewell—one last fuck-you to her colony.

Crimson stained the length of her tan body, yet she remained standing. Below the decks, the waters roiled and fins circled. After she finally passed out from the loss of blood, their bodies were tossed into the ocean so the predators could destroy the evidence.

Anserlee had only seen it done once and it made her tremor every time the memory crossed her path.

Suddenly from below, Andrew burst through the forest and dashed toward Myka with determined strides. Anserlee prepared to fly down and rescue her, but hesitated when Myka's eyes widened with what looked like hope.

Disappointment seeped through her. She could see how most women would be attracted to the rock star, but she had longed for Myka to be different. Though she'd noticed earlier that Myka seemed eager to spend time with him.

As she watched the two interact, she began to suspect something. The fierceness of their kiss startled her and her heart twisted with what resembled jealousy. She couldn't turn away, even with the guilt gnawing at her. She, unlike her sisters, didn't approve of their voyeuristic practices.

But she couldn't take her eyes off the two. Andrew's every move spoke of a quiet possessiveness that only came with time and familiarity—the way he kissed Myka firmly and then gently touched her nose or brushed away her hair.

There was none of the awkwardness that came between strangers.

Anserlee didn't know how it was possible, but she would bet her wing feathers that these two somehow already knew each other.

Her body unwillingly reacted to the scene playing out before her. She bit her lip between her front teeth, wishing it was her face buried between Myka's breasts. She mimicked Andrew's hands with her own until the tree branches shook under her as she climaxed in unison with Myka.

When her breathing slowed, she realized with a heavy heart that that girl and that boy had feelings for each other. And Anserlee knew nothing good could come from those emotions here in Pan. She silently vowed to help Myka pick up the pieces of her inevitable broken heart. Maybe then, in time, Anserlee would stand a chance.

She focused back on Myka when she saw Andrew's body stiffen with anticipation. She turned her head, not wanting to watch that part.

Through her reverie, an unusual silence echoed in her ears. The birds stopped singing and the squirrels stopped chattering, alerting Anserlee to possible trouble. She scanned the area and came up empty, but something was off. Nature never lied. Then she glanced back at Myka, and her heart slammed against her ribs.

Anserlee flew out of the thick, scraggly branches as fast as she could. But not fast enough. Andrew held Myka in the air by her throat, choking the life out of her. Myka's feet dangled in the air as her fists pummeled Andrew's face. Blood ran freely from his nose, dripping off his chin, down his chest, all the way to the waistband of his linen pants.

As she got closer, a song with an edge of hatred and jealously disturbed the air. Taken off-guard by the angry melody, she stumbled when she hit the ground. On her hands and knees, a song poured from her throat filled with love and light, but it was useless to pry his hands from Myka's neck. In the midst of the song, the controlled, Andrew, absorbed the strength of the controller, making him unusually strong. Anserlee's strength would not overpower that of the singer and the sung. But she could combat the orders with one of her own.

She focused all of her will and intent into Andrew's cold eyes. Behind their blue curtain, he struggled for control. But it wasn't enough, and Myka went limp.

"Fight!" she urged through her song. "You are stronger than this, Andrew!" she pleaded.

Relief flooded when whoever else was singing finally stopped and Andrew's grip loosened. Myka's flaccid body slid to the ground, unnaturally still.

As much as Anserlee wanted to chase down the criminal, she couldn't leave Myka.

"Oh God! What have I done?" Andrew fell to his knees and teetered back and forth. His nose had stopped gushing, but a crimson smear trickled.

"Back off!" Anserlee spat. "Give me room."

Andrew scooted away and buried his head in his hands.

Anserlee leaned in close with her cheek next to Myka's mouth as she watched and felt for her breathing. Her cold fingers pressed against her bruised throat, feeling for a pulse. Faintly, under the purple skin, a slight flutter tapped. But no breath.

She leaned Myka's head back and gently, firmly planted her lips, then exhaled. Her chest rose and fell with every breath Anserlee gave her, but nothing else happened.

She turned to Andrew between repetitions and, without the benefit of her Sirin abilities, ordered him to sing. He remained stunned, and Anserlee ordered him again. "Sing, damn you, sing! She needs a reason to come back to this godforsaken place."

He stood up with his head hung and sang low, deep down in his chest. The music flowed from his soul, pure, beautiful, and heartbreaking. The reverberation melted into her body and shivers rose on her arms as she continued to breathe for Myka.

It took her a few moments to recognize the old country song about love, loss, and a rose.

Andrew's voice cracked as his composure started to wane. She looked up at him between breaths and was shocked by the anguish warping his face.

The last line of the song escaped with barely a whisper. He fell back to his knees with his hands twisted in his hair while tears flowed from his bloodshot eyes.

Shock froze her limbs. This was far more than just *feelings*. This was love...and heartbreak. For a second, Anserlee stopped being jealous and felt every bone-crushing ounce of his pain. It clouded the air like a nightmare, suffocating her, pressing against her wings, making it hard to escape the darkness.

She turned back to Myka and pounded on her chest. "Breathe! Damn you! Don't you leave us!"

Over the cool draft, a cackle, sounding like that of a raven, echoed in the wind.

For the second time in one week, Myka stopped breathing. Here, in the in-between, life was easy, painless, and disconnected. Beneath her, while floating above, she watched and listened as Drew sang a song she loved and he hated. She'd spent hours of her life begging him to sing it for her, but it was the one thing he'd ever denied her, joking that he would only sing it over her dead body.

Oh no, Myka thought. *Am I dead?* If she was, it wasn't so bad. Her pain and heartbreak were a fraction, a shadow, of what they should've been.

Anserlee sat propped up on her knees, bowed over Myka. Her long, gray wings curled around her feet into the grass, flashing silver as feathers caught the light. She continued breathing for Myka, petting her forehead between sessions.

Slowly, Drew's voice became louder, steadily penetrating the fog that held Myka prisoner. His perfect voice faltered and cracked. He'd never done that before. When he fell to his knees, it startled her, then Anserlee began pounding on her naked chest.

What the hell are they doing? Myka thought, trying to retreat back into herself. *I like it here.*

Then a cackle-like laugh traveled over the breeze. A rage welled in the depths of her psyche. A fire of hate. An unfulfilled revenge. She would not leave Drew there, alone, to fend for himself amongst those whoring beasts.

She struggled to pull herself from the tendrils of fog wrapped around her. She didn't want to escape the comforting weight, but she had to, for his sake. It didn't want to let go, clinging to her like a mother's last embrace. A final goodbye. As she pushed farther into consciousness, the wisps grudgingly released. Cold air hit her body and jolted her further into reality, and for a brief moment, she regretted her decision to leave the safe, comforting sanctuary of death.

"Okay, okay," she rasped. Her voice scraped along her vocal cords like sandpaper over wood. She kept swallowing, despite the pain it caused, just to achieve some volume.

Finally, she gave up and gently touched Anserlee on the cheek. Her skin was hot and silky beneath Myka's chilly hands. Her eyes popped open in surprise, then pure joy bloomed on her face, replacing the agony and defeat.

A high-pitched, off-key, "Ohh!" escaped Anserlee before she started sobbing. She reached out behind her and yanked roughly on Drew's arm.

He looked first to her, angry, then to Myka. And despite the fact Myka had never seen him look worse, he'd never been more beautiful. Bathed in the evening sun, his scruff shone shades of deep red, gold, and black. When his swollen eyes met hers, they looked bluer set against their bloodshot background.

Disbelief supplanted his sorrow, and he leaned down and gathered her in his arms. Heat from his body melted into hers, erasing some of the chill from her clammy skin. He trembled as he held on to her. Pulling her cautiously into a seated position, he began rocking back and forth, holding her, chanting, "I am so sorry. So sorry."

Myka rested her head on his shoulder and held it there for a moment before kissing her way up his neck to his mouth. She tasted blood on his lips from where she'd had pummeled his face while trying to escape his grip.

She froze from the memory, and he mimicked her response. Then she shook her head quickly. That hadn't been him.

He started chanting again, "I am so sorry."

"It wasn't you," she whispered into his ear.

"I should've been able to control it," he said as his voice hitched. "I almost killed you. I thought I lost you."

"No, you didn't," Anserlee said, startling them both. Anserlee handed Myka her dress, and she pulled it over her head, followed by Drew's lavender flannel.

Myka had forgotten Anserlee was there. Her glorious face looked almost as bad as Drew's. Tears still ran freely, as did her nose. Myka reached out and pulled her down into the hug.

"*Rave* almost killed her," Anserlee said, holding tight to both of them. She backed out of the hug and grabbed Drew's chin, turning his head to her. "You did not do that. Do you understand me?" Drew started to disagree. "No!" she said in the same tone of voice she had used on Myka only once before. Next came the can of whoop ass if he wasn't careful. "You will not hold yourself responsible for the actions of others. I'm actually quite surprised at your ability to fight back. I could see your struggle." Her eyes danced over his face in awe, and she clasped his cheeks in her hands. "I've never witnessed that before."

Drew nodded numbly, having taken the scolding like a man.

"I think there may be more to *your* rock star than meets the eye." Anserlee let go of Drew's face and turned to Myka with her forehead wrinkled. "Now which one of you wants to tell me what's going on here?"

Myka let Drew tell their story since she could hardly squeak out a whisper.

Somewhere, somehow, they were going to have to trust somebody. Anserlee had saved Myka's life once, possibly twice, and she deserved the truth.

"Amazing," Anserlee said when Drew finished their story. "I have never heard of this happening before. Usually Sirins, even those on the outside with diluted blood, are repellents."

"Are you going to tell?" Myka chewed on her bottom lip.

"No," Anserlee said, shaking her head. "You two have enough to worry about."

"You mean you don't have to report back?" Drew asked.

"Well, of course I do. And I will stick to the truth."

Both of their shoulders fell.

"As much as I need to," Anserlee finished. "Mostly sticking to the truth is the safest way to lie. And while the Matriarchs can control me, they can't make me tell the entire truth." She smiled angelically, fluttering her long lashes.

"What about Rave?" Myka choked out.

"You two let me worry about her. Just please, don't leave your rooms tonight," she directed mostly at Myka. "I can't protect you if I don't know where you are." An irritated smirk played at the corner of Anserlee's mouth as if she was saying *I told you so* without speaking the words.

Myka shot up in bed, covered in sweat, while details of her nightmare slowly faded. She reached up and rubbed her neck, flinching in pain before realizing her terror had been real. Images of yesterday reeled through her head—Drew's strong hands clamped around her throat, lifting and squeezing all at once. The crushing pain and the panic of not being able to breathe. His blue eyes, flat and dead, stared straight through her. She'd swung her fists with everything he'd ever taught her. Her punches had connected with hard, unflinching bone, his nose cracking when she landed a fierce blow, and even in her nightmare, she felt the horror as blood gushed out. As she starved for oxygen, her energy had waned, and she'd stopped swinging. She'd tried pleading with her eyes, but he was gone and someone else was in control. Darkness had bled from her periphery and closed in until she passed out. And then she'd...died?

Logically, Myka knew Drew hadn't been calling the

shots, but emotionally, it didn't ease her fear. He'd almost killed her.

She laid back down trying to replay the good moments, but his vacant eyes kept sneaking into the picture.

Morning had arrived not soon enough, leaving her exhausted and wired at the same time.

Anserlee showed up and escorted Myka to her home to assist with her healing work again.

She was lost in the mundane task of grinding herbs when Drew ducked through the doorway, escorted by two raptors. Myka flinched, but tried to cover it with a smile. His eyes flashed with regret, pain, or sorrow. She quickly looked down, embarrassed by her initial reaction, and added oil to the mortar and pestle, inhaling the lavender deeply, hoping it would calm her anxiety. Today, she'd planned to avoid him so she could settle her nerves.

After the raptors left, an uncomfortable silence filled the room.

Anserlee huffed. "Oh, you two. We are not going to start this, are we?"

Neither of them answered.

"Drew, go sit next to her and help."

He pulled out one of the mismatched chairs and sat down as far away from Myka as he could.

Anserlee let them struggle in silence for all of fifteen minutes before she aggressively drew out a chair, scraping the legs across the floor. Her cheeks were flushed pink under her alabaster skin, giving her a childlike yet angry appearance. "Who's going to go first?" She glanced between them, dusting her hands off on her quilt-patched apron. When neither of them answered, Anserlee said, "Okay, Drew, you get to start."

He flattened his hands on the table and inhaled through his nose and exhaled out his mouth. Myka recognized the technique as one he used to calm himself before he got on stage. "She's scared of me, and I don't blame her." The muscles along his jaw flexed and his nostrils flared.

Anserlee didn't say anything, only waited for Myka to speak.

"I'm not scared of you," she said to Anserlee.

"Okay," Anserlee said. "Now let's try that again."

Myka tilted her head.

"Turn your chairs and face each other." Anserlee waited. "Now, please," she dictated in her therapist's voice.

They both obliged.

"Okay, Drew, try again, talking to Myka this time."

"You're scared of me. I saw it when I came in." He stared at his hands clasped together on his lap. The heavy platinum rings he usually wore were missing, leaving his fingers bare, with only tan lines as a reminder.

Myka wanted to reach out and grab his hand but she couldn't. "I don't blame you," she said.

He raised his eyes to her. "I blame myself."

She shook her head and finally looked at him. Bruises blackened under his eyes from his swollen nose and his eyelids were red and angry. "I'm not scared of you," she reiterated, this time with more confidence.

"But you blame me," he said.

"No, no…" she stuttered. "I just need a few days to clear my head." *Or erase the images that flash through my mind every time I look at you.* She'd died. And though he wasn't to blame, he was the weapon they'd used against her. It tortured her that she'd flinched when she saw him, because she wasn't scared of *him.*

But she was scared.

He clenched his hands tighter, the skin of his knuckles turning white. "I understand." He rubbed his fingers over his unshaven chin, making a sandpaper sound, before he slowly rose from the chair. Anserlee handed him a packet of something, whispered in his ear, and squeezed his arm before he walked out the door.

Myka wanted to yell at him to stop, to not give up so easily, but she couldn't because the other half of her *needed* him to leave. Her heart ripped from her chest as he closed the door without even looking back.

She glared over at Anserlee.

"Don't blame me." She held her hands in the air. "Now you both know what the problem is, and you can begin to fix it."

"I, I..." Myka got out before she started sobbing.

Anserlee rushed over and wrapped her in her arms. "Oh, sweet thing," she crooned, pulling Myka tight against her. She patted her back. "What you both need is some real sleep." She scurried away and brought back a mug filled with hot water and herbs. "Here. Drink this and go rest in my bed."

Myka gratefully climbed the ladder to Anserlee's loft and plopped down on her slightly too-short oval bed. She snuggled into her down pillow and fell asleep in fields of lavender and mint.

drew

Drew stood in front of the window, gripping the iron bars. Rain pelted the glass, but it didn't seem to bother the Sirins milling about on the boardwalks. Hate collected in his gut, a fire urging him to unleash, but he was utterly helpless here. He wasn't a fighter by nature. It wasn't that he didn't have the skills—he did—but he'd found he could charm his way through most situations. But this one was immune to both of his skills, leaving an emptiness inside his chest, a feeling of incompetence and uselessness. It was almost the worst thing he'd ever experienced, short of Myka breaking up with him. And short of killing her.

He exhaled, fogging up the glass. He turned away just as the rusted hinges on the door creaked, and it slowly opened. Drew's muscles flexed and dread filled the hollow space behind his ribs until Anserlee's head popped inside. His shoulders relaxed.

"How are you doing?" she asked at the same time he asked, "How is she doing?"

Anserlee huffed, though it came out more like a soft honk. She fluffed her wings and droplets of water peppered the floor. "She's stubborn, that one. I figured she'd come around by now."

It had been four days since he and Myka had their awkward encounter. Anserlee had checked in daily to give him updates. He appreciated her concern and had come to respect her advice. She wasn't like the other Sirins. She didn't make him uncomfortable, but he had his suspicions as to why.

"I told you—give her a couple more days." He dragged his fingers over his hair and rubbed the back of his neck. He hadn't been sleeping well the last few nights and his muscles ached.

"I think you're missing the gravity of the situation." She shut the door a bit harder than necessary, rattling the paintings on the wall.

"No, I'm not. I just know if I go to her before she's ready, I'll push her farther away. Remember, I tried to kill her—whether it was me or not, my hands were doing the work."

"Okay, fine. I'll give her a couple more days. That's it. But only because you know her better than I do. Then I'm pulling out the big guns."

An amused smile spread across his face. He had no doubt, despite her size, Anserlee had a set of big guns. "You do that."

"Does she shut down like this often? It's not a healthy coping mechanism to segregate one's feelings and not address them."

Drew shook his head. "It's not. And no, she doesn't do it often, but when she does..."

He paused for so long that Anserlee rolled her hand in

the air as if urging him to continue. "Would you like to finish what you were about to say, or do I have to ask?"

He took a deep breath and sighed. "The last time she shut down like this was when she broke up with me."

"Goodness, you said that was three years ago. We don't have three years. Once the two of you—well, you know—Rave will kill her, and the Matriarchs won't stop her. Or punish her." Anserlee twisted her hands in the pockets of her tunic.

"I know. But I'm not sure what to do," he said, his voice edged with helplessness. "She's an expert at pushing me away."

"Maybe I can help." Anserlee swept across the room and sat down at the small table. She gestured for Drew to follow. She pulled a couple of plates from her bag, a container of butter, a knife, and a loaf of bread. The smell of yeast and cinnamon swirled as she sliced a piece and slathered it with butter. "Eat." She pushed a plate in front of him. "And tell me more about it."

He took a bite and closed his eyes as he chewed. The food was the one thing he couldn't fault here. It was home-made, always fresh, and reminded him of his family's farm and his mom's cooking. A wave of homesickness washed over him, but he shoved it away to concentrate on his current problems. He swallowed the bread with a sip of water. "She left me the night we attended our first Grammy show. We'd been nominated but we didn't win. I was talking to some people, and she excused herself. Said she had to go to the bathroom. After she'd been gone for about, I don't know, twenty minutes, I asked the guys if they'd seen her. Nicky said she went back to the hotel room. I figured somehow, we'd gotten our wires crossed. But when I got to the room, she'd left me a note on the bed. She didn't even give me the courtesy of an in-person fuck-you. I'm sure you can figure out what it said."

Anserlee raised her brows as if she couldn't.

"The worst part was, I didn't even see it coming. I was completely blindsided. One second, I'd never been happier—then the next, my dreams crashed around me like an illusion. A house of cards. I've never felt so stupid." He curled his hands into the front of his hair and stared down at the table.

It had been three years ago, but the pain was like a phantom limb, and he could still feel it sometimes, stabbing, twisting, and warping his perception of the world. And now he was terrified after the latest events that they were finished for good. He didn't want to relapse into the darkness. He couldn't live through that hell again where hope sat just beyond his reach.

Anserlee laid her cold hand on Drew's arm. He looked up, meeting her sympathetic gaze. "Fuck," he whispered, the memory draining him. "I was getting ready to ask her to marry me." Though they hadn't been together long, he had been positive she was going to say yes. He would've bet his life on it—good thing he hadn't.

"Really?"

"Yeah. It was all set up. I had a jet ready to go and our bags packed. I'd even hired a body double so we could get out of there without the paparazzi following. Shortly after we met, I bought a small villa in Bacalar, Mexico on the Lagoon of Seven Colors. You should see it now. At the time, it wasn't anything fancy. It was pretty run-down. But as soon as the money started coming in from record sales and concerts, I had it remodeled to its original glory—hand-painted tiles, a courtyard full of flowers, and a swimming pool. I knew Myka would love its character. It was going to be ours and ours alone."

"You knew that early?"

"From the beginning." He'd practically had their life mapped out after their first unorthodox date at the emerald mine. He even had a keepsake to prove his commitment. He carried it with him to this day, though he'd left it behind at the lodge to keep it safe. He wondered if anyone had gone through his things and found it yet.

"Wow. Go on, please." She propped her elbows on the table, clasped her hands together, and rested them under her chin.

"I wanted her to have a sanctuary where she could let down her shield and be free." He tapped his heart. "I wanted to take care of her for a change, since she spent every waking hour taking care of me and the boys. I'm telling you—all the things she does for us. You'd be amazed. She orchestrates everything—schedules, photo shoots, interviews. Down to making sure we have snacks and peanut butter cups in our hotel rooms. Just so we can live the music. She's always in control, and I just wanted to be there when she finally let go. But instead of watching her twirl around the central courtyard in her bare feet"—or laying naked on the four-poster bed he'd found at an antique market—"she left me a letter with a bullshit excuse."

"What excuse?" Anserlee asked.

As a reminder that he wasn't enough, embarrassment flushed his cheeks. "That she couldn't manage the band and date me. And her job was more important to her."

"Bullshit is right!" Anserlee exclaimed, popping the side

of her fist on the table. Their plates jumped and the knife fell to the floor.

Drew laughed at her outburst, appreciating her reaction. It made him feel slightly better that she, too, could see through Myka's flimsy justification. "Exactly!"

"Has she told you the truth since?"

"Somewhat, but this mess is as much my fault as it is hers. When she broke up with me, I behaved like a heathen. Not toward her, but like a bull in rut."

"Ohhhh," Anserlee said, her forehead wrinkling. "That was stupid."

Drew nodded as he fetched the knife off the floor and set it on the edge of his plate. It was the biggest mistake he'd ever made.

"What did she say when you pressed her for the truth?"

"Basically, she admitted to letting me go so I could sow my wild oats."

"No, she didn't," Anserlee gasped.

"Yep. Then she said something about 'they,'" he said with air quotes. "In context, I'm thinking someone made her feel insecure about her looks? That's my best guess, and Nicky kind of hinted the same."

"That can't be it. She's gorgeous."

"I know that. And you know that. But the circles in which we run, Myka is—well, bigger than most." Anserlee opened her mouth, but Drew cut her off with a wave. "I love the way she looks. Every curve makes me happy. Every. Single. Fucking. One. But people can be so cruel. Especially when they're jealous. My mistake was thinking those bitches couldn't get to her because all I see is perfection. I'll take curves over bones any day of the week." Personally, he found the latest fashion craze, heroin chic, distasteful.

Tears welled in Anserlee's gray eyes. "You really do love her, don't you?"

He pressed his lips together and nodded ever so slightly. "I'm gone for her. I told you, have been since the beginning. When you know, you know."

"But you're so young."

"Sure. But to me, that just means we'll get more time together." He glanced at the table. "Or would have if things had gone as planned."

Anserlee let out a big sigh and muttered, "Well, I'm going to have to get you both out of here then."

He looked up and met Anserlee's gaze with a hint of suspicion. Why would she help them? "What do you mean?"

"I think I've figured out a way for you both to escape."

Drew stood up and slapped his hands on the table. "Then get her out of here! Get her out of here now. I can wait."

Anserlee placed a pale hand on top of his. "Sit back down so we can figure this out."

Drew dropped into the seat, crossed his arms, and studied Anserlee. Moments of all the times he'd seen them together played like a slideshow—the protective way she'd held on to Myka's arm when he'd been on the tower stage singing to everyone for the first time, the way her eyes never left Myka when he'd chosen to sleep with Forest for his audition, and her reaction when he'd accidentally killed Myka. Anserlee's behavior spoke volumes. And now, her offer to free Myka made perfect sense.

"You love her, too, don't you? And if she stays here, she'll most certainly die. But why put yourself in added danger by setting me free too?"

Anserlee licked her lips and swallowed as she nodded. "I

won't deny it. But after spending some time with you, I understand why Myka loves you. And now I have to get you both out of here, because Myka will never forgive me if I don't. Plus, I like you, too, even though...I hate you a little bit."

He cocked a brow with amusement. "Understandably. But I think we'll be friends regardless."

"I'd like to think we already are."

A lopsided grin lifted the corner of Drew's lips, and for the first time since he'd been marooned on Pan, he felt a sliver of hope grow in the darkness. "Agreed. Now how do we get her out of here?"

myka

Myka avoided Drew for the rest of the week, hoping time would combat her body's reaction to her fear. Helping Anserlee work distracted her from her mounting problems. She was truly one of the most compassionate, patient individuals Myka had ever known. Not once did she have an unkind word to say about any of the women who came to her for care. If it wasn't so genuine, Myka would've been annoyed.

She was content to help Anserlee and ignore her own fear. If she ignored *it, it* would go away. However, she did have a million questions she wanted to ask. But unfortunately, Anserlee's little medical practice was so busy they didn't have a moment alone. Until Anserlee finally lost her insurmountable amount of patience and closed up shop early, telling her last few clients they would need to come back tomorrow.

"Enough is enough!" Anserlee huffed on the fifth day of Myka avoiding Drew. "In a little more than a week, you and he are going to have to…" She furiously mixed one herb with another, mashing the contents together like they had personally offended her. "You need to toughen up and go see him." She stopped long enough to glare at Myka over the table where she'd been ordered to chop more herbs.

"Well, it's not like he's gone out of his way to come see me!" Myka yelled back. She had only seen glimpses of him being paraded around by the blonde bird lady.

"Oh, please," Anserlee said, her gray eyes flashing. "He thought it was best to give you a few days to calm down. I had hoped you would've asked to see him by now. But I didn't realize you were so obstinate. What is your problem? You know he had no control over his actions. I wish there were some way I could show you. Some way I could make you understand. Imagine being a puppet on a string. You control your mind but someone else controls your body."

Myka realized she was being unreasonable, but she was still scared. Every night, she woke covered in sweat, reliving the nightmare. Remembering as the love of her life killed her. "Why didn't he fight harder?" she whispered, ashamed of herself for even thinking that way. Logically, she knew it wasn't his fault. But if she was being honest, she had some pent-up resentment along with her fear. Somewhere in Myka's mind, she held on to that unreasonable assumption that true love conquered all. And he should've been stronger. She'd hoped with a few days of separation, her fear and resentment would fade.

Myka opened a bag of some kind of plant and sneezed as she poured it into the mortar. Weed remnants scattered everywhere. She wrinkled her nose, trying not to sneeze again.

"Fight harder?" Anserlee's tone dropped to a chilly octave. "He did. I was there. If he wasn't fighting, he would have snapped your silly little neck. Pop!" Anserlee clapped her hands together, and Myka shied away like a spooked horse. "That is the most control I have ever seen anyone have against us. And as for fighting harder, hasn't he been doing that for the last three years?" She tossed a rag at her, hard.

Myka stopped mid-motion and froze with her mouth agape as the rag hit her in the face and dropped to the table. "You two have been talking, I see." Her lips pressed together in a thin, firm line. She picked up the rag and swept the mess off the table into the garbage.

"Of course we have. We both care about you." She leaned across the table, grabbing Myka's hands. Anserlee's were so tiny and pale in comparison. "Don't you see? He *has* paid his price—a price, that it seems to me, he shouldn't have had to pay in the first place. Why couldn't—"

Myka scooted her chair out violently, sending it clattering to the floor. "The two of you have no business discussing our relationship." She didn't need to add more to her growing pile of anxieties. She stormed out into the miserable Alaskan drizzle before she said something she would regret.

"Gods! He said you were stubborn and when cornered you would shut down, but I assumed you weren't stupid," Anserlee said, flying out the door after her. *Yes, flying.* "You have officially crossed the line between the two. Get. Back. In. Here. Now," Anserlee ordered, every word a sentence of its own.

Myka stopped, careful not to slip on the wet planks. Others on the walkway paused and stared, some giggled and pointed. Large droplets of water dripped from the branches above and splattered on the mossy boardwalk.

"Don't make me come and get you. Because I promise you will not like it," Anserlee said, her voice quiet and dangerous.

Myka spun around and stomped past her back into the house, ignoring their growing audience.

Anserlee followed and gently shut the door, leaning against it. Myka stood in front of the hearth, warming her backside, with no inclination to sit down. She enjoyed towering over people. Her height intimidated some, but it didn't seem to faze Anserlee in the least.

"Are you done now?" Anserlee grabbed several oils and concoctions out of the cupboards.

Myka answered with silence.

"I see." Anserlee set multiple containers on the table. She carefully measured ingredients into a marble mortar before mixing them together with a twig covered in needles. She brushed her hands on her apron when she finished. "Sit. I need you out of the way." She added a few coals from the fire to her concoction and neon-blue puffs of smoke slowly spiraled from the meld. Whiffs of petrichor drifted under Myka's nose.

Anserlee chanted as she held the smoldering bowl in one hand while waving the scent throughout the room with her other. The smell grew even stronger.

Myka rescued the toppled chair from the floor and grudgingly sat down.

"There," Anserlee said, placing the bowl in the middle of the table and taking a seat across from her. "That will prevent anyone from overhearing our conversation. We have protection until the scent is gone."

"You know magic?" Myka leaned forward in the creaky chair. The concoction swirled around the window frames and the doorway, hiding in the cracks.

"Seriously?" she said. "You are on an island inhabited by Sirins, who swallow the souls of dead singers, give birth to them, and then grow them into who they were before, and you question magic? Besides, it's not really magic, per se, more like an intimate knowledge of how Mother Earth works."

Myka rolled up the long sleeves of Drew's lavender flannel. Despite being scared, angry, and embarrassed, she'd worn it every day. Because she loved him and wearing it made her feel...better. "Whatever." Myka settled into the chair and crossed her legs. *Let the battle of wills begin*, she thought.

Anserlee straightened up as if she'd heard Myka's silent challenge and cocked a dainty eyebrow. "Do you remember the men who sang that day on the stage before Drew?"

Myka folded her hands, wondering where Anserlee was going with this. She'd expected an immediate tongue-lashing. "Yes, I remember." Nothing could erase her Uncle James's voice from her head. She wasn't certain it was him, and she was holding out hope. She wasn't any closer to finding a way out for Drew and her, let alone anyone else.

"Wasn't it curious that they were hidden behind a curtain?"

"I didn't think about it." At the time, Myka hadn't given it a second thought, but now, it did seem strange.

"These men, these unfortunate humans, are our slaves. For sex, for entertainment, for anything we choose, they have no choice. And by that, I mean *no* choice. Over the years, our demands take a toll, not only on their bodies but on their entire essence, their souls. They start to waste away, a little at a time. It's almost imperceptible in the beginning, but soon, the changes become more apparent. First is the permanent deadening behind their eyes when we don't even have to sing to them anymore to get them to do *anything*. They lose their fight, their will, and accept that their only true escape from us is death. Then the physical changes start—the weight loss, the atrophied muscles, balding, and then soon, one by one, their teeth go. You can smell the disease that eats them from the inside out, rank with every dying breath they take. *We* are that disease."

With every word, every desperate sentence, Myka's desire to fight vanished.

"If you do not get past your fear and forgive Drew for something that was beyond his control, I have painted before you the future he will have. He will wither and waste away, all the while wishing to die." Her voice faded.

Tears pooled in Myka's eyes and stung the back of her nose. Bile burned her throat, tasting sour on her tongue. She tried interrupting, but Anserlee held her hand up fast and continued.

"With every day he stays, the more he will lose. The more you will *both* lose. Do you understand?" Urgency replaced the quiet compassion that usually swirled behind her eyes.

Myka nodded. Guilt and shame replaced her stubborn resolve. What had she been doing wasting precious time? Burying her head in the sand, trying to pretend none of this was happening? As foolish as it seemed—the answer was yes. That was exactly what she'd been trying to do. In her professional life, she never buried the problem because the band was worth fighting for. Personally, though she was tough on the outside, it was often a shield for a deeper issue —an insecurity that she wasn't worth fighting for, and if she ignored the problem, it would pass. She needed to pull herself together, because if she didn't, Drew was going to pay the price. And she couldn't allow that to happen, because of all the people she'd ever known, he was the one she would willingly die for.

When Anserlee didn't respond, Myka answered out loud. "I understand. I do. And I'll fix it."

"I appreciate that, but seeing how stubborn you are, I think the lesson needs to hit harder."

Myka's brows furrowed.

Anserlee removed the vase of fresh flowers from the table, then pushed the still-smoldering concoction to the middle and waved her hand over it, spreading the smoke. She set out three delicate plates, some fresh bread, butter, cheese, and berries.

A gentle knock came on the wooden door.

"Well, just to make sure you *really* understand, I've invited some company to dine with us for lunch. Come in, please. Take a seat at the table across from the young lady."

Myka heard shuffling from behind her but didn't look up until he sat down and folded his hands together on the table. She frowned in surprise—she'd expected Drew. Instead, an older man with dark-blond hair waited. Every vein in his hands stood out beneath his jaundiced, aged skin.

"James, please take a look at who's sitting in front of you," Anserlee said.

Myka's eyes snapped open wider and her mouth practically hit the floor. Her heart crashed against her ribs. Sitting in front of her was the remnants of her uncle. She started to rise, but Anserlee stopped her with a firm, frustratingly strong hand on her shoulder.

"Please, Myka, let's keep calm for James's sake, all right? It will be much easier for him that way."

The bread, which smelled so good only moments ago, no longer held any appeal. She wouldn't have recognized him if she didn't know who he was. His hair, even though it looked clean, lacked shine, and she feared if she touched him, his skin would feel like wax under her fingers. His eyes, behind his dated glasses, were sunken deep down in his skull and staring right through her.

Only once had Myka ever seen eyes like that. While performing one year in Germany, Burning Brenda had taken a tour of Dachau, the WWII concentration camp. There had been a wall of pictures, and all the victims had the same vacant expression as the one gazing back at her.

A sob of horror caught in Myka's throat.

"No, James, really look at her."

The tension in his face released and a hesitant smile rose. "Ana? Anastasia?" He said her mother's name. She looked like her mother, but her height and personality, she'd gotten from her father.

"No, Uncle, it's Myka."

"Myka, my little Myka? No," he said, shaking his head. "She's not here. I'm finally losing my mind. Thank the Lord," he said with such reverence it broke her heart. His smile widened into a manic grin, black gaping holes where his teeth should've been. He *wanted* to die. Death was better than living here amongst these monsters.

Myka's jaw clenched as rage built, shaking her muscles from within.

Anserlee sat down at the head of the table and grabbed

his hands. He flinched slightly. "No, you're right, this is your Myka."

"Why is she here?" His voice warbled feebly.

"That is a story I don't have time for."

"She needs to get out of here! Now!" he yelled, standing up from his chair. His eyes grew wild and panicked, darting between the two of them. The tendons in his neck strained under his sagging skin.

Anserlee started humming a sweet, calming tune, and he immediately sat back down. "I don't want to do that to you, James. I have been nothing but nice to you all these years and yes, we need to get her out of here. But first, I needed *her* to see the consequences of being here as long as you have. Plus, I thought you might want to see her, even if it was only for a little while."

"You're right." He held his hand up. "I'm sorry. This is the first time in years my mind has felt...clear, I suppose is the right word for it. So let me get this straight," he said to Anserlee. "*You* want to get her out of here?" He pushed up his glasses, yet somehow looked down at her.

Myka smiled softly, recognizing the gesture. Many years ago, she'd been on the other end of his interrogations.

"I understand that you have never compelled me, except for a moment ago, in all my years here, but you are one of *them*," he hissed. "Why should I believe you want to help?"

"Because I'm tired of all this. I don't like it. I never have," Anserlee said.

Uncle James's brows knitted together, and he shook his head. He had always been unusually perceptive and in tune with the world around him. It made him a phenomenal songwriter. "No." He waited for Anserlee to tell him everything.

She got up and paced around the cottage before she finally told James about Drew's and Myka's story.

From Drew's perspective.

They'd been having quite the chats while Myka had been avoiding her issues. Anserlee knew even more than Myka did. Drew had told Anserlee that he'd fallen in lust with Myka the moment he saw her and in love with her the night they sat around the campfire after they'd signed their first record contract.

After she'd broken up with him, he'd told her that he loved her and begged her not to leave him. But Myka had reasoned his confession away as panic. He hadn't loved her—not really. How could he? They were young. He just needed some time to see what else was available.

But hearing it from Anserlee opened her eyes to how blind she'd been. How easily other people's opinions had damaged her confidence.

Myka had lusted after Drew the second he opened his mouth, but she'd fallen in love with him unequivocally the first time they'd attended the Grammys. The same night she'd left him.

Her mind drifted back to the beginning of that evening. Before a few mean girls made her question her worth.

Drew arrived at her hotel door and let himself in with his own fancy keycard thirty minutes before he was due and plopped his long frame on her bed. He used the TV remote to flip through channels, landing on a wildlife documentary.

"You're early again." Myka tossed him a dirty look. She wanted him to see her all dressed up.

"Sorry, I like to watch you get ready. It calms me down. And besides, Tony and Gus kept beer-farting and stinking up the room."

"And what? You weren't joining them?" she asked, strutting by him in her undergarments that smoothed away any of the unwanted bulges.

"No, you know that."

She did know that, since he spent most nights with her, watching movies, making out, and ordering room service. Despite his rock star reputation, he knew she was a virgin and he wanted to take things slow, even when she'd begged him not to. She craved his touch.

Tonight, she wasn't going to accept "let's take this slow" for an answer. Just thinking about it made her body tingle and sigh. She finished her hair and threw on a third coat of mascara before slipping into her slinky purple dress.

"Here, zip this," she asked, standing in front of him.

He zipped the dress up slowly, then leaned in to kiss her neck. His lips were hot even on her flushed skin. A zing ran straight from her neck, directly to her nether regions.

He turned her around and placed his forehead against hers. "You're the only person I can imagine doing this with. You're the reason I'm here." He straightened up and pressed his finger to her lips before she could protest. The anxiety and fear were palpable behind his eyes. That man was not afraid to sing in front of thousands, but he was afraid to accept an award should they win.

That was when Myka fell in love with him. That unwavering cockiness, the ever-present shield of confidence he always wore, he stripped it away before her eyes and let her see directly into his heart. How unfortunate the timing was. If only he could have kept his heart hidden for a few more hours.

"Myka!" Anserlee snapped.

"What?" she answered, time-warping back to the present.

"Were you listening?"

She shrugged. "Not really. Didn't think I needed to."

"Well, you do! Drew and I have agreed on a plan to get you both out of here."

Myka sat up straighter and began to pay attention.

"James, are you willing to help us?" Anserlee asked.

"Like her life depends on it. Yes," he said. His frail hand clasped Myka's. She rubbed the back of his papery skin with her thumb. She wanted to squeeze but was afraid she might hurt him.

Anserlee rose from the chair, dusting fallen herbs and breadcrumbs off her gown. "Thank you, James, but you should probably go. I don't want anyone to see us all together like this again. I'll let you know more as soon as I can."

Uncle James stood and pushed his chair under the table. Myka didn't ask his permission before she wrapped him in her arms. The last time she'd hugged him, her head came to his mid-chest. Now she was a smidge taller.

"It has been a blessing to see you all grown up. You look so much like your momma. When you get home, please hug her for me and tell her in her sleep that I love and miss her." He kissed the side of her head.

Myka pushed away. "What do you mean? You're coming back with me!"

"No, child, I'm not. I'm broken, and I can't be fixed." He gripped her shoulders and stared her in the eyes.

"No! We can get you out and you can come back to us." Tears streamed down her face. She swiped at them with her sleeve.

"You don't understand. I can't go back to the world and let them see me like this. I'm a half-soul, only half of the man I used to be. I don't want to go back. I won't. But I will help you any way I can." Then he scuttled out the door, barely picking up his feet, without looking back.

"Drew told you James is my uncle, didn't he?" Myka stated the fact. "That's not the last time I'll see him, right?" She quizzed Anserlee as she quietly shut the door. She was not done arguing for his freedom.

"Probably," Anserlee said, cutting her off before she could protest. "For his safety and yours. If Rave gets any hint that you care for James, she'll use it to her advantage." She sat back down at the table and traced a finger around the rim of her water glass.

"Anserlee, why are you willing to help us? You completely avoided the question earlier. Because you're tired of all this, and you don't approve, doesn't seem like a good enough reason to risk your life."

She held Myka's gaze with her dove-gray eyes, her lashes almost touching her brows. "Don't you know?" she whispered. A flush spread over her skin.

"No." She paused, afraid she'd missed the obvious.

"Because, after spending so much time with Drew, I have decided I actually like him. Even though I'm jealous of him."

Of course she liked him. It was impossible not to. Myka could understand why she wouldn't want Drew to live the life her uncle was condemned to.

Wait. What?

Before she had time to think properly, she asked, "Jealous of what?" Myka's mouth dropped open as the reason finally dawned on her. "Oh. Oh..." she said, breaking her gaze and looking down at the table.

Myka picked a raw cuticle on her thumbnail. It wasn't like it was unusual, but she'd never had a woman that she thought of as a friend feel that way about her. Just to clarify she wasn't missing something, she asked, "So...you love me?"

"I'm in love with you, yes."

"Anserlee, that's not possible. We've only known each other for a week."

"And how long did it take you to fall in love with him?"

"Longer than a week." Though if she were being truthful, it wasn't much longer than a week. She'd fallen hard and fast.

"So you're telling me I don't know my own emotions? I'm over two hundred years old. I think I know how I feel." Anserlee crossed her arms.

Myka's eyes rounded with the news of Anserlee's feelings and her age. Though she should've suspected it, considering she was a supernatural creature. Why anything surprised her at this point was a mystery. "You're right. I'm sorry."

"So now you see," Anserlee said, getting up from the table.

"Yes, but sit down. I think we should talk about this." Myka grabbed Anserlee's soft, warm hand and pulled her back into her chair.

"Now you want to talk?" Anserlee said incredulously.

Myka sighed. She'd learned her lesson. "Yes."

"Are you angry?" Anserlee cocked her head slightly.

"No, no, of course not. I'm flattered."

A breath of air hitched in Anserlee's throat. "You are?" Her forehead wrinkled in surprise.

"Yes. I don't know how long ago you spent any time on my side of the world, but this isn't uncommon. And it's widely accepted in most circles."

"Well, it's been quite some time, and when we are in bird form, it's difficult to understand all that takes place. I have to be honest—there's a part of me that doesn't want to help you." Pain creased her eyes.

"Oh." Myka sucked on her thumbnail, trying to take the sting out of her bleeding cuticle.

"You're my friend, right?"

Myka nodded.

Anserlee pulled Myka's thumb away from her mouth and wrapped it with some gauze. Her touch was gentle, yet strong and sure. "I figured, in time, with no other options, you might come to feel the same about me as I do about you."

When Anserlee finished bandaging Myka's self-inflicted injury, she didn't release her hand. Myka's breathing slowed. She sat silent and waited for Anserlee to continue. The magic she'd conjured earlier had begun to wear off and Myka could hear Sirins chattering outside as they passed by.

"Then I got to know both of you, and I saw your love. Even if you did stay, there's no way, even in a million years, you could ever need me the way you need him. I just can't understand why you deny it at every turn. Silly." She shook her head. "Anyway, I can't compete with that. I would be the runner-up." Her wings drooped.

"Your life here has been hard, hasn't it?"

"Not always. But I've always been lonely. I'm not like most of the other Sirins. I'm a goose, born to mate for life in a world where that would never happen for me."

Sadness cloaked Myka's shoulders. Anserlee was her friend, and though she wasn't *in love* with her, she did love her. "I'm sorry. I don't know if this will make things better or worse, but if I didn't already love Drew, and I were here, you're the only one I could've loved." She squeezed her hand.

A tight-lipped smile flattened Anserlee's full lips before she got up and placed their dishes in the sink. She gripped the edge of the basin and said, "I don't know if that makes it better or worse, but we'll never know."

TWENTY-THREE

drew

Drew paced barefoot back and forth over the cold stone floor in his room like a caged lion. He didn't like the plan. He didn't like it at all. Because he didn't know what it was.

Anserlee had said the only way it would work was if he and Myka didn't know the details. She had a theory and that's all she would say. Otherwise, they were to stick to the schedule. In a little less than a week, he and Myka would have to *perform* in front of a live studio audience. Anserlee didn't seem to have a plan to get them out of *that* situation.

If someone had told him he would find himself in a predicament where he didn't want to have sex with Myka, he would've laughed in their faces. He couldn't even begin to count the ways and places his imagination had taken him. But this scenario wasn't one of them. And honestly, it made his chest tight.

He halted his pacing when he heard scuffling feet outside his door. A small knock preceded Myka's head peering around the corner. "Can I come in?"

Joy surged, replacing his moment of distress. "Of course," he said, instantly worried about her. She looked terrible. Her red, puffy eyes and dark circles stood out against her unusually pale skin. She'd lost the ten pounds she always complained about, but he didn't like what she'd gone through to get there. He preferred the extra weight. He loved soft curves over sharp angles. Especially hers.

He wanted to rush over and hold her while he, again, apologized, but he didn't want to spook her.

"Thanks." She closed the heavy door behind her. "Can we talk?"

"Yes, yes," Drew said, sounding on the edge of desperation. So many times, he'd wanted to talk, only to be shut down. "Come on, you want to have a seat on the...bed?" He offered her the only place in his room to sit beside the rickety chair made from birch trees. "Not that you have to sit there if, um, uh, you don't want to." He took a deep breath to calm his nerves. He didn't like feeling nervous around her.

"Yeah, can you sit too?" she asked.

He nodded and sat down on the messy bed, patting the spot next to him. Instead, she strolled over and stood in front of him.

"Sit," he insisted. He tapped the bed, worried she might pass out. He could see the outgrowth of her dark-blonde hair shadowing her skull as if it were a timeline counting the days that had passed.

She shook her head quickly as she brought a trembling hand up to his hair. "I like it. I haven't had a chance to tell you," she said, playing with the ends of his loose curls.

His breath hitched at her touch.

"As much as I hate to admit it, because *they* did this to

you, it suits you. I think we can work with this when we get back."

"Yeah, I think we can too." A sliver of hope pierced his darkness and a hesitant smile rounded his cheeks. She still wanted to escape. With him. And it sounded as if she might not quit the band after all. "Andrew Arie meets Alaskan Mountain Man," he laughed. "I might have to grow a full beard, though."

"No, this scruffy lumberjack look is all us poor women can handle," Myka said, her eyes darting down his bare chest and over his abs. She ran her fingers lightly over his three-day stubble, causing his pulse to falter.

He only shaved every few days. He wasn't comfortable with an old-fashioned straight razor and tended to accidentally cut himself. Plus, when he used something that sharp, they monitored him and took it away directly after he finished with it. He wasn't sure if they were worried he would use it on himself, or them. The latter was tempting and if he thought he could get away with it, he wouldn't hesitate to kill Rave or Gilda.

"I don't care about any of those other women." Drew placed his hand over hers, gripping tight. "The only one that matters to me is you." His voice was rough.

"I know." She pushed him to sit further back on the bed, and crawled onto his lap, straddling him. "I know that now."

She dipped her head forward and rested it in the crook of his neck while Drew wrapped his arms firmly around her back, positive she could feel his thrashing heart.

"Please forgive me," he whispered into her hair and inhaled the scent of the various herbs clinging to her.

"There's nothing to forgive. I know you would never

hurt me. I was being unreasonable and digging my head into the sand, hoping that if I ignored this nightmare, it would disappear."

He chuckled. "Well, it's good to know you haven't changed."

"Oh, I have. That coping mechanism isn't healthy, and I promise to work on it. But in this case, it kind of worked." She shrugged. "Apparently, you and Anserlee came up with a plan while I was away."

"I love you, Myka. I love you more than you know." He couldn't suppress those words any longer.

"No," she said, shaking her head. "I do know, because I love you the same. Can we just call all the hurt even and start over again?" She lifted her head and looked at him. Her eyes were so dark he couldn't differentiate her pupils from her irises. She clasped her hands behind his head.

"For now, yes, please, but eventually, I think we need to talk about it." Burying their past didn't seem like the smartest way to handle all of the pain they'd caused each other. But for now, he thought it was a good idea. It would be too much for them to tackle all their issues now. First, they had to escape.

Her lips parted and he could tell she was biting the inside of her cheek. She always did when she was nervous. "Okay. Once we get free of this nightmare, we'll lock ourselves in a room and bare our souls."

Drew's shoulders relaxed. As ominous as it sounded, he looked forward to that day.

Myka didn't know why she was so nervous. She could see the forgiveness they both deserved shining in his eyes. The hope lingering behind the deep-blue color said everything would be okay.

He leaned in and kissed her. His lips were soft, hot, and surprisingly gentle. She balled her fingers in his hair, pulling him hard into her, wanting him to punish her for behaving badly. For being so stubborn and turning a blind eye to the fact that all of this was her fault much more than it was his. But he denied her punishment and continued to gently tease her with his lips. His tongue danced inside her mouth as his hand cradled the back of her head. She remembered this kiss. It was eerily similar to the first one they'd ever shared. But she wasn't going to let it end there.

"Kiss me until I forget where we are," she demanded, not parting her lips from his.

He groaned deep in his chest, but because of the low, raspy tone of his voice, it sounded more like a growl. Her toes curled as he wrapped his hands around her waist and lifted her off of him, setting her down on the bed in his place. He stood tall above her and lifted her chin with one finger, forcing her gaze from his ripped stomach, up his chest, to his eyes.

"First, I need a promise from you, that you will never break my heart again. Because…" He looked away, anguish fleeting across his face. "I won't be able to recover from that kind of pain again. If we have any issues, we *have* to communicate. You can't shut down and run away. You *have* to promise me."

Normally, she'd never make a promise like that because life was unpredictable. But after what they'd been through, God would have to pry him from her cold, dead hands. Because she was never letting him go. "I promise to never break your heart again so long as you do the same. I won't survive it either. I promise to talk to you even when it's uncomfortable. I can't promise not to shut down, because that's how I process, but I promise not to run, and when I'm ready, we'll talk."

His lips turned downward in a thoughtful frown. "Okay. I can agree to that." He tucked her long bangs behind her ear, leaving behind a barrage of sparks. "Now that we're both standing in the flames, know from this moment on, no matter what happens on this island and beyond, *you're mine,*" he said so fiercely that shivers ran up her spine. He leaned down until they were nose to nose. "No matter what they make me do, it will always be you in my head. It will be your skin I taste on my lips, your body I hold beneath me." His tone softened. "You are mine, Myka, and I'm yours. I have been since the day I met you. Body, heart, and soul."

His pupils darkened as he waited for her to acknowledge. She nodded, spellbound, breath frozen as she waited for him. He crushed into her with a force she couldn't have imagined, a hunger in his kiss she didn't know existed. His lips claimed hers, leaving her no room to argue—not that she would have. Because she was, in fact, his.

He pulled away. "I need to know that I have your forgiveness for what they're going to make me do. Not only to you, but after…" Only the bobbing of his throat gave away his fear.

"Don't be silly. There will be *nothing* to forgive, but if you don't shut up and kiss me now, I might never forgive you for that!"

"Oh, I'm going to do so much more than just kiss you." His breath ran hot over her ear, sending anticipation flashing through her body, tightening her core.

His lips found the soft spot below her jaw, and she lifted her chin while inhaling a shiver. She reached for him to draw his body closer, but he chuckled against her neck and murmured, "Nope."

He untied the top of her linen dress and lifted it over her head. The material's soft caress tickled her skin. He ran his fingers down her sternum, over her cleavage, until they stopped on the front latch of her bra. He unclipped it with ease. She started to shimmy out of it, only for Drew to stop her.

"I don't want your help," he said, getting in her face. "You're going to let me do anything and everything I want, got it?" A dark brow rose in question. "I've been thinking about this for over three fucking years."

She nodded, her throat too twisted to speak. *Anything. Yes.* She was helpless.

"Good. Now that we're clear, you're going to sit there and not move for just a second."

He stood all the way up, stretched his long body, and walked across the room. His linen pants hung low on his hips, exposing the dimples in the small of his back on either side of his spine. His shoulders, wide and sculpted, flexed as he placed the birch chair under the handle for added security and locked the door. Then he grabbed a few more candles out of the cabinet. He lit them and placed two on each end table by his bed. He pulled the curtains shut and came back, stopping in front of her. The candlelight flickered over his abs and his hip muscles that continued down, hiding under his pants. She reached out to untie the flimsy cord, desperately wanting to see the growing bulge that was under them, only to have her hand swiped away.

A one-sided smirk teased his lips. "I know it's hard for you to relinquish control, but behave like I told you." He pushed her bra the rest of the way off her breasts and sighed as he stared. He licked the tip of his thumb and gently swiped it over her nipple.

She inhaled sharply as it puckered, and a bolt of electricity struck her core.

"Mine," he reminded her. Not that she was likely to forget.

He kissed her again, his hands burrowing into her short hair. He bit her lip, hard, causing her to flinch but not allowing her to pull away. "Mine," he whispered again, before his head dipped lower, kissing the sensitive skin along her neck.

The pace of her breathing increased as she anticipated his path to her breasts. His hands swept down her shoulders, grabbing on to her wrists as his lips brushed lightly over her already-taut nipple. His tongue flickered, hot and relentless, and her body screamed for release. His hands squeezed tighter, holding her prisoner, and his teeth bit down on her tender flesh, not as hard as on her lips, but enough to command her attention.

"Mine," he said, firmer this time.

"Yes," she said breathlessly.

He trailed his tongue to her other breast. As he feasted, he reached with both hands to rip open the side of her panties, then he did the same to the other side. When he released her nipple from his mouth, a small protest escaped her lips. He took a step back before pulling the material slowly out from between her legs, making sure the fabric brushed over her wet, pulsing center. He tossed them to the side. With one finger pressed against her sternum, he pushed until she was lying on her back. He swept kisses down her stomach, leaving behind a trail of flames. She was certain the moment his lips found home, she was going to combust.

In the three months they'd officially dated, they'd never gone this far. Never made it all the way to second base—hell, he'd never even seen her naked before they'd come to this godforsaken place. But this was a long time in the making, and she planned on enjoying every second of it.

Her throat hitched as he kneeled on the floor and lifted her dangling legs over his shoulders, his breath burning her exposed skin before he even touched her. Her mind became a tangled mess, only able to focus on the wanting and throbbing of her swollen clit and the aching deep inside.

Suddenly, at the door, came a series of knocks. The hits became louder and more insistent by the second. *Bang! Bang! Bang!* In rapid succession.

"Fuck!" Drew cussed. "What?" he hollered, still between her legs.

The door rattled as someone tried entering. "You need to open this door now," came a muffled voice from the other side.

"Why!?"

"Because I said so!" She sounded agitated and began pounding on the wood again.

"Give me a minute." Drew handed Myka her dress before grabbing his shirt. "Try to look casual," he said, before stalking angrily to the door.

Her mind, still a hot mess, tried to catch up to the unfortunate events. She quickly threw on her dress and rubbed her eyes fiercely, hoping to look as if she had been crying.

He turned and looked at her, frustration written all over his gorgeous face. "You ready?" he mouthed.

She nodded after she hid her bra and ruined panties under the bearskin rug next to his bed.

Drew grumbled as he removed the chair from under the door handle and opened it, but he didn't move aside. That didn't stop Gilda from barging past him and stopping in the middle of the floor. She scanned the area, eyes narrowing when her gaze fell on Myka sitting on top of the bed.

"What do you want, Gilda?" Drew demanded, taking her focus off Myka.

"What are you two doing?" Her sharp eyes darted back and forth between the two of them.

"Uh, what we were told. Getting to know each other." Drew crossed his arms, his tattoos flexing around his biceps, warping the art.

"Hmmm. Well, that's over now. Rave has convinced the Matriarchs that you two already know one another." She eyed Myka skeptically as if the notion of Drew knowing her was asinine.

Drew scoffed. "Well, that's ridiculous." He sounded bored.

She waved her golden hand in the air. "I agree, but it is not my decision. The two of you will no longer be spending any more time together until the audition."

"What do you mean? That's stupid. This is the first time I've seen Myka in a few days. Man, look at her, she's a wreck. She doesn't even want to do this."

"Really? Because Rave makes it sound as if the whore can hardly wait." Gilda wrinkled her nose.

Before she could protest, Drew jumped in. "Seriously, that's the pot calling the kettle black. She's young and scared. And it seems to me that the only people who are even nice to her are me and Anserlee. Go figure that she would find some comfort and protection in my arms. What did you," he said, measuring Gilda up and down, "creatures expect?"

She ignored him. "Whore, you need to leave." She snapped and pointed at the door.

"Hey!" Drew said, taking a big stride toward her. Sweet music hit the air. By his second step, he faltered and his eyes went vacant. "Yes, whore, you need to leave," he said, his voice sounding eerily robotic.

Myka bowed her head and scuttled away, leaving her belongings behind. The amount of time it had taken for Drew to obey Gilda was frightening. She wanted to cry but she needed to toughen up if they were going to escape.

She found Anserlee in her house, taking care of a long line of patients.

Her head cocked when Myka burst in. She caught an expression of confusion, but Anserlee quickly hid it away. "Oh, good, you're back. Put on an apron and help me."

In a daze, Myka obeyed and waited for Anserlee's next orders.

"Separate these herbs and put them into the teabags. Be careful, the measurements must be correct otherwise they won't work efficiently." Anserlee slid the ingredients and a recipe in front of her and went back to treating her patients.

Myka narrowed her focus, not wanting to screw up. After each bag was filled, she hand-labeled the concoction perfuming the air like a field of wildflowers and weeds.

Three hours later, as the last Sirin left, Anserlee mixed up some of her magic potion so no one could hear them, and Myka relayed the earlier events. Well, the parts that mattered anyway.

"So the two of you have come to terms with your predicament?" she asked. Most of the awkwardness between them was gone.

"Yes."

"So do you trust me?"

Myka hesitated for a moment, knowing that if she was going to trust anyone here, it was going to have to be Anserlee. "Yes."

"Good, because in order for you to escape, I'm going to ask you to do something you're not going to like. I need you to do it anyway. I have a plan, but first, I need to test a theory. Are you up for it?" She placed some fresh berries on the table before sitting down.

"I guess." Myka plopped a sweet blackberry in her mouth. It was the first thing she'd eaten all day.

"I need you to do exactly as I say, no questions asked. And tell no one. Not even Drew. Not because I don't trust him, but they can force him to talk. Agreed?"

"Ahh! I don't like letting go of control!" Myka said. With Drew, it was one thing, but this was something different.

"I know, but you have to for this to work."

They popped berries into their mouths with their pink-stained fingers as Anserlee told Myka what she needed to do.

"Tomorrow morning, early, you need to take your kayak and paddle to the nearest island off to your left."

"Wait. How do you know I have a kayak?" Myka tapped her fingers on the table.

Anserlee shrugged, her wings bobbing. "Initially, I didn't but Drew told me he had one and that he'd left it on the shore. When I went to make sure it was still there, I found two kayaks. A red one and a yellow one. I assumed one of them was yours. Am I wrong?"

Myka shook her head.

"Okay, then. Here's a map." She set a hand-drawn sketch on the table and pushed it in front of Myka. "You'll be leaving from this spot and going to that one." She connected the Xs on the map with her finger. She stopped Myka with a hard glare before she could protest. "You promised." She kept her mouth shut while Anserlee continued. "There, you will stay for one night. The next day, you'll head back when the sun is at the highest point in the sky. That's all you need to do."

Myka scowled. Leaving Drew behind tied her stomach in a knot, making her feel as if she'd swallowed a rock.

"I won't make you leave for good without him. I swear." Anserlee placed her hand over her heart.

"How am I going to escape without being caught?"

"I told you no questions. We agreed. I will only tell you what's necessary."

Myka weighed her options and quickly realized she really didn't have any others. Begrudgingly, she placed her and Drew's survival into the hands of someone who was supposed to be their enemy. But Anserlee had proven more than once that she wasn't like the rest of the Sirins. "Okay. I'll leave in the morning. I gotta go back to my room and grab some things."

"No, your belongings have already been brought here. I didn't know why earlier, but now I know—they want you watched at all times. Surprisingly, this will make it easier for you to leave." Anserlee pulled Myka's backpack from the closet and handed it to her.

Myka unzipped it and dug through her things. Her extra clothes and supplies, including her watch, were all still there, though messier than how she'd left them. "How is no one going to see me? Aren't there guards watching us?"

"Yes, but I have a way around that." Anserlee took the smoking concoction sitting on the table and poured some of its foul-smelling juice into a small bladder before adding hot water. She shook it and handed it to Myka. "When the time comes, you're going to need to drink all of it."

Her nose crinkled at the week-old garbage stench wafting from the container. She pinched it between her finger and thumb, holding it as far away as she could. "Can I ask, what's it going to do to me?"

"It's a concealment spell. Used in the smoke form, it keeps ears from listening; in the liquid form, it keeps people from seeing. You'll need to stick to the shadows because it won't make you completely invisible, just blurred. It'll last you approximately thirty-two hours, so altogether, that's how much time you have to get to one of the nearest islands and back without being seen. Once there, you're going to need to completely hide the kayak and yourself. If they spot you, the plan won't work. I will not raise the alarm until I 'wake up,'" she said with air quotes. "First, they'll search this island. Eventually, they'll suspect the use of the spell."

"But won't you get in trouble?"

"Not if you make it back in time. Outside of our bubble, we can only exist as birds, but with that comes unparalleled vision. You must find a cave or cabin of some sort where a bird cannot find you. Somewhere with solid walls where you can't wiggle the bushes or create any sort of movement. But it is important that when you do get back and show yourself, you need to be completely solid. That is the only way I can deny the spell has been used. Then you need to confess to trying to escape. Tell them you found a small cave near the shore, then tried to swim and failed."

"Won't they punish me?"

"No. The Matriarchs want you for the audition too badly to harm you yet. They will only laugh because there is no escape from here."

TWENTY-FIVE

myka

Early the next morning, Anserlee woke Myka from her restless sleep. She helped her dress in her own clothes, jeans, a T-shirt, and Drew's flannel, then slipped the backpack full of food and water over Myka's shoulders.

Myka checked her watch for the time as Anserlee made her drink every last drop of the gag-inducing concoction. It tasted like poison and a dirty dish sponge.

It only took moments for it to work. Myka blurred around her stomach first, then it progressed as it coursed through her veins. She held out her hands, wiggling her fingers, eyes growing bigger as she faded until she could see right through her skin to the other side. Anserlee rubbed more of it on Myka's clothes and backpack—it absorbed instantly like it was smoke instead of liquid—before she placed the remaining mixture inside Myka's pack.

"Rub this all over your kayak before you leave. Now go, quickly and quietly. Just because they'll have a hard time seeing you doesn't mean they won't be able to hear you.

Take the main path until you find the entrance to the complex, then stick to the left side of the wall until you hit the first path to your right. That will take you to the beach you washed up on." Anserlee pulled Myka down to her level and kissed her cheek. "Be safe, be strong," she whispered in her ear.

With an invisible rope, and a serious amount of strength for one so small, Anserlee lowered Myka out of her back window to the ground. When her feet hit the solid surface, she took off at a steady jog, wrapping her hands around the straps of her backpack to keep it from jostling. She'd noticed shortly after the drink took effect that she was clumsier than normal. It was hard to do things when you couldn't see where your feet were. Kind of like the opposite of being blind. She could see, but not herself.

The glow of dawn traced the edges of the mountains and trees, but it wasn't enough to light the trail. Barely able to make out the wide path, she had to be careful not to trip over exposed roots and rocks. Nerves spasmed in her gut, but by the time she came to the stone entrance an hour-ish later, the pains had faded and she started to adapt.

Just beyond the rock walls, covered in moss, stood three creepy totem poles—two on either side of the path and one directly in the middle. She slipped around to her left, stopping in front of the monstrosity. Birds, with their wings spread open, sat on top of screaming human men. Their talons gouged into their skulls as if they were about to carry them away like small prey. Cradled between the three poles was a round rock with a stone slab balanced on the highest point. It looked like an altar. She imagined it was where they left the unwanted baby boys to die in the elements. An offering to their sick gods.

She clenched her jaw to keep from screaming. It wasn't a problem she could solve at the moment, or probably ever, but it didn't stop the disgust and sorrow from winding through her heart.

As she passed by, she traced her fingers over the letters etched in the stone, wondering what it said. She whispered a small prayer for the lost souls, hoping they were in a better place.

A slight mist sprinkled her face while she followed the wall and stumbled upon the narrow trail, more like a tunnel. Less light filtered through the dense part of the forest, and she had to slow down in order not to trip. Bushes and trees crowded the overgrown path, forcing her to slouch to keep from knocking into the lowest branches. She startled occasionally as heavy drops of water, hanging precariously from the trees, found their way down the back of her neck.

After a few rough falls, she came to the end of the trail. Out in the open, the mist turned to a steady drizzle. Water leaked in through the holes in her rain jacket, compliments of her rough start here.

She traced the shoreline until she came to the campfire pit someone had made for her the day she'd washed up on the island. She had no idea who'd pulled her out of the ocean. Was it another Sirin? Because if Anserlee had saved her from the watery grave, surely she would've said something? She pressed her lips into a frustrated line. It was a mystery for another day.

She found her kayak, dragged it out from its hiding spot, and rubbed the smoky liquid thoroughly over the hard, yellow plastic as instructed. Once satisfied, she stuffed her backpack inside the waterproof sack that was still in the belly of the boat, secured it inside the compartment, and launched herself into the water. She headed to the nearest island to the left. It didn't look that far away, but she checked her watch to time the trip.

The ocean was remarkably calm, only minor swells with no whitecaps. The rain pattered her face and echoed on the kayak like knocking on a hollow wall. She paddled hesitantly, afraid she would hit the static barrier and be pushed around in a circle again. She braced herself for a direct hit, but this time, she passed right through with only her hair standing on end. It was strange, but Anserlee had insisted that Myka trust the process with no questions asked. She obviously knew something she and Drew didn't.

She settled into a hard pace, trying not to dwell on the fact that she was alone on this vast, foreboding ocean. Its waters reflected black and dense due to the lack of sunlight from the overcast sky. Heavy clouds obscured the mountain-tops, but visibility to the island stayed clear. Rain dripped off her nose and ran under the cuffs of her jacket, keeping her cool, but it did little to soothe her tired muscles. She pushed through the discomfort because her time was limited.

When she arrived on shore a couple of hours later, her arms shook with strain and her legs wobbled as she jumped out and pulled the boat from the water.

Gathering her strength, she gripped the rope and dragged it up the slight incline until she hit the tree line. She shoved the kayak into the bush and half-assed covered it with dead underbrush and ferns she ripped from the ground. She marked the spot with a cairn of stacked rocks so she wouldn't lose it.

Satisfied no one would discover it in its temporary hiding place, she walked the shoreline, scouting for a safe place to spend the next twenty-some hours. Her feet crunched over sharp mussel shells clinging to the rocks. Smelly seaweed and clear, dead jellyfish peppered the deserted beach. Skeletal trees, in shades of weathered gray, grew just beyond the rocky banks, defending the flourishing forest only a few feet away.

It didn't take long to stumble upon an old, abandoned shack covered in rotting siding. The roof was thick with moss and other plants. It would make for good cover, so she jogged back and dragged the kayak over the slippery rocks into the musty cabin. She pried open the door and then jimmied it back into place once she and the kayak were inside.

Shifty waves of muted light wove around the weathered plywood hanging haphazardly from the windows. Small puddles of water collected on the already-swollen wood floors, making her wonder how safe the foundation could possibly be. The cabin was flimsy, and she prayed the kayak wouldn't fall through the floor.

Exhausted, she found a dry corner and ate a bar made from berries, honey, and nuts, before she curled up and promptly fell asleep to the sound of lapping waves.

anserlee

"We will ask you again, where is the girl?" one of the three Matriarchs demanded. They stood in front of Anserlee with their heads turned slightly away, all in the same direction, but their large yellow eyes stared accusingly at her. Their spotted feathers were ruffled and puffed out.

"I told you already. I don't know. When I woke up, she was gone. First, I searched her previous accommodations, then both of the hot springs she's familiar with. After that, I raised the alarm." Anserlee had woken up in the morning and done exactly that so she didn't have to lie to them. She'd also made sure a few of her sisters saw her leave her house and head to the hot springs so she had witnesses if anyone questioned them.

"And what about the concealment charm sitting on the table? Hmmm?" The middle Matriarch clucked her tongue.

Anserlee focused on her breathing, making sure it stayed even, and maintained direct eye contact to avoid looking guilty. She dusted off her apron, having covered it in a plethora of fragrant herbs to hide her stress levels. "I was busy yesterday. I used it so I could talk with one of my patients to preserve confidentiality. It's well within my scope as a healer," Anserlee said, skewing the truth. She *had* concocted the charm for one of her clients that morning, but she didn't have to tell them she made more later.

"We are going to need a name." The third one tapped her long fingernail on Anserlee's forehead.

"If you must, but you realize that will shake the nest's confidence in me, and I am one of the few educated healers at this colony."

They took a moment to consider Anserlee's side of the events, then the middle one said, "You are right. For now, we will let her confidentiality remain. But we still have some concerns. We've had reports from multiple flock members that you have stronger-than-average feelings for the girl."

"And who told you that?" Anserlee asked, already knowing they wouldn't reveal their sources. She knew exactly who the culprits were—Rave and her minions.

"It does not matter who informed us. But is it true?"

"Yes, it's true. I find myself attracted to Myka." Anserlee stuck to the truth as much as possible. These three were experts in ferreting out lies. They would understand attraction far easier than friendship and love.

"Then it would reason that you would help her escape." They simultaneously sat in their nests, leaving her standing in front of the fireplace.

The flames began to scorch her feathers, so she stepped closer to the three despite her instinct warning her away. It wasn't like the Matriarchs were bad, but they weren't good either.

"I beg to differ. I want her to stay. After the event is over, she might find happiness with me. Why would I want her to leave?"

"Maybe you have hidden her away, so she is not the one to audition?" One of the Matriarchs raised a sly eyebrow.

"Mothers," Anserlee said, pressing her hand against her chest, not faking her astonishment. "I know better. I am one of the few who has witnessed the punishment for defiance. Ponder this—I have nothing to hide. If I was going to help her escape, do you think I would be stupid enough to leave the evidence sitting on my worktable? Surely, I would've cleaned up after myself. And I certainly don't want her to leave."

"Yes, Anserlee, you are clearly right, but it does not change the facts. You were the one who was designated to watch her. And she escaped from you," one said as they all nodded in unison.

Another one continued, "Whether you helped her or not is irrelevant at this point. Not keeping tabs on the prisoner is still punishable by silencing."

Even though she knew silencing was a possibility, Anserlee swallowed and a cold sweat beaded on her upper lip. She held her breath, waiting for the—

"But,"—one of them held up a finger—"we do agree that if she returns, your sentence should be lessened."

Anserlee hid her relief behind a small nod of acknowledgment.

When they'd been dispatched to the Caribbean, the Matriarch from Pan had believed that the guilty Sirins shouldn't have paid with their lives because the King of Rock 'n' Roll had returned. Anserlee had kept this detail in mind as she'd devised the escape plan. She had counted on her Matriarchs holding true to these principles. Now, all she could do was hope that Myka would make it back in time, so she didn't die.

"Yes, mothers, I understand." Anserlee's voice trembled, making her subtle accent more pronounced. "But I think you should know that Rave has far more motive for that girl's death than I do. I didn't say anything before, because I don't have proof—besides my instincts—but she has tried to kill Myka on more than one occasion. I have nothing to gain from Myka's death. But Rave does. She lusts over Andrew more than normal, and has since the moment he arrived. And she doesn't have the funds or skills to pay for his services anytime soon. If you won't take my word for it, ask Gilda."

"Again, Anserlee, you make a valid argument." The three turned back and forth between themselves, coming up with a collective decision without having to speak out loud. "We will look into it. But until then, you must spend the night in the dungeon to prevent your escape. You have always been a loyal subject to our nest, and a talented one. We hate to lose you. By our decree, the only way out of the silencing now is if the girl shows up tomorrow by the time the sun is at its highest point. Know that we all hope for this outcome. We shall take no joy or pleasure in your death."

The silencing would begin at noon. It was the same time Anserlee told Myka to head back to Pan. But the Matriarchs would draw the punishment out for hours using it as a warning for the other Sirins. The longevity would leave a window of safety for both of them. So long as Myka arrived by early evening, Anserlee would survive. If not, the colony would lose its Lead Healer.

Anserlee didn't take her treatment personally. It was how the Matriarchs were with everyone. No one was more important than anyone else. Even if Anserlee was the best healer on the island, or in the world, it didn't matter. The only things considered were the facts—not her past, not her future worth, only the now.

If Myka got back to the island in time, the facts would point in Anserlee's favor that she did not help her escape and her punishment would be lightened.

If not...well, she would die a most horrific death. The images of the silencing she'd witnessed were burned forever into her memory. A shiver spiked through her, remembering their raw, plucked wings, separated from their bodies, lying lifeless in a pool of blood, while discarded feathers blew aimlessly in the breeze and the water below roiled with sharks.

She pushed the nightmare away as two guards escorted her home to pick up a few comforts. She stuffed what she could—food, blankets, reading material—into a sack. They followed her down the circular stairs and locked her in an iron cell. The mothers weren't *yet* trying to punish her, only making sure she didn't fly away. Once she was a bird on the outside, the chances of finding her slimmed. Fleeing happened occasionally, but not often. Here, they could live for hundreds of years. Out there, they took on the lifespans of the birds they became. Some lived longer than others. As a goose, she'd have anywhere between ten to eighty years, depending on whether she lived in the wild or captivity.

She nestled down on the dirt floor, lit a candle, and cuddled into her blanket, preparing for a long night. She opened her journal, dipped her quill pen, and recorded yesterday's patient records as she did every day. Soon, the light shifted on the curved stone wall of her cell.

Rave waltzed around the corner and glanced over her shoulder, checking behind her.

Anserlee snorted and rolled her eyes. Rave didn't scare her.

"You hag," Rave whispered, wrapping her pale fingers around the iron bars. "You have no proof it was me that day in the meadow. You'll pay. I've never liked you, Anserlee. You're just so *good*," she said, as if it were a great offense. "It's sickening. I'm going to find Myka and make sure she never returns. I'm going to kill two birds with one stone, so the saying goes." She laughed wickedly before she retreated down the flickering hall.

If Myka didn't return in time, Rave would win. Not only would Anserlee lose her wings, and most likely her life, Myka would be semi-stranded on an island, and Rave would get her way with Drew. And if she knew anything about Rave, she was likely to traumatize him just because she could.

Anserlee set her quill aside and rested her head in the palms of her hands, praying for her plan to work.

myka

Myka woke up shivering with her teeth chattering. The humidity seeped into her bones, chilling her to the core. Tentatively, she stretched her limbs and hissed at the stabbing pins and needles. What she wouldn't give for a fire, but the chances were, someone would spot the smoke from the rusted potbelly woodstove.

Her pants were reasonably dry, but thanks to her tattered rain jacket, her shirt was still damp. She wriggled out of it and hung it over the rickety three-legged table, then wrapped the blanket tighter around her shoulders.

She prayed everything on Anserlee's end was going accordingly. She didn't like trusting her and Drew's future to anyone, but there was no other way. Like it or not, they were committed. Now, if she only knew what the plan was.

The concealment spell was the key, she was almost sure of it. Somehow, it allowed her to pass through the barrier unseen. But what she didn't understand was—why she couldn't know about the plan? In case she got caught so she had reasonable deniability, perhaps? And if that were the case, why couldn't she and Drew just leave together? Doubts about Anserlee's intentions crept forth in the quiet cabin. Though if Anserlee was lying to them, she was a world-class con artist. Myka's gut said Anserlee was trustworthy, so she decided, for now, to heed her intuition.

She shuffled to one of the boarded-up windows, stepping softly to mitigate the creaking floor, and peered out a crack. The overcast sky shielded the mountains across the small bay.

The pelting rain reminded her of her most pressing need—she had to pee. She squeezed her legs together and did the little dance, to no avail. The overgrown outhouse was at least fifty feet away. She was just about to take her chances when a muffled tapping on the roof, distinctly different from the cadence of the rain, changed her mind. She froze. There was no way to tell a regular bird from a Sirin, and Anserlee had told her the Matriarchs regularly sent out spies.

She slowly leaned away from the crack in the plywood. She might be somewhat invisible, but her body still blocked light.

A raven cawed, a deep and throaty rattle, sending shivers, which had nothing to do with the cold, running down Myka's spine. She had always loved ravens, fascinated by their eerie intelligence, ability to talk, and the beautiful oil-spill sheen of their feathers. She was having second thoughts.

She waited and waited and waited—which probably seemed longer than it was due to her urgent need—until she was positive the bird was gone.

Rummaging around the cabin, she found an old coffee

can and squatted over the rim. Thankfully, the pounding rain drowned out the sound of her full bladder.

She dug into her pack to note the time. She groaned. It was just past dinnertime. If only she could fast-forward the hours. To keep herself busy, she grabbed a homemade bar before sitting down on the cold floor.

Eventually, she fell into a fitful sleep, dreaming of the years with Drew after she'd broken things off. They had been some of the best and worst of her life. The band's success was incredible, partially due to their talent and partially due to their charisma—all of them had it in spades. It made many aspects of her job easier. People enjoyed collaborating with the boys. They took their jobs seriously but never stopped having fun. When they had arguments— and they could get heated—she'd taught them that they were only disagreements, not disrespect. Military service had instilled that lesson in her dad, and he'd passed it on to her. They'd always relied heavily on that philosophy in their family.

Seeing Drew with other women had broken her heart and torn her soul. Most nights, she'd cried herself asleep. But she'd buried her feelings deep and pretended she'd moved on. Only Nicky had been able to see through the illusion.

"Why do you do this to yourself?" he asked her one day out of the blue, about eight months ago. They stood side by side in his high-rise apartment, admiring the New York skyline.

"Do what to myself?" she asked, confused. She turned toward him.

"Torture yourself." The cityscape reflected in his sad brown eyes.

"Nicky, if you've got something to say, just say it already," she said, not amused by his evasiveness.

He reached out and held her shoulders. While she was always calm and controlled, Nicky was calm and serene. "It's not your face that gives you away, but your heart. I can feel the pain radiating from you. I've always been able to. It's so vast, it makes me feel queasy sometimes."

Her eyes opened wide and then narrowed. "What are you talking about?" She felt her control slip away with her anger. It was a very touchy subject for her. Only Nicky dared approach it, and even then, he was taking his life in his hands.

"You either need to tell him how you feel...or leave. Find somewhere you can forget about him. Your opportunities are endless. With your talent and connections, you could work with anyone. I know you love your country music," Nicky said. His expression twisted in amusement at her taste in music.

"I don't want to leave you guys." Her anger vanished, replaced by a surge of fear—fear of leaving and fear of the unknown. But mostly fear of leaving Drew. "Do you want me to go?" she whispered.

"No. God, no. You're my girl, my sanity amongst the chaos. But it hurts me to see you this way." His highlighted hair fell into his face, and he swept it backward out of his eyes.

"How can you even tell? I've been good." She bit her bottom lip.

"I know. You've successfully hidden it from everyone, especially Drew. He still pines for you even though he thinks you hate him. Hell, he hates himself sometimes. Why do you think he behaves the way he does? It's to get your attention. You two need to stop torturing each other and move on with your lives—one way or another."

She stiffened up. If Drew still had feelings for her, she was going to have to leave. Because she would not be able to resist him. And what would happen when he got bored with her and found someone new? She was pretty sure she'd die of a broken heart. The first time around, even though it was her choice, had emotionally destroyed her.

"That's not true. He's moved on. He's fine," she snapped.

"Your ability to lie to yourself is impressive."

Her mouth hung open and anger flushed her cheeks. He was walking a thin line. "Are we done yet?"

"For now." Nicky patted her shoulder and gave it a good squeeze before he walked away, leaving her a prisoner within her pain.

Later, in her car, she bawled. She hadn't realized her emotions had been obvious to anyone. Nicky was right—she needed to move on or leave. And she couldn't move on without leaving.

She woke up again in the cold, dark cabin, lethargic and sad.

Shortly after that conversation, Drew had started flirting with her again. She didn't know if Nicky had had *the talk* with him too, but from the way he'd started behaving, it was a reasonable assumption. Their latest incident at the Alaskan resort had given her an excuse to leave.

If she would've been brave enough to talk to Drew earlier, they might never have ended up in this situation. Even after breaking his heart and giving him the excuse to be free, he'd always treated her kindly, even when she had been indifferent toward him.

At first, he'd begged her to explain—pleaded with her not to leave him, but she'd shut him down cold. Allowing cracks in her exterior would've been devastating. Because at the time, she'd given credence to the cruel words those women had spoken. Nicky hadn't been wrong about her ability to lie to herself—it was the only way she could maintain her icy demeanor. The only way she could be near Drew and not love him. Sadly, she'd failed. She'd loved him even when she'd hated him. But she'd always hated herself more —in the beginning, because she'd believed the ugly words. And now, because she'd been too stubborn and embarrassed by her actions to have a conversation with Drew once she'd realized those women were trash. If she could go back and do it all over again, she would've stepped out of that bathroom stall and given them the ass-chewing they'd deserved.

Tears leaked down her cheeks. She had to get her and Drew out of this situation. And she needed to do it soon. She checked her watch again and groaned. It was only four in the morning.

She peered out the crack to find the view blocked by a dense fog rolling over the rocky beach. She could hear the waves lapping on the shore, but she couldn't see the water's edge. The eerie hush and thick mist unnerved her. How was she supposed to get back to Pan if she couldn't see where to go? She wanted to fall asleep so time would pass quicker, but already having slept off and on for endless hours, her body was sore and achy.

She scooted the dining table out of the way, its rickety legs hesitating over the waterlogged boards. She moved into a down dog position, trying to calm her pounding heart and freaking-out brain. *Breathe. Clear your mind.* She found solace in the poses and continued until around six.

The fog was even thicker. She couldn't see anything past the leaning front porch. A few large *whooshes* out in the ocean, followed by some slaps, caught her attention. A hint of a song floated through the air.

She stopped breathing and cocked an ear toward the door, afraid the Sirins might have found her. But it didn't sound human or aviary. More like a high-pitched cow singing to a howling wolf. It faded away slowly, like whatever it was, was getting farther away. But between that and the nearby seagull cries, Myka stayed inside.

Boredom forced her to explore the cabin, but there was nothing much to find—a few canned goods that had probably been left here before she was born, a package of damp matches, and mice turds. As Anserlee had instructed, she placed the bladder that held the magic potion in one of the drawers. Bringing the evidence back to Pan would've been stupid.

Hours later, she finally checked her watch again. It was close to time. Though it was still partially overcast, the sun had successfully burned off most of the fog, but with it came the blustering wind. The ocean waves had picked up. Anxiety gnawed a hole in her stomach and sweat collected under her armpits and boobs. Being no expert kayaker, she was scared. Terrified. But fear didn't stop her.

She ran her fingers over the shell of the boat until she found the opening. She stuffed her backpack in the waterproof bag and threw it in the belly before putting on her life jacket.

With the rope firmly in her grip, she dragged it down the rickety steps onto the beach. Its hard-plastic shell vibrated over the rocky shore, but the slope did most of the work. Her rubber boots kept her feet mostly dry as she waded into the murky water. The waves crashing on the shore almost knocked her over, but she managed to hop into the kayak.

Before she was able to secure the neoprene skirt, the next wave hit and toppled the boat. The frigid water stole her breath. Sputtering salt and seaweed, she frantically searched for the kayak's shadow. The surf had pushed it to the shore, though now, it was slowly coaxing it out again. She dove for it and grabbed it with cold, blue fingers. Kayaks, especially those full of water, were heavy. She pulled it onto the beach, tipped it over, emptied the water, and launched immediately. She couldn't give herself time to think about the dangers, or she wouldn't have been strong enough to try again. Mentally or physically.

Myka concentrated hard on keeping the kayak's nose heading straight into the waves. This time, she waited until she was farther out to secure the neoprene skirt. Once past the shore break, she gripped the paddle tight with her shaking hands. A deluge of water ran from her hair, down her cheeks and neck, into her already sopping-wet shirt.

She fought against the current and the swells, steering straight into them. Her arms tired quickly. The higher the sun crawled into the sky, the more the wind picked up and the bigger the white caps became. On the high point of the wave, she could see land ahead, but on the low part, it completely disappeared. The island, which didn't seem that far away, got smaller instead of larger.

Focused on the physical exertion, she didn't have time for fear. Sweat mixed with ocean water poured from her brow, burning her eyes and cracked lips. The elastic on the raincoat, where it rubbed against her wrists and armpits, chafed. She wanted to remove it, but thanks to the life jacket, and the fact that every time she stopped paddling, the boat turned sideways, she couldn't. Her throat screamed for water, but again, she couldn't stop.

The purr of a small plane engine droned in her ears, but

even if she wanted to flag them down, she couldn't. She was invisible.

An unusual number of birds passed overhead, but thanks to the choppiness of the waves, her shadow was well skewed on the surface.

A small, dark head popped out of the water a few feet in front of her and then disappeared. She stifled a scream, trying to remember what dangerous creatures lurked in this ocean. But the most dangerous thing was the temperature and the likelihood of going into hypothermia if she capsized. Then the creature popped up again. *Whew.* It was only a seal.

The seal swam beside the boat, easily keeping Myka's pace. She was so close she could see the whiskers on her nose. It was nice to have company, but Myka wondered how she could see her. Maybe she was a supernatural creature too? She laughed, realizing how ridiculous that notion was. Or at least it would've been a month ago.

Baba had not only imparted Myka with tales of Sirins, but she'd also told her about the legend of the Selkies—a Celtic folktale of beings that were half human and half seal. On land, they were able to remove their skins and live like humans. But according to the lore, their homes were near Scotland and Ireland, not Alaska.

Thankfully, tales about Selkies, while often sad, were much more pleasant than the Sirins.

A beam of sunlight stabbed through a break in the clouds and sparkled over the seal's coat as her back broke the surface. Every once in a while, she would disappear for a few minutes. Myka was surprised by how sad she was to see her go, then relieved when she popped her head above the ocean and peered at her with her big, black eyes.

With every stroke of the paddle, Myka's fingers cramped and her wrists locked. Her biceps burned and started to shake. The seal swam ahead and glanced back like she was cheering her on, pushing Myka forward and then waiting for her to catch up.

The radio static reached Myka's ears long before she caught a glimpse of the bubble. She almost laughed that she was so happy to see that damn thing. It glimmered like an oil slick on the water, moving and slithering with a life of its own. Her eyes involuntarily closed as the kayak broke through the barrier. Inside, the waves let up slightly, and she paddled to the same shore she'd washed up on originally.

Before pulling her boat to safety, she waved at the seal. With her flipper, the seal waved back. Myka rubbed her eyes and shook her head. Dehydration was making her delirious.

She hurried as fast as her exhausted body could travel, trying to be watchful of her movements. At that moment, she was thankful for the noisy waves whitewashing the sound of her dragging the kayak over the beach and burying it in the underbrush. The wind concealed her ruffling amongst the bushes. She took her time getting back since she couldn't reveal herself until fully visible.

With the top of the tower barely visible, she waited in the forest, leaning against a tree. She was afraid if she sat down, she'd fall asleep from exhaustion. Every few minutes, she checked her skin. It had taken her much longer to get back than she'd estimated, but she still hadn't completely appeared.

A bloodcurdling scream startled Myka and shook her to the core. Then it came again, louder, and more wretched than before. Who would have cause to scream like that? The answer was clear. Myka looked down at her hands again and pleaded for them to return to normal. A faint shimmer of color, from clothing to flesh tone, started to fill in the outline of her form. She was not quite there, but so close. If she ran in now and was caught like this, they would kill Anserlee for sure. Her stomach and jaw clenched at every scream and she had to keep swallowing to prevent herself from vomiting.

She stared at her hands and feet as if looking at them would make them solidify. They were the only parts left that weren't solid. It took everything inside her not to bolt.

Finally, after *forever*, she fully appeared.

She scooted past the totem poles and ran to the base of the tower. No one was around.

Myka hollered loudly in between the weakened screams. Soon, a brown head peeked over the side, left for a moment, and then two others swooped down and scooped her up. They dragged her to the middle of the tower and shoved her to the ground where the three Matriarchs awaited.

Anserlee was kneeling on a circular platform, chained to the floor by her wrists and ankles. Her head hung low, her chin resting on her heaving chest. Strands of sweaty hair stuck to her cheeks and the remainder spilled over her shoulders. Silver feathers, the hollow shaft tipped with crimson, were scattered across the decking, fluttering in the breeze. Blood stained her hands and seeped from the tips of her wings, smearing the wood like a child's finger painting.

Myka contained the sob building behind her ribs. She'd made it. Barely. All of her earlier misgivings about Anserlee's intentions vanished. The only person who would put themselves through that kind of torture was someone fueled by love.

"Well, we are certainly pleased to see you." One of the three Matriarchs approached Myka, glaring with her amber eyes.

Myka stood up and brushed off her hands.

"Yes," said another. All of them had their hair braided around their heads and woven with jewels like a crown. "We would have been very sore to have lost our most accomplished healer."

Anserlee raised her head and closed her bloodshot eyes in relief when she saw Myka. A small blue-winged woman unlocked Anserlee's chains and helped her off the floor.

"Where have you been?" one Matriarch hassled Myka, tapping her uncomfortably on her sternum with a long, sharp fingernail that looked more like a talon, yellow at the base and black at the tip.

Standing this close to the creature, Myka could see a soft, transparent down covering her face.

"I ran away. What do you think?" Myka straightened her spine and glared down at the diminutive beast.

"And why did you come back?" She blinked rapidly, tilting her head jerkily from side to side. She stepped back so she didn't have to look up at Myka quite as much.

"Because I couldn't get out." Myka bit down on the inside of her cheek to keep from crying. Or screaming. Or at least that's what she wanted it to look like. Anything to conceal her lies.

"Where did you hide?"

She tilted her chin upwards and crossed her arms.

"Hmmm, it doesn't really matter. We will get it out of you eventually," one threatened, "but only after your usefulness is expended."

They turned toward one another when Rave swooped in

from above. Her feet landed gently on the ground and her wings glinted in the sunlight. Her windblown hair and flushed cheeks only accentuated her beauty. "Mothers," she said, bowing her head to them. "I found this." She flicked Myka an evil smile with angry eyes.

A bad feeling bubbled inside Myka's gut.

"Explain this," one asked, shoving a picture in Myka's face. In her hand, she held the photo of Drew and her at the Grammys.

Myka's eyes narrowed to slivers but she refused to speak.

The Matriarch turned her back and held the picture under Anserlee's nose.

Anserlee reached up and took it with a trembling hand.

"Anserlee, did you know about this?"

"I suspected but had no proof. You know I do not like making accusations without the evidence to back up my theory." Her voice was strained and scratchy from the screaming.

"Yes, we know." They nodded in unison, and one of them snatched the photo from Anserlee.

Myka's heart kicked and resentment flared. The picture belonged to her, and she tried snatching it, but the Matriarch was too quick and slapped her hand, hard, leaving her flesh stinging.

Taunting her, the Matriarch wiggled it under her nose. "Again, girl, explain. Or we will just get Andrew to spill. That will be easy enough."

They were right. So Myka started yelling, "Of course we know each other. I'm the manager of Burning Brenda. How do you think I got here? All of us were on vacation together! Thanks for fucking ruining it!" Spit flew from her lips. Myka probably should've tempered her outburst, but if she seemed too calm, she might look suspect. And it felt good to give them a piece of her mind.

One wiped her cheek with the back of her hand. "Why didn't you tell us?"

"Because you're chicken shits, and I don't like you. Plus, I figured the less you knew, the better for me."

The three pinched their lips and blinked rapidly, obviously irritated by her outburst. One looked to the other, who looked to the other, then said, "Well, I guess it makes sense to move up Andrew's audition to tomorrow. After that, you will no longer be needed." They licked their lips with red, pointed tongues and smiled at Myka like they were offering her cake instead of threatening her life.

Wild cheers broke out in the crowd.

Sweat collected under Myka's breasts and at the small of her back, making her damp clothes even more uncomfortable. "What difference does that make to me?" Myka hollered. "You stopped letting me see him days ago."

The three exchanged a guarded look. "We gave no orders for your visitations to be cut short. Interesting." One raised a sharp eyebrow. "Anyway, Steller's jays, take the girl and Anserlee back to her nest, and stay posted."

anserlee

Anserlee inhaled sharply and smothered a scream when her sisters gently lifted her off her feet. Her head bobbed to her chest as they flew her home and dropped her off in front of her house.

"Thank you," she said, her voice hoarse. She shuffled slowly inside and sat down at the table with the front door still open.

Her sisters' faces held compassion and fear—it was the first time this flock had witnessed the song silencing. Thankfully, they hadn't seen the entire ritual, as she once had.

"Our pleasure, Anserlee." One of them threw a log into the hearth and started a fire. "You sit tight, and we'll fetch the girl." Their blue wings disappeared out of the doorway as they shut it.

Before they'd carried her home, the Matriarchs had commanded them to stand watch over Anserlee all night. Or at least until she was stronger. They weren't afraid she or Myka would escape—the guards were posted for their safety. She'd seen the look that passed between them when they heard Drew and Myka's visitations had been cut short. Anserlee now knew the order had not come from the Matriarchs. She had a reasonable guess who it had come from, but, alas, it was not her problem at the moment. At least the guards would ensure she and Myka slept safely for tonight.

Anserlee looked up when the door to her cottage opened. Myka limped through and closed it softly behind her. She took off her tattered raincoat and hung it on the rack.

"Here," Anserlee said, wincing as she rose from the table. "Let me make us some tea and then we can both sleep easier."

"No," Myka insisted. "You sit. I'll make us some."

Anserlee began to protest.

"Don't." Myka held out the palm of her hand. Her skin was red and angry from the drying effects of the salt water and the cold. She scratched her fingers through her matted hair, messing it up. "I'm already up. I can bring the herbs to you so you can measure properly."

Myka hobbled across the floor. Elation fluttered in Anserlee's chest, edging out most of her pain. If Myka hadn't returned in time... She didn't want to think about it. But the horrific event repeated itself regardless.

As she'd knelt before the Matriarchs, pulling out her own feathers one at a time, she'd begun to worry that she'd condemned both of them to die—her by silencing and Myka from exposure. Alaska was a dangerous place if you weren't prepared.

"Do you think we're safe?" Myka said, setting two mismatched mugs on the table. "I've never seen anyone look as angry as Rave did up there."

"Honestly, no," Anserlee said. "But there are guards posted outside our door and there will be others watching. If she's going to make a move, I don't think it will be tonight. She's lost her shot at you until this is over. I do believe the Matriarchs have their suspicions about her now."

Myka picked the proper herbs from the cabinet and handed them to Anserlee before she grabbed the kettle bubbling over the fire and poured hot water into the mugs. She stoked the fire and then sat down at the table.

They embraced silence for a few minutes, holding on to their steaming cups, waiting for the tea to steep and cool down.

"That rock in front of the totem pole is the sacrificial altar, isn't it?"

Anserlee gripped her cup tighter with shame. "It is." Another practice she didn't agree with. To give the Gods time to accept the full moon offering, Sirins were forbidden from the area until the following evening. But most of the time, when she went back to check on the baby boys, they were gone. She often wondered if it was really the Gods that had taken them or if the Matriarchs came back later to dispose of the problem. Or, the scenario she hoped for, if someone else out there had secretly saved them.

"There's something carved into the stone. What does it say?" Myka tapped her fingers on the mug.

"'A blissful death awaits those who follow the Sirins' song.'"

"Hmm, I think that might be a bit of an exaggeration," Myka said dryly.

"I believe you may be right."

"Can I do anything for you?" Myka asked, leaning forward. "Do you want me to clean up your wings?"

Small drops of blood spattered the floor, mirroring Anserlee's path through the house. "Not tonight. They're feeling better already. We heal quickly, and tomorrow, we can go to the hot springs and both clean up." Anserlee finished her tea, needing it to dull her raw emotions. "We'd better get to the loft before we fall asleep on these chairs."

They climbed the ladder, Myka insisting Anserlee go first. She helped Anserlee out of her bloodied tunic and into a softer nightgown before stripping down and doing the same. When she laid down in her nest, Myka covered her with blankets, tucking them around her like she was a child. It wasn't often someone took care of Anserlee. Matter of fact, she wasn't sure anyone had in the last century.

After Myka finished using the facilities, she started making a bed for herself on the floor.

"Can you just sleep with me tonight?" Anserlee asked, her voice frail and exhausted. Just for tonight, she wanted to pretend Myka was hers. She wanted to feel her breath on her cheek. Feel her heartbeat against her chest.

"Of course, but won't I hurt you?" Myka brushed a lock of hair from Anserlee's forehead.

The path of her finger tingled over her chilly skin. She clenched her teeth, but not from the pain. "No, I'm good. I just don't want to be here alone."

"Okay," Myka said, scooting in behind her wings, gently pulling the covers over them.

"Anserlee, I am sorry it took me so long to get back," Myka whispered. "I ran in the moment the draft wore off."

Her breath was hot on the back of Anserlee's scalp. She had to restrain the shiver that trickled through her feathers as she tried to contain her racing heart and rapidly beating pulse. She'd heard of these feelings, mostly in the books she'd read, but she'd never experienced them herself. They were exhilarating and uncomfortable. But mostly, they brought a tightness to her chest and a lump in her throat because she knew those feelings would never be reciprocated.

"I know. I have never used that potion on a human before, and I needed to make sure you were hidden."

"What were they doing to you up there?" Myka asked softly.

Anserlee paused for a moment.

"You don't have to tell me if you don't want to." Myka reached up and petted her hair.

Ironically, goose bumps peppered Anserlee's skin. The hardest part was knowing Myka actually cared about her. What if she were to throw caution to the wind and turn around and kiss Myka? Would she respond? Would she run? And if she did respond, would Anserlee be able to live with just one night? And when the time came, would she be strong enough to let her go?

She closed her eyes, her lashes tickling her cheekbones, and swallowed back her turmoil. "They started the beginnings of the song silencing, making me tear out my own feathers."

Myka gasped and stopped stroking Anserlee's hair.

"That part is more psychological than painful. Don't stop, please." She set her hand over Myka's.

Myka resumed. "Really? Because from where I was, it sounded horrific. Why were they punishing you if they couldn't prove you gave me the potion?"

"They weren't punishing me for the potion; they were punishing me for your *escape*. I was supposed to be watching you."

"Oh. So having me near really didn't make it easier on you—only more dangerous. Why did you do it then? You don't need to take unnecessary risks," Myka admonished in a harsh whisper.

"It is the only way we are going to get you out of here." And thanks to their successful test run, Anserlee's theory had been confirmed. She figured she could survive knowing Myka was safe. That she was loved and taken care of. Therefore, Drew had to go too. Though having gotten to know him, she might have helped him escape whether Myka was here or not. She'd like to think so, anyway. He was a good man, and she could see why Myka was head over heels in love with him.

"You're coming with us," Myka said firmly. "I can't leave you here. If they find out you helped us, they'll kill you."

"If I come with you, I'll have to live and die as a bird. And even if I could live in your world as I am, I have wings." Anserlee inhaled a slow breath and exhaled it gently. Late-afternoon shadows crawled over the wooden walls. Flecks of dust and tiny feathers floated in the dying light.

"How long do geese live?"

"In the wild, perhaps at best, twenty years. But because I'm a Sirin, I'd probably have thirty to forty years. In captivity, it would be longer."

"Oh," Myka whispered. "Still, though, there must be another way. We only need to figure it out. Is there anything I can do?"

"No," Anserlee said. She had to change the subject. The sensations traveling through her body, the ache deep inside, was not going away no matter how deep she buried them. Between the soft caress and the caring in Myka's voice, it was enough to break Anserlee's will.

It took a great amount of strength not to take what was within her reach. If Anserlee were to make a move, Myka would reciprocate. Anserlee felt it in her bones. But it wouldn't be because she loved her in the way she wanted—it would be payment for a debt. Though in Anserlee's eyes, there was no debt to be repaid. The sacrifice had been freely given. But Myka wouldn't see it that way.

Anserlee suppressed her emotions and hardened her resolve. Unrequited love was far more painful than she'd imagined, worse than what she'd experienced from the song silencing, but the idea of Myka staying here and suffering for the rest of her short life was unbearable. Unthinkable. Anserlee might not get the life she desired, but she could make sure Myka had a chance to live hers.

"But you will have to go through with the live audition tomorrow night. Honestly, the sooner that gets over with, the better. Rave will be more focused on getting Drew away from the others than killing you."

"Why? Why does it have to be me? Honestly, I'm surprised the Matriarchs didn't punish me, or worse, for being so disrespectful."

"I can only make assumptions about their reasons. But once they make up their minds, they don't back down. I'm not sure if it's a matter of principle or if it's a leftover from the animal kingdom. Once the alpha decides, there's no turning back. They probably moved up the audition because you were mouthy. Once you're done with it, they won't care who kills you."

"Yeah, I figured." Myka was quiet for a moment, then said, "How does this all work? Give it to me straight. I need some facts in order to fortify my wall."

Anserlee understood the need, but she still didn't want

to talk about it. She didn't approve of their practices. But Myka was right—to be prepared, she needed to know what she was up against. "First, Drew is given the entire evening to demonstrate what a night with him will be like. It's...I suppose, what you would consider marketing. I told him not to make it too fabulous since that will only increase his starting price."

Myka sniffed.

"And I need to bid on him."

"What? Why?" Myka asked, starting to sit up until Anserlee hissed in pain.

"Calm down! Because it is going to be a lot easier to get him out of here if I have a night alone with him? Remember?"

"Yes, you're right. It still hurts to think about it." Myka's words were sharp.

Yes, it does, Anserlee thought. "Then when the two of you are done, you'll be escorted back to your room, or here, or if the Matriarchs choose, back to the dungeon."

"Why back there?"

"Well, they don't take kindly to being screamed at by anyone, let alone a human female. You did call them chicken shits. And *no* Sirin is a chicken. Matter of fact, some of us eat chicken," Anserlee said, her voice beginning to slur as the tea took hold.

"Cannibals," Myka teased. "But you don't eat chicken, do you." It wasn't a question.

Anserlee shook her head and giggled, making her sound a bit like a cooing dove, before she drifted off to sleep.

myka

Muted light, shining through the dingy glass, caressed Anserlee's flawless skin in a buttery glow. She looked so young with her face relaxed and her stress buried in slumber.

Myka hoped someday Anserlee would find the kind of love she deserved. She had the makings of a perfect partner. She was kind and caring—though no pushover. She was quick to laugh and quicker to laugh at herself. She was smart and capable, yet humble.

Honestly, she reminded Myka much of Drew in terms of personality. Though physically, they couldn't have been more different. She was feminine and dainty. He was not. Though both were truly as beautiful on the inside as they were on the outside. An unusual combination, especially in the music industry and, it seemed, in the Sirin's world.

Anserlee's feathery eyelashes began to flutter as she woke up. "Ugh, is it morning already?" she asked, pulling her hair out of her face. She scrubbed her tiny hands over her pink cheeks. "Well, let's get to it."

They made it to the hot spring and both of them sighed heavily as they slipped into the steaming water. They stayed in longer than necessary, but Anserlee looked so much stronger after they got out. Myka certainly felt restored. Her muscles no longer groaned and screamed in protest.

The day blew by with all of Anserlee's pampering. Once Myka was dolled up and ready to go—or not—Anserlee said, "This is how it's going to work." She took Myka's hand in hers and led her out of the cottage to the tower. "I am taking you early to avoid the others. Make yourself comfortable, but don't try to leave. I have to lock you in. I'm leaving guards posted outside the door just to make sure you don't get any unwanted visitors."

A wave of dizziness swept over Myka, leaving her light-headed. The nerves in her stomach were working overtime and eating really wasn't an option. "Okay." She placed her hand on the cold stone wall for balance.

"Next, I will let Drew in, and then everyone else will arrive. You're not to begin until you hear the chimes. After that, you'll have all night."

They marched up the half-circle stairs until they came to the fourth floor—the audition floor. On the far side, where the stairs began again, was a solid oak door with a heavy wooden beam across it. It prevented escape, but not entrance. A sparkling wall of floor-to-ceiling windows lined the rest of the half-circle and Myka had to stop and catch herself. Her heart battered inside her chest, but not from exertion.

Tiered stone benches lined the other side of the space—spectator seats. Her limbs buckled. She held on to the cold wall as she shuffled to the glass and peered through. Before she could get a good look inside, Anserlee pushed Myka past the door, away from the windows, making her stay put until she had it open.

Once ready, Anserlee motioned for Myka to enter.

She hesitantly stepped over the threshold.

A huge four-poster bed sat front and center against the back curved wall. On one of the bedside tables rested a dark bottle—wine, she assumed—and two fluted glasses. The final remnants of evening light stabbed through the outside windows, and danced on the crystal, throwing a soft shimmer over the fluffy white blankets and poufy white pillows. Two fur rugs, resembling polar bear skin, flanked the bed, and another lay in front of the roaring fireplace. Above the polished wood mantel hung a gilded mirror with a vase of fresh wildflowers reflecting in the surface.

This was, by far, the most beautiful room she'd ever been in. Despite the beauty, a cold, terrified shiver trembled in her bones. She looked at the wall of glass to see the spectator seats but was surprised instead by her own image. The glass was mirrored. And though she felt gross just standing in the room, she looked incredible.

Earlier, Anserlee had laced Myka into a white whale-boned corset that pushed her large breasts higher and made her waist tiny. The white, flowy skirt tiered down in bundles of lace until it reached the floor, slightly longer in the back. She'd dusted her skin with gold powder, added shiny pink lips, a dash of blush, and kohl liner to her already dark eyes. She'd smoothed her platinum hair down and tucked her long bangs behind her ear. She gave Myka some gold earrings but wouldn't give her the necklace to go with it. She said her décolletage was more than enough. Instead, she tied a white, velvet ribbon around her neck with the bow dangling down her back.

Myka stared at herself in the mirror with her mouth parted.

"I am good, aren't I?" Anserlee said, shaking Myka out of her trance.

"Yeah, you are." Myka's knees buckled and she sank to the floor. "I have wanted this day for so long...but not like this...never like this." Tears of anger, sadness, and hopelessness filled her eyes as she gripped the white lace in her fists.

Anserlee knelt in front of her. Light from dozens of candles on the high shelf echoed in her big, gray eyes. "Don't let them see you cry. Don't you dare give them the satisfaction. Besides, you will ruin all this fabulousness I've created." She set a cool hand on Myka's bare shoulder.

"You're right," she said, dabbing the corners of her eyes. "It's too bad you can't live on the outside. People would pay you handsomely for your gifts. All of them," she said, getting up off the floor and looking out the interior windows. "I ca-can't see out," Myka stuttered. The wood fire crackled and popped, but its homey smell brought little comfort.

"I know. It makes it easier to forget. Plus, the walls are treated so sounds cannot get in or out. They can't sing to Drew while he's in here. Do you hear me? You're safe so long as you're inside."

Myka nodded.

"Nor will they be able to hear you. The Matriarchs will be here too. I know you hate them, but I guarantee nobody will step out of line while they're present."

Relief flooded her shoulders. At least nobody could try to kill her while she and Drew were inside these walls. "Still, forgetting them is not going to be possible." Myka wrenched her sweating hands together.

Anserlee frowned. "I know. I have to go fetch Drew now.

When this," she said, rolling her eyes and shaking her head, "is all over, you need to go directly back to your room and stay there. Bar the door and *do not* let anyone enter but me. I have to stay behind so I can arrange the soonest possible time slot. The two of you will have a good fifteen minutes before the chimes ring," Anserlee said. She placed her cool hand on Myka's forearm and squeezed. "Remember, that man loves you. Live in that blessing if you can."

Myka paced around the room until Drew walked in and shut the door. He stopped and stared at her with an intensity that absconded her breath. He hooked his thumbs through the belt loops of his ratty jeans, ones she'd bought him, and stared. His tattoos stood out more than usual due to the lack of sun on his golden skin. His hair, still damp, curled slightly around his ears.

"You..." He paused, shaking his head, running his hands through his hair and mussing it up. "I don't even have words. Good God, woman, do you know what you do to me?" He closed the distance between them in a heartbeat, gathering her in his arms and pressing her tight against him. He smelled good, like lemongrass, spruce trees, and sweet fresh air. "I don't know how I am going to do this slowly," he murmured into her hair. "Do you know how often I dream of holding you in my arms? How long I have waited for this moment?"

"As long as I have?" she whispered back.

"So, like, from the second I saw you?" He pushed her back so he could look her in the eyes.

She arched her eyebrows. "Yeah, pretty much."

"You're beautiful and you fucking smell good." He smiled and leaned in, inhaling deeply. Anserlee had rubbed her skin with coconut and vanilla, making it soft and smelling like a tropical destination.

"You're pretty handsome yourself," she said in the understatement of the year.

The shadow from the flames rolled over his chiseled face and his blue eyes looked as black as hers in the low light. He grabbed the hem of his shirt and fiddled with the edge. "Yeah, well, I felt more comfortable in my own things."

She ran her fingers over his scruff and quirked the corner of her lips.

"I thought you liked it?" he said, looking worried.

She smiled. "I love it. You're the sexiest man alive. And you're mine."

He pulled her in close and whispered in her ear, his breath scorching her neck, "That I am, my love. Always."

The bells rang. She almost chuckled as the riff from a popular rock song began to play in her head. Two emotions rolled up her throat—excitement and repulsion. She wondered how they managed to occupy the same space.

myka

Myka snuck a glance toward the windows, but Drew grabbed her chin, his calloused finger rough on her skin, and turned her face back toward him. "No," he said, "look at me." He leaned in and placed a warm, slow kiss on her lips. Longing ran through her body like an ember fueled by a slow breeze. He paused with his forehead against hers. "I need you to be present—only with me. I promise you, soon enough, I'm going to make you forget they exist. Okay?" He smirked, but there was a possessiveness in his eyes she hadn't noticed before.

A rush of headiness waved over her body. He stepped back, and she had to stop herself from following.

He reached for the bottle of wine on the side table next to the bed. "I've been waiting for this moment since the first time I saw you," he said, popping the cork. He took a healthy swig before he poured them each a glass and handed her one. The burgundy color looked eerily like blood. "Maybe not like this, but..."

"Me too." She grimaced after tasting the sickly sweet

wine. It didn't matter if she didn't like it—she was going to drink it anyway. She downed the glass like a shot of tequila.

"Really? Since the moment you saw me?" he flirted, pouring her more wine.

"Well, until I got to know you," she joked. "I don't want your ego exploding."

"Don't worry, I have you to keep it under control." He clinked their glasses together.

He was just distracting her from their audience, but she appreciated the gesture, though she doubted she'd be able to forget about them.

"No, but seriously." He finished his wine before setting their glasses down. "I have wanted you from the second I saw you, but I loved you from the second I *saw* you." He placed her hand on his chest and pressed it against his heart. Its rhythm thumped soothingly under her palm. "You broke my heart once, so please, *please* don't do it again," he begged, his usual cockiness gone, replaced by a fever of worry and desperation. "You're a goddess, and I worship at your feet. I will not survive without you."

"I already promised you, Drew. I will never leave you." She'd already given him the keys to her heart. "From here on out, I'm at your mercy."

He leaned into a hug, and she rested her cheek on his warm chest. He stroked the shell of her ear. "From now on, it's you and me. Us against the world. Never again will we make rash decisions without figuring it out together. I love you. And only you. I have since the beginning." He pushed her back so he could look at her, his expression serious.

"I'm sorry I listened to them. I should've never."

Lines formed between his brows. "Are you finally ready to tell me who they are?"

With nothing left to lose, she laid her heart bare and spilled her insecurities. "That night at the Grammys, when I went to the restroom, I just happened to overhear a conversation. They said I was a fat cow, and that I got my job because of who my uncle was."

The muscles in his jaw flexed and his nostrils flared, but he let her finish.

"That eventually you'd get bored with me, and I'd find my way back to the herd. I should've ignored them. I'm so—"

He pressed a finger against her lips and shook his head. The intensity behind his eyes held her hostage. "Well, that explains a lot. Fucking bitches," he growled. "I'm so sorry you had to go through that, though I wish you would've talked to me about it then. But I understand. And how can I blame you? It's not like we haven't watched other musicians behave poorly." He cupped her face and stroked her cheek with his thumb. "But I'm not like other musicians. I hope you can see that now. I hope you can see that I love you more than you'll ever know. And that those bitches were just jealous because you're beautiful, and intelligent, and independent as hell. I wish you could see yourself through my eyes. I need you to know they don't hold a candle to you. Tell me you understand?"

She nodded. The guilt she carried in her soul lightened, but it would never disappear. It was a lesson forged in stubbornness, pride, and stupidity. And she wasn't likely to forget it.

"Good. We'll talk more when we get home, okay? Because your lips are making it very hard for me to focus."

Her mouth parted, begging silently for him. She, too, needed his lips on hers. Every nerve bubbled in anticipation.

The electric buzzing she always felt while near him was worse than normal, as if it couldn't be contained by these tainted walls. Over the years, the stones had probably witnessed their share of sex and violence—but this? This was love. A once-in-a-lifetime unbreakable bond.

"I don't know how I'm going to do this slowly," he repeated, his raspy tone rolling over her body, leaving behind a wave of desire. "You look so..." His eyes rested on her sky-high cleavage thanks to the corset and her skin tingled under his hungry gaze.

He reached into his back pocket, and to her delight, pulled out his portable cassette player.

She covered her mouth. "Are you kidding me?" She should've known he'd pack it with him. He didn't go anywhere without music.

"I made them give it back to me for tonight." He put the headphones over her ears and hit play.

She choked back a laugh at his song choice, tears clouding her vision. "Would you do anything for love?"

"Apparently, I would." His eyes flickered to the windows. "Even that." He shrugged and smirked, holding out a hand. "Dance with me."

She pulled the headphones off and hung them around her neck. She turned the volume up so he could hear the music too before she took his hand. He twirled her to him, his chest pressed against her back. He began to sing along. His breath tickled her neck and, as always, his voice triggered something primal within her, something that bypassed her conscious mind and traveled directly to her soul. It filled her with love, desire, hope, and the feeling of being home in his arms. Exactly where she was meant to be.

They swayed to the music. When the song picked up

tempo, he twirled her away, and she started to sing with him, their own duet. Out of the corner of her eye, she saw the door open slightly.

She stiffened until she remembered the Matriarchs were out there, but even though they didn't like her, they wouldn't let anything happen. Not yet. They probably wanted to hear the duet too. Just because Myka *chose* not to sing in front of audiences didn't mean she lacked talent. She was part Sirin, after all, and she was quite gifted in her own right.

The only time Drew broke eye contact was when he pulled her back into him for the slow parts. His body, warm and hard against hers, made it difficult to remember the lyrics. By the time the eight-minute song finished, they were laughing so hard they collapsed onto the fur rug.

After they caught their breath, Drew got up and shut the door before he came over and helped her off the floor. "That's part of the reason I love you, you know."

"What's that?" She fluffed the skirt of her dress.

"Around me and the guys, you're so goofy, and you really don't care if you make a fool out of yourself or not. I find that incredibly sexy." He pushed her long bangs out of her face and tucked them behind her ear. His fingers burned a path over her skin.

He leaned in and kissed her ever so gently, rubbing his lips back and forth, tickling like butterfly wings. Then he ran his lips over her jawline and kissed the sensitive spot below her earlobe. Her pulse quickened and her breath hitched. He lifted his head and winked at her before he got them more wine.

"What is going on? Are we going to do this or what?" She

slapped her hands on her hips, desperate to keep him nearby.

"Oh yeah, we're going to do this, but Anserlee said we need to make it last, so certain people won't be able to afford my...well, you know. Because otherwise, I would have you on this floor right now," he whispered into her ear, "with my face buried between your legs."

She gasped. The fire already burning between her thighs flared. He spun around again, and this time, brought back the bowl full of berries, set it on the floor next to the wine, and patted the rug for her to sit down.

He popped a ripe berry into his mouth and she watched, mesmerized, as he chewed. "Did I embarrass you?" He hadn't shaved today and the sexy scruff along his jaw outlined his perfect lips.

"Uhhh, maybe, but not really," she said, even though he might have.

"Good, and good, because I meant it. By the end of this night, I want..." He paused and took a deep breath. He closed his eyes and shuddered as if he were mapping out a plan. "Oh, yeah. But for now, I want to talk. Like we used to. I miss that so much." He held a berry up to her lips, his gaze deepening as she opened her mouth and he set it inside.

"Mmmm, that's way better than the wine," she sighed.

He leaned forward and kissed her. His tongue, sweet like wild strawberries, gently slid over hers. "Yeah, way better than the wine," he said, his voice huskier than normal.

They talked, snacked on berries and cheese, and drank wine well into the night. The sun had finally set and the light from the full moon glowed over Drew's face. She couldn't stop staring at him as he spoke. The cadence of his voice had a calming effect, but as time passed, the tension between them increased. The air charged as if it were full of static and any sudden movement might ignite a spark. Her heartbeat throbbed continuously between her thighs. She shifted position to relieve the sensation but only made it worse.

A slow, cocky smirk formed at the corner of his mouth before he scooted closer. He trailed his finger over her bottom lip. The tender flesh tickled under his touch and her breath grew shallow. With all four fingers cupped under her chin, he drew her forward pressing her lips to his. He devoured them meticulously, fanning the flames licking her skin.

He pulled her up to standing, his lips never leaving hers, and ran hot kisses down her neck before finding their way to the top of her breasts. She shuddered and a tiny moan escaped as her nipples puckered almost uncomfortably.

"I want you out of this thing," he growled as he spun her around.

Her ribs expanded gratefully when he unlaced her corset. She held on to it as he turned her to face him. Her eyes flickered to the windows and shame stabbed when she remembered they were there.

"Hey," he said sharply. "Only me, remember?" His voice softened.

She nodded, staring again at his swollen, berry-stained lips. She swallowed and he smiled as if he knew what she'd been thinking.

"Take off your shirt," she whispered.

He raised one eyebrow in a dare. "Take it off for me."

Myka glanced down at her dangling corset and hesitated for only a second before she let it drop to the rug. She brought her eyes back to his, but he was focused on the rise and fall of her bare breasts.

The hunger on his face made her knees weak but she managed to take a step forward. She ran her fingers slowly up his washboard stomach, memorizing every ridge and valley, before pulling the shirt over his wide shoulders. She buried her face in the material and inhaled deeply. Then she went to put it on.

"Uh-uh," he said, grabbing it from her and tossing it across the room. It hit the wall and slid to the floor in slow motion.

Her eyes, again, flickered toward the windows.

He shimmied them around so her back was facing their audience.

"Now, I'm going to make you forget they're even there." He set his hands on either side of her waist and tugged the skirt over her hips. It fell to the floor and pooled like a fluffy white cloud beneath her feet. A flicker of surprise passed behind Drew's eyes. Underneath, she had nothing on. Flames from the fire warmed her naked skin.

She gnawed on her bottom lip and undid his button fly, one at a time, concentrating hard on the task. She smiled when his breath hitched, a thrill rushing through her that she had the same effect on him that he had on her. His jeans dropped to the ground and he stepped out. She caught her finger under the elastic of his boxers and then snapped it back.

"Scared?" he asked.

"Freaking terrified," she said as he slid his drawers off. She wasn't scared of the sex—she feared the emotional commitment it would mean later should they escape their circumstances. She already loved him—and after this, no matter what happened, she always would. From here on out, he held her heart in his hands, and with it, the power to crush it. She had to trust he felt the same way. She had, after all, promised never to break his heart again. She'd meant it.

They both stood back and stared. She drank in his glorious form.

He looked like a statue carved from marble bathed in silver moonlight. Shadows from the candlelight and flickering fire danced over the hard-muscled planes of his long, lean body. His penis, as large as she'd suspected from what little they had accomplished, jutted proudly from the nest of dark curls.

They crashed together—lips, arms, and legs. He trailed kisses down her neck, slowly making his way to the swell of her breasts before taking her already-hard nipple into his mouth. Sparks flared and a small moan escaped as he lavished attention on the tiny bud while his other hand slipped between her legs. He teased her clit with long, slow strokes, fueling the hot ember into a raging inferno. She didn't know where to focus as everything quivered and pulsated in a frenzy.

Right before her body gave her what she wanted, he stopped. She let out a small, pathetic whine.

He chuckled and scooped her up, carrying her to the bed. He laid her on the covers and climbed on top of her, his weight imprisoning her. Every inch of her skin trembled as he kissed her collarbone and trailed his burning lips down her stomach to the insides of her thighs. Her breath shallowed and her skin flamed. With the coax of his hand, he spread her legs further. Her center throbbed and ached as he nipped and licked everywhere but there. She arched her back, a silent plea to end her misery. His tongue flicked her swollen clit and stars burst behind her closed eyes. As he feasted on her flesh, sucking and pulling, rolling the mass of nerves around his mouth, he slid his large finger inside, curling into a spot that made time freeze. And just as he'd promised, the world vanished and the only thing that existed was ecstasy. Her fists clenched the down comforter as her moans and whimpers turned to cries. Her hair stuck to her sweaty forehead.

"Don't stop," she begged. "Please, Drew, don't stop."

He added another finger and pumped his hand as his tongue worked mercilessly. Her back arched as the intensity built until the only thing that mattered was the fireworks exploding inside.

Her heart continued to slam against her ribs even after she finished. He sidled up next to her and kissed her gently with the taste of her still on his lips. He pulled back the covers and they crawled under, facing each other.

"I didn't know," she said, at a loss for words.

"Didn't know what? That it could feel like that?"

"No. That it could get even better than the last time. I mean...wow."

"Fuck, baby, if you think that was good, just wait. That was an appetizer."

"I don't think anything can get better than that," she whispered, the sparks of her orgasm still warming her.

"Oh, it can. But not tonight, not with them watching. Not without protection."

Until that moment, she'd truly forgotten they were there. An eerie shiver slithered over her as she remembered. "What do you mean?"

"If you get pregnant here and we don't get out... I don't want to even think about the consequences," he said.

"Oh, my sweet, naïve little rock star," she said, batting her eyelashes. "I took care of that a while ago. Like right after we started dating."

"Huh?" He propped himself up on an elbow, hovering above her, moonlight sharpening his cheekbones.

"You know, just in case. I wasn't the one who wanted to take it slow." She smiled and twirled his soft hair around her finger as she nibbled on her bottom lip. "And you? Are you...?" She could feel her cheeks burn. She didn't want to bring it up, but she wasn't sure Anserlee would have a cure for an STD.

He lightly flicked the tip of her nose. "Yes, I'm clean. I was tested a while ago. And I haven't slept with anyone in over eight months. Haven't you noticed?"

"I might have, but I was trying not to." Because that had made it harder for her to stay away.

"I stopped seeing other people when Nicky hinted you might be softening when it came to matters of the heart. Specifically, you and me."

"Well, it looks like we're both out of excuses."

"You know, you're just making this harder on me," he whispered. "I want you. I want you so fucking bad it hurts. But not like this. Your first time is *not* going to be with them as witnesses."

"Please. I want this. What if we don't get out of here?" Desperation replaced her need for privacy. Realistically, she knew this might be their only chance. If she died, she wanted—no, she *needed*—to feel his body inside of hers.

"I'm going to do everything in my power to get us out of here," he said, nudging her chin up so he could kiss her. Her body instantly responded and desire surged, perhaps worse than before.

One by one, the candles had begun to burn out, and the fire had died down to only glowing red coals. Her hand traveled over his rock-hard abs to the fine trail of hair under his belly button. She reached her hand around his cock, which twitched, and he inhaled sharply through his nose, releasing his breath between his teeth. Under her palm, his pulse beat furiously. She didn't expect his skin to be so velvety soft and hot as she stroked him. He bit down where her neck and shoulder met as he positioned himself on top of her. Her legs spread farther and her hips rose to meet him.

"No," he whispered, "that's only for us."

He slid his penis slowly through the spreading wetness between her thighs until her clit ached.

"Please, Drew, please," she pleaded.

He whispered again, "Whatever you do, make this convincing." He rolled his hips forward and pinched her nipple hard.

"Ouch," she hissed as he chuckled. "What was that for?"

"Authenticity. You're a virgin. That first part is supposed to hurt, but now that we've got that out of the way..."

Even though he wouldn't give her what she wanted, she didn't have to convince anyone of anything. Just his hard shaft rubbing against her was enough to make her climax a second time.

As they lay in the bed, both of them breathing hard, she heard the door squeak open.

"Remember," Drew said quietly, "no matter what happens from here on out, I love you. Always."

Her heart kicked her ribs, and she started to protest. It sounded eerily like a goodbye.

"Get up!" someone squawked loudly.

Drew crawled out of bed and grabbed his black T-shirt off the floor, tossing it to Myka.

"You, girl, get out," Gilda said without even looking at her. Her focus was solely on Drew standing naked in front of her.

She put it on and snatched her skirt before she quickly scurried out the door, back to her room. This was the part she couldn't bear to witness. The image of him with anyone was going to kill her. She'd already spent every night of the last three years picturing him with someone else and hating him for it—but hating herself worse.

drew

D rew stood rigidly in front of Gilda, sweat gathering at the base of his neck. His stomach tossed wildly, but he willed his face to stone. There was no way he would let her know how severely she got under his skin.

Gilda ordered him, without singing, to follow her out the door. He defiantly put on his pants before he complied. She motioned for him to step onto a stone platform in front of the wall of windows. Candlelight slithered over her fingernails, black and sharpened to points.

Rows upon rows of elegantly dressed Sirins stood as he took to the pedestal and turned to face them. Most wore brilliant-colored gowns decorated with sparkling jewels. Their wings and long hair eerily reminded him of a church choir comprised of angels. Some of them looked to be carved from alabaster, others sculpted from bronze or onyx. Each one was more beautiful than the last. *Or in this case,* Drew thought, *each one more repulsive than the last.*

Excited chatter filled the curved room as the women

eyed him hungrily. Their predatory gazes crawled over his skin, making the hairs on his arms and the back of his neck rise. They had seen him naked before, and even though he had on jeans, they'd never been allowed this close.

He felt like a slab of beef dangling amongst a pack of ravenous carnivores. Some of the women studied him with an air of disdain while others practically drooled. They kept raising their noses in the air like they were trying to catch his scent. A couple of them, in the back row, started making out and began touching each other intimately. Their fast-paced moans turned into orgasms, echoing throughout the room. His Adam's apple bobbed violently, trying to hold back the bile burning his throat.

"Quiet!" Gilda yelled, silencing the rowdy group. She crossed her arms over her black leather bodice. The material absorbed the surrounding light and contrasted with the spun-gold color of her hair.

Drew spotted Anserlee in the corner by herself, her plain cotton gown standing out amongst the finery. She nodded almost imperceptibly to him, and that one small gesture strengthened his determination to make it through the coming horror. She had a plan. And he had to hope it was a good one. She'd told him earlier when she brought him to this room that the first part of her plan had been successful, proving her theory to be true. But she still couldn't tell him what it was.

"To all of you who will be bidding for the services of Andrew Arie, pick a feather now," Gilda said. She plucked a long, golden quill from the end of her wing and held it up. It sparkled like twenty-four-carat gold in the torchlight. Most of the women followed suit. Anserlee winced as she pulled out hers. He could only imagine she was still sore after her ordeal.

Once everyone had a feather, Gilda turned the auction over to the Matriarchs and took her place amid the rest of the Sirins.

Drew had to physically keep his hands from balling into fists. Rave was his last choice to sleep with, followed closely by Gilda, who was inspecting every inch of him, raising her eyebrow occasionally in appraisal, followed closely by licking her lips.

"Let the bidding commence!" said one of the Matriarchs while she tossed her hands in the air. Her bracelets clinked as they slid up her raised arms.

All three were dressed identically in loose white gowns with gems dangling from their hair and draping onto their foreheads like a set of jeweled bangs. Braids and knots and feathers threaded through the rest of their locks.

"We will be using only gold and precious stones for this auction, no service trading," said another in the trio. A sound of disappointment wailed through the air. "At least for the first month's services. We shall reevaluate then."

A tightening wound through Drew's chest and the flames of the torches hanging from the stone walls dimmed and then brightened as his vision faded. He flexed his fists to keep his blood pumping. If he didn't get out of here, he would become a sex slave for the rest of his pathetic life. Until that moment, he hadn't completely understood the gravity. It was as if he were waking from a nightmare only to find he wasn't actually dreaming. He knew Myka's fate would be death. Rave was not going to allow her to live— nor would Gilda. On more than one occasion, he'd heard her nasty comments about *the whore*. And if sleeping with a few of these creatures would save Myka's life, he'd do it a million times over. Other people had survived worse.

His greatest concern was getting the love of his life safely home.

The creatures switched to a language Drew didn't understand. It sounded familiar, angry, and lyrical all at the same time. And then the auction began.

All the feathers waved in the air, except for the Matriarchs, until one by one, only four feathers remained—Gilda's being one of them, Rave's another, Anserlee's not.

A ball of panic strangled his throat, making it hard to swallow. He wiped his sweating palms on his jeans.

"And the first night's services belong to Gilda!" one of the Matriarchs hollered after all other feathers hung defeated.

Gilda, her head tilted arrogantly, handed her feather to one of the owls. She stopped in front of Drew and slowly walked around him, her eyes feasting on what was now hers. He refused to look at her and instead stared above everyone's heads. He flinched when she ran a fingernail over his stomach and down to his crotch, her talon rasping loudly on the denim. She gave his dick a firm squeeze. His nostrils flared, and he clenched his teeth to keep from screaming. He didn't know if he could do this. But then if he didn't do what she wanted, she would sing to him and possibly make him do things he really couldn't imagine.

Four feathers later, Anserlee strolled to the front and surrendered her gray plumage to the owls. He jumped as she smacked him on his ass before she left the room. He should have expected it since those before her had all touched him in a degrading way. Though with Anserlee, it felt forced.

Drew didn't pay attention to the bidders after that.

Anserlee had said their evening together would be his night to escape.

"And that wraps up the auction!" one of the Matriarchs cheered, raising closed fists over her head. All of the Sirins, chatting loudly, hashing over the events, exited the room leaving him alone with the Matriarchs.

"Not quite," Drew said, casually stuffing his hands into his pockets. They'd promised him if he didn't perform to his full abilities, which meant taking Myka's virginity, they'd kill her. "If you touch one hair on Myka's head, I'll kill myself."

The Matriarchs glanced at each other, their eyes narrowing and an evil smile twisting their lips. "For now she's safe. But eventually, you won't care."

He didn't argue, because after seeing the wasted remnants of the men here, he knew they weren't lying. But, if everything went as planned, freedom was only a few days away. All he had to do was survive sleeping with Gilda, two Sirins he didn't recognize, and Rave and her two cronies, who'd pooled their resources together.

THIRTY-TWO

anserlee

After Anserlee successfully placed a bid, she hurried down the stairs to Myka's room with plans to sleep there. It was the safest place to be, with barred windows and only one door to lock.

Immediately after the audition, the Matriarchs had called off the protective guard. Myka was no longer useful and just another mouth to feed. From here on out, she was deadweight, deemed worthless, and the only Sirin that cared if she lived was Anserlee. So much so, she was willing to risk her life.

She unlocked the door and tiptoed in, hoping Myka would be asleep. A few candles wavered in the dark room, illuminating the crying heap curled in the center of the bed. The mattress trembled with every wave of despair.

Jealousy gnawed at her stomach. As twisted as it was, she wished Myka were crying over her. She mentally chastised herself for the bitter emotion and inhaled a deep breath. She exhaled the ugliness and fluffed her wing feathers, trying to prepare for what lay ahead.

"Hey, hey, now," Anserlee fussed as she climbed up on the high bed and sank into the cushy down.

Myka curled into a tighter ball and began crying harder, having a hard time catching her breath. Anserlee sat up against the headboard and petted Myka's silky hair until the hysterics subsided.

"You ready to talk?" Anserlee asked when the sobs became only hiccups.

Myka shook her head.

"Well, that doesn't really matter because we are going to talk before these wounds fester." She hopped off the bed and wet a cloth before handing it to Myka. "Here, this is for your eyes. And have a drink of water." She filled a cup and forced Myka to sit up. "Better?" she asked after a minute.

Myka nodded.

Anserlee crawled back up on the bed and nested into the blankets. "Okay then, I need to fill you in on the plan," Anserlee said. She needed to give Myka something to focus on other than her pain. "I have Drew on day five," she started.

Myka's bloodshot eyes grew big in the dim candlelight. Kohl eyeliner and black mascara stained the delicate skin under her eyes.

"Look, you know the deal. We can't avoid the subject, but you also know this is temporary. We're going to get you both out of here." Anserlee cupped Myka's chin. Her skin was red and blotchy from crying. "I need you to be present. Drew needs you. Both of your lives depend on you. This heartbreak that you think you're suffering from is pointless," Anserlee admonished.

Myka's brows furrowed.

She reached up and pushed Myka's bangs out of her

eyes. Her finger tingled at the touch. Try as she might, she couldn't suppress her feelings for the woman. And when you loved someone, you did everything in your power to make them happy. Even at your own expense.

"Ahh, but..." Myka stuttered.

Anserlee snapped her fingers and pointed at Myka. "No, you listen to me. I will not sit here and watch you cry for someone who loves you more than he loves himself. The next few days are going to be far harder on him than you! Imagine having strange men grope you, feel you, do anything they want to you, and you have to convince them you're enjoying it!" Anserlee paused and glared, allowing the severity to sink in. "I'm not sure you could do it. But Drew will survive for you. Because he loves you. Your man is going to be a whore for the next week. How do you think he's feeling right now? Sick, sick to his core. And you are lying here crying and accomplishing nothing. You need to stop crying now. He's going to do this and not allow it to affect him. You need to do the same. Because once you're free from here, your ability to move past this will determine the rest of your lives." Though her tone was angry and harsh, all she wanted to do was lean in and kiss Myka's soft, pouting lips. Kiss some of her pain away. And though Myka was a woman, Anserlee's powers were bound to trickle through. If she thought it would make things better, she would help Myka forget the last hour she'd spent crying.

Anserlee had been there earlier, watching with the others, standing in the corner alone. She desperately wanted what they had. Love. Chemistry. Passion. Trust. Friendship. Even on the outside looking through the glass, their bond was intense. And that undeniable bond was what stopped Anserlee now. Even with her abilities, she couldn't compete with that kind of love. She was happy for them, yet devastated at the same time.

"Well, this is not the talk I expected us to have," Myka hiccupped.

"What talk did you think we would have?" Anserlee asked, cocking her head to one side, curious.

"I figured you'd let me wallow in my misery for more than an hour."

Anserlee gently tapped the tip of Myka's pink nose. "We don't have time for that. Besides, it's not doing you any good. The outcome will be the same."

"Then I thought we would talk about what happened tonight in the room with Drew," she said, hesitating on his name.

"No, no, we don't need to talk about that if you don't want to. I was there." Anserlee gritted her teeth, remembering the heavy breathing and the moaning encompassing the spectators' room as they all watched and some actively participated.

"Yes, don't remind me. But I need to tell you that we didn't...well, you know. He said we weren't going to do *that* with everyone watching, that *that* would be for us alone. But I'm worried now. I thought we had to, or they would kill me."

"No. Either way wouldn't make a difference. Rave is going to try and kill you no matter what."

"Yeah, you're probably right."

"I told the owls I wanted to keep you for myself, and they have no problems with that, but they won't help keep you alive. They don't care."

Myka shrugged. "Figures. So what do we do now?"

"I am going to kill you myself," Anserlee said.

myka

Myka awoke the next morning to soft, gray feathers tickling her nose every time she inhaled. Anserlee was curled around her, her arm and wing draped over her shoulder. She could feel her chest rise and fall as she quietly snored in, then exhaled, sounding like the coo of a dove.

Her eyes burned from crying and her mouth felt like she'd eaten a wad of cotton. She scooted out from under Anserlee's wing and grabbed the empty glass from the night table. She filled it up in the sink and hastily drank three full glasses before splashing water on her face. Cold droplets ran down her neck into her nightshirt, making her shiver in the cool air. She jumped when someone beat loudly on the door.

Anserlee shot up from her sleep and looked around, panicked. Long strands of hair stuck to her cheek. When she spotted Myka, she visibly relaxed. "Who is it?" she asked loudly, her voice rising at the end.

"It's Gilda! The Matriarchs want to see the both of you

immediately. I will meet you up there," Gilda shouted through the door.

"What do they want? What should we do?" The glass in Myka's hand trembled and water sloshed over the side.

"I don't know, but we have to go. Try to stay calm and talk as little as possible," Anserlee said.

Myka stepped into the white skirt from the night before and threw on Drew's black T-shirt, tying the excess material into a knot over her stomach. They were the only clothes she had. She lifted the collar of his shirt and pressed her nose to the material, letting his scent fill her lungs—a reminder that she would do anything for him.

"Come on." Anserlee yanked her hand.

Despite being so little, she successfully dragged Myka up some flights of stairs until they came to a huge double door with iron fittings. She unlatched the lock to let them into the Matriarchs' quarters.

Ornately carved furniture, tapestries, artwork with gilded frames, and weapons straight out of a dungeon spanned the oddly shaped room. But the strangest thing was the hole in the center of the ceiling.

From behind, Anserlee wrapped her tiny arms around Myka's waist. She glanced over her shoulder as Anserlee stretched out her wings and flew through not one but two circular openings until they landed on the top suite. Her strength was eerie and made Myka a bit uncomfortable.

There, the Matriarchs waited for them, nestled in front of a dying fire. Down feathers floated lazily in the air, hovering in the beams of sunlight stabbing through the windows. The soft glow blurred the outlines of the three, making them appear like birds in a nest.

"Mothers." Anserlee bowed her head.

Myka simply stared at the floor, nervous about where to look. Her hands, hanging by her sides, trembled. A soft breeze blowing up from the hole in the floor ruffled her skirt, and the dust bunnies swirled helplessly in the draft. She gripped the hem of Drew's shirt, attempting to hide her anxiety.

"There have been questions brought forth that perhaps Andrew did not fully perform his duties last night. Is this true?"

Myka's chin snapped up in time to see them simultaneously cock their heads.

She ignored the question.

One of them rose and walked over to her, her feet jerking slightly with every step. Her eyes, orbital and unblinking, locked on Myka. Except for those creepy eyes, the three lacked the usual range of facial expressions. She snatched Myka's arm in her dry, papery hand. It was surprisingly warm on her cool skin, but goose bumps rose from her touch anyway. Bad goose bumps. Like the kind warning you to run.

"Oh," the Matriarch said as if she was actually surprised, "he didn't do as was promised. Thankfully, he's already admitted to it."

"You're not going to kill her, are you?" Anserlee jumped in.

"No, Anserlee, we have promised her to you for all your years of dedicated service. And the boy vowed to take his own life if we killed her. We don't want to have him guarded all the time, so we promised to leave her alive. But..." The Matriarch looked at Anserlee, then Myka. "We didn't promise not to have her punished."

All three smiled in tandem. Their cheekbones sharpened and their thin lips disappeared beneath their beakish noses.

A shock of terror wove through Myka, dumping an overload of adrenaline into her system. Nausea watered in her mouth.

"And what shall the punishment be?" Anserlee said, sighing as if she'd suspected this was coming.

"Tonight, she shall have a front-row seat to Drew's debut with Gilda."

Myka's stomach heaved and twisted before it ricocheted all the way to her throat. She couldn't even swallow. Knowing Drew would be with other women was bad enough, but watching it would be torture. Ten lashes with a whip, starvation, isolation. She would do anything for love —but she wouldn't do *that* to even her worst enemy.

"I will accompany her this evening," Anserlee said indifferently.

"Please," Myka begged them. "Please, anything, just not this."

"And that is exactly why this is the punishment you need. He is ours now. Not yours." The Matriarch's words were firm but not angry.

The back of her nose stung as hot tears filled her eyes, threatening to spill over the dam. She bit the inside of her cheek until blood ran over her tongue.

"Oh, Anserlee, you're not to be there. You bring her far too much comfort. You may escort her there and back to her room. We know you fear for her safety. You are both dismissed."

Myka wanted to scream, the words itching in her throat. *"I will not do this, you fucking bitches!"* But her life was worthless, and she was afraid if she opened her mouth, they would prove just how worthless it was. The only reason they hadn't already killed her was because Drew had threatened suicide. They didn't want to lose him. Neither did Myka. And it was the only thing keeping her mouth shut.

Though it didn't stop anger from flaring. It blazed up her cheeks to the tips of her ears. But she couldn't control it any more than she could control the beating of her heart.

"Anserlee," one said calmly, as if Myka wasn't a threat.

"Myka!" Anserlee snapped while grabbing Myka's hand. "Don't make me hurt you." Concern and something more serious sat behind her eyes. Though Myka hadn't even moved, Anserlee put downward pressure on her wrist as a reminder of what she was capable of.

Myka hissed, winching as pain shot up her shoulder.

"Come with me now." Anserlee wrapped her arms around Myka's waist before flying her down to the door.

When they got out, Myka said, "Why would you let them do this?"

She pointed a finger at Myka's face and whispered angrily, "Seriously? You don't get it, do you? The only reason they left you alive is because it's more convenient for them. For now, anyway. Eventually, Drew will forget you even exist, then they'll probably have you killed if you continue to behave like this!"

"I didn't do anything!" Myka hissed.

Anserlee's gray eyes tightened into slivers. "You were thinking about it!"

"So now they're the thought police?!"

Anserlee hauled Myka back to her room-slash-prison and pushed her inside before the outside lock clicked into place.

Myka pounded on the door, splitting her knuckles

open, leaving behind a trail of blood on the wood. She screamed for what seemed like hours until finally, exhaustion set in. The palms of her hands smarted from slapping the door after she couldn't stand the pain in her fists any longer.

Soon, her anger turned to defeat and she gave up.

She rinsed her raw hands in the sink, flinching at the cold water. The small slivers of wood stuck under her skin started to sting after the adrenaline wore off. It wasn't Anserlee she was angry with, but the temper tantrum had made her feel more composed somehow.

Leaning against the rough stone, she let her legs slide out from under her until she was sitting on the floor. She knocked her head on the surface and focused on their conversation from the night before.

The plan.

"What?" Myka had asked, confused. Not only by what Anserlee had said, but by the ridiculous look on her face after she announced that she was going to kill Myka herself.

Anserlee chewed on her bottom lip, unable to hide her excitement. "I have a potion, of sorts, that will make you sleep, deep. To the untrained eye, you will appear dead. I learned it years ago when I made a trip to the Caribbean. The Sirins there taught me. They make it from a puffer fish. I brought some home with me, but I've never needed it until now."

"And the owls won't know?"

"No, I don't share everything with them. Honestly, at this point in time, they won't even care." She shrugged, her wings mimicking her shoulders. "They don't believe anyone can escape from their colony. The arrogance on their part is imperative for my plan to work."

"So what is your plan?" Myka asked, thinking about the

original star-crossed lovers, Romeo and Juliet, and how that poisoning fiasco ended.

"In four days, I am going to give you the death draft. I will lay you to rest in a far-off cave, where you will wake and then drink the elixir that makes you invisible. After, you must paddle out to the same island as before, wait three days, and then come back to help Drew escape."

"Phew, that sounds complicated. Why can't I just stay here and wait?"

She tapped Myka's bottom lip with a cool finger. "Because I need you out of the way and safe. That way, I only have Drew to worry about."

"Then why don't I leave sooner?"

"Because four days from now is when Rave and her groupies have a date with Drew."

Myka cringed at the word groupies. It brought everything closer to home. "I don't want her to have him," Myka said, lowering her voice to a dangerous whisper.

"You don't get it, do you? You don't have a choice, and besides, this will work to our advantage. It will be so much easier to hide you if Rave isn't watching."

"I don't care! Please, not her!"

"I am sorry, but I will need her and her friends kept busy. And Drew is the only distraction strong enough to work."

Myka narrowed her gaze accusingly. "I thought she didn't have enough money to buy him?"

"She bought him with the help of the two raptors that accompany her all the time."

Myka looked away and scrubbed her fingers through her short hair. "I'm sure this won't be his first foursome."

Anserlee slapped her not so lightly on the arm. "Hey, knock it *off. Not his choice, remember? Not. His. Choice." Anserlee stared Myka down, forcing her to turn away.*

"The moment you hold him in your arms again, you're going to have to wipe the slate clean or you will never fix this. You promised him you could do that. But even if you can't, neither of you deserves a life spent here. So we're going to get you out. I just have to keep you from doing anything stupid for the next four days."

The door creaked and Anserlee stuck her head through the opening. "Are you done throwing your temper tantrum?"

"Yes," Myka said groggily, since she'd somehow fallen asleep. She was still cranky but not violent. For the moment, anyway.

"Good, because we need to get you up there soon." Anserlee glided over and helped Myka off the stone floor. Her limbs were stiff from the hard, cold surface.

The thought of Drew having sex with someone else was a torture she'd been putting herself through for the last three years. But *watching* him with someone else—that was a whole new level of hell.

"Already?" She was surprised she'd been asleep that long. Though the last couple of nights had been tough. And tonight—tonight, was going to be the worst.

"Yes," Anserlee said. She sat Myka in a chair and began fussing with her hair.

"Is he going to know I'm there?" Myka's voice cracked.

"No, the punishment is only for you." Anserlee tossed her long braid back over her shoulder.

"Why? He lied too."

"Yes, but he's their pet now. They'll tread lightly for as long as they can. They don't want to break his will if they can help it. They last longer that way." Anserlee pushed a fur blanket into Myka's hands.

She cringed when her skin cracked open and started bleeding again.

"Seriously?" Anserlee sniped. "Here, let me bandage those so you don't get blood all over the fur." She went to the cupboard and gathered a few things in her arms, then carried them back to the table. She dabbed Myka's knuckles with goo, then wrapped her hands in gauze, huffing and glaring between steps.

"How am I going to do this? How is he going to..." Myka ignored the discomfort as she muttered under her breath. It was going to be bad enough that she had to watch. But poor Drew. Her chest quivered with a suppressed sob. His part of the situation wasn't just sexual assault—it was full-on rape. Over and over again. Whether he complied willingly or not.

Anserlee stopped and stared into Myka's eyes. She placed her cool palms on Myka's feverish cheeks. "You'll figure it out. Because that's what he would do for you."

"You like him, don't you?"

A soft honk-like snort escaped as she released Myka's face. "Yes, I do. And sometimes I wish I didn't, or I might consider keeping you here for myself. I know in time you could love me," she whispered.

Myka's heart squeezed at the agony and loneliness in Anserlee's tone. The last thing she wanted to do was cause her pain in any way. "Oh, Anserlee, I already love you, just not like you need me to."

A sad, tight smile curled her lips. "I know."

Anserlee led Myka up the circular stairs, their footsteps matching the pulse hammering under her jaw. They stopped on the fourth floor, and she rested her hand against the stone wall to steady her legs. The room was empty, and despite the orange glow of the torches, a cold void settled in her bones. She shivered.

"I can't help you now. Be strong," Anserlee said, setting her down on the bench. She kissed the top of her head, lingering for a moment, and squeezed her shoulder before she left her alone.

Drew was already in the auditioning room, separated from her by a one-way mirror like the interrogation room of a police station. She didn't know which was worse—being on that side or this one.

He paced, running his fingers through his thick hair in frustration or impatience. Or fear. She knew that tick well. He always paced when things weren't going his way or were taking too long. He reminded her of those tigers at the zoo who wore ruts along the borders of their cages, searching for an exit.

At least he didn't know she was here.

She looked over at the stairwell, as two Sirins dressed in brown leather entered and sat on either side of her like she needed a babysitter.

"I can't wait until we get him," one Sirin purred.

They were trying to goad her. She clenched her teeth and denied them the satisfaction as she stared straight ahead into the room. The fluffy white bed looked ever so inviting.

She could almost hear the crackling of the fire and the smell of the wood smoke and fresh flowers.

These women would never get the chance to sleep with him, Myka vowed.

"I know!" the other one said. "I'm so pleased you, me, and Rave pooled our money together so we could afford him so early on. I mean, with his schedule, he's going to wear down fast. It'll be fun to share him while he's fresh."

Bile shot to the back of her throat. She swallowed it, but the bitterness remained. These were Rave's henchmen. She'd never looked at them closely before. Somewhere along the way, they'd all started to look the same. When everyone was so beautiful, how did you tell them apart?

"I know, right? I can't wait to have that fucking huge dick deep in my throat and my cunt clenching around him." She rolled her hips forward and sighed as if she were imagining it.

The other one reached between her legs and pressed her hands to her crotch. "I don't know why we never thought of this before. But then again, no one has ever fetched a price like his." She sounded surprised at their own stupidity.

Myka's breath caught in her chest as she actually looked at the Sirin talking. Dark chestnut hair hung over her shoulder to her waist in shiny, loose ringlets. Myka cowered at the animosity dancing behind her chocolate-colored eyes.

She glanced away and back into the room just in time to catch Drew downing the entire bottle of berry wine. She gagged, remembering how disgustingly sweet it was, but a peace settled over her as she realized he needed to be drunk to get through it. Oh, how she yearned for a bottle of her own.

The two raptors bantered back and forth on what they

were going to do to him during their session, but Myka ignored them. She shut down her emotions more efficiently than she ever had. She pretended this was a business deal, simply a transaction. She'd performed so many of those in the past and it only worked if nothing was personal. Later, while alone, she would process everything. But not here. She would *not* give them the satisfaction.

Until Gilda walked up the stairs wearing nothing but black lace-up leather boots and long matching gloves. The soft patch between her legs was slightly darker than her golden hair and metallic wings. She carried a black bag and a whip over a bare shoulder. Myka wanted to say, *"Nice boots. Are those to cover your ugly fucking feet?"* But Gilda would make Drew pay for Myka's comment. So she kept her mouth shut and stared ahead.

Gilda entered the room like a drill sergeant, her tiny, athletic body straight and rigid. Her hair, braided into a hundred tiny strands, spilled like a river of gold over her shoulders, brushing the back of her knees.

One of the raptors locked the door behind her as Gilda began laying her equipment out on the table. Ball gags, nipple clamps, brass knuckles, polished knives, and shit Myka didn't even recognize.

Drew didn't seem surprised by her lack of clothing or what was in the bag. He looked bored. *He expected this,* Myka thought. Her heart tripped, and she swallowed back the rising nausea. As strange as it seemed, she would have done anything to trade places with him. Anything to keep him safe. She would rather bear the pain than watch him hurt.

The things that went on in that room were far too grave for her to recant.

She tried closing her eyes, but each time she did, her

guards elbowed her violently in the ribs. Afraid they might break one and hinder their chances of escaping, she forced herself to watch. Sweat dampened under her arms and breasts and rolled down her spine. Her chest trembled as she gulped air.

Occasionally, even the two raptors, who were giving a detailed play-by-play, went silent, too stunned to report. They held her in place with a death grip on each arm. Blood, from their nails digging into her skin, ran down her biceps and dripped off her elbows onto the bench.

She welcomed the pain, though it did little to distract from the horrors going on in that room. Her guts flipped and she swallowed constantly, trying not to throw up. She wasn't successful and quickly turned and vomited behind her. Once she finished, they forced her to sit straight so she could continue watching the show. Tears, born of hate and anger, flowed in rivulets over her cheeks.

If she ever had the opportunity, she'd scorch this nightmare to the ground with all of the Sirins inside. She'd take great pleasure in watching them burn alive. God, she fucking hated them.

At the end of the night, Drew lay broken on the floor, naked and defeated. Gilda crouched down next to him, her legs spread wide for all to see, the mess of blood and semen glistening on her inner thighs. She pulled off her gloves, yanking one finger at a time. She threw them on the floor and grabbed a handful of his sweaty hair, pulling his head back violently. She whispered something in his ear. He looked up through the mirrored window, straight at Myka. She bit down hard on her inner cheek, crunching the skin between her teeth. Even though she knew he couldn't see her, Gilda had told him she was there—the ultimate punishment for both of them.

Gilda got up and kicked him with the toe of her leather boot. He rose slowly, the pain obvious, and stood with his back facing the windows. She dug a black talon into his skin between his shoulder blades. He flinched but didn't move. One letter at a time, she carved her name into his flesh. Trails of crimson blood ran down his back and over his buttocks. His hard body covered in tattoos contrasted sharply with his curled shoulders and head hung in shame. Even in the dim candlelight, Myka could count the bruises, lashes, and teeth marks.

Finally, the bells rang, and Gilda's time was over. She packed her bag and opened the door for him.

He exited the audition room, leaving behind bloody footprints. As he passed within feet of Myka, he wouldn't even look at her, so she began to sing their song. He lifted his dead eyes, shining with unshed tears. She blew him a kiss and signed, *"I love you."* His face relaxed slightly, and he nodded his head.

myka

Today was the day Myka was destined to die. Nerves beat in the hollow of her chest, and she felt twitchy and irritable. The last three days had dragged by in a flash, which she didn't know was possible.

Moments where she'd replayed Drew's torture ran slow like molasses, but when she remembered she was about to meet her demise, the day sped forward, like skipping chapters in a book.

She hadn't seen Drew since his encounter with Gilda and, to be honest, that was probably a good thing. If she had to endure being repeatedly raped, she certainly wouldn't want him witnessing it. She could only assume he'd feel the same. As much as she wanted to see him, she wanted it to be when this nightmare was over. She couldn't bear to have him ripped from her grasp again. When they got through this, she was never going to let him go.

Never.

She could only pray he'd feel the same.

She sat at the table in Anserlee's house, watching her

friend concoct the potion that would kill her. Anserlee's delicate hands mixed this and mashed that, somehow gracefully ignoring the smell wafting from the brew—rotting fish, sour milk, metal, and blood.

Anserlee hummed as she stirred while Myka put things away when she was finished with them. Or sometimes before she finished, which caused her to yell and insist that Myka sit down. But she couldn't, because when she sat down, it was too easy to dwell. Myka was an emotional basket case and keeping busy helped.

She didn't want to think this was the last time she would ever see Anserlee. She would never again behold her downturned gray eyes that made her look a tiny bit sad even with a bright smile on her lips. Never again would she stroke her glorious angel wings as she slept at night. And never again would she face the wrath of the tiny woman standing in front of her.

"Are you okay?" Anserlee asked after she'd put the last ingredient back in the cabinet. "You're just standing here, in the way."

"No, I am not okay," Myka admitted, sitting down, closing her eyes, concentrating on breathing. She didn't want to cry anymore. Her eyes and the skin around them hurt. In all of her twenty-four years put together, she'd never cried this much. She'd always thought of herself as tough, solid, and perhaps intimidating at times. For the last month, she'd been reduced to a blubbering mess, and it needed to stop.

"What's going on? Are you having second thoughts? We can do this. I have it all worked out," Anserlee said in one big breath. Even sitting in this chair, she barely looked down at her.

"Anserlee," Myka whispered, her voice straining, "how am I never going to see you again? Isn't there any way you can come with us?"

"Oh, sweetheart, you won't see me again. Or if you do, you won't know it's me for sure, and neither will I, not really, not like I know you now." Anserlee clasped Myka's hands in her firm grip. "As much as I want you both to stay here, you can't. They will kill you, and in time, they will do worse to Drew. I can't tell you how many times I imagined escaping with you, but there's no way that can happen. I cannot live in my Sirin form outside the bubble that imprisons us. And if I could, remember I have wings. They would be quite conspicuous."

"I know, but we'd figure out the wings. I'm telling you, we'd come up with something amazing," Myka said.

Anserlee shook her head, sadness clouding her eyes.

Myka's chin fell to her chest before she glanced back at Anserlee. "But I am going to miss you. More than miss you."

"I am going to miss you too. And Drew too. But letting you go..." Anserlee whispered, tears pooling, "is going to be the hardest thing I've ever done."

They sat there for what seemed like forever, just staring at each other. Myka memorized every beautiful angle of Anserlee's heart-shaped face—her tiny nose, perfect skin, and the longest eyelashes she'd ever witnessed. She never wanted to forget anything about her. Especially her heart.

Anserlee reached out and slid a finger over Myka's cheek. "Can I, please, just once, so I will know, so I can remember when you're gone," she whispered, her accent heavier than normal.

Myka nodded. How could she deny her? After everything Anserlee had sacrificed, it was the least she could do. And

Drew wouldn't mind—not in a case like this. Not with Anserlee.

Anserlee leaned closer and pressed her soft, cool lips to Myka's burning skin. She wove her tiny hand behind Myka's head, cradling it gently. Jolts of electricity shocked through her, and she could see how a man, or woman, could get addicted to this. Every emotion Anserlee had for Myka tingled through their contact, from the tips of her ears to the balls of her feet. In her lips, Myka could feel how dearly Anserlee loved her, how much she was going to miss her, and how desperately she desired her.

Physically, Myka's body responded, and she trembled beneath Anserlee's touch. But emotionally, all she felt was sorrow. To love someone so deeply and not have it returned was torture in itself. She supposed Drew could relate. Though even when Myka had pretended to be indifferent to him, she hadn't been. Watching him struggle through their breakup had been painful for both of them.

Anserlee ran her fingers down Myka's neck to her shoulder, where she squeezed one final time, then pulled back from the kiss. "I knew it." Anserlee hung her head, her silvery-brown hair falling over her face. With her hands still on Myka's shoulders, she said, "I knew it the second I saw you. If I didn't already like Drew, I would hate him." She bit down angrily on the last few words. Her lashes fluttered and her chin trembled. "Okay, so I might hate him a little bit right now."

Though Myka could never return her love, Anserlee still deserved a love of her own. In Pan, that was never going to be a possibility. "Are you sure there's no way for you to come with us?" Myka asked. "I'm not supposed to be able to escape, yet you figured out a way."

Anserlee glanced at the ceiling, blinking quickly, her eyes shiny. She stood up and propped her hands on her hips. "If only there was a way. But as of right now, I don't know of any, and I have never heard of any."

"But you also said there was no way for me to leave, or Drew, but you knew there was. How did you know?"

"I can't tell you that exactly, but I have long suspected there was a loophole. Obviously at some point in time, someone must've escaped, otherwise you and Drew would not exist. And if I ever find a way to escape, I promise, I will find you." She placed a long kiss on Myka's cheek before she pulled away.

Myka's heart sank, and guilt cloaked her shoulders.

"Uh-uh," Anserlee said. "I don't want to see you sad. I'm going to be fine."

Myka knew that to be a lie. But because Anserlee loved her, and loved Drew a little bit too, she'd lie to protect their hearts.

"What will they do to you when Drew escapes on your watch?"

"Nothing. He's not going to escape on my watch. I have everything figured out. You only need to trust me."

Myka did trust her. With her life.

Anserlee tried to hide a falling tear as she turned away to grab the smelly concoction off the table. "Now, I need you to drink this. It's not going to hurt. When you wake up, you will be in a small cave very close to where your kayak is. You need to rub the paste—"

"I know, I know," Myka said, setting her fingers over Anserlee's. "We've been over this part already. Like a million times." She stood up to her full height and leaned down to claim a tight hug. "I do love you, Anserlee. So very much, that I'm afraid words don't exist to describe my feelings. You're my angel. And I'll never forget you." Before she could chicken out, she pulled away and downed the disgusting drink.

The last things Myka remembered were Anserlee's bloodshot eyes with tears streaming down her face.

THIRTY-SIX
anserlee

Anserlee caught Myka's body before she could crash to the floor completely. She had known the potion would work fast, but she hadn't expected it to work quite that quickly. She prayed she'd mixed the right proportions for Myka's size. She'd gone over the formula a thousand times, and even though she was sure it was correct, it didn't stop her from worrying.

She laid her gently on the creaking wooden floor and sat down at the table, collecting herself while going over the schematics in her head. *Again.* The plan, which Drew had nicknamed their "Hail Mary," was now irrevocably in play.

After about an hour, she knelt next to Myka and placed her hand on her devastatingly frigid cheek. Her skin, always so warm, was now akin to cold, dead flesh. She felt for a pulse and was horrified and relieved not to feel one. It was all part of the plan, this being the most dangerous. But Myka had been warned again and again, and yet had still insisted that they go through with it. They really didn't have any other choice if Myka and Drew were to survive.

Once Anserlee was confident Myka was in a deep enough state to fool the Matriarchs, she picked up her flaccid body and flew her to the top floor of their tower. She stood in front of the owls with Myka dangling from her arms. Her head lolled without support and her long legs almost reached the floor.

"What do we have here?" One of the Matriarchs got up from her nest and poked Myka's arm like you would poke a dangerous snake with a stick.

"She's dead," Anserlee said quietly.

"How?" The Matriarch hesitantly touched Myka's skin. "Oh, she is very cold."

"I don't know, but I have my suspicions," Anserlee said through clenched teeth, determined to play the part of grieving avenger.

"Lay her down," one of the others said, getting up from her nest. She laid her hand on Myka's cheek, then lifted one of her arms and let it fall to the floor in a loud thunk.

Anserlee flinched.

"How do you know for sure she is dead?" the one still seated asked.

"She has no heartbeat, and she's not breathing." Anserlee attempted to sound respectful.

"Any other ways to tell?"

"Here, come look in her eyes." Anserlee lifted one of Myka's eyelids. "See?" She shaded Myka's pupil with the other hand then took it away to see if her eyes would dilate. "They're frozen." Myka's almost-black irises helped with that test.

"So she won't feel this then?" The three looked to one another then nodded in unison, only moments before the one closest to Myka pulled out a small knife and stabbed her in the leg.

Anserlee yelped, startled by the Matriarchs' actions. "What are you doing?" But Myka didn't move. Anserlee stared at the pearl knife-handle sticking out of Myka's thigh.

"Just making sure."

"What? Making sure she's dead? I assure you she is. But why in the Gods' names would you question that?" Anserlee crossed her arms to keep her heart where it belonged.

"Because Rave has been making quite a racket about your feelings for the humans," one said. "*Both* of them," all three said in tandem.

Anserlee gathered her composure with a deep breath. "Of course she is. She's the one I suspect of killing Myka, though I don't like making accusations without proof. If I were the three of you, I might question her motives with Drew also. Rave doesn't like to share."

Rave really didn't like to share, and Anserlee suspected she might try to kill Drew after she had him a few times. Though Anserlee wouldn't bring this to the Matriarchs' attention because she didn't want them sending out a raptor to follow Rave. The next part of her plan hinged on no witnesses.

"I realize you may have trust issues with me right now, but if you look at the facts, all those issues stem from the same Sirin. I know over the years she has caused this nest far more trouble than I ever have. Now, with your permission, I'm going to take Myka and give her a proper burial. Alone." Anserlee huffed before she picked Myka up and flew down the large hole in the floor.

As much as it pained her, she was thankful Rave and her

buddies had Drew this evening to keep them occupied. He was a strong man—both physically and emotionally. She didn't have to reach far to see why Myka loved him so deeply. She suspected she, too, had succumbed to the charms of the lead singer of Burning Brenda. After having spent so much time with him, it was hard not to. She was certain if anyone could survive with only a little damage—it was Drew. He would power through in order to keep Rave and her buddies busy so Anserlee could see Myka to safety.

Out in the open, it was much easier to fly with Myka in her arms than to walk. Wispy white clouds skated slowly across the sky, filtering the bright sun. Treetops swayed gently in the cool wind and calmed her angry, flushed skin. Very rarely did she make false accusations. Rave hadn't killed Myka, but she needed the Matriarchs to think she might have.

Currently, Rave and her minions were with Drew so the Matriarchs would wait until tomorrow morning to question her. That would allow Myka time to wake up and paddle to safety without being seen. She didn't worry about Rave's accomplices because they were lazy. Without Rave by their side to dictate their every move, and after their long night with Drew, they would sleep the day away.

She landed as gently as she could, which wasn't as graceful as she'd expected. Myka flew out of her arms like a rag doll and crashed onto the beach then rolled a few times. Anserlee's arms shook from the strain of the extra weight and her wings drooped, dragging on the ground. She hadn't realized how tired she was until she stopped. She brushed some sand and rocks off Myka's face before she picked her back up again. The knife surprisingly hadn't moved much— if anything, it was stuck deeper.

Myka was going to wonder what had happened to her while unconscious, and nobody would be there to explain how she'd gotten a stabbed leg, scraped face, and dirt in her hair. Anserlee hated to think about how much that leg was going to hurt when she woke up.

Beach pebbles crunched underfoot as she dodged the larger rocks, careful to not twist her ankle with the extra load. Water lapped onto the shore as the tide rolled in. The cave wasn't too far away, and Anserlee managed to get Myka there without dropping her again.

She placed her on the damp floor inside the cave. The evening sunlight penetrated the darkness enough for her to see. Water dripped from the ceiling, plopping soundlessly onto the wet sand. Quickly, she drew out the pearl-handled knife and let Myka bleed freely for a moment. She hadn't wanted to remove it in front of the Matriarchs because dead bodies didn't bleed like live ones did.

She took out the portable healing kit she carried and bound Myka's leg with herbs and a tight wrap. She tucked more bandage material in the supply pack that she'd left here earlier this week, along with the kayak. Then she hid the knife inside a small pocket of Myka's coat.

Anserlee dragged Myka's body to a cavern further back, leaving a smudged trail of sand behind, but she wasn't worried because the incoming tide would cover the tracks. She lifted Myka onto a high, wide shelf burrowed deep in the cave. She was confident that with tonight's weather forecast, the water would never make it that high. She crawled up after her and propped the pack under Myka's head. Then she hauled the kayak up and placed it between Myka and the edge of the shelf.

A fat tear rolled down her face. She hoped everything

would go according to the plan. She petted Myka's hair and kissed her lips one last time.

As she stood at the mouth of the cave, not looking back, she whispered, "The price of love is pain. And my dearest Myka, I'd pay it again, just to make sure you were safe."

THIRTY-SEVEN
drew

ater in the afternoon, Drew had a date with Anserlee and finally with freedom—no more unwanted nights doing unspeakable things. He'd just gotten back from an unescorted dip in the hot springs to wash off the filth that stained more than his skin. Those scars would take longer to heal. To keep away any unauthorized contact with their latest pet, the Matriarchs had assigned him two guards. In exchange for not touching him, they had been granted a free night on the first of the month.

They stood sentry outside his room.

Instead of pacing, like usual, he sat on the bed, absent-mindedly stroking the fur blanket. He had a feeling that years of therapy would not erase all the hell he'd been through in the last few weeks.

This morning, he'd heard the rumors of Myka's death, and while worry ate a hole in his stomach, Anserlee had promised him it wasn't true, but part of the plan. Myka was hidden and safe.

Just one more night. Just one more night, he kept repeating in his mind. He took comfort that his last night would be spent with Anserlee, and he wouldn't have to sleep with her. Though honestly, he would've rather slept with her than any of the others. His night with Gilda would haunt him for life, he was sure of it. He'd been afraid Rave and her groupies were going to be worse—which was setting the bar ultra-high but in comparison, they'd been mild.

Rough sex with a trio wasn't outside of his wheelhouse. To maintain a semblance of control, he'd done most everything Rave and her buddies had wanted without them singing.

Gilda was another story. At first, he'd tried to obey her commands without her using her voice, but eventually, they reached a point where he couldn't. He'd figured once he hit his breaking point, Gilda would be satisfied. He was wrong. Very wrong.

His stomach churned at the memory. But the worst part was, Myka had witnessed the entire scene. He could only hope she could get past the horrors that had taken place. What he went through was bad enough. He couldn't fathom being on the other side. Watching as someone hurt her? That would've been so much worse.

He ran his finger through his damp hair and pulled on his jeans when a short knock pounded on the door. In walked Anserlee, carrying a small quilted bag.

"Hey," he said, relieved that it was her. He didn't think he could tolerate anyone else.

"Hey," she replied after she shut the door. "We have a few things to go over before we leave."

"Anserlee, we've been over this a thousand times." He held his hand up as she started to protest. "We go on our *date*, dinner by the ocean, you make me drink some nasty shit, then I get in the kayak and I head to my left, find an old cabin on the beach, hang out there until the next night, then paddle back to help Myka escape. Correct?" he said, barely above a whisper. He was taking no chances of being overheard.

"Yes, that's right. But I have a letter with instructions in it that you'll need to follow once you get to the island. It is imperative. *Im-per-a-tive,*" she said, drawing the word out and using her index finger to gesture the importance of her words, "that you read it *only* then. If you read it before the proper time, you will be stuck here forever, and Myka and I will be put to death. And you'll wish for the same fate." She joined him on the bed and clutched his hand, patting it like someone older might do. "You might be tempted to read it sooner, but if you do—"

"I gotcha, Anserlee. I won't read it until I get to the island. You have my word."

She handed him a wad of cotton coated in something resembling beeswax. "Alright then. So long as I have made my point clear. Here, you will need to stuff these in your ears."

"What are they?"

"Filters, for lack of a better term. They're treated with a substance that will muffle our voices when we sing. These will help you resist should you hear our call. Whatever you do, don't take them out until you reach the island. You'll be far enough away once there."

"Do the Matriarchs know you know all of this?"

"Of course not. We healers like to keep our secrets." She smiled innocently, fluttering her long lashes.

He shuddered as he stuffed the filters into his ears. The sensation of cotton balls was his version of nails on a chalkboard and shivers spread along his arms. "Okay, now sing to me, Anserlee. I want to get accustomed to how they work."

She looked surprised and slightly offended.

"What?" he asked, raising a dark eyebrow. "I need to be prepared."

"Well, let's do it when we get outside. We might as well make it work for us. When we get out there, make a spectacle. When I start singing, I want you to comply, then as we get further from the nest, try to break away from my control." She shook her head and pursed her lips as if she did not approve.

"What?" Drew asked again, throwing on a tunic shirt.

"I don't like doing this. I made a promise to myself, and to you, that I would never sing to control you."

"Yeah, but I'm asking you to break that promise so I can be prepared if need be."

"Well, if everything goes according to plan, there will be no need."

And how often does everything go according to plan? he thought, noticing the stiff set of her shoulders and knotted muscles in her jaw. He set a hand on her shoulder and squeezed as they walked out the door, downstairs, and then outside.

Sirins milled about on the boardwalks above their heads. They peered down curiously over the side of the platform, making it sway precariously to one side. But that didn't matter so much when none of them would fall to their deaths—even though nothing would make him happier. So many beautiful, winged women and he wanted to smash their perfect heads. Excluding one.

He stopped and looked up at all the women. "I hate you

fucking freaks! Know this—I will never, of my own free will, fuck any of you!"

"Drew, knock it off!" Anserlee yelled. She was so tiny, wearing her little lace-up boots and stomping at him furiously while standing there with her hands on her hips, glaring up at him. Her hair blew around her face, getting stuck to her lips, and she had to spit it out. He almost laughed, and then he did because it would only help their charade.

"Drew, stop this, I don't want to sing to you. I want you to do this willingly."

"Never." He scowled down, towering over her. "I fucking hate you as much as I hate them." The venom in his tone was convincing, and she stepped back.

"Fine, you give me no choice then. I paid a lot of gold for you." She smiled and her gray eyes sparkled. She inhaled deeply, the front of her wool sweater straining under her breath, and she sang.

A form of ecstasy flooded his veins instantly and unhindered his conscious mind, the one that said, *maybe you should think about this first?* Only this was a new kind of ecstasy—a better one, a more addicting one. His mind numbed and his body tingled like little carbonated bubbles tickling every cell in his being. He felt light and carefree, with no worries, no problems.

Anserlee's voice was the sweetest yet, and he would deny her nothing. He imagined all the ways he would pleasure her and in turn pleasure himself. He hurried to follow her closer, desperate to reach out and touch the soft feathers on her angel wings. He wanted to stroke his hands over her flawless skin. His mouth ached, needing to kiss her perfect porcelain doll lips. But her song firmly prevented it. He was to follow and follow only.

She walked like a dancer, gracefully moving down the narrowing trail to the ocean. The afternoon sun shone through the thick trees, spattering her silvery hair with flecks of gold. His fingers twitched with the desire to run them through the long strands blowing in the breeze.

Then—something began to nag his subconscious, but he shoved it away, preferring the company of bliss. Until they hit the shore and a red kayak awaited him.

Images of a tall, curvy blonde slammed into his head painfully, like a hammer beating on the back of his skull. Her black eyes bore deep into his blue ones. Then memories of his lips all over her golden skin began to play. There...she was the nagging in the recesses of his mind; she was his reason to fight.

His eyes snapped fully open, and he stopped and studied the tiny woman in front of him. He no longer yearned for her as he had mere moments ago. He squinted his eyes and bowed his head, trying to concentrate through the heavenly voice in his ears. Urging him to forget Myka and let go...

She told him to come to her, to hold her, but he didn't want to. She was not his enemy, but she wasn't his lover. She insisted that he come to her. *Kiss her. Love her.* He took a tentative step forward then said, "*No!*"

His control snapped back with a sting like a rubber band.

"Anserlee! What are you doing?" he hollered.

"Shhhh, only what you asked me to," she said, hurrying to him. "You did it! It took you long enough." Lines between her eyes formed under her displeasure.

He clasped his hands in front of his lips in the prayer

position. Molten lava crept under his shirt, up his neck, and warmed his face as he remembered his desires.

"Hey, don't sweat it," she said with a finger in the air. "You will now have a better shot at resisting the others if the need arises. With me, you didn't have hate to fuel your emotions."

"Ugh!" he growled, shaking his head, trying to erase the embarrassing images. They made him feel weak and pathetic.

"I am not going to lie to you," Anserlee said. "I might've enjoyed the wicked images going through your mind. But the same as you, I like Myka more." She smiled.

"Bullshit. You love Myka, or you wouldn't be doing this."

"True," she said as she laid out a blanket on the rough sand. "Though I might have a tiny crush on you too." She patted a spot next to her and started taking food out of her bag. "I'd like to think that I would've taken an interest in you without Myka here, but the truth is, I wouldn't have. I never have before. I keep my head down and do my part for the community. I am ashamed of my complicity, though, I thought you should know. But the others are all half-souls, not a full soul like you. They wouldn't be able to integrate into society. They would be discovered, and that would be disastrous for not only us but humans also. So many of us live just on the outskirts of discovery all the time."

"What do you mean?" Drew polished an apple on his shirt as he sat down and took a huge bite. The fresh juice ran down his face, and he wiped it off with the back of his hand.

"Here." Anserlee laughed with a soft honking, giving him a cloth napkin. "I mean, humans at some point in time have seen us. Where do you think tales of angels came from? That was before we were trapped here."

"Oh," Drew said, completely at a loss for words. Horror, then acceptance, rolled through him. That's exactly what he'd thought the first time he saw them.

"Don't get me started on the Sea Sirens—they aren't locked up like we are. But their voices, while captivating, aren't capable of the complete control we wield. Plus, they can't create half-souls, they can just enthrall men. And usually, only the weak-minded of your species capitulate to their wishes."

"Shit! Are you for real?"

"Yes, I'm for real. You have to watch out for the Selkies and Bigfoot around here too."

"And werewolves and vampires?" He threw his apple core into the ocean. Seagulls jockeyed for positions, screaming at one another.

"Yes. I'm surprised you're questioning it after all you've seen. As for werewolves, we call them shapeshifters, and please be careful—there are a lot of them in Alaska. And I've heard of vampire-like creatures, but I have never seen one for myself. I believe they stick closer to Europe."

"Fuck me," Drew said, rubbing his hand along the back of his neck.

They sat quietly while Drew processed the impossible. Gentle waves caressed the shore, and a cool breeze carried the scent of seaweed, salt, and fish.

"Are those anyone we need to worry about?" He pointed at the seagulls, still arguing over the apple core.

"No, none of us here are seagulls. They lack the necessary brain power." They chuckled together. "Around here, we have a lot of birds of prey—owls, hawks, eagles, and so forth."

"And you're a goose," Drew said, pulling his knees to his chest and hugging his arms around them.

"Yes. I'm surprised you figured that out. Did Myka tell you?" She cocked her head to one side. These minor actions constantly reminded Drew that they were part bird, not fully human. They moved differently than humans—more graceful at times, but some of their movements were jerky, halted. It was as if they forgot, sometimes in their human form, that they had eyes on the front of their heads instead of on either side.

"No, but my mom is sort of a bird whisperer. Any injured birds in the immediate area are brought directly to her. She fixes up the ones she can, then releases them back into the wild. If they're too much for her skills, she takes them to the vet, then takes them home to recover. I grew up with birds everywhere. Once, we had a duck that would attack people on command. I tried naming him Pecker, but for some reason," Drew laughed, "unbeknownst to me at the time, my mother wouldn't allow it. She insisted on Mr. Peck. Hey," Drew held his hands up, "I was young."

It took a minute for Anserlee to stop full-on honk-laughing before she wiped the tears from her eyes and asked, "But how did you figure out what I was?"

"Seriously?" he said, pointing his nose down at her. "Your name is Anserlee. Anser is the genus for gray geese." He shrugged at her surprised expression. "My mom has a wall in her office dedicated to all the birds she's rescued. Pictures of them with their scientific names hang like wanted posters. Her favorite bird of all time is a Graylag goose. Cecilia, she still has her. Spoiled ass bird, doesn't really like anyone but my mom. We call her the guard goose, of course, among other things." Drew smirked.

"You know, I knew there was a reason I liked you so much!" She bumped his arm with her shoulder. "And now we know what side of the family your Sirin blood comes from." Anserlee handed him a slice of bread with butter. "Here, eat. You're going to need your strength."

Drew pulled the bread apart, and flakes from the crunchy crust scattered on his lap. He closed his eyes and savored the perfection. Besides Anserlee, this was the only thing he would miss.

"By the way, how do you get butter and milk here?"

"Well, you've heard of eagles attacking calves before, right?"

He nodded with his mouth full.

"Let's just say, not all of them are killed and eaten. We get all kinds of things that way. One time, one of the raptors brought back a small dog. She had it for about six years before it died."

They finished their meal in a comfortable silence, watching as the afternoon light rode the waves, only to be swallowed a second later in the ocean's black abyss.

"Well, it's probably time," Anserlee said, getting up from the blanket. She dusted off her hands and held them out to help Drew up. Tiny bits of cotton flew up in the cool breeze, then settled in the water, on the shore, and tangled in Anserlee's hair.

"You know, I'm going to miss you," he said, pulling her into a hug. He wrapped his arms around her and held tight. He petted her soft wings and kissed the top of her head. He breathed in deeply, never wanting to forget the smell of lavender and mint that clung to her at all times. "I have so much to say to you, but I just can't find the words. You'll always be my guardian angel. If you ever figure out a way to escape, find us. We will protect you. Out there, I can protect you."

Her head nodded into his chest. "Alright, into the kayak you go." She shoved him away and dried her tears. "Your rain gear and life jacket are right there. I packed you a bunch of things inside a waterproof sack and put it in the boat's compartment. Now, once you get through the barrier, paddle hard. I don't want there to be any chance of you hearing us sing. I'm going to change into a goose and escort you out beyond the barrier, but after that you're on your own."

Drew yanked the kayak over the gravel beach and pushed it into the water before he got in. Even now, with the sun below the earth, there was still enough light to see the island he needed to reach.

"Bottoms up." He tipped his head back to drink the potion Anserlee had given him earlier.

"I knew it!" came a screech from beyond the trees. "Get Anserlee! I will take care of him!" Out of the bramble, Rave flew toward them, leading her two cronies.

Anserlee stumbled backward, falling hard into Drew, knocking the invisibility potion out of his hands. Blue, smoking liquid soaked quickly into the wet sand and a small wave washed over the bladder before Drew could reach down to save it.

"Shit," he whispered, holding on to Anserlee. "What do we do now?"

"It's okay," Anserlee said under her breath. "You don't actually need the potion to escape through the barrier; it was just another measure of safety."

"Well, well, well, what do we have here?" Rave said. Her black hair swirled in the wind, slapping the two Sirins behind her. "The illustrious Anserlee helping our boy toy escape. I told the mothers not to trust you! I can't believe *they* didn't believe me."

Anserlee turned her back on the three Sirins stalking toward them and threw her arms around Drew. She pulled him close and whispered, "You have to kill Rave." He stiffened up. Her voice trembled, "If you don't, I will certainly die."

The thought of killing someone turned his stomach, but for Anserlee, he wouldn't question her orders. "Consider it done." Though he had no idea how.

Anserlee instructed, "Get her into the water and drown her. She can't swim. Then get out of here! I will take care of the others."

"Take her to the Matriarchs!" Rave shouted. "Don't kill her—I want to enjoy her silencing."

The two bronze-haired beasts grabbed Anserlee by each arm and began pulling her away. She ripped one arm out of their hands and turned back to Drew. She said nothing but just nodded before she walked away.

He knew what he had to do.

myka

The *tap tap tap* of water dripping on Myka's forehead, rolling down the side of her face, into her already-wet hair, woke her from the drug-induced death. She sat up in darkness to the sound of rolling waves splashing onto the side of the cave.

Anserlee had prepared her for the conditions she would wake up in. What she hadn't prepared her for was that even though she'd sat up and the water had stopped tapping on her forehead, her head hadn't stopped pounding. Myka's swollen tongue felt like sandpaper on the roof of her mouth, and she had a hard time swallowing. Except for her hair and face, she was dry, but due to all the moisture in the air, she shivered from the cold. She felt around for the pack beside her, but her coordination had yet to return. Between the numbness in her hands and the violent shivers, her dexterity was at an all-time low. Pins and needles shot up her limbs, but as the feeling returned to her legs, the pain became quite apparent. A spot on her left leg screamed in pain, throbbing with every beat of her heart. She reached down to find a bandage wrapped around the outside of her rain pants.

Of all that is holy, what happened to me while I was dead?

She rubbed her hands together, warming them enough to find her flashlight. She shone it inside the bag until she came upon the leather bladder containing the invisibility potion. Anserlee said she was to leave when the sun rose and the tide rolled out, which looked to be soon, judging by the faint haze of orange light feebly reaching inside the cave. She was to paddle as hard as she could and get to safety, wait for three full days, then come back to rescue Drew. With the pain in her leg, she wasn't sure how she was going to get into the kayak, let alone come back. *Baby steps,* she told herself. She would do this for him. One step at a time.

She opened the potion and gritted her teeth through the pain as she rubbed it all over the top of her kayak and clothes. Even though she was freezing, sweat poured from her clammy skin. She breathed deeply, trying to concentrate on the task.

Plugging her nose, she took a long swig of the stinky liquid, swallowed hard, then downed the rest without stopping.

She pushed the kayak off the edge of the cave shelf, and it landed with a splat on the wet sand. She threw down the rest of her gear and hopped off, landing on her good leg. The jarring impact stole her breath away. It couldn't be worse than childbirth, right? If millions of women could go through that and not die, she was going to survive this.

She dragged the plastic boat, limp by limp, to the opening of the cave and slid it into the water before slowly hopping in. Not once did she look at her leg. What she didn't know definitely hurt.

The *thump, thump, thump* of pain did not stop as she paddled, but it did subside slightly. The early-rising sun crept over the mountains, outlining the dense tree line in its warm glow. Gentle waves rose, then hung for a few seconds before they fell off into the quiet ocean.

By all standards, it was a calm, peaceful morning, but a barely contained panic strained at every nerve fiber in her system. Every splash from jumping salmon sent her into fight or flight. She didn't calm down until she saw the glistening of the morning sun reflecting off black seal fur. Her little head popped above the water a few feet from her kayak. Though she didn't know if it was *her* seal, or just another seal, Myka took comfort in her presence. Her dark eyes seemed so human, so comforting. She jetted toward the island like she knew where Myka was headed, so she followed. Myka could hear the static from the bubble barrier long before she could see its oily, shimmering skin. Her hair, longer now, began to rise away from her head, responding to the electricity in the air. Her paranoia increased, and she felt like eyes were upon her even though Anserlee had promised no one would be looking for her.

She was dead.

The second she passed through, her hair fell and everything became clearer. A calmness eased the tension corseting her ribs, like now that she'd broken through to the other side, they couldn't hurt her anymore. But that was far from the truth. They still had Drew and Anserlee. They could inflict far worse than physical pain.

Birds darted in and out of the sea. Anserlee had told her that the ocean birds were safe. None of them were Sirins. Plus, she and her kayak were invisible, laying down another layer of safety. Somewhere far, far above, she could hear a jet engine whine.

Tears streamed down her face as she paddled furiously. She was almost there. But Drew would not be waiting for her on the island, and she would have to return to Pan. Dread curled in her chest. Getting in that kayak to go back would be one of the hardest things she'd ever do. Maybe after a few nights, she would have the strength she needed. And even if she didn't, she'd go back anyway.

She made it safely to the island, and with every hurdle she accomplished, a small weight lifted from her shoulders. After pulling the kayak out of the water, she waved to the seal, and again, the seal waved back with a flipper. She shook her head wondering if maybe her seal had escaped captivity, or if Myka was so lonely she was assigning human actions to something that was perfectly normal for a wild seal. She dragged the kayak over the rocks and stuffed it behind the tree line, covering it with old brush and logs. Once satisfied it was hidden from prying eyes, she limped down to the shore, scanning for the seal. Not finding her friend, she let out a deep breath of disappointment. She missed her company already. She wished she had asked Anserlee if there were other creatures lurking in the world, living on the outskirts of society.

Anserlee had said the Sirins wouldn't be looking for her, but she decided to be cautious anyway. She stumbled back to the original shack she'd stayed in and passed out.

AFTER A FEW HOURS' NAP, SHE HOBBLED AROUND TO THE OTHER side of the island. In just a week since she'd last been here, the trees had turned from green to gold and orange, gilding the mountainside in fall colors. Leaves rained down, landing gently along the tree line. She pulled her hands inside the cuffs of her sweatshirt to ward off the brutal chill in the air.

She found a nice, sheltered cove with a fresh water stream where she could have a fire and not be in a direct line of sight of the Sirins. Because they thought she was dead, she should be okay, but her paranoia wasn't completely satisfied.

As she gathered rocks for her firepit, her heart kicked at every sound, from splashing in the water to birds cawing above. She filled her leather canteen in the stream, dug through the pack for the small pot, and put the water over the cozy fire she'd started. While waiting for it to boil, she rewrapped her injured leg. Due to Anserlee's expert knowledge of herbs, the injury seemed like it was doing well. Once satisfied the water was safe to drink, she poured herself a cup of tea and snuggled down into the sand.

She pulled the letter Anserlee had left her, the one she was not supposed to open until after she was safely past the barrier, from her pocket. Late-afternoon light painted the rough paper in sepia tones. She loosened the wax seal with her fingernail and unfolded it.

The beautiful cursive lettering echoed in her head as she imagined Anserlee's voice reading the words.

MY DEAREST MYKA,

If you're reading this, you're safe, and I need you to stay that way. I'm in the process of getting Drew out of Pan, which I can see *now isn't much of a paradise if you are human. No matter what happens, you are never to come back here. Yes, read that line again. <u>Never</u>. The only way I got you through the barrier was because of your intense desire to return and save Drew. That is the loophole I discovered thanks to the King of Rock 'n' Roll. He likes to disappear from his life with the Sirins, only to return of his own free will later. He gets out because he doesn't want to leave forever. That's why I couldn't tell you and Drew—because if you knew the truth, my plan wouldn't work.*

At this point in time, Drew is under the same instructions you were—paddle out and return later. He carries a letter of his own. He should be only a day behind you. If for some reason we fail, (stop panicking and keep reading), you must leave your little island. But <u>Do Not</u> come back here. I will get him out. I promise. Build a huge fire and someone will rescue you. I know you well enough to know, right now, you are arguing with me, but you know I'm right. If you come back here, you will die, as will I. I am willing to sacrifice my life for yours, but the question is, are you willing to sacrifice mine for his? The Gods willing, we will never have to find out.

You are the greatest gift I have ever known. My perception of life has forever been altered—again, a gift from you and a gift from Drew. I will love you to the end of time. My heart is yours, yours is his, and both of yours are mine.

Love always,

Anserlee

SADNESS AND RELIEF SWIRLED TOGETHER IN AN EDDY OF EMOTIONS. No questions asked, she would've gone back for Drew despite the dangers, but thanks to Anserlee, she didn't have to. Myka's chin quivered, and tears dripped from her face onto the ink, smearing the words.

But not going back meant she would never see Anserlee again.

With the cuff of her sleeve, she dabbed softly at the tears on the page. Carefully, she folded the letter, the only physical reminder she would ever have of her friend, before storing it in the envelope for safekeeping.

THIRTY-NINE

drew

Drew stood calf deep in the ocean, holding on to his kayak as he watched Rave's two cronies escort Anserlee away. He didn't know for sure where they were taking her, but if he had to guess, it would be directly to the Matriarchs to tattle on them. And that would be a death sentence to Anserlee. There was no way he was going to allow that to happen. He'd never killed anyone before, and in his wildest dreams, he'd never thought he would have to, but if it came down to Myka's life, Anserlee's life, and his own, he'd do what he had to. Which, according to Anserlee, was to kill Rave.

"Hey, soldier, looks like it's just you and me now," Rave said in her deep, throaty voice with a sultry dark eyebrow raised. "Let's up the game from the other night. I don't really like to share, but that was the only way I was going to get you...until this opportunity presented itself. Luck be a lady."

Drew said nothing. He would not play a part until she sang.

"Hmmm, no love for Rave? You know I can change that,

right? You sure seemed to like it the other night." She advanced slowly, her hips rolling seductively. The late-afternoon light shimmered on her wings, reflecting black, then deep green to navy blue. Her lips stood out like slashes of blood against her pale skin, and what he'd once thought was beautiful now looked like a pin-up nightmare.

"I would rather we did this the old-fashioned way. But"—she raised her hands in the air like a white flag—"it's your choice."

"You know I'll never do this willingly," Drew said. "Besides, the Matriarchs will come looking for you as soon as your goons deliver Anserlee to them."

"Oh, you see, I've planned for just that. My goons, who are red-tailed hawks and some of the most efficient predators on earth, have taken her straight to prison; they will do nothing, and tell no one, until I'm done with you. And ohhh, the plans I have for you," she said, stopping only a few feet away from him at the shoreline.

He had to bide his time and not play his hand until the last possible moment.

"Come." She beckoned him with a finger. She wasn't singing to him, only asking him. She really did want to do this the old-fashioned way.

He stepped back and folded his arms.

"That's how it's going to be? Don't you remember last night? I'm sure you do. I do," she said, chewing on her bottom lip.

A song slipped quietly from her; the pull wasn't there but the words were. Usually, it was the opposite. Like he knew what to do, and he didn't have to be told. Not this time. Now he could hear her commands amongst the melody.

"Come," was all she said.

So he did. He started forward, pulling his kayak with him. He didn't want to let it go because it was his ticket out of here.

He stalked up to her, pushing her back one step at a time, pressuring her away from the water. He stared down from his towering height and did his best impression of a heroin high. Not that he would actually know how that felt because he never touched the hard stuff. But he'd witnessed enough of it.

"Kisssss..." she commanded, sounding more like the snake she was than a bird.

He closed his eyes and conjured Anserlee's face. Not Myka's—he couldn't do that. But Anserlee wouldn't mind. Both were tiny with huge wings and if he could keep his eyes closed the whole time, he might succeed.

He leaned in slowly and brushed her lips softly with his.

She shuddered and caught her breath. "Again, again," she chanted.

Softly, gently, he licked her bottom lip and sucked on it as he pulled away. Her hands found his hard chest and worked their way under his shirt then down into the pockets of his pants. When she grabbed hold of the letter Anserlee had tucked away, he jerked but quickly composed himself. He nuzzled her neck even though she hadn't commanded it. It didn't seem to matter to her. She tilted her head for easier access. He clenched his teeth, trying not to gag from her scent. She smelled eerily like the chicken coop his mother had made him clean when he misbehaved as a kid. No time-outs or spankings for him. Only good old-fashioned manual labor. He'd never regretted it—that hard work had helped him become the man he was.

He stopped breathing through his nose and kissed her neck, cold from the Alaskan air, and then made a path all the way to her earlobe.

"What is this?" she asked, remembering she had something in her hand.

Drew tried to play cool. "A letter," he whispered in her ear, flicking her earlobe with his tongue.

"Stop," she sang.

He did as he was told, but not because he actually wanted to. He couldn't let her have that letter. According to Anserlee, it would condemn them both.

"Do we have to?" he growled. "I want you. I'm going to rock your world." He knew from the last night, she particularly enjoyed corny sayings like you might see in a porn film. Cheesy *bow-chicka-bow-wow* music played in his head while her tune played in his ears.

Her eyes closed as she took a deep breath. "Don't worry, soldier, we have all night." She opened the wax seal with a sharp fingernail. He went to reach for it, but she ducked out of his way so quickly he barely saw it happen. "No, no, big boy, I want to see this." She wagged her finger at him.

She wasn't singing, so he dashed toward her, grabbing at the letter.

"Must be terribly important to you. This is going to be fun." She spread her wings and lifted off the ground, out of Drew's reach. She took her time unfolding it, obviously enjoying the frustration he couldn't hide.

"Give me the letter, Rave, or I won't give you what you want," Drew said, glaring up at her.

"Oh, you're so cute down there. Like you have a choice." She laughed.

Wind from her wings fluttered over his face as she hovered out of arm's reach.

"You might be surprised, Rave. Now give me the fucking letter!" Drew yelled, knowing it wasn't going to help.

She tilted her head back and gurgled with glee. "Oh, this is fun, watching you struggle. You're completely at my will. And what's even more entertaining is that you already know that." She began to read. "This is good, so good," she mumbled as she scanned the letter. "Your turn." Her smile verged on maniacal.

"No!" he shouted, plugging his ears and shoving the cotton deeper inside.

"Don't be stupid, that doesn't work." And she sang. "Take your fingers out of your ears and listen."

Drew stood immobile on the ground, frozen in panic. Anserlee had told him the plan would fail if he knew the contents of the letter—but if he gave away his secret, Rave would know her voice no longer worked on him. His heart hammered against his rib cage.

He had two choices, neither good. Get the letter, get off the island, and leave Rave alive which would guarantee Anserlee's death. Or pretend longer, get Rave in the water, kill her, and figure out another way off the island.

Though his initial reaction was to run to Myka at any cost, she was off the island and safe, whereas Anserlee was sure to die if he let Rave live. He couldn't, in good conscience, let her sacrifice be wasted. He took his hands away from his ears. He would find another way off this hellhole.

"'My dearest Drew,'" Rave began reading with a fair amount of drama in her voice. "'If my plan has worked, you're safe with Myka on the other island. The only way through our protective barrier is to want to return. It only keeps you here if you want to escape forever. I needed you to think Myka was still here so you would come back to save her. That's why I couldn't tell you about the plan—if you knew, it wouldn't work. When you arrive on the other island, Myka is waiting for you on the far side. I checked just to be sure she was safe. You never need to come back! You are free, my dear friend. In all our time together, I've come to know what an incredible man you are, and I am going to miss you so very much. Take care of Myka, make her happy. That is my wish. Love always, Anserlee.'" Rave's cackle floated in the air, echoing off the mountains. "This is rich," she said. "This letter has everything in it I need to convict Anserlee and to finish off Myka."

"Myka's safe—you read it yourself." So long as he knew Myka was out there safe, waiting for him, he could go on. He would find another way out. But first, he had a job to do— one that he was starting to look forward to. If someone had ever said that he'd have the desire to kill a person, especially a woman, he would've laughed. Violence had never come naturally to him even though he loved martial arts. But anyone who practiced knew it was about controlling oneself, not harming others. Though thanks to his years of study, he had the tools he needed.

"She's not safe yet. Not until she is far from here."

"Yes, she is. You know it, and I know it. Off this island, all you are is a fucking bird. A fucking crow, to boot. And even if you order your goons to help, seriously, they're only hawks."

"You're right, with only the three of us, we would be useless. But with this letter, I have the proof I need to dispatch our militia. And I don't know if you've seen Gilda in her raptor form, but it's impressive. Even more so than with her whips and chains." Rave glided to the ground, setting down out of arm's reach. "She has an army of birds."

He felt the blood drain from his face and a sheen of sweat bead on his skin. Gilda frightened him no matter what form she was in.

"If you've never seen a golden eagle up close, get ready for a treat. Their talons are the size of my hand, and their beaks are made for ripping flesh. First, she plucks out the eyes, then the tongue, and after that, she goes for the belly, flaying the innards. And Gilda is particularly brutal. Oh, but you know that already, don't you?" she said, sounding sorry, but not.

He hung his head, pretending to wallow in shame. Somehow, he needed her to refocus without it seeming obvious. None of those horrible things would happen if he could just get her in the water and kill her.

"Ohhhh, you poor boy. Checking out, are you? We have better things to do anyway. Come here and show me what you got," she challenged.

Drew raised his eyes in defiance. He needed her to sing —to believe she was in charge. His guts twisted, and he hoped his acting skills were up to par.

"Come to me," she sang. "Love me all night. Do to me what you would do to the one you love."

Slowly, he took a step toward her, then another, never taking his eyes off her. He reached out and touched her bottom lip, dragging his finger lightly over her sensitive flesh. A tiny moan escaped from her. He cupped her cheek in his large hands and brushed a piece of wayward hair off her forehead, tucking it behind her ear. His hands pretended to memorize the contours of her face, touching her skin gently, skimming lightly to her neck. The tie at the front of her linen gown pulled apart easily, revealing her large breasts.

He shut down his emotions as best he could. One step at a time, he walked around Rave as she stood frozen, her breath escaping in short bursts. He dragged her hair over her shoulder, then maneuvered between her dark wings. They trembled beneath his touch. He kissed the exposed skin of her neck and growled deep in his throat before he bit her hard enough to make her gasp.

He plucked a feather from her wing, causing her to yelp, but he knew she liked a little pain with her pleasure. Back around front, he took her gown between his hands and gradually ripped the fabric down the middle, exposing her lusciously curvy body that made him want to puke.

"Take it off," he said.

She wiggled out of her destroyed gown. It fell to her feet, leaving her only in brown leather boots. With her own feather, because touching her cramped his stomach, he ran it over her skin, over her erect nipples, between her legs, causing little whimpers of pleasure. He dropped the feather in the water and watched as the tide pulled it away. He yanked his shirt over his head and closed his eyes when she bit her lower lip.

Finally, wanting to get this over with, he leaned in and kissed her panting mouth, hard, rough, scraping teeth, biting lips. All of his anger and disgust poured into that one kiss, and she loved it. He picked her up, and she wrapped her naked legs around him, her pussy hot, wet, and repulsive against his abs. He began to slowly back into the water.

Her head popped up out of the kiss when a wave hit her wing tips. "What are you doing? Stop!"

He did. "I've never taken anyone in the water. Can't you

be my first?" he asked, boring his eyes into hers. Let her confuse his hate with passion.

"I don't like water," she said hesitantly.

"Oh, yeah! That'll be even more fun. What's sex without a little danger?" he asked, not moving before he had permission. She needed to believe she was in control. He gripped her hair tightly and squeezed her ass. He was so close to where he needed her. "Please," he begged in a whisper.

She thought for a few beats before nodding.

He smiled at her hungrily, not for her pleasure but at her demise.

He backed up slowly, one step at a time. Even with adrenaline pumping through his system, he needed to do this quickly. The Alaskan water was so damn cold, he was losing feeling in his legs.

"Not too deep," she stuttered. It was the first time he'd ever seen her nervous.

"Oh, baby, I'm going to fuck you so deep, my dick is going to come out your throat," he growled into her ear. She noticeably relaxed in his arms. "I'm going to make you come harder than the crashing waves." He felt dirty, sick, and perverse.

Before he had time to think about what he was going to do next, he pulled her in tight and reached around, pinning her wings. His grip firm, he dove straight into the frigid water. The cold hit him like a punch to the face, but he held on with all his strength to the struggling woman in his arms. He knew from experience how strong these women were so he needed to get her in the water where she couldn't touch the bottom. He kicked with everything he had until they were well away from the shore.

She fought, kicking and punching, and even with the

water buffering her blows, they still found their mark. Because of the cold, he barely felt her nails digging into his skin, ripping his flesh. She tried holding on to him as he pushed her away, farther out into the ocean, with his long arms. He backed off, treading water and feeling sick as she screamed for help. Begging him to save her. And almost looking surprised that he didn't. Her arms flapped wildly in the ocean, and she choked and sputtered on salt water. Her wings, which gave her an advantage in the air, did nothing to help her once she was waterlogged.

Ravens were not made to swim.

Getting as close as he dared, he grabbed the end of her long hair and held her under until she stopped struggling. Then he held her under for another minute, the longest minute of his life, just to be sure she was dead.

Tears poured from his eyes, mixing with the cold ocean, as he swam for shore. He dragged her lifeless body onto the beach, pulling her over the rough rocks, well out of the way of the ocean's tide. He stood there shivering violently.

Her lips, once so red and vibrant, were now gray-blue. They contrasted morbidly against her pale skin. Her dark, open eyes stared vacantly through hair that stuck to her face and wrapped around her neck like strands of seaweed trying to strangle her.

Drew leaned over and vomited until there was nothing left, before falling to his knees and dry-heaving for good measure. When he turned back around, she was no longer human but in her true form, a black raven, so much larger than he would have guessed.

FORTY

drew

The setting sun brandished the sky in corals, pinks, and purples. The mountains in the distance glowed with a rosy blush. Drew built a fire and plucked another feather from Rave's dead body before he delicately laid her on the red-hot flames. Charring feathers made him gag again, but there was nothing left to vomit.

He was empty inside, physically and spiritually void. He would keep her feather with him forever to remind himself of the irreparable damage murder did to your soul. Even though he'd done it to protect those he loved, he was terrified he would never grant himself forgiveness. But if that was the price he had to pay to keep Myka and Anserlee safe, so be it. He'd live with that burden, along with all the other ones he'd racked up on this hellhole.

By the firelight, he reread Anserlee's letter. Once he finished, he placed it into the flames to burn the evidence. He didn't know how long he sat there staring, crying, but not feeling any pain, as he rubbed that lone black feather back and forth across his hand.

Finally, he tucked it into his pocket. Not knowing what else to do, he got into his kayak. If the letter was right, he wouldn't be able to get through, but he had to try.

As he paddled out, he chanted in his head that he was coming back for Anserlee after he got Myka out of Alaska for good. But it didn't work. The oily barrier recognized his lie and pushed back every time he tried blowing through.

Drew floated around aimlessly for hours. It wasn't like he could be washed into the open ocean. The constant rocking of the boat almost lured him to sleep. Despite his mind reeling, his body was exhausted. The deep, bloody fingernail scratches in his skin began to sting now that the adrenaline had worn off, and he could see bruises in the shape of small hands starting to form.

His heart kicked when something hit the side of the hard-plastic boat.

"What the fuck," he sputtered, jolting awake.

On the other side of his kayak, a shiny head with large eyes stared at him. Moonlight reflected in their glossy orbs.

"Oh, thank God!" he sighed. "Hey, little one, I've had a rough day. How about you?"

Her head nodded up and down, splashing water.

Drew shook his head quizzically; he needed some sleep. "Did you just answer me?"

The seal did it again, then started to swim for shore. He turned his head and watched her go, sad to lose the only company he had.

He was surprised when she turned and barked at him.

"You're cute," he said. "But you're a seal. I don't know how you're going to help me." He laughed, thankful for the moment of reprieve from his guilt.

She barked again, louder this time, and slapped the water with a flipper.

"You're just a... Wait... And they're just birds..." he said, pausing, questioning everything he should know. He remembered Anserlee had said there were far more beings in the great wide world than humans.

He turned his kayak and followed the seal back to the island. Once onshore, he climbed out of the boat, pulling it away from the incoming tide.

She stopped in front of an old, washed-up log and looked up at Drew, then down at the log, up again, then down.

"Do you want me to sit?"

She nodded and barked.

"Fuck, I'm losing my mind," he said as he capitulated, propping his elbows to his knees and placing his head in his hands. "I hate this place."

"As do I," came a voice with a Celtic lilt from behind him.

Drew shot up off the log and stumbled backward. His nerves were not going to take much more of this.

Out of the trees walked the most beautiful creature he'd ever seen—and that was saying a lot after being stranded on an island with Sirins, even if he hated all but one.

Her long black hair hung over the front of her shoulders, brushing her kneecaps. Her skin flashed slightly like the inside of an abalone shell rotating in the light. A smile tugged at the corners of her perfect pink lips, exposing a set of tiny fangs, and lit up her round ebony eyes. She obviously wasn't human but something more. Over one arm, she carried what looked like a blanket. She held up her other hand, long, delicate fingers extended, and said, "Don't be afraid. I'm here to help."

"To tell you the truth, I'm too tired to be that afraid," Drew admitted, trying to control the shaking of his hands, not from fear, but bone-deep exhaustion.

"Yes, I suppose you should be. But even though you are, we must hurry. Eventually, someone is going to come looking for you." Long legs led to bare feet that seemed to crunch painlessly over the sharp rocks as she ventured closer. She grabbed his kayak and started dragging it up the shore. When she stopped in front of him, she tossed his waterproof bag at his feet.

"Hurry where? I can't leave here. For now, I'm a prisoner."

"With my help, you can escape. I can get you to the island where your pretty lassie waits."

He sat up straighter. "You mean Myka? How do you know all of this? And what are you and why do you want to help me? And where are you taking my kayak? I'm gonna need that," he interrogated.

"Relax. I'm hiding it so they can't find it." She gave the boat a hard shove, sliding it into the forest as the bushes trembled under the force. She returned her attention to him and brushed off her hands. "Helping you escape grants me vengeance." She stretched out to her full height with her chin tilted regally. "Let's just say they took my love from me. And I can take you from them."

He cocked his head cautiously toward her. That didn't sound good, but a quick death would be preferable to his other option.

"Not like that! I can help you escape. You are as much like me as you are like them. Didn't they tell you that you and your girl should not like each other, let alone love one another? You should be polar opposites. Like magnets that repel."

He nodded.

"It is because you, Andrew Arie, are also part Selkie. You are one of a kind, as far as I know. Your Selkie blood negates, or more like balances your Sirin blood." Her mouth turned down into a sad frown.

"Excuse me," Drew interrupted. "What's a Selkie?"

"I'm a Selkie—half human, half seal. I'm Eislyn. But if you want to get out of here, we need to do it now. I fear they are coming!"

"Okay, okay. How?" he said, throwing caution to the wind, suspecting he was hallucinating.

"Get undressed. All of it. Toss your wet clothes and shoes into the bushes, and then put this on. It was my husband's pelt, and with it, you'll be able to pass through the barrier. For it will no longer recognize that you're human." She handed him the heavy fur blanket she carried with her. "Just wrap it around your shoulders and follow me."

Desperation urged him to follow her insane directions without question. He threw the blanket over his shoulders and instantly warmed up as if he'd stepped into a sauna. "Now what?" He wondered how a blanket was going to help in this situation. Though it was quite toasty.

But instead, his question came out as something akin to a seal's bark. *Hmmm.* "What the fuck?" he said, freaking out. Again, it came out as a bark, except at a much higher octave this time.

"Relax," he heard a voice in his head. "At least this way, no one will know who you are. Now look up."

A dozen or so large raptors started circling in the air

above them. Moonlight reflected on the golden feathers of the largest bird. Drew knew there was no mistaking who that was. Her wings must have spanned a good eight feet, and he could see her sharp, black talons clearly with his new, much sharper vision. Deeper-seated than a mere human instinct, fear stabbed under his skin urging him to run.

"Come. We must go," Eislyn said.

He ripped his gaze from the sky to find her back in her seal form. Though she looked different, her eyes remained the same.

Her whiskers twitched as she nudged his neck with her nose. "They'll be no danger to us in the water, but here on land, we are free game, and she prefers her meat raw."

Drew took his first steps, difficult with only flippers, and landed on his snout. He sneezed in the sand.

"Shift your weight to the front," she instructed. "Now hurry." She grabbed his waterproof sack in her teeth and carried it into the water as he followed.

The abyss swallowed them easily. He was surprised at how clear his vision was under the surface. What was so dense and absolute from above was murky and green but visible below. He stayed by her side as they got close to the living bubble that protected this island from the rest of the world. *Or protects us from them*, he thought.

"You're right," he heard her say in his head.

"Huh?"

"You're right. That bubble ahead protects you. Otherwise, Sirins would rule the world. The only people who could stop them would be other women, because they're not affected by the Sirins' song."

Drew tensed up, expecting his head to bounce off the

shiny oil barrier, but instead, he passed through it like it wasn't even there.

"Good thing they can only leave in their bird forms then."

He rose out of the ocean to take a breath. While walking in this body was cumbersome, swimming was exhilarating. He cut through the cold waters like a torpedo. Salmon and other fish veered out of his way as he shot through the air and dove back into the water, twisting and twirling with unwavering amounts of energy. Once he had burned off some steam, he slowed down and swam alongside her.

"So, what's your story? You seem to know mine," he asked in his mind.

"Oh, mine is so very similar to yours, except yours has a happy ending," she said.

He could feel the sorrow in her words cut like a knife through his heart.

"Centuries ago, my love, Ronan, and I came to shore on this island to celebrate our union. We knew to watch out for these creatures, but we didn't know about this island and these Sirins," she said, as if admonishing herself for not knowing better. "They sang for him, and he followed. Even though we're supernatural, when our men are in their human forms, the Sirins' song can easily lure them."

"Centuries ago?"

"Yes."

At this point, why did things surprise him?

Visions of Eislyn and Ronan's last moments together flashed through Drew's mind like he was watching a movie trailer. Empathy curled in his heart. The pain she carried seemed fresh and raw. A wound that had never healed.

Though distraught, she continued. "At first, they didn't realize he was a Selkie. We're naturally stronger than humans and our resistance to the Sirins' song diminishes after a while. So after they got what they wanted, they killed him and left him on the shore for me to find."

Again, as if watching it through her eyes, he witnessed images of Ronan lying dead on the shore. A narrow but deep slit ran from one side of his neck to the other. Dried blood stained his pale skin all the way down his long legs to the tips of his feet.

"Good God, I'm so sorry." He wondered how she did it, how she went on.

"Thank you. I feel your pain for me. But I go on because I want my revenge," she growled angrily. "I deserve it. For so long, all I've wanted to do was kill them, but there's only one of me and so many of them. So I bid my time, and I wait."

"Are you saying, everything I feel and think, you know?"

"Yes, and I must tell you, helping you feels so much better than killing. I know, because I can feel your misery. Your very being is tainted with what you think was murder. But you are wrong. That was self-defense, not murder. Sometimes in the supernatural kingdom, or anywhere, for that matter, it's kill or be killed."

He didn't disagree, but he wasn't used to living by those rules.

She chuckled, but didn't comment on his thoughts. "You are now forever part of my world. You shall walk in this life a human, but know that you are family."

Rocks and sand along the sea floor became visible as they got closer to the shore. Drew's throat tightened with emotions, but neither could he project exactly what he was feeling any more than he could speak the words out loud.

"Now go, Andrew Arie. Son of my heart's blood. You are free to be with your love."

"What are you going to do now? Now that you have avenged Ronan?"

"The same thing I have been doing for more years than I can count—saving the baby boys that the Sirins leave out as sacrifices to die in the woods. Your kayak is going to make that so much simpler."

"Huh. That solves the mystery of how some of us got here, doesn't it?"

"Yes. But I believe there are more of us supernaturals helping. No community approves of what the Sirins do—not to the men so much, but to the babies. What kind of monsters do that?"

"I don't know where to begin or how to thank you."

"I know. I feel your heart."

When he was within standing distance of the shore, all it took was a wish, and the seal skin dropped away from his body, leaving him naked. And cold. His limbs felt awkward and useless in the water.

"Now wrap the skin around me and go." She let go of his bag and pushed it toward him with her nose. "Oh, and stay away from the Caribbean. Hawaii is safe, as are Fuji and Tahiti." A laugh tickled the back of his mind like wind-chimes in the distance.

He could still hear her inside his head, though he was human again. He draped the pelt over her back, and it disappeared, becoming her own. She bowed her head in thanks before she dove away.

"Goodbye! And thank you!" he yelled, the words thick on his tongue.

"Always, son of my heart's blood. Always," a whisper formed like a memory.

He grabbed his bag from the water and walked onto the shore, rolling her final words around in his head. *Son of my heart's blood.* Was he?

Myka gimped, pacing aimlessly along the cold, gray shoreline. The moon, high in the sky, cast its eerie light over the bleak, dreary scene. Though it was the end of August, no rain had fallen in the last couple of days, but that didn't make her feel any better. If there had been rain, she might have taken off her dirty, stinky clothes and danced naked in its downpour.

The sheer mind-wrenching anxiety building up in her head was about to break free. Anserlee had said within a day. It had been a day, and she was going stir-crazy, inventing one disturbing scenario after another. And if he didn't show up, she wasn't sure she'd be able to leave. Though she knew she had to for Anserlee's sake. Her heartbeat lagged.

If they hadn't killed her friend already, they would certainly do so if Myka showed back up on that island alive. How would she ever know what happened to her? She imagined the possibilities, none of them pleasant.

Being on Pan had violently opened her eyes to all the

things she didn't know. Or had been too blind to see. It wasn't like there hadn't been sightings of all kinds of strange things, stories that were so far-fetched no one believed, because if they did, they were labeled crazy, stupid, freaks, and liars.

If she were lucky enough to be rescued, she would have to come up with something more plausible. Like pirates. Because, of course, that was easier to believe. At least she had the limp, but she'd be damned if she ever got a fucking parrot. She was afraid her outlook on most birds was forever altered.

She went back into the woods to search for dry wood, but not too far, since it was still dark. She didn't like spending any time in the thick forest. The mosquitoes were huge and voracious, and she didn't have any bug repellent. On the shoreline, the constant breeze kept them at bay. Plus, she now questioned *what* or *who* could be in those woods.

She'd slept most of the day, which she'd needed. Her leg felt better after the rest. She'd taken a peek under the bandage earlier and it seemed fine—not red or hot, though it still ached. So now, she was not tired, but instead, uncomfortably restless. She almost missed the pain because the physical discomfort had kept her mind occupied. Her stomach growled but she couldn't bear to choke down another nut-berry bar. Besides, food wasn't always staying put, and she didn't want to waste it. She didn't know how much longer she'd be stuck there.

She walked down the slope to the rocky beach with her arms full of damp wood. Did nothing ever dry out in this blasted state? But the fire was still going strong thanks to packing matches in plastic bags and Anserlee sending dry moss.

She would always be Myka's guardian angel. Tears welled up in her eyes every time she thought of her. Myka looked up, trying to keep the darn things from flowing over, only to see something big and blurry lumbering toward her about a hundred yards down the beach.

Bear! Shit... *No. Moose!* Wait? *I'm on an island*, raced through her head. What were the chances of a bear or moose being out here? She willed her heart to slow down. She'd not seen signs of either. She had grown up in upstate New York, where both species lived.

She wiped her eyes, clearing away her tears so she could see better.

She blinked hard not trusting her vision because it wasn't an animal walking on the shore. It was a human. "Drew?" A whisper escaped from her throat. "Drew?" she screamed.

His head came up and he raised his hands high and waved.

Her heart squeezed and air rushed from her lungs. She dropped the stack of wood and ran as fast as her limping leg allowed.

A long thirty seconds later, she crashed into his outstretched embrace. They hung on to each other for dear life, sobbing.

She stood back and looked into the face of the man she loved, making sure he was really there. Then he collapsed, like a giant falling redwood, into the rough sand at her feet. She kneeled beside him, yelling and slapping his face. She was in such a frenzy she didn't even realize he'd grabbed her hands.

"Myka, Myka, stop! I'm alive. I just ain't got nothin' left right now," he slurred. "Let me sleep for a while."

"Come on," she said, pulling him up, half-dragging him to the fire.

She glanced up at the sky, worried the Sirins might find them because of the smoke, but Anserlee had assured her this island was far enough away that Drew wouldn't answer the Sirins' call. But would that stop them from coming for them in their bird bodies?

He was shivering and his skin felt cold to the touch, so she decided the risk was worth it. She'd keep the flames small.

He practically dropped onto the blanket, and she covered him with another. She coaxed him to drink a tiny bit of water, and then he promptly fell asleep. As he snored lightly, she unlaced his sneakers, the ones she'd bought him for this particular trip, and laid them upside down on some rocks beside the fire. Her breath hitched as she caught sight of an angry wound on his hand. Curious if that was the extent of his injuries, she pulled his shirt off over his head so she could inspect the rest of his body. Claw marks, red and jagged, gouged from his neck and down his torso. Faint bruises in the shape of handprints outlined his wrists, along with more scratches, though they were better hidden amongst his tattoos. She dabbed the herb concoction Anserlee had made over his wounds, then lifted him up just enough to swipe some over the letters carved into his back. His skin was healing but still thick with crusted blood. She swallowed hard at the memory, though her mouth was dry. She laid him back down and unbuttoned his jeans.

Relief swept through her at finding no scratches or bruises as she worked the denim down one leg a little, then the other leg a little, until she finally had them off. She left on his boxer briefs because even though she'd already seen all of him, it felt weird taking those off without his permission. She covered him back up and kissed his forehead.

To keep them warm, she recovered her discarded wood and stacked it neatly by the fire. She stoked the flames only a little and watched, mesmerized, as smoke and ash swirled in the breeze. Convinced it would last a while, she scooted her lap under his head and leaned against a piece of skeletal driftwood. Only a few moments ago, this land and this day had seemed so bleak, gray, and hopeless, but now felt like a dream come true.

Firelight flickered over his skin. She pushed his hair off his face to see more. His ocean-logged hair felt gritty and gross between her fingers, but she didn't care. She couldn't believe he was real. She traced his jawline with her finger, running it over his five o'clock shadow. He must have shaved that morning. His long lashes were tipped white from the salt water, and she carefully wiped them with the edge of her sleeve. She couldn't stop touching him. She ran her hand down his neck and rested it on his chest. The feel of his beating heart brought a quivering smile to her face. *Were they finally safe?*

Moonlight gleamed over the snowcapped mountains in the distance, its silver light dancing along the serrated peaks into the blackened treetops. Myka wanted to believe she wouldn't hold this land partially at fault, but she probably would. She had known Alaska was dangerous the second she laid eyes on her, but that was the problem with dangerous things. Moth meet flame. She dropped her eyes to Drew's face once again. Only this time, she was going to dive headfirst into the fire.

FORTY-TWO

drew

Drew loved the feeling of Myka's hand resting on his chest, so he kept his eyes closed for a minute longer to savor the moment. Then he reached up and clasped her hand in his.

"Good morning, sleepyhead," Myka said.

He peered into her eyes and stared. She looked tired but content. About an inch of dark-blonde hair had grown from her roots—a gentle reminder of how long they'd been in Pan.

He knew at some point he was going to have to get up, even if he wasn't ready. His body ached, but it felt so good to have Myka all to himself. Once they reached safety, all hell was going to break loose. Having dealt with the paparazzi a time or two, Drew knew how ugly the press could get. But he'd take a crazy photographer any day over a scorned Sirin. They needed to leave before the Sirins thought to look further away than their own island. Myka might be dead to them, but he, their prized pet, was only missing. And the

Matriarchs knew there was a way for their pets to escape, even if it didn't happen often.

"We gotta get out of here," he said before he was any more tempted to pull her into his arms and not let go. All he wanted was her, but after everything he'd done, he didn't feel worthy. He had blood on his hands.

"Yeah, I know, but there's no hurry, right? Except we might run out of food." Her smile didn't reach her eyes. "Is there something wrong?"

"Uh, things over there didn't go according to plan. They know something. I don't know what, but as I left, they were already searching, probably for me."

"Oh, okay," she said, pulling her hand away. Tiny wrinkles creased between her brows. "Is Anserlee safe?"

"Honestly, I don't know." He sat up and groaned as he slowly got up from the ground. His muscles were tight and sore, and the scratches on his chest burned. At least the pain distracted him from the healing scars on his back where Gilda had carved her name. They itched like mad, and he couldn't wait to get home so he could have them covered up with tattoos.

He held his hand out to Myka and pulled her up off the sand. Once she was standing, he dropped her hand and grabbed his jeans and shirt from the log.

"Is there any clean water around here?" He wanted to rinse the salt water off his body.

"Yeah, come on," she said. She grabbed the small cooking pan and their bags before she headed down the beach.

He slipped on his shoes and stepped up beside her, offering her an arm for support, desperate to touch her. They'd made a promise that once this was over, they'd put the past behind them. But after everything that had happened, he'd understand if she didn't want him any longer.

"Why are you limping?" His breath came easier when she accepted his help.

"Honestly, I don't know. I woke up with a stab wound or something." Then she proceeded to tell him her story and all about the help she'd received from an unusual seal.

Drew informed her that Eislyn was, in fact, not really a seal.

"Are you serious?" She pressed her free hand to her mouth. "That makes me so happy. Not only to know that I'm not crazy, but wow—a Selkie. So cool, and answers so many questions."

"I was curious," he hesitated. He wanted his hunch to be true so desperately that he almost didn't want to share it in case he was wrong. "She called me son of my heart's blood, do you think—"

She gasped. "That you're Ronan's great, great, and then some great-grandson? Yeah. It's the only thing that makes sense. Wow, how cool is that? What a small world, don't you think?" Myka asked.

He basked in the strangeness of it all as they meandered to a small freshwater stream without spawning salmon. They hiked up inside the tree line for cover.

"This is the best spot I've found. I bet this will be the cleanest, coldest bath we've ever taken." She pulled a bar of soap out of her pack and wiggled it in the air.

His eyes lit up. "Soap! Who would've ever thought I'd be this excited to see a bar of soap?" He removed everything but his boxers before he dipped a toe in the creek. "Fuck, I think that's colder than the ocean," he exclaimed. "This is not going to bode well for my ego," he muttered under his breath as he waded in. He glanced back at Myka as she hopped in, naked as the day she was born. He quickly looked away.

"Here, let me help you," he said after she'd finished soaping up. He held the pan filled with water. "You ready?" he asked, before he poured it over her head a few times.

"Ahhh! Holy mother of everything! You're right. It's cold!" Her teeth chattered. "Your turn," she said, only seconds before she poured water over his head. "Not to worry—your ego's intact as far as I'm concerned," she assured him.

He tried laughing but he was too cold. The muscles along the back of his neck seized causing a temporary headache to form. "Again, again," he said before he could wimp out.

When they were done, they wrapped themselves in the blankets and ran back to the campfire, their coverings flowing behind them like superhero capes, cackling like fools.

When they caught their breath, they both stopped laughing and just stared at each other in an awkward silence. She turned abruptly and pulled a toothbrush and paste out of her pack and handed them to him.

"No, you go first," Drew said.

"I did, this morning before you woke up."

"Oh," was all he managed to say.

She stared for a long beat as if waiting for him to say something, anything, but the words were lodged in his throat. She looked away and grabbed clothes from her pack —a pair of jeans and a sweatshirt.

He walked away from the campsite and brushed his

teeth, thinking he didn't know how to move forward. After all the things he'd done, would she be able to forgive him? Could he forgive himself?

He didn't know where to begin. Though it could be said that what happened to him wasn't his fault, it didn't stop the shame from following overhead like a dark cloud. He put the toothbrush back in the bag and brushed his hands together to warm them up. He would do this later when the words were there. The longer he put this off, the better. They were going to have to stay on this island until they were rescued, so there was no need to make an uncomfortable situation worse.

He pulled on his jeans, but before he got them buttoned, she whispered so quietly he almost missed it, "So that's how it's going to be?"

Drew stopped with a black T-shirt halfway on. Abruptly, he changed his mind about waiting this out in silence. He was not going to make the same mistake twice. He pulled down his shirt and finished buttoning his pants.

"No, you're right. This time, the choice is truly in your hands." He reached up to tuck her windblown hair behind her ear, but he stopped. He had to get this over with. "I have done unspeakable things. Unspeakable things have been done to me," he said, studying the soft planes of her face, memorizing every curve. He shuddered inside, knowing he may never kiss those lips again. "I love you. I will always love you. But I'll also understand if you can't get past all that has happened. I'll do whatever you ask of me"—he paused, swallowing—"even if that means walking away from the only woman I've ever loved." He hoped the desperation didn't show on his face. He didn't want her to stay with him out of pity, and he didn't want her to stay because she was afraid of what would happen to him if she left. He was broken, but he wasn't hollow. Yet.

She stared at him for a long minute. His heartbeat slowed to a dangerous pace.

"Good. Now that we got that load of crap out of the way." She propped her hands on her hips.

His eyes popped open in surprise.

"I love you, Andrew Arie. And nothing that you did or was done to you could ever stop that. I thought we discussed this already?!" A gust of blustery wind blew her bangs back into her eyes as she grabbed him by the front of the shirt. "We can talk about everything that happened over there...or not. We can do it now or we can do it later. Whatever! I will never forgive you for what happened over there."

Drew shook his head in confusion. Had he missed something?

She tapped his chest with a finger. "Because, you dumbass, there is nothing to forgive!" she yelled. "Do you understand me?"

He raised his hands in the air. "Yes, but you don't get it."

Her face pinched. "I know, and I probably never will. Not really. But I was there for some of it. Do you want to talk about it?"

His teeth ground together. He knew at some point he was going to have to talk about the horrors he'd lived through, but he didn't want to burden her with more. At least not now. "I don't. You saw the worst of it. And I'm not ready to relive any of it."

The worry in her eyes sharpened.

"I think once we get home, I'll talk with the boys. You know Nicky's been through something similar."

She nodded. "Is that going to be enough?"

"If it's not, I promise I'll start seeing a professional. Okay?"

"Okay," she agreed, but she didn't look convinced.

"But there's something else you need to know."

Her brows knitted together.

"I killed somebody. I killed Rave," he said, finally breaking eye contact and staring out over the ocean. The sun glinted on the surface of the dark-green waters.

She leaned her head against his chest. "Thank you."

"What?" he said, pushing her back so he could see her eyes.

"I said thank you. Thank you for doing what you had to do to get back to me. I'm not sure I could live without you."

He pulled her back into his arms and rested his hand on the nape of her chilly neck. Her tears soaked through the front of his shirt. "You don't hate me?" His voice was unsteady.

She shook her head still buried in his chest. "I've never hated you. Even when I wanted to, I couldn't. I love you. I will *always* love you."

His shoulders dipped with relief, and the binding he'd created around his emotions broke free, allowing him to breathe, truly breathe, for the first time in days. "Thank God. I don't know what I would've done without you. From now on, it's you and me. Always." He stepped back and got down on one knee as pink stained her cheeks. "Myka, this isn't how I'd planned on doing this. I had so many great ideas, but I can't wait for the perfect place or the perfect timing any longer."

Her smile widened, and she covered it with a trembling hand.

"I want you. But most importantly, I need you. Myka Vukovic, will you marry me?"

She got down on her knees and barreled into him. "Yes! You know I will!"

"We'll get you a ring when we get back. I want that to be the first thing we do, okay?" Though they hadn't found an emerald at the emerald mine on their first date, he'd bought her one shortly after. Even then, he'd known she was the one. But, because of all that had taken place, he wanted to buy her a new one. A fresh start.

"Ha-ha. The first thing I'm going to do is take a hot shower," she said with a smirk on her lips.

"Am I invited?"

Her lips parted and she nodded. "You're the VIP."

He pulled her hard into him and crushed his lips against hers. He buried one hand in her hair and rested the other on the small of her back as he drew her in close. As always, she felt right in his hands. He trailed kisses down her neck before forcing himself to stop at her shoulder. He didn't want things to get carried away; this wasn't the time or place. They needed to get out of here.

The beating of her heart pounded in tandem with his as he took a deep breath and released it slowly. He needed to control himself. He had waited three years for her. He could wait a little longer.

FORTY-THREE

myka

"What are you doing?" Myka asked as Drew pulled away.

He cupped her cheek, his thumb stroking her skin as he stared at her with smoldering blue eyes. "Baby, we got time, all the time in the world, to do this."

"No!" She stomped her foot in the sand. It had less impact than she'd intended. "I have waited years for this, for you. Only you. I don't want to wait one more minute! Please. It seems like every time we get close, the rug is pulled out from underneath us. I can't let that happen again."

"Are you sure? Because we could get a nice room somewhere when we get out of here, and I could make it perfect. Besides, I think we need to stay on guard."

"Why? We're off the island. Out here, they're just birds," she reasoned.

He cocked his brow as if he didn't necessarily agree with her.

349

"What I want is you. I don't care where. I need you," she practically begged. The aching and burning and throbbing between her thighs was making it hard to think.

She backed off a half step, remembering the trauma he'd been through. She couldn't believe how selfish she was acting. She just wanted him to know that she desired him and nothing that had been done to him could ever change that.

"Oh, my gosh, I'm so sorry. You're probably not ready. I didn't even think," she said.

He lifted her chin and ran his thumb along her bottom lip, his eyes searching for answers. Shivers skated over her, inside her, basically everywhere. She'd waited too long for this, too long for him, but if he needed time to heal, she'd wait.

"It's not a question of being ready. I've loved you for so long—I just want to make sure we're safe," he said before he kissed her.

She was expecting the kiss to be hard, fast, intense, but what she got was slow, gentle, and exploratory, like he was memorizing her with the contours of his lips.

He pulled away, and something like a whine escaped from her. He held his finger to his lips, shushing her, and searched the sky. He cocked his head as if listening. After a minute, he said, "Now, where were we?" He grabbed the ties on the front of her sweatshirt and yanked her close.

As his eyes roamed her face, a smile curled his lips. She mirrored his expression, excited, yet still a bit nervous. To keep her racing heart under control, she tried breathing calmly through her nose.

His hands trailed to the hem of her sweatshirt and with her help, they lifted it over her head. He tossed it onto the blanket lying next to the campfire. Sparks of wood popped and sputtered while ashes flew away on the breeze. She tugged the hem of his T-shirt, hinting that it was his turn. He obliged.

Pressing her palm onto his bare chest, she closed her eyes. The ever-present buzz when they were near each other intensified. Her body, internally and externally, felt as if it were vibrating. If she stood there long enough, concentrating on the sensation, she was sure it, alone, was enough to get her off in her heightened state.

He clasped his hand over hers and squeezed tight before he ran his hands under her shirt. His fingers glided along her rib cage as he guided her tank top up over her arms.

"Are you sure?" she asked as he tossed it aside.

"Yes. This. This is what heals me." He touched her cheek and smiled.

"How can you be this okay?"

"Because I have you."

She arched a brow.

"No really. If I had to go through that a million times just to end up here, with you, I'd do it all over again. You don't understand, I'd traverse the seven levels of hell just to hold you."

"You already did." Her voice broke.

He chuckled. "True. Now if you don't have any objections, I'd like to collect my prize." He ran his thumb over her bottom lip, pulling it open as his fingers dropped down her chin and traced the hollow of her throat.

"You are impossibly cocky."

He grinned. "But you love me."

"Until the end of time," she said, unsnapping the top button of his pants. His breath hitched. She popped open the next one, and the next one, and slid his jeans to the ground.

Even with all the bruising and scratches, his body was heavenly. His thighs were muscular, his ass rock hard, and his stomach, a washboard of perfection. With light pressure, she explored his abs with her fingers and hooked them into the elastic band of his boxer briefs, slowly sliding them off.

Finally, she was going to get what she wanted. She wrapped her lips around his straining cock, circling the salty tip with her tongue. With long strokes, back and forth, she took more of him in her mouth, sucking while cupping his balls. He groaned and buried his hands in her hair. When he'd had enough, or he couldn't take it anymore—she wasn't sure which—he gently pulled her up and kissed her deeply before turning her around.

He undid her bra with deft fingers, letting it drop to the blanket below. His hands were rough and cold, but they still burned a path over her skin as he ripped her ugly, linen panties, compliments of her captors, and tossed them into the fire.

He pulled her backward into him, the length of him pressing against her behind, hard and hot. His arms wrapped around her, warming her with his naked body as they watched and listened to the soft splash of the incoming tide.

"I love you," he murmured, kissing her neck. The gentle but nippy breeze only added to the tingles coursing through her. He slid his hands under her breasts and circled her already-taut nipples with his thumbs. Her knees buckled as she leaned her head back, inhaling the ocean air. The pounding between her legs silenced the rest of the world. He helped her to the blanket and tucked her sweatshirt under her head.

He knelt and straddled her, resting his weight on her thighs. "You sure?" he asked. The sun, now having risen high above the trees, bathed his body in gold, the tip of his cock glistening in light. His hair waved more than ever from the salt water, and the scruff on his jaw sparkled red in the rays.

"Yes. Positive. But only if you're ready."

"You need to stop. I told you already—*you* are what I need. It's just...I thought this should be special, you know."

Her body demanded relief. The need for him to be inside of her was overwhelming. Exquisitely excruciating. "You're what makes it special," she said. "Not the location. Please. I don't want to wait any longer."

He bent over her and lightly feathered his lips over hers. "Okay. Okay. But we're going to take this slow."

"No, now," Myka begged, her hips pushing up to meet his.

He groaned against her neck, slowly rubbing his length over her wet, pulsing center.

"Please," she begged again, spreading her thighs farther apart, about to combust from the flames.

Denying her wishes, he scooted downward, dragging his tongue along her collarbone and over her ribs. He dipped it into her belly button and nipped her skin, kissing her stomach while traveling lower, until his lips were on her hip. Her body flexed and her insides tightened as he rolled his thumb slowly in circles over her swollen flesh, driving her mad. A mere second away from coming, he stopped, then laughed when she protested.

His voice, that deep growling tone, vibrated over her

skin as he murmured with his mouth pressed against her inner thigh, "I've waited a long time for this, too, and I have *no* plans for you to ever forget this moment."

With his fingers, he spread her open and licked along her opening, stopping to flick her clit. Lights flashed behind her closed eyes as he repeated the process, then took the sensitive bud into his mouth and started sucking. Her fists gripped the blanket beneath her and she spread her legs wider.

"Grab the back of my head and ride my face," he said.

She froze.

"Do it now," he ordered firmly.

Surprised by his bossiness, but not entirely unpleased, she gripped his hair and pressed his face hard against her. He slid two fingers deep inside and lightly circled her anus with his other hand. She inhaled sharply but didn't stop him. This area wasn't her expertise, and while she didn't like his past, there was no denying he'd learned a lot during the last three years.

He devoured her flesh, curling his fingers, hitting just the right spot, as she rose higher and higher. Her nipples puckered, her toes curled, her back arched. Her core clenched and her breathing paused just as she started to tumble over the edge. Abruptly, he stopped.

"Are you trying to kill me?!" she whimpered. Her pulse whooshed in her ears, making it hard to hear.

"No. But I don't want you thinking someone can ever replace me." He gave her clit another quick lick, causing her body to involuntarily twitch.

"I think you're torturing me because I broke up with you."

"Well, I'm not going to deny that I'm enjoying being in control for once."

"You're mean," she said.

"I'm not," he said, crawling up her body until the tip of his penis nudged her entrance.

Once again, he slid through her wetness, teasing her.

"Please," she whispered, her body ready to implode, begging for release.

"What you deserve is a spanking and probably more. When we get back, I plan to take my revenge slowly, but because we may be on a time limit now, we'll save it for another day."

Carefully, as if she would break, he slipped inside, his girth and length filling her, stretching her walls. She tensed up from the pain, so he stopped and leaned his forehead against hers, breathing together.

He kissed the hollow of her throat and took her breast in his hand, bringing her nipple to his lips. Sparks of pure desire negated the pain. He reached between her legs and started stroking her clit. She arched harder, not willing to wait another moment longer, and grabbed his ass, pulling him deeper inside.

"Fuuuuck," he moaned, his breath spilling on her neck. "You okay?"

She nodded. "Better than okay. Please don't stop. I can't bear this much longer."

He chuckled and thrust his hips forward, burying himself to the hilt. With his mouth indulging her breasts, then switching to her lips, he pumped slowly, rhythmically. Pleasure she hadn't known existed swelled throughout, building in tiny increments, each push coaxing her orgasm up, up, and over the edge. She threw her head back as wave after wave pummeled her body. He reached down and covered her mouth to muffle her screams.

He collapsed on her chest, both sweating and breathing heavily.

"God, woman, I love you," he whispered into her ear after. "I want to do that every day for the rest of my life—probably multiple times a day, if you want the truth."

They gathered wood and tree branches with fir needles and piled them carefully onto the fire. It was a bold move, knowing the amount of gray smoke billowing from the flames would attract the attention of the Sirins. They also hoped it would attract a rescue team. They lined the beach with white rocks spelling out SOS, then sat down on the shore and waited.

Myka didn't honestly think they'd have to wait long. They weren't that far away from Sitka.

She'd suggested they could kayak out, but he finished telling her of the amazing events leading up to and following his escape, ending with only having one kayak. Eislyn needed the other one to help the baby boys escape.

They talked about what they would tell the world. Because of Drew's fame, the tabloids were going to be frantic with a capital F. Their stories needed to be the same, so they agreed to take Anserlee's advice and stick to the truth as much as possible.

They had each flipped their kayaks and washed up on the same small island. *Check.*

Myka found Drew injured. *Check.*

They waved down a small boat. *Check.*

Unfortunately, their rescuers were not friendly, but a boat full of women, all foreign falconers, who figured out who Drew was and decided to ransom him after all the searching died down. *Check.*

They only kept Myka alive to ensure Drew's cooperation. *Check.*

They set up a home base on the island to wait out the searching frenzy. Myka and Drew eventually stole their kayaks back and escaped. *Check.*

They island-hopped slowly so the falconers couldn't find them. *Check.*

Because they were careless, they didn't pull both kayaks far enough in and the tide took one out while they slept. *Check.* As if they'd be that stupid, but they couldn't find a better excuse.

They built an SOS fire and prayed for rescue. *Check.*

They hashed out the minor details over and over. Even if their story was far-fetched, it was far more believable than the truth.

As they sat on the shore, watching the cloud of smoke fill the air, they soon heard the buzzing of a small engine in the distance. They clambered from the ground and ran, waving their jackets over their heads. A small red and white plane circled the cove.

The tiny aircraft set down on the calm ocean just off the shore, then floated in. Tears filled Myka's eyes when she recognized the burly pilot.

"Christ Almighty! Am I glad to see the two of you!" Paul

yelled as he tied the plane to a large piece of driftwood. He jogged toward them. Denali, his husky, beat him to it and started jumping and barking.

Myka fell into his giant bear hug. "Can we please get out of here?"

"Damn right. Let's get your things and go home," Paul said, patting Drew heartily on the back.

Suddenly, Denali's bark changed from frantic to fierce.

"Hey, girl, what's the matter?" Paul asked her, scanning the shoreline for danger.

Both she and Drew automatically looked to the sky, knowing where the danger hailed. Coming straight toward them flew a flock of different kinds of birds.

Myka pointed in the air, and Paul's squinty eyes grew two sizes. "What the hell is that?"

"That is our cue to go," Drew said urgently, handing Myka her pack.

"Yeah, I think you're right. Come on." Paul and Denali ran down the beach toward the plane with them following.

"Hop in!" Paul yelled.

Drew lifted her up onto the float, and she opened the door. He handed her Denali, and she helped the dog into the back seat as screeches, screams, and a high-pitched call filled the air above. Massive black shadows passed over the ground like pterodactyls.

As Myka pulled herself inside the plane, something hit the back of her head with such force that stars burst into her vision. A scream ripped from her throat, mingling with those of the raptor. Talons, sharp as a razor's edge, scraped her scalp, feeling as if they'd sliced through her skin all the way to her skull. Drew grabbed the raptor by its tail and threw it off, but not before the bird ripped out two wads of her hair by the roots.

Another huge shadow skimmed over the calm ocean surface. Myka looked up to see outstretched yellow feet with dagger-like spurs aimed straight at Drew's head. Before she could shout a warning, the massive golden eagle hit Drew on his back. He slammed into Myka, pushing her into the plane headfirst. Gilda—it had to be her—seized a hold of Drew's pack and was trying to pull him off the float. The massive span of her wings pumped violently backward, curving inward with every stroke.

Myka frantically searched the plane for something to hit her with. In the rear seat was a fishing pole, a shotgun, and a stick about a foot long and two inches in diameter with a leather strap attached to the end. She thought about going for the gun, but was afraid she might hit more than the bird. She grabbed the stout stick and wrapped the leather toggle around her wrist. Wind, dust, and tiny feathers from the eagle's wildly flapping wings made her eyes water and sting as she tightened her grip on the baton and *crack, crack, cracked* it down on Gilda's thick yellow legs. The shock waves from the blows reverberated up Myka's arms. The bird screamed, the sound shrill in Myka's ears.

On the other side of the plane, Paul cussed up a storm as Drew pushed himself into the front seat and slammed the door to keep the birds from entering the cockpit.

"Give me that stick," he shouted, "and stay in here!"

"Here," Myka said, handing him the twelve-gauge shotgun instead. "Fuck the stick!"

She had no problem giving Drew the gun. He'd grown up on a farm and spent plenty of time at the rifle range.

He half crawled over Paul's seat and swung the door open.

Myka plugged her ears as he pulled the trigger. A loud bang echoed, and the birds scattered, but none fell out of the sky. Myka's ears rang like she'd been hit in the head with a bell.

The shot gave Paul enough time to free the plane and jump in. He started up the engine just as some of the smaller birds threw themselves into the windshield. They clawed at the glass. "I don't know how we're going to lift out of here if they keep doing that! Why are they doing that? If they hit one of the props, we're going down."

"Myka, hop in the front, then crack the door open for me," Drew said as he folded his long body over the seat into the back with her. "Put those headphones on."

"What are you going to do?" She climbed into the front.

"I'm going to start shooting. That should make them think twice." He loaded another round into the chamber. "Take these and hand them to me as I need them." He passed her a box of shells.

"Are you okay with that?" He was already suffering from killing Rave.

"I have no problem with it," he snarled through clenched teeth.

Myka put on the headphones and lifted the hood of her rain jacket, not wanting to distract Drew with the blood all over the back of her head. She popped open the door slightly, giving him just enough room to wield the shotgun, then she shimmied as far away as she could while still holding the door.

Paul talked to someone on his radio, asking for help, as he maneuvered the plane further from the shore.

"Get ready for it," Drew said two seconds before he fired.

Birds scattered, and a couple fell into the ocean.

Again, Drew fired, but the birds had significantly backed off. She felt sorry for Denali, who had no ear protection.

"All right, shut the door. We're going to try this," Paul said.

They took off slowly, and though the birds followed them, they stayed at a distance.

"What the hell was that?" Paul exclaimed through the headset.

"That is a very long, completely unbelievable tale," she said to Paul with a straight face. His hat, which she'd never seen him without, was missing, and rivulets of blood ran down his face from the gouges in his bald head.

Denali sat in the back, on Drew's lap, shaking and panting heavily. He petted the fur between her ears.

Blood from Myka's scalp wound ran freely down the back of her neck into her shirt. She began to feel lightheaded as her mouth watered and lights flashed in her peripheral vision. Like an echo chamber far off in the distance, she heard Drew call her name. Slowly, she drooped to the side, relieved they were on their way home.

myka

Myka woke up later, snuggled in a warm bed with Drew's strong arms around her. She inhaled the smell of his normal cologne, cedar and spice, and exhaled relief. Though her body was sore, they were alive. All in all, she felt pretty good thanks to the extra-strength painkillers and glass of water sitting on the end table.

Rain pounded on the windows, blurring the treetops outside their room. They were safe in the top suite of Barb and Paul's lodge.

Slowly, the fuzzy details of last night came back to her.

She remembered Drew carrying her up the dock, despite his own injuries. He'd held her hand as Barb, a former nurse, stitched up her head by the fireplace downstairs. Once they got her upstairs, Drew helped her in the shower. He'd protested, but she hadn't wanted to crawl into bed with blood all down her back.

Gently, she reached up and touched her skull. She hissed in pain as her fingers bumped the bandage covering what she assumed were stitches. After the unfortunate events, she wasn't growing her hair out anytime soon.

Drew woke up and stretched. "Hey, baby, how you doin'?" he asked in his fake Brooklyn dialect that always made her smile.

"Happy to be alive, I think." She turned to face him, cringing with the movement. "But worried about Anserlee. Worried about what we're going to tell people and if they'll believe us."

"Well, we're probably going to wonder and worry about Anserlee forever." He rested his hand on her cheek. "And as for people believing us, well, they either do or they don't. Personally, I don't really give a shit."

"Should we tell everyone the same thing? Or should we dare tell the truth to some?"

"You know, I think maybe we should tell the truth to the guys. They were out there, too, and saw both of us disappear into thin air. Paul and Barb too. I have a feeling after what Paul just witnessed, he might believe us. Sometimes you just gotta have faith."

"Yeah, you're right. That seems to be the underlying lesson of my life," she grumbled.

Drew crawled out of bed wearing only a pair of black boxer briefs. Tattoos spanned his arms and dipped slightly onto his shoulders, but underneath where the ink stopped, she got a clear view of where Gilda had etched her name into his skin. The wounds were red and raised but didn't look inflamed.

Rage and sorrow clogged Myka's throat. She swallowed. "God, Drew, I'm so sorry."

"No worries." He grabbed something out of the top drawer of the dresser and snuggled back under the covers.

He propped a pillow behind her, helping her sit up, then one behind himself.

"What are we going to do about that?"

He shrugged. "I've been meaning to get another tattoo. I just didn't know what I wanted. But now, I've been thinking about a set of gray wings—for Anserlee."

Myka bit down on her bottom lip as tears collected. "Yeah, I think she'd like that. Maybe I'll get a matching set."

The smile that spread across Drew's face settled the rage boiling behind her ribs.

"I'd love that, and she'd love it too. I know she would. As for what happened over there, for now it's in the past. I'll take some time later to deal with it, but right now, I want to concentrate on the future. So happy thoughts only, okay?"

She nodded. It wasn't her right to tell him how to deal with his pain. And if he wanted to focus on the future, she wasn't going to stop him.

"I know I promised to take you ring shopping when we get home, but first, I want you to see this." With a shaking hand, he opened a box lined with black velvet. Inside sat a simple but beautiful, large emerald ring in a platinum setting.

"Oh my goodness, that is—" She glanced up into his dark-blue eyes, her hand pressed against her chest. "It's perfect. How? Where did you get this? When did you..." She shook her head, trying to clear her brain as she pieced together a timeline. "Wait, we broke up. You brought this with you?"

"What? I had two weeks on an island to get you to love me again. I just thought it would be *this* island."

"Your cockiness never ceases to amaze me." She elbowed him lightly.

"Yeah, but you love me, right?" That growl in his voice curled her toes and turned her insides to mush.

"Words don't exist for how much I love you." She tugged him in for a kiss. His lips were hot and gentle, as if he feared she would break.

He pulled away and held up the ring. "So? Is that a yes? You like it?"

"A million times, yes," she said.

He slipped it onto her finger, and she held it up. "I love it." Muted morning light glittered over the surface, throwing a rainbow of colors onto the log walls. "When did you have time to buy it?"

"Baby, this was custom-made years ago. I had it with me the night you ditched me."

She inhaled sharply. "You were going to ask me to marry you then? We'd only been dating a few months."

"You still don't get it, do you?" He leaned over. "Since the moment I met you, you were the only one. When I'm around you, my body hums, it..." His eyes squinted as he tried to find the words.

"Buzzes," she finished for him.

"Yeah. You feel it too?" The surprise in his eyes turned to hope.

She nodded. "I love you," she whispered, again admiring the ring on her finger.

"I love you, too, baby. Are you ready to go home? Or do you want me to get the guys back out here? They know we're safe, and so do our families. I figured we'd have a press conference when we got home. The world can wait, as far as I am concerned."

She buried her head into his chest. "I wanna go home."

epilogue

After sitting down and sharing the truth with Barb and Paul, who took the news surprisingly well and promised to keep their secret safe, Drew and Myka flew in a private jet home to New York.

They decided not to tell their parents the truth but to stick to their original story to keep their lives less complicated. But to Nicky, Gus Gus, and Tony, they owed the truth. After all, they'd been there. Their heads had been messed with, and their hearts had been broken too.

Thanks to the tabloid-feeding frenzy, their new album, *Rise of the Sirin*, skyrocketed to the top of the charts. The subject matter was dark and often heartbreaking, but because the band had no way of discussing their experiences in therapy, they used songwriting as their outlet. Doing so allowed them to work through the trauma and create something unforgettable. Even their harshest critics folded under the pressure.

As a result, Burning Brenda set up a charity for people

who'd experienced sexual abuse—men, women, and children.

One day, out of the blue, while the band was on tour, Drew got a strange phone call from his mother. She told him a goose with a letter tied to her leg addressed to him and Myka had shown up on her front porch. She thought it was probably a good idea if they came home and explained what the hell was going on.

Myka and Drew dropped everything to fly home.

Wandering around his parents' house, following Drew's mother, was a beautiful, gray goose with an orange beak surrounded by white feathers. She softly honked as they unfolded the note and read.

My dearest Myka and Drew,

If you're reading this, all is well. I have safely made it to your mother's house. Thank you, Drew, for the idea. I will have to reside the rest of my days in this body, but I have come to terms with that, and I am happy to do so.

Drew, I am sure you are curious about how I managed to escape after I was thrown in prison. My emergency backup plan worked. The next morning, the mothers sentenced me to song silencing for your escape—or, at that time, they assumed your death. I'd heard of Rave's absence, and I'd hoped you'd made it off the island. But I didn't know for sure until Gilda came back with the report that both of you had slipped through their hands. My information, and my freedom, are all due to James's courage and loyalty to his family. Within the uproar, he was able to steal the keys to my cell and set me free mere hours before I was to be executed.

Myka, your Uncle James sends his love and asks that you not worry about him. But we all know that won't happen.

Now I need you both to let go of the life you think I should have and accept the life that I've chosen. I have no regrets. I love the two of you more than you can know, and this way, I will no longer have to miss you.

Yours forever,

Anserlee

Myka's chin trembled, and tears welled in Drew's eyes. Together they dropped to the floor and opened their arms. Anserlee, with her wings outstretched, waddled into their embrace. She plopped in Myka's lap and burrowed her head under Myka's short bob. Drew grabbed Myka's hand and let out a deep breath. "She's home. She's safe."

Myka's face scrunched with pain, but she nodded. Though it wasn't the outcome they wanted, it was the best they could hope for.

After the final tears had been shed, and Anserlee had settled into her nest for the night, Drew and Myka sat down with their families and told them the unbelievable truth. Whether they believed or not didn't bother them. Of course, Baba already knew the truth.

The End

(Or is it?)

Myka scooted across the couch holding some photos. "Look at these," she said, her voice filled with excitement. She pulled the blanket under her chin to ward off the winter chill.

To warm her up, Drew hit the on button for the gas fireplace, and the flames whooshed to life. He peered at the first picture. "Wow. That's cool. What is it I'm looking at, exactly?" He glanced up. The Christmas lights decorating the tree reflected a confetti of color in her dark eyes.

She tucked her hair behind her ear. It had grown out into a cute bob over the last year and a half. "Apparently, *Rise of the Sirin* inspired this tattoo artist to draw mock-ups of our nightmare. As disturbing as it sounds, they're amazing." She flipped through the other photos, her emerald engagement ring sparkling. They'd set a wedding date for the end of May to get married in Sedona, Arizona. Far away from the ocean.

"How did you get them?"

She handed him the pictures. "Nicky. His tattoo artist is

friends with her. And Nicky knows you've been looking for the right person. He showed them to me, and I loved them. We thought you should take a look."

Drew stared at the artist's beautiful renditions of Sirin wings in shades of gold, black, bronze, and, of course, silver. Some of the other pictures were a bit more disturbing and sent a barrage of shivers over his arms—sly ravens, vicious eagles, razor-sharp talons, and bloody names carved into skin.

"You okay?" Myka rested her hand on his leg.

"Yep." He, Nicky, Gus, and Tony had spent hours working through his trauma. Not once had they made him feel less than for the awful things he'd experienced. They'd made him feel stronger, telling him that not very many people could've survived with so few scars. Except for the one on his back, the rest were hidden. Never gone, but manageable.

Most of their fans believed Drew had taken his and Myka's "captured by pirates" story and rebranded it into a fantasy world to make it more palatable and lyrical. Little did they know.

"You've been talking about getting the scars on your back covered up for over a year. I thought this one would be perfect." She tapped the one he was staring at.

A purple guitar sat in front of a pair of beautiful silver wings. Though he had tattoos on his arms, most of his back was free other than Gilda's name. He hated it—but at times, he wasn't ready to let it go. It was a reminder of everything he'd been through and that he'd survived because of all the people he loved.

"You're right. That's exactly what I've been looking for. It would be a perfect tribute to Anserlee." And though

Gilda's name would never be completely erased, it would be buried under the angel wings of the woman who'd sacrificed everything to save them.

Tears pooled in Myka's eyes, making them shine like polished obsidian. "I thought so too."

"I'm ready. Can you reach out to the tattoo artist and schedule an appointment?"

She bit down on her bottom lip and made a funny face.

"You already did, didn't you?" He raised a brow and crossed his arms.

She nodded and shrugged. "What? I knew the second I saw it—it was the one. The artist is a huge fan of Burning Brenda, and she's here in New York this week as a guest artist. I thought it would be the perfect Christmas present."

"Why didn't you tell me earlier?"

She cocked her head. "Because you know how you are. You would've hemmed and hawed until it was too late. If you don't want it, I can cancel the appointment. I'll pay her for her time, and with this kind of talent, I'm sure she can sneak someone else in at the last minute."

"No. I want it."

She kicked her feet and smiled as if she knew exactly how this conversation would go. "Cool. The car will be here at five to pick us up."

After Drew's security team cleared the alley behind the tattoo studio for safety, the driver let him and Myka out of the back seat. Lack of privacy was one of the prices of fame.

"Welcome." A small woman with short, black hair and deep-brown eyes opened the back door and ushered them inside. She was wearing an old flannel and cutoff denim shorts. Her knee-high combat boots afforded her a few inches, but she couldn't have been an inch over five feet tall.

The old wood floors creaked underfoot as they walked down a long hallway into the main room. Pictures of spectacular tattoos, some black and gray, others a rainbow of colors, hung on the exposed brick. Brown leather furniture and the black ductwork in the ceiling yielded an industrial vibe.

"I'm Pippin," she said, shaking Myka's hand first before offering it to Drew. Her grip was warm and firm. Though her skin was tan, a spattering of dark freckles peppered her nose and cheeks, giving her that eternal youthful look. The studded dog collar around her neck and the piercings in her nose added to the effect. "I've been so excited to meet you both. Obviously, I'm a huge fan. When Myka called me, I didn't believe it was really her."

"That happens," Drew said.

"So, she filled me in on what we'll be working around. Are you sure you're ready?" Pippin asked, rolling up the sleeves of her flannel.

"Yes."

"Okay then. Take off your shirt and lie down right there." Pippin tapped the leather bench.

Grabbing his T-shirt by the collar, he yanked it off and set it in Myka's outstretched hand. She stuffed it into her purse and sat down on one of the provided recliners.

Pippin's eyes barely gave his washboard abs a moment of her time.

Leaning back, he hissed when his skin hit the cold

surface. "Kind of late to get started on a piece this big," he said.

"Nah, I'm nocturnal by nature. And I don't need you awake if you can sleep through something like this."

Drew probably wouldn't be able to sleep, but after Pan, his definition of pain had been altered.

"This is going to be chilly," she warned.

The smell of alcohol burned his nose as she cleaned and shaved his back before she started sketching out her plan. He closed his eyes and relaxed. As she worked, she sang along with the radio. Her voice was sweet, and it reminded him of Anserlee.

Once she finished, she said, "Okay. Stand up and take a look in the mirror." She placed a handheld mirror in his palm and pointed to the full-length one at the back of the room. Myka went with him.

"Wow." Myka trailed her fingers down his arm as they both stared. "It's perfect," she whispered.

Drew swallowed back the emotions trying to surface. "It is. Black and gray? Or color?"

"Black and gray with a tiny haze of purple?" she said.

"Sounds good." He leaned down and kissed her soft lips. "You gonna get one too?"

"Yes, but not today."

"I love it." Drew handed Pippin the mirror, and Myka sat back down, pulling a book from her purse.

Pippin took a deep breath and crossed her arms. She nodded her head ever so slightly and chewed on her bottom lip.

His brows furrowed. "Everything okay?"

She sighed and dropped her arms to her sides. "Yes. *And no*. We gotta talk."

Drew's forehead wrinkled and warning bells started tolling. When they'd arrived, he hadn't gotten the stalker/creeper vibe from her, and he was pretty good at picking them out of a crowd.

"I'm just not sure if you're going to believe me—or admit it if you do."

Myka dropped the footrest of the recliner and sat forward.

"Fuck it," Pippin said. She blew her long bangs from her forehead with a puff of air. "I know all those songs on *Rise of the Sirin* are true. Every single one of them."

There were fans who claimed the songs were real and that Sirins, vampires, and all kinds of supernatural creatures existed. The conspiracy theories were abundant. And they weren't wrong, but just like Pippin predicted, they would never admit it.

He stepped back and folded his hands over his stomach, disappointment twisting. He'd really been looking forward to covering up Gilda's name.

Myka rose from the chair and stood slightly behind him, catching the belt loop on his jeans with her finger.

Without warning, Pippin turned around and pulled off her flannel shirt. Two raised scars, angry and red, vertically paralleled her shoulder blades. "I know because I used to be one of them," she said quickly, as if she didn't want to say the words but had to.

"What the fuck!" was Drew's initial reaction. Bile shot to his throat and his fists clenched.

Myka grabbed his arm gently, holding him back.

She raised her hands. "I wasn't like them. I swear. That's part of the reason I got banished."

His shoulders relaxed a fraction, and he unclenched his fists.

She put her shirt back on and turned around. "I'll understand if you don't want to go through with the tattoo. But I thought it was only fair that you know what I am. Or what I was. If you don't believe me, I can always show you my feet."

"They cut off your wings," Myka said, stepping forward, ignoring her last comment.

"They did."

"Why?"

Pippin swallowed and tucked her hands into her pockets. "I was on watch when the King of Rock 'n' Roll disappeared from our island. And even though I saw him leaving, I didn't stop him." She shrugged. "I might've let him go."

"Wait," Myka said. "Anserlee told me about this. She accompanied one of her Matriarchs to somewhere in the Caribbean."

"Long, light-brown hair, heart-shaped face, silver wings, and big gray eyes?" Pippin asked.

Myka and Drew exchanged a look.

"Yes. That's her," Myka confirmed.

Pippin smiled sadly. "I remember her. She argued for the Matriarchs to lessen our punishments. But it didn't matter to them that he'd returned, because he'd escaped on our watch. All the other Sirins died, but somehow, after they dumped us in the ocean, I washed up on shore. The island was almost deserted, but a few people lived there, and they saved me."

"Just when I think life can't get any stranger," Drew said, running his fingers through his short hair.

"I know, right?" Pippin agreed, her voice lightening.

Drew looked at Myka, and she nodded.

"Now let me really blow your mind," Drew said. "Anserlee is with us."

Pippin's dark-brown eyes widened, and her mouth dropped open. "How?"

"She's still in her bird form. But you're living proof it doesn't have to be that way, does it?" Drew asked.

Something like hesitation and a bit of fear traveled over her face. "It doesn't. But the price she'll have to pay is losing her wings."

Myka's complexion blanched, and Drew grabbed her arm, pulling her in close. "Coming from someone who's been there, was it worth it? You don't have to lie to me or soften the blow," Drew said.

"At first, I would've said no." Pippin paused for a beat. "But now that I have a pretty cool life, yes, I'd do it again."

"Okay, let's get this tattoo started, shall we? You can tell me your story and maybe we can discuss options for Anserlee's future."

acknowledgments

A big thank you to my friends and family. Your support means the world. Especially you, Geri. Remember that time on the beach in Hawaii as I read the first draft to you and a stranger asked what book we were reading and where he could get it???!!! It's a memory I'll never forget.

And you, Mandi, because who else could come up with the band name Burning Brenda and have such a wild/meaningful story attached?

Shannon and Ruth—thank you for double-checking my Sitka facts. Because while I lived in AK—I've never been to Sitka, so any inconsistencies are on me.

To Jessica McKeldon and Rachel Throp—thank you for making me look smart. Or at least smarter!

To my cover designer, Ivy, how do you nail perfection the first time around?

To my character artist, Leraynne S., your talent defies my expectations.

To Kelli Maxwell of Ember Marketing Group—thank you for reaching out to me and saying—*I can sell this!* Good, because I'm not very good at it...

Thank you to all my alpha/beta readers and my critique groups, because honesty can be hard. *Here's my baby—tell me all the ways in which you hate it-lol!* Despite the pain, it's much appreciated.

And last, but certainly not least, thank you to all the readers. You make this journey possible!